THE
CHEMIST
STEPHENIE MEYER

sphere

SPHERE

First published in Great Britain in 2016 by Sphere
This paperback edition published in 2017 by Sphere

3 5 7 9 10 8 6 4 2

Copyright © 2016 by Stephenie Meyer

The moral right of the author has been asserted.

A CIP catalogue record for this book
is available from the British Library.

ISBN 978-0-7515-7004-5

Printed and bound in Great Britain by
Clays Ltd, St Ives plc

Papers used by Sphere are from well-managed forests
and other responsible sources.

Sphere
An imprint of
Little, Brown Book Group
Carmelite House
50 Victoria Embankment
London EC4Y 0DZ

An Hachette UK Company
www.hachette.co.uk

www.littlebrown.co.uk

THE
CHEMIST

She wasn't going to let them *win*. There was no way she would give them such an easy resolution to their problem. They would probably get her in the end, but they were going to have to *work* for it, damn them, and they would bleed for it too.

W/D

Also by Stephenie Meyer

Twilight
New Moon
Eclipse
Breaking Dawn

Life and Death: Twilight Reimagined

The Short Second Life of Bree Tanner

The Host

*This book is dedicated to
Jason Bourne and Aaron Cross*

*(and also to Asya Muchnick and Meghan Hibbett,
who gleefully aid and abet my obsession)*

THE
CHEMIST

CHAPTER 1

Today's errand had become routine for the woman who was currently calling herself Chris Taylor. She'd gotten up much earlier than she liked, then dismantled and stowed her usual nighttime precautions. It was a real pain to set everything up in the evening only to take it down first thing in the morning, but it wasn't worth her life to indulge in a moment of laziness.

After this daily chore, Chris had gotten into her unremarkable sedan—more than a few years old, but lacking any large-scale damage to make it memorable—and driven for hours and hours. She'd crossed three major borders and countless minor map lines and even after reaching approximately the right distance rejected several towns as she passed. That one was too small, that one had only two roads in and out, that one looked as though it saw so few visitors that there would be no way for her not to stand out, despite all of the ordinariness she worked to camouflage herself with. She took note of a few places she might want to return to another day—a welding-supply shop, an army surplus store, and a farmers' market. Peaches were coming back in season; she should stock up.

Finally, late in the afternoon, she arrived in a bustling place she'd never been before. Even the public library was doing a fairly brisk business.

She liked to use a library when it was possible. Free was harder to trace.

She parked on the west side of the building, out of sight of the one camera located over the entrance. Inside, the computers were all taken and several interested parties were hanging around waiting for a station, so she did some browsing, looking through the biography section for anything pertinent. She found that she'd already read everything that might be of use. Next, she hunted up the latest from her favorite espionage writer, a former Navy SEAL, and then grabbed a few of the adjacent titles. As she went to find a good seat to wait in, she felt a twinge of guilt; it was just so tawdry, somehow, stealing from a library. But getting a library card here was out of the question for a number of reasons, and there was the off chance that something she read in these books would make her safer. Safety always trumped guilt.

It wasn't that she was unaware that this was 99 percent pointless—it was extremely unlikely that anything fictional would be of real, concrete use to her—but she'd long ago worked her way through the more fact-based kind of research available. In the absence of A-list sources to mine, she'd settled for the Z-list. It made her more panicky than usual when she didn't have *something* to study. And she'd actually found a tip that seemed practical in her last haul. She'd already begun incorporating it into her routine.

She settled into a faded armchair in an out-of-the-way corner that had a decent view of the computer cubicles and pretended to read the top book in her pile. She could tell from the way several of the computer users had their belongings sprawled across the desk— one had even removed his shoes—that they would be in place for a long while. The most promising station was being used by a teenage girl with a stack of reference books and a harried expression. The girl didn't seem to be checking social media—she was actually writing down titles and authors generated by the search engine. While she waited, Chris kept her head bent over her book, which she had nestled in the crook of her left arm. With the razor blade hidden in her right hand, she neatly sliced off the magnetic sensor taped to the spine and stuffed it into the crevice between the cushion and the arm of the chair. Feigning a lack of interest, she moved on to the next book in the pile.

Chris was ready, her denuded novels already stowed away in her backpack, when the teenage girl left to go find another source. Without jumping up or looking like she'd rushed, Chris was in the chair before any of the other lingering hopefuls even realized their chance had passed.

Actually checking her e-mail usually took about three minutes.

After that, she would have another four hours — if she wasn't driving evasively — to get back to her temporary home. Then of course the reassembly of her safeguards before she could finally sleep. E-mail day was always a long one.

Though there was no connection between her present life and this e-mail account — no repeat IP address, no discussion of places or names — as soon as she was done reading and, if the occasion called for it, answering her mail, she would be out the door and speeding out of town, putting as many miles between herself and this location as possible. Just in case.

Just in case had become Chris's unintentional mantra. She lived a life of overpreparation, but, as she often reminded herself, without that preparation she wouldn't be living a life at all.

It would be nice not to have to take these risks, but the money wasn't going to last forever. Usually she would find a menial job at some mom-and-pop place, preferably one with handwritten records, but that kind of job generated only enough money for the basics — food and rent. Never the more expensive things in her life, like fake IDs, laboratory apparatus, and the various chemical components she hoarded. So she maintained a light presence on the Internet, found her rare paying client here and there, and did everything she could to keep this work from bringing her to the attention of those who wanted her to stop existing.

The last two e-mail days had been fruitless, so she was pleased to see a message waiting for her—pleased for the approximately two-tenths of a second it took her to process the return address.

l.carston.463@dpt11a.net

Just out there—his real e-mail address, easily traceable directly to her former employers. As the hair rose on the back of her neck and the adrenaline surged through her body—*Run, run, run* it seemed to be shouting inside her veins—part of her was still able to gape in disbelief at the arrogance. She always underestimated how astonishingly careless they could be.

They can't be here yet, she reasoned with herself through the panic, her eyes already sweeping the library for men with shoulders too broad for their dark suits, for military haircuts, for anyone moving toward her position. She could see her car through the plate-glass window, and it *looked* like no one had tampered with it, but she hadn't exactly been keeping watch, had she?

So they'd found her again. But they had no way of knowing where she would decide to check her mail. She was religiously random about that choice.

Just now, an alarm had gone off in a tidy gray office, or maybe several offices, maybe even with flashing red lights. Of course there would be a priority command set up to trace this IP address. Bodies were about to be mobilized. But even if they used helicopters—and they had that capability—she had a few minutes. Enough to see what Carston wanted.

The subject line was Tired of running?

Bastard.

She clicked it open. The message wasn't long.

> Policy has changed. We need you. Would an unofficial
> apology help? Can we meet? I wouldn't ask, but lives
> are on the line. Many, many lives.

She'd always liked Carston. He seemed more human than a lot of the other dark suits the department employed. Some of them—

especially the ones in uniform—were downright scary. Which was probably a hypocritical thought, considering the line of work she used to be in.

So of course it was Carston they'd had make contact. They knew she was lonely and frightened, and they'd sent an old friend to make her feel all warm and fuzzy. Common sense, and she probably would have seen through the ploy without help, but it didn't hurt that the same ploy had been used once in a novel she'd stolen.

She allowed herself one deep breath and thirty seconds of concentrated thought. The focus was supposed to be her next move—getting out of this library, this town, this state, as soon as possible—and whether that was enough. Was her current identity still safe, or was it time to relocate again?

However, that focus was derailed by the insidious idea of Carston's offer.

What if...

What if this really was a way to get them to leave her alone? What if her certainty that this was a trap was born from paranoia and reading too much spy fiction?

If the job was important enough, maybe they would give her back her life in exchange.

Unlikely.

Still, there was no point in pretending that Carston's e-mail had gone astray.

She replied the way she figured they were hoping she would, though she'd formed only the barest outline of a plan.

> Tired of a lot of things, Carston. Where we first met, one week from today, noon. If I see anyone with you, I'm gone, yada yada yada, I'm sure you know the drill. Don't be stupid.

She was on her feet and walking in the same moment, a rolling lope she'd perfected, despite her short legs, that looked a lot more casual than it was. She was counting off the seconds in her head, estimating how long it would take a helicopter to cover the distance between DC and this location. Of course, they could alert locals, but that wasn't usually their style.

Not their usual style at all, and yet...she had an unfounded but still pressingly uncomfortable feeling that they might be getting tired of their usual style. It hadn't yielded the results they were looking for, and these were not patient people. They were used to getting what they wanted exactly when they wanted it. And they'd been wanting her dead for three years.

This e-mail was certainly a policy change. If it *was* a trap.

She had to assume it was. That viewpoint, that way of framing her world, was the reason she was still breathing in and out. But there was a small part of her brain that had already begun to foolishly hope.

It was a small-stakes game she was playing, she knew that. Just one life. Just her life.

And this life she'd preserved against such overpowering odds was only that and nothing more: life. The very barest of the basics. One heart beating, one set of lungs expanding and contracting.

She was alive, yes, and she had fought hard to stay that way, but during her darker nights she'd sometimes wondered what exactly she was fighting for. Was the quality of life she maintained worth all this effort? Wouldn't it be *relaxing* to close her eyes and not have to open them again? Wasn't an empty black nothing slightly more palatable than the relentless terror and constant effort?

Only one thing had kept her from answering *Yes* and taking one of the peaceful and painless exits readily available to her, and that was an overdeveloped competitive drive. It had served her well in medical school, and now it kept her breathing. She wasn't going to let them *win*. There was no way she would give them such an easy resolution to their problem. They would probably get her in the end, but they were going to have to *work* for it, damn them, and they would bleed for it, too.

She was in the car now and six blocks from the closest freeway entrance. There was a dark ball cap over her short hair, wide-framed men's sunglasses covering most of her face, and a bulky sweatshirt disguising her slender figure. To a casual observer, she would look a lot like a teenage boy.

The people who wanted her dead had already lost some blood and she found herself suddenly smiling as she drove, remembering. It was odd how comfortable she was with killing people these days, how satisfying she found it. She had become bloodthirsty, which was ironic, all things considered. She'd spent six years under their tutelage, and in all that time they hadn't come close to breaking her down, to turning her into someone who enjoyed her work. But three years on the run from them had changed a lot of things.

She knew she wouldn't enjoy killing an innocent person. She was sure that corner had not been turned, nor would it be. Some people in her line of work—her former line—were well and truly psychotic, but she liked to think that this was the reason her peers were not as good as she was. They had the wrong motivations. Hating what she did gave her the power to do it best.

In the context of her current life, killing was about winning. Not the entire war, just one small battle at a time, but each was still a win. Someone else's heart would stop beating and hers would keep going. Someone would come for her, and instead of a victim he would find a predator. A brown recluse spider, invisible behind her gossamer trap.

This was what they had made her. She wondered if they took any pride at all in their accomplishment or if there was only regret that they hadn't stomped on her fast enough.

Once she was a few miles down the interstate, she felt better. Her car was a popular model, a thousand identical vehicles on the highway with her now, and the stolen plates would be replaced as soon as she found a safe spot to stop. There was nothing to tie her to the town she'd just left. She'd passed two exits and taken a third. If they wanted to blockade the freeway, they'd have no idea where to do it. She was still hidden. Still safe for now.

Of course, driving straight home was out of the question at this point. She took six hours on the return, twisting around various highways and surface roads, constantly checking to be sure there was no one following. By the time she finally got back to her little rented house — the architectural equivalent of a jalopy — she was already half asleep. She thought about making coffee, weighing the benefits of the caffeine boost against the burden of one extra task, and decided to just muscle through it on the vapors of her energy supply.

She dragged herself up the two rickety porch steps, automatically avoiding the rot-weakened spot on the left of the first tread, and unlocked the double dead bolts on the steel security door she'd installed her first week living here; the walls — just wooden studs, drywall, plywood, and vinyl siding — didn't provide the same level of security, but statistically, intruders went for the door first. The bars on the windows were not an insurmountable obstacle, either, but they were enough to motivate the casual cat burglar to move on to an easier target. Before she twisted the handle, she rang the doorbell. Three quick jabs that would look like one continuous push to anyone watching. The sound of the Westminster chimes was only slightly muffled by the thin walls. She stepped through the door quickly — holding her breath, just in case. There was no quiet crunch of broken glass, so she exhaled as she shut the door behind her.

The home security was all her own design. The professionals she'd studied in the beginning had their own methods. None of them had her specialized skill set. Neither did the authors of the various novels she used as implausible manuals now. Everything else she had needed to know had been easy to pull up on YouTube. A few parts from an old washing machine, a microcontroller board ordered online, a new doorbell, and a couple of miscellaneous acquisitions, and she had herself a solid booby trap.

She locked the dead bolts behind her and hit the switch closest to the door to turn on the lights. It was set in a panel with two other switches. The middle was a dummy. The third switch, the farthest from the door, was patched into the same low-voltage signal wire as the doorbell. Like that fixture and the door, the panel of switches was newer by decades than anything else in the small front room that was living area, dining room, and kitchen combined.

Everything looked as she'd left it: minimal, cheap furnishings—nothing big enough for an adult to hide behind—empty counters and tabletop, no ornaments or artwork. Sterile. She knew that even with the avocado-and-mustard-vinyl flooring and the popcorn ceiling, it still looked a little like a laboratory.

Maybe the smell was what made it feel like a lab. The room was so scrupulously sanitary, an intruder would probably attribute the pool-supply-store scent to cleaning chemicals. But only if he got inside without triggering her security system. If he triggered the system, he wouldn't have time to register many details about the room.

The rest of the house was just a small bedroom and bathroom, set in a straight line from the front door to the far wall, nothing in the way to trip her. She turned the light off, saving herself the walk back.

She stumbled through the only door into her bedroom, sleep-walking through the routine. Enough light made it through the mini-blinds—red neon from the gas station across the street—that she left the lamp off. First, she rearranged two of the long feather pillows on top of the double mattress that took up most of the space in the room into the vague shape of a human body. Then the Ziploc bags full of Halloween costume blood were stuffed into the pillowcases; close up, the blood wasn't very convincing, but the Ziplocs were for an attacker who broke the window, pushed the blinds aside, and shot from that vantage point. He wouldn't be able to detect the difference in the neon half-light. Next, the head—the mask she'd used was another after-Halloween-sale acquisition, a parody of some political also-ran that had fairly realistic skin coloring. She'd stuffed it to roughly match the size of her own head and sewn a cheap brunette wig into place. Most important, a tiny wire, threaded up between the mattress and box spring, was hidden in the strands of nylon. A matching wire pierced through the pillow the head rested on. She yanked the sheet up, then the blanket, patted it all into shape, then twisted together the frayed ends of the two wires. It was a very tenuous joining. If she touched the head even lightly or jostled the pillow body a bit, the wires would slip silently apart.

She stood back and gave the decoy a once-over through half-closed eyes. It wasn't her best work, but it *did* look like someone was asleep in the bed. Even if an intruder didn't believe it was Chris, he would still have to neutralize the sleeping body before he went on to search for her.

Too tired to change into her pajamas, she just stepped out of her loose jeans. It was enough. She grabbed the fourth pillow and pulled her sleeping bag out from under the bed; they felt bulkier and heavier than usual. She dragged them into the compact bathroom, dumped them in the tub, and did the bare minimum of ablutions. No face-washing tonight, just cleaning the teeth.

The gun and the gas mask were both under the sink, hidden beneath a stack of towels. She pulled the mask over her head and tightened the straps, then clapped her palm over the filter port and inhaled through her nose to check the seal. The mask suctioned to her face just fine. It always did, but she never let familiarity or exhaustion make her skip the safety routine. She moved the gun into the wall-mounted soap dish within easy reach above the bathtub. She didn't love the gun—she was a decent shot compared with a totally untrained civilian, but not in the same class as a professional. She needed the option, though; someday her enemies were going to figure her system out, and the people coming for her would be in gas masks, too.

Honestly, she was surprised her shtick had saved her this long.

With an unopened chemical-absorption canister tucked under her bra strap, she shuffled the two steps back into the bedroom. She knelt beside the floor vent on the right side of the bed she'd never used. The vent cover grille probably wasn't as dusty as it should be, the grille's top screws were only halfway in, and the bottom screws were missing altogether, but she was sure no one looking through the window would notice these details or understand what they meant if he did; Sherlock Holmes was about the only person she *wasn't* worried would make an attempt on her life.

She loosened the top screws and removed the grille. A few things would be immediately obvious to anyone who looked inside the vent. One, the back of the vent was sealed off, so it was no longer functional. Two, the large white bucket and the big battery pack probably didn't belong down there. She pried the lid off the bucket and was immediately greeted by the same chemical smell that infused the front room, so familiar she barely noted it.

She reached into the darkness behind the bucket and pulled out, first, a small, awkward contraption with a coil, metal arms, and thin wires, then a glass ampoule about the size of her finger, and, finally, a rubber cleaning glove. She positioned the solenoid—the device she'd scavenged from a discarded washing machine—so that the arms extending from it were half submerged in the colorless liquid inside the bucket. She blinked hard twice, trying to force herself into alertness; this was the delicate part. She put the glove on her right hand, then pulled the canister free from her bra strap and held it ready in her left. With the gloved hand, she carefully inserted the ampoule into the grooves she'd drilled into the metal arms for this purpose. The ampoule rested just under the surface of the acid, the white powder inside it inert and harmless. However, if the current running through the wires that were attached so tenuously atop the bed were to be interrupted, the pulse would snap the solenoid shut, and the glass would shatter. The white powder would turn into a gas that was neither inert nor harmless.

It was essentially the same arrangement that she had in the front room; the wiring was just simpler here. This trap was set only while she slept.

She replaced the glove and the vent cover and then, with a feeling that was not quite buoyant enough to be called relief, lurched back to the bathroom. The door, like the vent, might have tipped off someone as detail oriented as Mr. Holmes — the soft rubber liners around all the edges were definitely not standard. They wouldn't entirely seal the bathroom off from the bedroom, but they would give her more time.

She half fell into the tub, a slow-motion collapse onto the puffy sleeping bag. It had taken her a while to get used to sleeping in the mask, but now she didn't even think about it as she gratefully closed her eyes.

She shimmied herself into the down-and-nylon cocoon, squirming till the hard square of her iPad was nestled against the small of her back. It was plugged into an extension cord that got power from the front-room wiring. If the power fluctuated along that line, the iPad would vibrate. She knew from experience that it was enough to wake her, even as tired as she was tonight. She also knew that she could have the canister — still in her left hand, hugged tight against her chest like a child's teddy bear — unsealed and screwed into place on the gas mask in less than three seconds, despite being half awake, in the dark, and holding her breath. She'd practiced so many times, and then she'd proved herself during the three emergencies that had not been practice. She'd survived. Her system worked.

Exhausted as she was, she had to let her mind tick over the evils of her day before it would let her be unconscious. It felt horrible — like phantom-limb pain, not connected to any actual piece of her body, just *there* anyway — knowing they'd found her again. She wasn't satisfied with her e-mail response, either. She'd come up with the plan too impulsively to be sure of it. And it required her to act more quickly than she'd like.

She knew the theory — sometimes, if you ran headlong at the guy holding the gun, you could catch him off guard. Flight was always her favorite move, but she didn't see a way out of the alternative this time. Maybe tomorrow, after her tired brain had rebooted.

Surrounded by her web, she slept.

CHAPTER 2

As she sat waiting for Carston to show, she thought about the other times the department had tried to kill her.

Barnaby — Dr. Joseph Barnaby, her mentor, the last friend she'd known — had prepared her for the first attempt. But even with all his foresight, planning, and deep-rooted paranoia, it was just dumb luck in the form of an extra cup of black coffee that had saved her life.

She hadn't been sleeping well. She'd worked with Barnaby for six years at that point, and a little more than halfway through that time, he'd told her his suspicions. At first she hadn't wanted to believe he could be right. They were only doing their job as directed, and doing it well. *You can't think of this as a long-term situation,* he'd insisted, though he'd been in the same division for seventeen years. *People like us, people who have to know things that no one wants us to know, eventually we become inconvenient. You don't have to do anything wrong. You can be perfectly trustworthy. They're the ones you can't trust.*

So much for working for the good guys.

His suspicions had become more specific, then shifted into planning, which had evolved into physical preparation. Barnaby had been a big believer in preparation, not that it had done him any good in the end.

The stress had begun to escalate in those last months as the date for the exodus approached, and, unsurprisingly, she'd had trouble sleeping. That particular April morning it had taken two cups of coffee rather than the usual one to get her brain going. Add that extra cup to the smaller-than-average bladder in her smaller-than-average body, and you ended up with a doctor running to the can, too rushed to even log out, rather than sitting at her desk. And that's where she had been when the killing gas filtered through the vents into the lab. Barnaby had been exactly where he was supposed to be.

His screams had been his final gift to her, his last warning.

They both had been sure that when the blow came, it wouldn't happen at the lab. Messy that way. Dead bodies usually raised a few eyebrows, and smart murderers tried to keep that kind of evidence as far removed from themselves as possible. They didn't strike when the victim was in their own living room.

She should have known never to underestimate the arrogance of the people who wanted her dead. They didn't worry about the law. They were too cozy with the people who made those laws. She also should have respected the power of pure stupidity to take a smart person completely by surprise.

The next three times had been more straightforward. Professional contractors, she assumed, given that they'd each worked alone. Only men so far, though a woman was always a possibility in the future. One man had tried to shoot her, one to stab her, and one to brain her with a crowbar. None of these tries had been effective because the violence had happened to pillows. And then her assailants had died.

The invisible but very caustic gas had silently flooded the small room—it took about two and a half seconds once the connection between the wires was broken. After that, the assassin was left with a life expectancy of approximately five seconds, depending on his height and weight. It would not have been a pleasant five seconds.

Her bathtub mixture was not the same thing they'd used for

Barnaby, but it was close enough. It was the simplest way she knew to kill someone so swiftly and so painfully. And it was a renewable resource, unlike many of her weapons. All she needed was a good stock of peaches and a pool-supply store. Nothing that required restricted access or even a mailing address, nothing that her pursuers could track.

It really pissed her off that they'd managed to find her again.

She'd been furious since waking yesterday and had only gotten angrier as the hours passed while she made her preparations.

She had forced herself to nap and then drove all the next night in a suitable car, rented using a very weak ID for one Taylor Golding and a recently obtained credit card in the same name. Early this morning, she'd arrived in the city she least wanted to be in, and that had turned her anger up to the next level. She'd returned the car to a Hertz near Ronald Reagan National Airport, then walked across the street to another company and rented a new one with District of Columbia plates.

Six months ago, she would have done things differently. Gathered her belongings from the small house she was renting, sold her current vehicle on Craigslist, purchased a new one for cash from some private citizen who didn't keep records, and then driven aimlessly for a few days until she found a medium-size city-town that looked right. There she'd start the process of staying alive all over again.

But now there was that stupid, twisted hope that Carston was telling the truth. A very anemic hope. It probably wouldn't have been enough motivation on its own. There was something else—a small but irritating worry that she had neglected a responsibility.

Barnaby had saved her life. Again and again. Every time she survived another assassination attempt, it was because he had warned her, had educated her, had made her ready.

If Carston was lying to her—which she was 97 percent sure he was—and arranging an ambush, then everything he'd said was a lie.

Including the part about her being needed. And if they didn't need her, that meant they'd found someone else to do the job, someone as good as she had been.

They might have replaced her a long time ago, might have assassinated a whole line of employees for all she knew, but she doubted it. While the department had money and access, the one thing it had in short supply was personnel. It took time to locate, cultivate, and train an asset like Barnaby or herself. People with those kinds of skills didn't grow in test tubes.

She'd had Barnaby to save her. Who was going to save the dumb kid they'd recruited after her? The newcomer would be brilliant, just as she had been, but he or she would be blind to the most important element. Forget *serving your country,* forget *saving innocent lives,* forget the *state-of-the-art facilities* and the *groundbreaking science,* and the *unlimited budget.* Forget the seven-figure salary. How about not being murdered? No doubt the person now holding her old position had no idea that his or her survival was even in question.

She wished she had a way to warn that individual. Even if she couldn't spend all the time Barnaby had devoted to helping her. Even if it could be only one conversation: *This is how they reward people like us. Get ready.*

But that wasn't an option.

The morning was spent on more preparations. She checked into the Brayscott, a small boutique hotel, under the name Casey Wilson. The ID she used wasn't much more convincing than Taylor Golding's, but two of the phone lines were ringing as she registered, and the busy desk clerk wasn't paying close attention. There were rooms available this early, the clerk told her, but Casey would have to pay for an extra day, as check-in did not begin till three. Casey agreed to this stipulation without complaint. The clerk seemed relieved. She smiled at Casey, really looking at her for the first time. Casey controlled her flinch. It didn't matter if this girl remembered Casey's face; Casey would make herself memorable enough in the next half hour.

Casey used androgynous names on purpose. It was one of the strategies she'd gleaned from the case files Barnaby had fed her, something the real spies did, but it was also common sense, something the fiction writers had figured out as well. The logic was that if people were searching this hotel for a woman, they would start with the clearly female names in the register, like Jennifer and Cathy. It might take them another round to get to the Caseys and the Terrys and the Drews. Any time she could buy for herself was good. An extra minute might save her life.

Casey shook her head at the eager bellman who stepped toward her offering his services and wheeled her single piece of luggage behind her to the elevator. She kept her face turned away from the camera over the control panel. Once inside the room, she opened the bag and removed a large briefcase and a zipper-top black tote. Other than these two things, her suitcase was empty.

She took off the blazer that made her thin gray sweater and plain black pants look professional and hung it up. The sweater was pinned in the back to make it formfitting. She removed the pins and let the sweater bag around her, changing her into someone a little smaller, maybe a bit younger. She removed her lipstick and rubbed off most of her eye makeup, then checked the effect in the large mirror over the dresser. Younger, vulnerable; the baggy sweater suggested that she was hiding in it. She thought it would do.

If she'd been going to see a female hotel manager, she would have played it slightly differently, perhaps tried to add some fake bruises with blue and black eye shadow, but the name on the card at the desk downstairs was William Green, and she didn't think she would need to put in the extra time.

It wasn't a perfect plan, and that bothered her. She would have liked to have another week just to review all the possible repercussions. But it was the best option she could set in motion with the time she'd had. It was probably overly elaborate, but it was too late to rethink it now.

She called the desk and asked for Mr. Green. She was connected quickly.

"This is William Green—how can I help you?"

The voice was hearty and overly warm. She immediately had the mental image of a walrus of a man, bushy mustache included.

"Um, yes, I hope I'm not bothering you..."

"No, of course not, Ms. Wilson. I'm here to help in any way I can."

"I do need help, but it might sound a little odd...It's hard to explain."

"Don't worry, miss, I'm sure I can be of assistance." He sounded extremely confident. It made her wonder what kinds of odd requests he had fielded before.

"Oh, dear," she dithered. "This might be easier in person?" She made it into a question.

"Of course, Ms. Wilson. Fortunately, I will be available in fifteen minutes. My office is on the first floor, just around the corner from the front desk. Will that suit?"

Fluttery and relieved: "Yes, thank you *so* much."

She put the bags in the closet and carefully counted out the bills she needed from the stash in the large briefcase. She slipped this into her pockets, then waited thirteen minutes. She took the stairs to avoid the elevator cameras.

As Mr. Green ushered her into his windowless office, she was amused to see that her mental image had not been that far off. No mustache—no hair at all except for the barest hint of white eyebrows—but in all other ways very walrus-y.

It wasn't hard to play frightened, and halfway into her tale of her abusive ex-boyfriend who'd stolen the family heirlooms, she knew she had him. He bristled in a very male way, looking as if he wanted to rant about the sort of monsters who hit little women, but he mostly held his peace aside from several *Tut-tut, we'll take good care of you, you're safe here* kinds of assurances. He probably would have helped her without the generous tip she gave him, but it certainly didn't hurt. He swore to tell only the members of the staff who were part of her plan, and she thanked him warmly. He wished her well and offered to bring the police in, if that would help. Casey confessed with great sadness how ineffective the police and the restraining orders had been for her in the past. She implied that she could handle this alone as long as she had the help of a big, strong man like Mr. Green. He was flattered, and he hurried out to get everything ready.

It wasn't the only time she'd played this card. Barnaby had suggested it initially, when their escape plan had reached the fine-tuning stage. At first she had bristled at the idea, offended in some obscure way, but Barnaby was always practical. She was small and female; in a lot of people's heads, that would always make her the underdog. Why not use this assumption to her advantage? Play the victim to keep from being one.

Casey went back to her room and changed into the clothes she'd kept inside the briefcase, trading her sweater for a tight, black V-neck tee and adding a thick black belt with intricately braided leatherwork. Everything she took off had to fit back into the briefcase, because she was leaving the suitcase and she wouldn't be returning to this hotel.

She was already armed; she never went out without taking some precautions. But now she moved to the high-alert version of her personal protection, arming herself to the literal teeth — or to the tooth, really; she inserted a fake crown full of something much less painful than cyanide but just as deadly. It was the oldest trick in the book for a reason: It worked. And sometimes the last move you had was permanently extracting yourself from the hands of your enemies.

The big black tote bag had two ornamental wooden pieces at the apex of the shoulder strap. Inside the tote was her special jewelry in little padded boxes.

Every piece was one of a kind and irreplaceable. She would never again have the access to acquire ornamental tools like these, so she was very careful with her treasures.

Three rings — one rose gold, one yellow gold, one silver. They all had small barbs hidden under clever little twisting hatches. The color of the metal indicated which substance coated the barb. Very straightforward, probably expected from her.

Next, the earrings, which she always handled with delicate care. She wouldn't risk wearing them for this part of the journey; she would wait until she was closer to her target. Once they were in, she had to move her head very deliberately. They looked like simple glass globes, but the glass was so thin that a high note could shatter it, especially as the little spheres were already under pressure from the inside. If anyone grabbed her by the neck or head, the glass would burst with a quiet pop. She would hold her breath — which she could do for a minute fifteen, easy — and close her eyes if possible. Her attacker would not know to do that.

Around her neck went a largish silver locket. It was very conspicuous and would command the attention of anyone who knew who she truly was. There was nothing deadly about it, though; it was just a distraction from the real dangers. Inside was a photo of a pretty little girl with fluffy, straw-colored hair. The child's full name was handwritten on the back of the picture; it looked like something a mother or an aunt would wear. However, this particular girl was Carston's only grandchild. Hopefully, if it was too late for Casey, the person who found her body would be a real cop who, due to the lack of identification, would be forced to dig into this evidence and bring her murder around to the doorstep where it ultimately belonged. It probably wouldn't really hurt Carston, but it might make things inconvenient for him, might make him feel threatened or worry that she'd released other information elsewhere.

Because she knew enough about hidden disasters and classified horrors to do much more than inconvenience Carston. But even now, three years past her first death sentence, she hadn't grown comfortable with the idea of treason or the very real possibility of causing a panic. There was no way to foresee the potential damage of her revelations, the harm they might cause to innocent citizens. So she'd settled for just making Carston *think* that she had done something so reckless; maybe the worry would give him an aneurysm. A pretty little locket filled with drippings of revenge to make losing the game more palatable.

The cord the locket was attached to, however, *was* deadly. It had the tensile strength of airline cable in proportion to its size and was easily strong enough to garrote a person. The cord closed with a magnet rather than a clasp; she had no desire to be lassoed with her own weapon. The wooden embellishments on her tote's shoulder strap had slots where the ends of the cords fit; once the cord was in place, the wooden pieces became handles. Physical force wasn't her first choice, but it would be unexpected. It gave her an advantage to be ready.

Inside the intricate patterns of her black leather belt were hidden several spring-loaded syringes. She could pull them individually or flip a mechanism that would expose all the sharp ends at once if an attacker pressed her close to his body. The mix of the different substances would not blend well in his system.

Scalpel blades with taped edges were tucked into her pockets.

Standard shoe knives, one that popped forward, one to the rear.

Two cans labeled PEPPER SPRAY in her bag — one containing the real thing, the other with something more permanently debilitating.

A pretty perfume bottle that released gas, not liquid.

What looked like a tube of ChapStick in her pocket.

And several other fun options, just in case. Plus the little things she'd brought for the unlikely outcome — success. A bright yellow, lemon-shaped squeeze bottle, matches, a travel-size fire extinguisher. And cash, plenty of it. She stuck a key card in the tote; she wouldn't come back to this hotel, but if things went well, someone else would.

She had to move carefully when she was in full armor like this, but she'd practiced enough that she was confident in her walk. It was comforting to know that if anyone caused her to move less carefully, he'd be the worse for it.

She left the hotel, nodding to the clerk who had checked her in, a briefcase in one hand and the black tote over her arm. She got into her car and drove to a crowded park near the middle of the city. She left the car in an adjacent strip mall's lot on the north side and walked into the park.

She was quite familiar with this park. There was a bathroom near the southeast corner that she headed into now. As she'd expected, midmorning on a school day, it was empty. Out of the briefcase came another set of clothes. There was also a rolled-up backpack and some more accessories. She changed her clothes, put her previous outfit in the briefcase, and then shoved it and the tote into the large backpack.

When she walked out of the bathroom, she was no longer immediately recognizable as a *she*. She slouched away toward the south end of the park, loose-kneed, concentrating on keeping her hips from swaying and giving her away. Though it didn't appear that anyone was looking, it was always smarter to act like someone was.

The park started to fill up when lunchtime approached, as she'd known it would. No one paid attention to the androgynous kid sitting on a bench in the shade furiously texting on a smartphone. No one came close enough to see that the phone wasn't on.

Across the street from the bench was Carston's favorite lunch spot. It was not the meeting place she'd suggested. She was also five days early.

Behind the men's sunglasses, her eyes scanned the sidewalks.

This might not work. Maybe Carston had changed his habits. Habits were, after all, dangerous things. Like the expectation of safety.

She'd sifted through the advice that both the factual accounts and the novels had given on disguises, always focusing on the commonsense stuff. Don't slap on a platinum wig and high heels just because you're a short brunette. Don't think *opposite;* think *inconspicuous.* Think about what attracts attention — like blondes and stilettos — and avoid it. Play to your strengths. Sometimes what you believe makes you unattractive can keep you alive.

Back in the normal days, she'd resented her boyish frame. Now she used it. If you put on a baggy jersey and a pair of well-worn jeans a size too big, any eyes looking for *woman* might slide right over *boy.* Her hair was short as a boy's and easy to hide under a ball cap, and layered socks inside a pair of too-large Reeboks gave her that puppy-pawed look of the average teenage male. Someone who really looked at her face might notice some discrepancies. But why would anyone look? The park was filling with people of all ages and sexes. She did not stand out, and no one hunting for her would expect her to be here. She hadn't been back to DC since the department's first attempt to murder her.

This wasn't her forte — leaving her web, hunting. But it was, at least, something she'd put some thought into beforehand. Most of what she did in an average day took only a small part of her attention and intelligence. The rest of her mind was always working through possibilities, imagining scenarios. It made her slightly more confident now. She was working from a mental map that had been many months in the creation.

Carston had not changed his habits. At exactly 12:15 he sat down at a metal bistro table in front of his café. He'd picked the one that was angled so he could be completely covered by the umbrella's shade, as she'd expected. Carston had once been a redhead. He didn't have much of the hair anymore, but he still had the complexion.

The waitress waved to him, nodded toward the pad of paper in her hand, then went back inside. So he had a usual order. Another habit that could get you killed. If Casey had wanted Carston dead, she could have managed it without his ever knowing she had been here.

She got up, shoved the phone in her pocket, and slung her backpack onto one shoulder.

The sidewalk led behind a rise and some trees. Carston couldn't see her here. It was time for another costume. Her posture changed. The hat came off. She shrugged out of the jersey she'd layered over the T-shirt. She tightened the belt and rolled up the bottom inches of the jeans, turning them into a boyfriend-cut look. The Reeboks came off and traded places with the slip-on ballet–slash–athletic shoes from the backpack. She did all this casually, as if she were hot and just stripping down a bit. The weather made it believable. Bystanders might have been surprised to see a girl under the masculine clothing, but she doubted this moment would linger in anyone's memory. There were too many more extreme styles on display in the park today. The sunshine always did bring out the freaks in DC.

Her tote went over her shoulder again. She dropped the backpack behind an out-of-the-way tree while no one was looking. If someone found it, there was nothing inside that she couldn't live without.

Decently certain that no one could see her, she added a wig and then, finally, carefully, she threaded her earrings into place.

She could have confronted Carston in her boyish garb, but why give up any secrets? Why let him connect her to her surveillance? If he'd even noticed the boy, that is. She might need to be a boy again soon, so she would not waste the persona now. And she could have saved some time by wearing the costume from the hotel, but if she'd made no changes to her appearance, the image of her captured by the closed-circuit security cameras at the hotel could be easily linked to the footage from any public or private cameras picking her up now. By spending extra time on her appearance, she'd broken as many links as she could; if someone was trying to find the boy, or the businesswoman, or the casual park visitor she was now, he would have a complicated trail to follow.

It was cooler in her female outfit. She let the light breeze dry the sweat that had been building up under the nylon jersey and then walked out to the street.

She came at him from behind, taking the same path he had just a few minutes earlier. His food had arrived—a chicken parm—and he seemed to be totally absorbed in consuming it. But she knew Carston was better than she was at appearing to be something he was not.

She dropped into the seat across from him with no fanfare. His mouth was full of sandwich when he looked up.

She knew that he was a good actor. She assumed he would bury his true reaction and display the emotion he wished before she could catch sight of the first. Because he didn't look surprised at all, she assumed she'd taken him completely unawares. If he *had* been expecting her, he would have acted like her sudden appearance had shocked him. But this, the steady gaze across the table, the unwidened eyes, the methodical chewing—this was him controlling his surprise. She was almost 80 percent sure.

She didn't say anything. She just met his expressionless gaze while he finished masticating his bite of sandwich.

"I guess it would be too easy to just meet as planned," he said.

"Too easy for your sniper, sure." She said the words lightly, using the same volume he had. Anyone overhearing would think the words a joke. But the two other lunch groups were talking and laughing loudly; the people passing by on the sidewalk listened to earphones and telephones. No one cared what she was saying except Carston.

"That was never me, Juliana. You must know that."

It was her turn to act unsurprised. It had been so long since anyone had addressed her by her real name, it sounded like a stranger's. After the initial jolt, she felt a small wave of pleasure. It was good that her name sounded foreign to her. That meant she was doing it right.

His eyes flitted to her obvious wig—it was actually quite similar to her real hair, but now he would suspect she was hiding something very different. Then he forced his eyes back to hers. He waited for a response for another moment, but when she didn't speak he continued, choosing his words carefully.

"The, er, parties who decided you should...retire have...fallen into disfavor. It was never a popular decision to begin with, and now those of us who were always in disagreement are no longer ruled by those parties."

It could be true. It probably wasn't.

He answered the skepticism in her eyes. "Have you had any... unpleasant disturbances in the past nine months?"

"And here I was thinking that I'd just gotten better at playing hide-and-seek than you."

"It's over, Julie. Might has been overcome by right."

"I love happy endings." Heavy sarcasm.

He winced, hurt by the sarcasm. Or pretending to be.

"Not so happy as all that," he said slowly. "A happy ending would mean I wouldn't have contacted you. You would have been left alone for the rest of your life. And it would have been a long one, as much as that was in our power."

She nodded as if she agreed, as if she believed. In the old days, she'd always assumed Carston was exactly what he appeared to be. He had been the face of the good guys for a long time. It was almost fun now in a strange way, like a game, to try to decipher what each word actually meant.

Except then there was the tiny voice that asked, *What if there is no game? What if this is true...if I could be free?*

"You were the best, Juliana."

"Dr. Barnaby was the best."

"I know you don't want to hear this, but he never had your talent."

"Thank you."

He raised his eyebrows.

"Not for the compliment," she explained. "Thank you for not trying to tell me his death was an accident." All of this still in the lighthearted tone.

"It was a poor choice motivated by paranoia and disloyalty. A person who will sell out his partner always sees the partner as plotting in exactly the same way. Dishonest people don't believe honest people exist."

She kept her face stony while he spoke.

Never, in three years of constant running, had she ever spilled a single secret that she'd been privy to. Never once had she given her pursuers any reason to think her a traitor. Even as they tried to kill her, she had remained faithful. And that hadn't mattered to her department, not at all.

Not much did matter to them. She was distracted for a moment by the memory of how close she had been to what she was looking for, the place she might have reached by now on her most pressing avenue of research and creation if she hadn't been interrupted. That project had not mattered to them, either, apparently.

"But the egg is on those disloyal faces now," Carston continued. "Because we never found anyone as good as you. Hell, we never found anyone half as good as Barnaby. It amazes me how people can forget that true talent is a limited commodity."

He waited, clearly hoping she would speak, hoping she would ask something, betray some sign of interest. She just stared at him politely, the way someone would look at the stranger ringing her up at a register.

He sighed and then leaned in, suddenly intent. "We have a problem. We need the kind of answers only you can give us. We don't have anyone else who can do this job. And we can't screw this one up."

"*You*, not *we*," she said simply.

"I know you better than that, Juliana. You care about the innocents."

"I used to. You could say that part of me was murdered."

Carston winced again.

"Juliana, I'm sorry. I've always been sorry. I tried to stop them. I was so relieved when you slipped through their fingers. *Every* time you slipped through their fingers."

She couldn't help but be impressed he was admitting all of it. No denials, no excuses. None of the *It was just an unfortunate accident at the lab* kind of thing she had been expecting. No *It wasn't us; it was enemies of the state.* No stories, just acknowledgment.

"And now everyone is sorry." His voice dropped and she had to listen hard to make out his words. "Because we don't have you, and people are going to die, Juliana. Thousands of people. Hundreds of thousands."

He waited this time while she thought it over. It took her a few minutes to examine all the possible angles.

She spoke quietly too, now, but made sure there was no interest or emotion in her voice. Just stating obvious facts to move the conversation forward. "You know someone who has vital information."

Carston nodded.

"You can't take him or her out, because that would let others know that you are aware of them. Which would expedite whatever course of action you would prefer not to happen."

Another nod.

"We're talking about the bad stuff here, yes?"

A sigh.

Nothing worked the department up like terrorism. She'd been recruited before the emotional dust had entirely settled around the hole where the Twin Towers used to stand. Preventing terrorism had always been the main component of her job — the best justification for it. The threat of terrorism had also been manipulated, turned and twisted, till by the end she'd lost a lot of faith in the idea that she was actually doing the work of a patriot.

"And a large device," she said, not a question. The biggest bogeyman was always this — that at some point, someone who truly hated the United States would get his or her hands on something nuclear.

That was the dark shadow that hid her profession from the eyes of the world, that made her so indispensable, no matter how much Joe Citizen wanted to think she didn't exist.

And it *had* happened—more than once. People like her had kept those situations from turning into massive human tragedies. It was a trade-off. Small-scale horror versus wholesale slaughter.

Carston shook his head and suddenly his pale eyes were haunted. She couldn't help but shudder a little internally as she realized it was door number two. There were only ever two fears that big.

It's biological. She didn't say the words out loud, just mouthed them.

Carston's bleak expression was her answer.

She looked down for a moment, sorting through all of his responses and reducing them to two columns, two lists of possibilities in her head. Column one: Carston was a talented liar who was saying things he thought would motivate her to visit a place where people were better prepared to dispose of Juliana Fortis forever. He was thinking quickly on his feet, pushing her most sensitive buttons.

Column two: Someone had a biological weapon of mass destruction, and the powers that be didn't know where it was or when it would be used. But they knew someone who did.

Vanity carried some weight, shifting the balance slightly. She knew she was good. It was true that they probably hadn't found someone better.

Still, she would put her money on column one.

"Jules, I don't want you dead," he said quietly, guessing her train of thought. "I wouldn't have contacted you if that were the case. I wouldn't *want* to meet with you. Because I am certain you have at least six ways to kill me on your person right now, and every reason in the world to use one of them."

"You really think I would come with only six?" she asked.

He frowned nervously for a second, then decided to laugh. "You make my point for me. I don't have a death wish, Jules. I'm on the level."

He eyed the locket around her neck, and she suppressed a smile.

She returned to her light voice. "I would prefer it if you called me Dr. Fortis. I think we're past the point of nicknames."

He made a hurt face. "I'm not asking you to forgive me. I should have done more."

She nodded, though again, she wasn't agreeing with him, she was just moving the conversation along.

"I am asking you to help me. No, not me. To help the innocent people who are going to die if you don't."

"If they die, it's not on me."

"I know, Ju—Doctor. I know. It will be on me. But who's to blame won't really matter to them. They'll be dead."

She held his gaze. She wouldn't be the one to blink.

His expression shifted to something darker. "Would you like to hear what it will do to them?"

"No."

"It might be too much even for *your* stomach."

"I doubt it. But it doesn't really matter. What *might* happen is secondary."

"I'd like to know what is more important than hundreds of thousands of American lives."

"It's going to sound horribly selfish, but breathing in and out has sort of trumped everything else for me."

"You can't help us if you're dead," Carston said bluntly. "The lesson has been learned. This won't be the last time we'll need you. We won't make the same mistake again."

She hated to buy into this, but the balance was shifting even more. What Carston was saying *did* make sense. She was certainly no stranger to policy changes. What if it was all true? She could play cold, but Carston knew her well. She would have a difficult time living with a disaster of this magnitude if she thought there was any chance she could have done something. That was how, in the beginning, they'd roped her into possibly the worst profession in the entire world.

"I don't suppose you have the files on you," she said.

CHAPTER 3

Tonight, her name was Alex.

She'd needed to put a little distance between herself and DC, and she'd ended up in a small motel just north of Philadelphia. It was one of half a dozen that lined the interstate on the way out of the city. It would take any tracker a while to search all of them, even if he first somehow narrowed down her position to this part of town. She'd left no trail to even get a hunter to Pennsylvania. Regardless, she'd be sleeping in the bathtub tonight as usual.

There was no table in the small room, so she had all the files laid out on the bed. Just looking at them exhausted her. It had not been a simple matter of having Carston FedEx them somewhere.

The information was ready, Carston had told her. He'd been hopeful that she would meet with him, and he would have brought the files with him if he'd been expecting her. She insisted on hard copies, and he agreed. She gave him the delivery instructions.

The difficulty was breaking the connection on both ends.

For example, she couldn't just have Carston dump the files into a trash can and hire someone to pick them up for her—it was too easy for people to keep an eye on that trash can. The watchers would see the person who picked the files up and then follow that person. That person could take the files to a separate drop spot before she came near them, but the eyes would already be there. Somewhere along the line, the package had to be out of the observers' sight long enough for her to perform a complex little shell game.

So Carston had, as instructed, left a box for her at the front desk of the Brayscott Hotel. Mr. Green was ready. He thought Carston was a friend who had stolen back those family heirlooms from the violent ex, who was surely following him. Mr. Green had given her the code so she could remotely watch the hotel's video surveillance feed from an Internet café miles away. Just because she hadn't seen people following Carston didn't mean they weren't there, but he appeared to simply deliver the box and walk away. The manager did a good job of following all her instructions, most likely because he knew she was watching. The box went into the service elevator and down to the laundry, where it was transferred to a maid's cart, delivered to her room, and then put into her inconspicuous black suitcase by the bike messenger to whom she'd given the key card and five hundred dollars. The bike messenger had taken a circuitous route, following the instructions she'd given him over a cheap prepaid phone that she'd already disposed of, and eventually dropped the box with a confused salesperson at the copy store across the street from the café.

Hopefully, the watchers were still back at the hotel, waiting for her to walk through the front door. Probably they were smarter, but even if there were ten watchers, there wouldn't have been enough to follow every stranger who walked out of the hotel. If one had attached himself to her messenger, he would have had a hard time keeping up. She could only cross her fingers that no one was watching now.

She'd had to move fast. That next hour was the most dangerous part of her plan.

Of course, she'd known there would be some kind of tracking device hidden in the materials. She'd told Carston she would scan for a trick like this, but perhaps he'd guessed that she didn't have the tech to do that. As quickly as possible, she made a set of colored duplicates. It took fifteen minutes, much too long. The duplicates went into the suitcase, and the originals into a paper bag that the girl at the counter gave her. She left the box in the garbage there.

The clock was really against her now. She'd climbed in a cab and had the driver head toward a rougher part of DC while she looked for the first place that would give her the privacy she needed. She didn't have time to be picky, and she ended up having the cabbie wait for her at the end of an unsavory alley. It was the kind of behavior he would definitely remember, but there was no help for it. They could be watching her already. She hurried to the bottom of the dead-end alley — what a place to be caught! — stepped behind a dumpster, and cleared a spot on the broken asphalt with her foot.

The sound of movement behind her made her jump and spin around, her hand on the thick black belt at her waist, her fingers automatically seeking the thin syringe hidden farthest to the left.

Across the alley, a dazed-looking man on a bed of cardboard and rags was watching her with a mesmerized expression, but he said nothing and made no move to either leave or approach. She didn't have time to think about what he would see. Keeping the homeless man in her peripheral vision, she turned her focus to the bag of original documents. She pulled her lemon-shaped squeeze bottle out of her handbag and squirted it into the paper bag. The smell of gasoline saturated the air around her. The man's expression didn't change. Then she lit the match.

She watched the burn carefully, the fire extinguisher in her hands now in case the flames started to spread. The homeless man seemed bored by this part. He turned his back to her.

She waited until every scrap was ash before she doused the flame. She didn't know what was in the files yet, but it would assuredly be very sensitive. She had never worked on a project that wasn't. She rubbed the toe of her shoe across the black and gray powder, grinding it into the pavement. There wasn't a fragment left, she was sure. She tossed a five to the man on the cardboard before she ran back to the cab.

From there it was a series of cabs, two rides on the Metro, and a few blocks on foot. She couldn't be sure that she'd lost them. She could only do her best and be ready. Another cab landed her in Alexandria, where she rented a third car on a third brand-new credit card.

And now she was outside of Philly in this cheap hotel room, a heavily perfumed deodorizer warring with the smell of stale cigarette smoke, staring at the neat stacks of paper laid out on the bed.

The subject's name was Daniel Nebecker Beach.

He was twenty-nine. Fair-skinned, tall, medium build, medium ash-brown hair with longish waves—the length surprised her, for some reason, perhaps because she so often dealt with military men. Hazel eyes. He was born in Alexandria to Alan Geoffrey Beach and Tina Anne Beach née Nebecker. One sibling, Kevin, eighteen months older. His family had lived in Maryland for most of his childhood, except for a brief stretch in Richmond, Virginia, where he had gone to high school for two years. Daniel had attended Towson University and majored in secondary education with a minor in English. The year after graduation, he'd lost both parents in a car accident. The driver that had hit them was killed as well; his blood alcohol concentration had been .21. Five months after the funeral, Daniel's brother was convicted on drug charges—manufacturing methamphetamine and dealing to minors—and sent to serve a nine-year sentence with the Wisconsin Department of Corrections. Daniel had married a year later, then gotten a divorce two years after that; the ex had remarried almost as soon as the rushed divorce was final, and she'd produced a child with the new husband—a lawyer—six months after the wedding. Not terribly hard to read between the lines on that one. During that same year, the brother died in a prison fight. A very long rough patch.

Daniel currently taught history and English at a high school in what most people would consider the wrong part of DC. He also coached girls' volleyball and oversaw the student council. He'd won Teacher of the Year—a student-voted award—twice in a row. For the past three years, since the divorce, Daniel had spent his summers working with Habitat for Humanity, first in Hidalgo, Mexico, then in El Minya, Egypt. The third summer, he'd split his time between the two.

No pictures of the deceased parents or brother. There was one of the ex — a formal wedding portrait of the two of them together. She was dark-haired and striking, the focal point of the photograph. He seemed almost like an afterthought behind her, though his wide grin was more genuine than the expression on her carefully arranged features.

Alex would have liked the file to be more filled out, but she knew that, with her detail-oriented nature, she sometimes expected too much of less obsessive analysts.

On the surface, Daniel was totally clean. Decent family (the self-destructive cycle that had led to the brother's death was easy enough to understand in light of the parents' crash). The victim in the divorce (not uncommon for the spouse of a crusading teacher to realize that the salary would not support a lavish lifestyle). Favorite of the underprivileged kids. Altruist in his free time.

The file didn't state what had first caught the government's attention, but once they'd scratched that surface, the dark came seeping out.

It seemed to have begun in Mexico. They hadn't been watching him then, so it was only the bank numbers that told the story. The forensic accountants had put together a well-documented history. First, his own bank balance, which had sat at just a couple of hundred dollars after the divorce, was suddenly plus ten grand. And then a few weeks later, another ten. By the end of the summer, it was sixty total. He went back to work in the States, and the sixty grand disappeared. Maybe a down payment for a condo, a fancy car? No, nothing visible, nothing on the record. The next year, while he was in Egypt, there were no sudden increases in his finances. Had it been gambling? An inheritance?

That alone wasn't enough to catch anyone's attention without some kind of a tip-off, but she couldn't locate the catalyst in the file. Even with an explicit tip, someone in the accounting department had to have been putting in overtime or else was very, very bored, because despite the lack of urgency, the financial analyst had hunted down that original sixty thousand dollars like a bloodhound with his nose to the ground. Eventually he found it — in a new bank account in the Caymans. Along with another hundred thousand.

At this point, Daniel's name was put on a list. Not a CIA or FBI or NSA list — an IRS list. Not even a high-priority list at that. His name wasn't very near the top; he was just someone to look into.

She wondered for a moment how his brother's death had affected him. It looked like he had logged some fairly consistent visits to the brother, his only family left. Wife runs out, brother dies. Seemed like a decent recipe for pushing someone deeper into his bad choices.

The money kept growing, and it was in no way consistent with what a drug mule or even a dealer might make. Neither job was so well compensated.

Then the money started to move and became harder to trace, but it added up to about ten million dollars in Daniel Beach's name bouncing around from the Caribbean to Switzerland to China and back again. Maybe he was a front, with someone using his name to hide assets, but as a general rule, the bad guys didn't like to put those kinds of funds into the hands of unwitting schoolteachers.

What could he be doing to earn it?

Of course they were watching his associations at this point, and it paid off quickly. Someone named Enrique de la Fuentes showed up in a grainy black-and-white photo taken by the security camera in the parking lot of Daniel Beach's motel in Mexico City.

She'd been out of the game for a few years, and this name didn't mean anything to her. Even if she had still been with the department, it probably wouldn't have been a part of her usual caseload. She had done some occasional work on the cartel problem, but drugs never got the red lights flashing and the sirens screaming the way potential wars and terrorism did.

De la Fuentes was a drug lord, and drug lords — even the scrappy, upwardly mobile kind — rarely got any attention from her department. Generally the U.S. government didn't much care if drug lords killed each other, and usually those drug wars had very little impact on the life of an average American citizen. Drug dealers didn't want to kill their customers. That wasn't good for business.

She had never in all her years, even with the high-security clearance that was a necessary part of her job, heard of a drug lord with an interest in weapons of mass destruction. Of course, if there was a profit to be made, you couldn't count anyone out.

Profiting from the sale of was quite a different kettle from *unleashing,* though.

De la Fuentes had acquired a medium-size Colombian outfit in a hostile (to put it mildly) takeover in the mid-1990s and then made several attempts to establish a base of operations just south of the Arizona border. Each time, he'd been repelled by the nearby cartel that straddled the border between Texas and Mexico. He'd become impatient and started looking for more and more unorthodox methods to dispose of his enemies. And then he'd found an ally.

She sucked in a breath through her teeth.

This was a name she knew — knew and loathed. Being attacked from the outside was horrific enough. She felt the deepest revulsion for the kind of person who was born to the freedom and privilege of a democratic nation and then used that very privilege and freedom to attack its source.

This domestic-terrorist ring had several names. The department called them the Serpent, thanks to a tattoo that one of their late chiefs had possessed — and the line from *King Lear.* She'd been instrumental in shutting down a few of their larger conspiracies, but the one they'd accomplished still gave her the occasional nightmare. The file didn't say who had made the first contact, only that an accord had been reached. If de la Fuentes did his part, he would receive enough money, men, and arms to take out the larger cartel. And the terrorists would get what they wanted—destabilization of the American nation, horror, destruction, and all the press they'd ever dreamed of.

It was bad.

Because what was better for destabilization than a deadly, laboratory-created influenza virus? Especially one you could control.

She could tell when the narrative shifted from the analysts' point of view to the spies'. Much clearer pictures.

The spies were calling it TCX-1 (no notation in the files on what the letters stood for, and even with her rather specialized background in medicine, she had no idea). The government was aware that the TCX-1 superflu existed, but they thought they'd eradicated it during a black ops raid in North Africa. The lab was destroyed, the responsible parties apprehended (and executed, for the most part). TCX-1 hadn't been heard of again.

Until it showed up in Mexico a few months ago, along with a supply of the lifesaving vaccine, already incorporated into a new designer drug.

She was starting to get a headache, the kind that was extremely localized. It was a hot needle stabbing directly behind her left eye. She'd slept a few hours after checking in and before diving into the files, but it hadn't been enough. She made the short walk to her toiletry bag beside the sink, grabbed four Motrin, and swallowed them dry. She realized two seconds later that her stomach was totally empty, and the Motrin would no doubt burn a hole through the bottom as soon as it hit. In her bag she always had a stash of protein bars, and she quickly gnawed her way through one as she returned to her reading.

The terrorists knew they were always being watched, so what they'd given de la Fuentes was information. De la Fuentes would have to provide the manpower—preferably innocuous, unremarkable manpower.

Enter the schoolteacher.

From what the best analytical minds could piece together, Daniel Beach, all-around good guy, had gone to Egypt and acquired TCX-1 for a hungry, unstable drug lord. And he was clearly still part of the plot. From the evidence available, it appeared he would be the one dispersing TCX-1 on American soil.

The inhalable designer drug containing the vaccine was already in circulation; valued customers would never be in danger, and perhaps this was a second part of the plot. Even the most unstable drug lord had to be pragmatic where money was concerned. So maybe noncustomers would learn just where salvation waited — and that would create a whole new desperate clientele. Daniel Beach was no doubt immune by now. It wasn't a difficult job to circulate the virus; it would be as simple as wiping an infected swab across a surface that was regularly handled — a doorknob, a countertop, a keyboard. The virus was engineered to spread like the proverbial wildfire — he wouldn't even need to expose that many people. Just a few in Los Angeles, a few in Phoenix, a few in Albuquerque, a few in San Antonio. Daniel already had hotel reservations in each of these cities. He was due to embark on his deadly journey — ostensibly to visit more Habitat for Humanity sites as a preparation for next fall's school field trip — in three weeks.

The Serpent and de la Fuentes were attempting to orchestrate the most debilitating attack that had ever been perpetrated on American soil. And if it was true that de la Fuentes already had the weaponized virus and the vaccine, they had an excellent chance of success.

Carston hadn't been kidding. What she'd originally thought had been an act to play to her sympathies now appeared to be an amazing demonstration of self-control. Of all the potential disasters that had crossed her desk — back when she'd had a desk — this was one of the very worst, and she'd seen some bad things. There had even been one other biological weapon with the potential to do this kind of damage, but that one had never made it out of the lab. This was a feasible plan already in progress. And it wasn't hundreds of thousands of people dying they were talking about here — it would be closer to a million, maybe more, before the CDC could get control of the situation. Carston had known she would discover that fact. He'd deliberately downplayed the disaster so that it would sound more realistic. Sometimes the truth was worse than fiction.

The stakes were higher than she'd expected. This knowledge made it harder for her to justify her own little low-stakes game. Was the tight focus on saving her own life even defensible in the face of this kind of horror? She'd held a hard line in her conversation with Carston, but if there was any chance this story was more than a trap, did she have any choice but to try to stop it?

If Daniel Beach disappeared, de la Fuentes would know someone was onto him. Odds were, he would act sooner than he'd planned, ahead of schedule. Daniel had to talk, and he had to talk quickly. And then he had to go back to regular life, be seen, and keep the megalomaniac drug lord calm until the good guys could take him out.

In the beginning, it was standard operating procedure for Alex's subjects to be released into the wild for a short time. This was a major part of her specialty; Alex was the best at retrieving information without damaging the subject. (Before Alex, Barnaby had been the best and only man for the job.) The CIA, the NSA, and most similar government sections had their own teams for interrogating subjects who were slated for disposal after the information was acquired. Over time, as she proved more successful than even the best of the other teams, Alex had gotten a lot busier. Though the other sections would rather have stayed insular, kept the information with their own people, the results spoke for themselves.

She sighed and refocused on the now. Eleven pictures of Daniel Beach lay in a row across the pillows at the head of the bed. It was hard to reconcile the two sides of the coin. In the early pictures he looked like a Boy Scout, his softly waving hair somehow projecting innocence and pure intentions. But though it was obviously the same face in the spies' photos, everything was different. The hair was always hidden under hoods or ball caps (one of her own frequent disguises); the posture was more aggressive; the expressions were cold and professional. She'd worked on professionals. It took time. Possibly more than one weekend. She looked at the two matching but contradictory faces again and wondered briefly if Daniel had an actual psychiatric disorder or if it was a progression she was looking at, and the innocent no longer existed at all.

Not that it mattered—yet.

The headache felt like it was searing a hole through the inside of her eyeball. She knew it wasn't the hours of reading that had caused it. No, the decision looming in front of her was the source of the pain.

She gathered up all the files and stuffed them into a suitcase. The decimation of the population of the American Southwest would have to take a backseat for a few hours.

She was in a different car than she'd started out with that morning. Before checking into the motel, she'd returned the rental in Baltimore, then taken a cab to York, Pennsylvania. The cabbie dropped her a few minutes' walk from the house where a man surnamed Stubbins was selling his three-year-old Tercel, as advertised on Craigslist. She'd paid cash and used the name Cory Howard, then driven to Philly in her new ride. It was a trail that *could* be followed, but it would be very hard to do.

She drove several miles away from her motel, then chose a little dive that seemed to be doing brisk business. That was desirable for two reasons. One, she would be less memorable in a crowd. Two, the food was probably edible.

The dining area was packed, so she ate at the small bar. The wall behind the bar was mirrored; she could watch the door and front windows without turning around. It was a good perch. She had a greasy burger, onion rings, and a chocolate malt. All were delicious.

While she ate, she turned off her brain. She'd gotten pretty good at that over the last nine years; she could compartmentalize almost anything. And while she focused on the food and watched the people around her, the headache subsided to a dull throb. Over the course of the meal, the Motrin finally won and the pain dissolved completely. She ordered a piece of pie for dessert—pecan—though she was completely stuffed and could only pick at it. She was stalling. Once the meal was over, she'd have to make a decision.

The headache was waiting for her in the car, as she'd known it would be, though it was not as sharp as before. She drove randomly down the quiet residential streets, where anyone following her would be obvious. The little suburb was dark and empty. After a few minutes she wandered closer toward the city.

There were still two columns of possibilities in her head.

The first column, that Carston had been lying in order to lure her to her death, was beginning to seem more and more unlikely. Still, she had to stay alert. This whole story could be fiction. All the evidence and coordinating departments and separate analysts with their differing writing styles and the photographs from around the world—it could be a very detailed, elaborate setup. Not a foolproof one, either, since they had no way of knowing she wouldn't just walk away from it.

But why would Carston have all this info prepared if he'd hoped to get her to a prearranged meeting? They could have killed her easily there without all this window dressing. A ream of blank paper was all you would need if you expected your mark's brains to be on the pavement before she could open the briefcase. How quickly could this kind of thing be thrown together? She'd given him no time to manufacture it on the spot with her early arrival. Who was Daniel Beach in this scenario? One of their own? Or an unsuspecting civilian Photoshopped into the exotic scenes? They had to know she would be able to verify some of this information.

They'd offered her a plan of action in the final file. In five days' time, with or without her, they would pick him up during his regular Saturday-morning run. No one would miss him until school began again Monday. If anyone did happen to look for him, it might appear that he'd taken a little holiday. If she agreed to help, she would have two days to get the information they needed, then she would be free to go. They hoped she would consent to keep in some form of contact. An emergency e-mail address, a social network site, the classifieds even.

If she didn't agree to the job, they would do their best without her. But trying to leave the informant physically unmarked would be slow...too slow. Failure was hard to contemplate.

She almost salivated at the thought of all the goodies waiting for her back at the lab. Things she could never get her hands on out here in the real world. Her DNA sequencer and polymerase chain reactor. The already fabricated antibodies she could stuff her pockets with if the invitation was on the up-and-up. Of course, if Carston was for real, she wouldn't need to steal those things anymore.

She tried to imagine sleeping in a bed again. Not carrying a pharmacy's worth of toxins on her body at all times. Using the same name every day. Making contact with other human beings in a way that left nobody dead.

Don't count on it, she told herself. *Don't let it go to your head and impair your judgment. Don't let hope make you stupid.*

As pleasant as some of her imaginings were, she hit a wall when she tried to visualize the steps she would need to take to make them happen. It was impossible to see herself walking back through the shiny steel doors into the place where Barnaby had died screaming. Her mind totally refused to construct the image.

The lives of a million people were a heavy weight, but still an abstract idea in many ways. She didn't feel like anything could push her hard enough to get her through those doors.

She would have to go around them, so to speak.

Only five days.

She had so much work to do.

CHAPTER 4

This operation was murdering her nest egg.

That thought kept circling in the back of her brain. If she lived through the next week, and nothing changed in regard to her working relationship with the department, she was going to have serious financial issues. It wasn't cheap changing lives on a triannual basis.

Just acquiring disposable funds in the first place had been a major procedure. She'd had money—the salary had certainly been a factor in her choice to do the job in the beginning, and earlier than that, she'd inherited a decent insurance payout when her mother had died. But when you work for powerful paranoids who probably note it in your file when you switch toothpaste brands, you can't just withdraw all your money and put it in a shoe box under the bed. If they weren't planning to do anything to you before, you might have just given them a motive. If they were, you just made them decide to accelerate their plans. You could try withdrawing all your money on the way out of town, but that limited your ability to pay for any advance preparations.

Like so much of it had been, it was Barnaby's scheme. He'd kept her in the dark about the details to protect the friend or friends who helped him set it up.

In the cafeteria located a few floors up from the lab, she and

Barnaby had let themselves be heard talking about a promising investment situation. Well, Barnaby had called it promising and worked to convince her of it. There was nothing remarkable about the conversation; various versions of it were probably taking place by watercoolers in several normal offices at the same moment. She played being convinced, and Barnaby loudly promised to set it up. She wired money to an investment firm—or a company that sounded very like an investment firm. A few days later, that money was deposited—minus a 5 percent "commission" to compensate those friends for their time and risk—in a bank in Tulsa, Oklahoma, in the name of Fredericka Noble. She received notification of this new account in an unmarked envelope placed in a copy of *Extranodal Lymphomas* at the county library. An Oklahoma driver's license for Fredericka Noble, with her own picture on it, was also in the envelope.

She didn't know where Barnaby's drop was. She didn't know what his new name was going to be. She'd wanted them to leave together—the vast aloneness of running was already part of her nightmares then—but he had thought that unwise. They'd both be safer separated.

More investments, more little envelopes. A few more accounts were created for Freddie, but there were also accounts and IDs for Ellis Grant in California and Shea Marlow in Oregon. All three identities were strong creations that would hold up under scrutiny. Freddie had been blown the first time the department found her, but this only made her more careful. Ellis and Shea were still safe. They were her prized possessions and she used them carefully and sparingly so as not to contaminate them by any association with Dr. Juliana Fortis.

She'd also started buying jewelry—the good stuff, and the smaller the better. Canary diamonds that looked to her eyes like nothing more than yellow sapphires but that cost ten times as much as their clear counterparts. Thick gold chains; heavy solid-gold pendants. Several loose gems she pretended to be planning to set. She knew all along that she would never get back half of what she paid, but jewelry could be carried easily and later converted to cash under the radar.

From a pay phone, Freddie Noble rented a small cabin just outside Tulsa, using a new credit card that would be paid from the Tulsa bank account. The cabin came with a sweet older landlord who sounded happy to bring in the boxes she mailed there—boxes full of the many things she would need when she walked away from her life as Juliana Fortis, everything from towels and pillows to her unset jewels to reflux condensers and boiling flasks—and collected his rent without commenting on her absence. She left a veiled hint here and there that she was planning to leave a bad relationship; it was enough for the landlord. She ordered supplies from library computers, giving an e-mail address she never accessed on her laptop at home.

She did everything she could to be ready, and then she waited for Barnaby to give the signal. In the end, he did let her know that it was time to run, but not the way they'd planned it.

That money, so carefully hoarded for so long, was now flowing through her fingers like she was some entitled trust-fund brat. One big spree in hopes of gaining her unlikely freedom, she promised herself. She had a few tricks for making real money, but they were dangerous, involving risks she could ill afford but would have no choice but to take.

People needed medical professionals who would break the rules. Some just wanted a doctor who knew how to oversee the administration of a treatment that was not approved by the FDA, something they'd picked up in Russia or Brazil. And some people needed bullets removed but didn't want it done in a hospital, where the police would be notified.

She'd maintained a floating presence on the web. A few clients had contacted her at her last e-mail address, which was now defunct.

She'd have to get back on the boards that knew her and try to get in touch with some contacts without leaving any new trails. It would be hard; if the department had found the e-mails, they probably knew about the rest. At least her clients understood. Much of the work she did for them ranged from quasi-legal to totally criminal, and they would not be surprised by occasional disappearances and new names.

Of course, working on the dark side of the law added other dangers to her already overloaded plate. Like the midlevel Mafia boss who found her services very convenient and thought she should set herself up permanently in Illinois. She'd tried to explain her carefully composed cover story to Joey Giancardi without compromising herself — after all, if there was money to be made by the sale of information, the Mob wasn't exactly known for its loyalty to outsiders — but he was insistent, to put it mildly. He assured her that with his protection, she would never be vulnerable. In the end, she'd had to destroy that identity, a fairly well-developed life as Charlie Peterson, and run. Possibly there were members of the Family looking for her, too, now. It wasn't something she lost sleep over. When it came to manpower and resources, the Mob couldn't touch the American government.

And maybe the Mob didn't have time to waste on her anyway. There were lots of doctors in the world, all of them human and most of them corruptible. Now, if he'd known her real specialty, Jocy G would have put up more of a fight to keep her.

At least Joey G had been good for changing her jewels into cash. And the crash course in trauma medicine couldn't hurt. Another perk of working in the underground: no one got too upset about your low batting average. Death was expected, and malpractice insurance wasn't necessary.

Whenever she thought of Joey G, she also remembered Carlo Aggi. Not a friend, not really, but something close. He'd been her contact, the most constant presence in her life then. Though he was stereotypically thuggish in appearance, he'd always been sweet to her—treated her like a kid sister. So it had hurt more than the others when she hadn't been able to do anything for Carlo. A bullet had lodged in his left ventricle. It was too late for Carlo long before they'd brought his body to her, but Joey G had still been hopeful; Charlie had done good work for him in the past. He was philosophical when Charlie had pronounced Carlo dead on arrival. *Carlo was the best. Well, you win some, you lose some.* And then a shrug.

She didn't like to think about Carlo.

She would have preferred a few more weeks to think about other things—to fine-tune her scheme, consider her vulnerabilities, get the physical preparations perfect—but Carston's plan gave her a deadline. She'd had to divide her limited time between surveillance and organizing a workspace, so neither had been perfectly done.

It was likely that they'd be watching her in case she tried to make a move without them. After her early visit to Carston, they would be anticipating it. But what choice did she have? Report for work as expected?

She'd seen enough to bet that Daniel would follow the same pattern today as he had the past three. Something about his almost identical outfits—similar jeans, button-down shirt, casual sport coat, all featuring only minor differences in hues—made her suspect that he was a creature of habit in his public life. After school, he would stay past the final bell to talk to students and work on his lesson plan for the next day. Then, with several folders and his laptop in a backpack over his left shoulder, he would head out, waving to the secretary as he passed. He would walk six blocks and get on the subway at Congress Heights around six, just as the commuting mayhem was at its worst. He had a straight shot up the Green Line to Columbia Heights, where his tiny studio apartment was located. Once there, he would eat a frozen dinner and grade papers. He went to bed around ten, never turning the TV on as far as she'd seen. It was harder to follow what happened in the morning—he had rattan shades that were basically translucent when lit from inside, but opaque in the morning sun. He hit the street at five for a morning run, returned an hour later, then left again after another thirty minutes, headed for the subway station three blocks away, longish curly hair still wet from his shower.

Two mornings ago, she'd followed his exercise route as best she could from a safe distance. He held a strong, fast pace—obviously an experienced runner. As she watched, she found herself wishing that she had more time to run. She didn't love running the way others seemed to—she always felt so exposed on the side of a road, no car to escape in—but it was important. She was never going to be stronger than the person they sent after her. With her short legs, she wouldn't be faster, either, and there was no martial art she could learn that would give her an advantage over a professional killer. But endurance—that could save her life. If her tricks could get her past the crisis moment, she had to be able to keep going longer than the killer could keep chasing. What a way to die—winded, muscles quitting, crippled by her own lack of preparation. She didn't want to go out that way. So she ran as often as she could and did the exercises she could manage inside her small homes. She promised herself that when this operation was over, she would find a good place to jog—one with plenty of escape routes and hidey-holes.

But his running route—like the apartment and the school—was too obvious a place to make her move. The easiest way to do this would be to grab him off the street as he was finishing his run, worn out and unfocused, but the bad guys would know this too. They would be prepared for her. The same was true for the walking portion of his journey to school. So it had to be the Metro. They would know the Metro was another possible option, but they couldn't cover every line, every stop, while also watching each leg of his commute.

There were cameras everywhere, but there was only so much she could do about that. When it was over, her enemies would have a million clear shots of what her face looked like now, three years later. Not much change, in her opinion, but they would still, no doubt, update her file. That was all they would be able to do, though. Her former position with the department had given her enough familiarity with the mechanics of snatching a target off the street to know that the difficulties were a lot greater than the average espionage TV series would lead one to believe. The purpose of the Metro cameras was to help catch a suspect *after* the crime. There was no way they'd have the resources and manpower to act on the coverage in real time. So all the cameras could tell them was where she *had* been, not where she *would* be, and without that information, the footage was useless. All the usual discoveries the tapes could help with—who she was, where she'd gotten her information, what her motive was—were things they already knew.

In any case, she couldn't think of a less risky option.

Today her name was Jesse. She went with a professional look— her black suit with the V-neck black tee underneath and of course the leather belt. She had another, more realistic wig; this one chin-length and lighter, a mousy blond-brown color. She held this back with a simple black headband and added glasses with thin metal rims that didn't make it look like she was hiding but still subtly disguised the shape of her cheekbones and forehead. Her face was symmetrical with small features; nothing stood out. She knew that as a general rule, people overlooked her. But she also knew she wasn't so generic-looking that someone specifically searching would fail to recognize her. She would keep her head down whenever she could.

She brought a briefcase rather than her tote; the wooden details from her shoulder strap snapped into place on the handle of the briefcase. It was lined with metal, heavy even when empty, and could easily be used as a bludgeon if necessary. The locket, the rings, but not the earrings. She would have to do a bit of manhandling, and the earrings wouldn't be safe. The shoe knives, the scalpel blades, the ChapStick, the various sprays...almost full armor. Today it didn't make her feel more confident. This part of the plan was far outside her comfort zone. Kidnapping wasn't something she'd ever imagined needing to do. In the past three years, she hadn't thought of a scenario that didn't boil down to either kill or escape.

Jesse yawned as she drove through the dark streets. She'd not been getting enough sleep, nor was sleep going to figure largely in the next few days. She had a few substances that would keep her awake, but the crash could be delayed for only seventy-two hours at most. She would need to be hidden very well when that crash came. She hoped it wouldn't be necessary to use them.

There were plenty of spaces available in the economy parking lot at Ronald Reagan. She pulled into one near the shuttle bus stop, where most people would want to park, and waited for the bus to arrive. She knew this airport better than any other. She felt a long-missing sense of comfort kick in—the comfort of familiar surroundings. Two other passengers showed up before the shuttle, both of them with luggage and tired faces. They ignored her. She rode the bus to terminal three, then doubled back on the pedestrian bridge to the Metro stop. This route took her about fifteen minutes at a brisk walk. Nice thing about airports—everyone walked fast.

She'd debated wearing boots with wedge heels, going for a different height, but then decided she would be walking—and possibly running, if things went badly—too much today. She wore the dark flats that were half sneaker.

As she joined the crowd heading down to the Metro platform, she tried to keep her face hidden as much as possible from the ceiling cameras. Using her peripheral vision, she searched for a likely group to join. Jesse was sure that the watchers would be looking for a lone woman. A larger group—any group—was a better disguise than makeup or a wig.

There were several clusters of people heading to the tracks with her as the first wave of rush hour began to crowd the escalators. She chose a trio, two men and one woman, all in dark business suits and carrying briefcases. The woman had shiny blond hair and was a good nine inches taller than Jesse in her high-heeled, pointy-toed pumps. Jesse edged her way around a few other parties until she was somewhat hidden between the woman and the wall behind them. Any eyes examining the new quartet would naturally be drawn to the tall blonde. Unless those eyes were specifically looking for Juliana Fortis.

Jesse's quartet moved purposefully through the crowd, claiming a spot near the edge of the platform to wait. None of the others in the group seemed aware of the small woman moving in tandem with them. There were too many close-packed bodies for her proximity to be noticeable.

The train raced into view, whipping past and then jerking to an abrupt stop. Jesse's group hesitated, looking for a less crowded car. She contemplated abandoning them, but the blonde was impatient, too, and she forced her way into the negative space of the third car they considered. Jesse pushed in close behind the woman she'd been following, her body pressed against both the blonde and another, larger woman behind her. She would be all but invisible between them, uncomfortable as the position might be.

They rode the Yellow Line up to the Chinatown station. There she left the trio and joined a new couple, two women who could have been secretaries or librarians in their buttoned-up blouses and cat-framed eyeglasses. They rode the Green Line together up to the Shaw-Howard station, Jesse's head cocked in the direction of the shorter brunette, pretending to be absorbed in a story about last weekend's wedding reception that hadn't included an open bar, of all the nerve. Mid-story, she left the secretaries on the train and melted into the crowd exiting the Metro. She did a quick U-turn through the densely packed ladies' room and then joined the crowd heading down to the tracks for the next train. Timing would be everything now. She wouldn't be able to hide inside the herd.

The shrill wail of the approaching train had Jesse's heart bouncing up into her throat. She braced herself; it felt like she was a sprinter crouched at the blocks, waiting for the gun to fire. Then she shuddered at the metaphor in her head—it was only too possible that a gun was actually about to fire, but this one would have real bullets and wouldn't be aimed at the sky.

The train shrieked to a stop, and she was on the move.

Jesse power-walked down the line of cars, elbowing through the flow of passengers as the doors whooshed open. Scanning as fast as she could, she searched for the tall frame with the floppy hair. There were so many bodies ducking past her, blocking her view. She tried to put a mental X through every head that didn't match. Was she moving too quickly? Not quickly enough? The train was leaving by the time she got to the last car, and she couldn't be positive he wasn't on it, but she didn't think he was. By her calculations of his last two arrivals, he was most likely on the next train. She bit her lip as the doors closed. If she'd blown this one, she'd have to try again on his next trip. She didn't want to have to do that. The closer the time got to Carston's plan being put into action, the more dangerous this would be.

Rather than linger in plain sight, she continued briskly toward the exit.

She did another circuit through the restroom, wasting a little time pretending to check the makeup she wasn't wearing. After counting to ninety in her head, she rejoined the stream of commuters on their way to the tracks.

It was even more crowded now. Jesse chose a spot close to a group of suited men at the far end of the platform and tried to blend in with the black fabric of their jackets. The men were talking about stocks and trades, things that seemed so far from Jesse's life that they might as well have been science fiction. The next train was announced and she got ready to walk and scan again. She stepped around the traders and examined the first car as it came to a stop.

Moving fast, Jesse's eyes ran through the next car. *Woman, woman, old man, too short, too fat, too dark, no hair, woman, woman, kid, blond . . .* The next car—

It was like he was helping her, like he was on her side. He was right beside the window, looking out, standing tall, with the wavy hair very much in evidence.

Jesse gave the rest of the occupants a quick once-over as she walked toward the open doors. Many business types—any one of them could have been hired by the department. But there were no obvious tells, no extra-wide shoulders that didn't quite fit into normal-size suit coats, no earpieces, no bulges under the jackets, no eye contact between riders. No one wore sunglasses.

This is the part, she thought to herself, *where they try to bag us both and haul us back to the lab. Unless this is a setup, in which case Daniel and his innocent curly hair will be one of them. He might be the one to shoot me. Or stab me. Or they'll try to get me off the train to shoot me somewhere in private. Or they'll knock me out and throw me on the tracks.*

But if the story is all true, they'll want us both alive. They'll probably try something similar to what I'm about to do to Daniel. Then they'll cart me off to the lab and my odds of ever walking out again are . . . less than encouraging.

A thousand other bad endings raced through her head as the doors closed behind them. She walked quickly to stand beside Daniel, sharing the same pole for balance, her fingers close below his paler, much longer fingers. Her heart felt like someone was squeezing it in a tight fist; it got more painful in direct proportion to her proximity to the target. He didn't seem to notice her, still staring out the window with a faraway look, a look that didn't change as they pulled into the darkness of the tunnel and he could see only reflections from inside the car. Nobody in the car made any move toward them.

She couldn't see any of the other guy in Daniel Beach, the one she'd seen pictures of in Mexico and Egypt, the one who hid his hair and moved with aggressive assurance. The abstracted man next to her could have been an Old World poet. He must be an incredible actor...or was it possible that he was legitimately psychotic, suffering from dissociative identity disorder? She didn't know what to do with that.

Jesse tensed as they neared the Chinatown stop. The train lurched into the station, and she had to grip the pole tighter to keep from swinging into Daniel Beach.

Three people, two suits and one skirt, exited the train, but none of them looked at Jesse. They all hurried past, moving like they were late for work. Two more men got into the car. One caught Jesse's attention — a big man, built like a professional athlete, wearing a hoodie and sweatpants. He had both hands in the front pouch of the hoodie, and unless his hands were the size of shoe boxes, he was carrying something in them. He didn't look at Jesse as he passed her, just went to the back corner of the car and grabbed an overhead strap. She kept him in the corner of her eye in the reflection, but he didn't seem interested in either herself or the target.

Daniel Beach hadn't moved. He was so absorbed in his distant thoughts that she found herself relaxing beside him, as if he were the one person on the train she didn't have to guard against. Which was foolish. Even if this wasn't a trap, even if he was exactly who she'd been told he was, this man was still planning to become a mass murderer in the very near future.

The athlete pulled a boxy pair of headphones out of his sweatshirt's big pocket and covered his ears with them. The cord led back down to the pocket. Probably to his phone, but maybe not.

She decided to make the next stop a test.

As the doors opened, she bent down as if to fix the nonexistent cuff on her pants, then straightened suddenly and took a step toward the door.

No one reacted. The athlete in the headphones had his eyes

closed. People got on, people got off, but no one looked at her, and nobody moved to block her exit or suddenly brought up a hand with a jacket awkwardly draped over it.

If her enemies knew what she was doing, they were letting her do it her way.

Did that mean it was real or that they just wanted her to believe it was for now? Trying to think around their circles made her head hurt. She grabbed the pole again as the train started moving.

"Not your stop?"

She looked up, and Daniel Beach was smiling down at her — the perfectly sweet, guileless smile that belonged to the school's most popular teacher, to the Habitat for Humanity crusader.

"Um, no." She blinked, her thoughts scrambling. What would a normal commuter say? "I, uh, just forgot where I was for a minute. The stations all start to blur together."

"Hold on. The weekend is only eight or nine hours away."

He smiled again, a kind smile. She was more than uncomfortable with the idea of socializing with her subject, but there was a strange — possibly counterfeit — normality about Daniel that made it easier for her to assume the role she needed to play: Friendly commuter. Ordinary person.

She snorted a dark little laugh at his observation. Her workweek was just beginning. "That would be exciting if I got weekends off."

He laughed and then sighed. "That's tough. Law?"

"Medicine."

"Even worse. Do they ever let you out for good behavior?"

"Very rarely. It's okay. I'm not much for wild parties anyway."

"I'm too old for them myself," he admitted. "A fact I usually remember around ten o'clock every night."

She smiled politely as he laughed, and tried to keep her eyes from looking crazed. It felt both creepy and dangerous to be fraternizing with her next job. She never had any interactions with her subjects beforehand. She couldn't afford to look at him as a person. She would have to see only the monster—the potential million dead—so she could remain impassive.

"Though I do enjoy the occasional quiet dinner out," he was saying.

"Mm," she murmured distractedly. It sounded like an agreement, she realized.

"Hi," he said. "My name is Daniel."

In her surprise, she forgot what her name was supposed to be. He held out his hand and she shook it, tremendously aware of the weight of her poisoned ring.

"Hi, Daniel."

"Hi…" He raised his eyebrows.

"Um, Alex." Whoops, that was a few names back. Oh, well.

"Nice to meet you, Alex. Look, I never do this—ever. But… well, why not? Can I give you my number? Maybe we could have that quiet dinner sometime?"

She stared at him in blank shock. He was hitting on her. A man was hitting on her. No, not a man. A soon-to-be mass murderer working for a psychotic drug czar.

Or an agent trying to distract her?

"Did I scare you? I swear I'm harmless."

"Er, no, I just…well, no one has ever asked me out on a train before." That was nothing but the plain truth. In fact, no one at all had asked her out for years. "I'm at a loss." Also true.

"Here, this is what I'll do. I'll write my name and number down on this piece of paper and I'll give it to you, and when you get to your stop, you can throw it in the next trash can you see, because littering is wrong, and immediately forget all about me. Very little inconvenience to you—just that extra few seconds with the trash can."

He smiled while he spoke, but his eyes were down, focused on writing his information on the back of a receipt with a no. 2 pencil.

"That's very considerate of you. I appreciate it."

He looked up, still smiling. "Or you don't have to throw it away. You could also use it to call me and then spend a few hours talking to me while I buy you food."

The monotone voice overhead announced the Penn Quarter station and she was relieved. Because she was starting to feel sad. Yes, she was going to have a night out with Daniel Beach, but neither of them was going to enjoy it very much.

There could be no room for sadness. So many innocent dead. Dead children, dead mothers and fathers. Good people who had never hurt anyone.

"It's a dilemma," she answered quietly.

The train stopped again, and she pretended to be jostled by the man exiting behind her. The appropriate needle was already in her hand. She reached out as if to steady herself with the pole and grabbed Daniel's hand in a move designed to look accidental. He jerked in surprise, and she held on tight like she was trying to keep her balance.

"Ouch. Sorry, I shocked you," she said. She released him and let the tiny syringe slide out of her palm into her blazer's pocket. Sleight of hand was something she'd practiced a lot.

"No worries. You okay? That guy really knocked you."

"Yes, I'm fine, thank you."

The car started moving again, and she watched as Daniel's face quickly lost its color.

"Hey, are *you* okay?" she asked. "You look a little pale."

"Um, I...what?"

He glanced around, confused.

"You look like you're going to pass out. Excuse me," she said to the woman in the seat beside them. "Can my friend sit? He's not feeling well."

The woman rolled her enormous brown eyes and then looked studiously in the other direction.

"No," Daniel said. "Don't...bother about me. I'm..."

"Daniel?" she asked.

He was swaying a little now, his face dead white.

"Give me your hand, Daniel."

Looking bemused, he held out his hand. She gripped his wrist, moving her lips in an obvious way as she looked at her watch and pretended to count to herself.

"Medicine," he muttered. "You're a doctor."

This part was closer to the scripted version, and it made her more comfortable. "Yes, and I'm not pleased with your condition. You're getting off at the next stop with me. We're going to get you some air."

"Can't. School... can't be late."

"I'll write you a note. Don't argue with me, I know what I'm doing."

"'Kay. Alex."

L'Enfant Plaza was one of the biggest and most chaotic stations on the line. When the door opened, Alex put her arm around Daniel's waist and led him out. He draped one arm over her shoulder for support. This didn't surprise her. The tryptamine she'd injected him with made people disoriented, acquiescent, and quite friendly. He would follow her lead as long as she didn't push him too hard. The drug was distantly related to a class of barbiturates that laypeople called truth serum and that had a few effects similar to Ecstasy; both were good for breaking down inhibitions and inducing cooperation. She liked this particular synthesis because of the confusion. Daniel would feel incapable of decision making and therefore would do whatever she told him to until it wore off—or unless she asked him to do something that really pushed against the walls of his comfort zone.

This was easier than she'd hoped, thanks to the unexpected tête-à-tête. She'd planned to stick him, then play the old *Is there a doctor in the house? Why, yes,* I *happen to be a doctor!* routine to get him to go with her initially. It would have worked, but he would not have been this docile.

"Okay, Daniel, how are you feeling? Can you breathe?"

"Sure. Breathing's good."

She walked quickly with him. This drug rarely made anyone sick, but there were always exceptions. She glanced up to check his color. He was still pale but his lips hadn't taken on the greenish hue that would presage nausea.

"Do you feel sick to your stomach?" she asked.

"No. No, I'm fine..."

"I'm afraid you're not. I'm going to take you to work with me, if that's okay. I want to make sure this isn't serious."

"Okay...no. I have school?"

He was keeping pace with her easily despite his disorientation. His legs were about twice as long as hers.

"We'll tell them what's happening. You have a number for the school?"

"Yes, Stacey—in the office."

"We'll call her while we walk."

This would slow them down, but there was no help for it; she had to allay his concern so he would stay docile.

"Good idea." He nodded, then pulled an old BlackBerry out of his pocket and fumbled with the buttons.

She took it gently from his hand. "What's the last name for Stacey?"

"It's under 'Front desk.' "

"I see it. Okay, I'll dial for you. Here, tell Stacey you're sick. You're going to the doctor."

He took the phone obediently, then waited for Stacey to answer.

"Hello," he said. "Stacey. I'm Daniel. Yes, Mr. Beach. Not feeling so good, going to see Dr. Alex. Sorry. Hate to dump this on you. Sorry, thanks. Yes, get better, for sure."

She flinched a little when he used her name, but that was just habit. It didn't matter. She wouldn't be Alex again for a while, that was all.

It was a risk, taking him out of school. Something de la Fuentes might notice if he was keeping close tabs on his messenger of death. But surely he would not raise the alarm to critical over one missed Friday. When Daniel showed up intact Monday morning, the drug lord would be reassured.

She took the phone from Daniel and pocketed it.

"I'll hold this for you, okay? You look unsteady and I don't want you to lose it."

"Okay." He looked around again and frowned at the giant concrete ceiling arcing overhead. "Where are we going?"

"My office, remember? We're going to get on this train now." She didn't see any faces from the other train in this car. If they were following, they were doing it from a distance. "Look, here's a seat. You can rest." She helped him settle, surreptitiously dropping his phone by her foot and then nudging it farther under the seat with her shoe.

Tracking a cell phone was the very easiest way to find someone without having to do any work. Cell phones were a trap she'd always avoided. It was like volunteering to tag yourself for the enemy.

Well, she also didn't really have anyone to call.

"Thanks," Daniel said. He still had one arm around her, though now, with him sitting and her standing, it was at her waist. He stared up at her dizzily and then added, "I like your face."

"Oh. Um, thank you."

"I like it a lot."

The woman sitting next to Daniel looked over at Alex and examined her face. *Great.*

The woman seemed unimpressed.

Daniel leaned his forehead against her hip and closed his eyes. The proximity was disconcerting on a few different levels, but also oddly comforting. It had been a long time since any human being had touched her with affection, even if this affection had come out of a test tube. Regardless, she couldn't let him fall asleep yet.

"What do you teach, Daniel?"

He angled his face up, his cheek still resting on her hip.

"Mostly English. That's my favorite."

"Really? I was horrible at all the humanities. I liked science best."

He made a face. "Science!"

She heard the woman beside him mutter, "Drunk," to her other neighbor.

"Shouldn't have told you I was a teacher." He sighed heavily.

"Why not?"

"Women don't like that. Randall says, 'Never volunteer the information.'" The way he said the words made it clear he was quoting this Randall verbatim.

"But teaching is a noble profession. Educating the future doctors and scientists of the world."

He looked up at her sadly. "There's no money in it."

"Not every woman is so mercenary. Randall is dating the wrong type."

"My wife liked money. Ex-wife."

"I'm sorry to hear that."

He sighed again and closed his eyes. "It broke my heart."

Another twinge of pity. Of sadness. He would never say these things, she knew, if he weren't high on her Ecstasy–truth serum hybrid. He was speaking more clearly now; the drug wasn't wearing off, his mind was just adapting to working around it.

She patted his cheek and made her voice cheery. "If she was that easily bought, she probably isn't worth crying over."

His eyes opened again. They were a very gentle hazel, an even mix of green and soft gray. She tried to picture them intense — fitting under the baseball cap of the self-assured man meeting with de la Fuentes in the photos — and failed.

She didn't know what she would do if he actually had dissociative identity disorder. She'd never worked with that before.

"You're right," he said. "I know you are. I need to see her for what she really was, not what I imagined she was."

"Exactly. We build up these ideas of people, create the one we want to be with, and then try to keep the real person inside the false mold. It doesn't always work out well."

Gibberish. She had no idea what she was saying. She'd been in one semiserious relationship in her whole life, and it hadn't lasted long. School had been prioritized before the guy, just like work had been prioritized before everything else for six years. Like how she now prioritized breathing over everything else. She had a problem with obsessiveness.

"Alex?"

"Yes?"

"Am I dying?"

She smiled reassuringly. "No. If I thought you were dying, I would have called an ambulance. You'll be fine. I just want to double-check."

"Okay. Will I have to have blood taken?"

"Maybe."

He sighed. "Needles make me nervous."

"It will be fine."

She didn't like that this bothered her—lying to him. But there was something about his simple trust, the way he seemed to ascribe the best motives to everything she did . . . She had to snap out of it.

"Thank you, Alex. Really."

"Just doing my job." Not a lie.

"Do you think you'll call me?" he asked hopefully.

"Daniel, we're definitely going to spend an evening together," she promised. If he hadn't been drugged, he would have heard the edge in her voice and seen the ice in her eyes.

CHAPTER 5

The rest went almost too smoothly...did that mean something? Her paranoia level was already so high, it was hard to say if this new worry elevated it or not.

He got into the cab at the Rosslyn station without protest. She knew how he felt—she and Barnaby had tried out most of the non-lethal preparations to have some concrete experience with what they could do. This one was like dreaming a pleasant dream, where problems and worries were for someone else to figure out, and all one needed was a hand to hold and a nudge in the right direction. In their notes they'd nicknamed it *Follow the Leader*, though it had a more impressive name on the official reports.

It was a relaxing trip, and if it weren't for the fact that she desperately needed her inhibitions, even back then, she might have indulged again.

She got him talking about the volleyball team he coached—he'd asked if he'd be back at school in time for practice—and he spent the entire cab ride telling her about the girls until she felt she knew all their names and their strengths on the court by heart. The cabbie paid no attention, humming along to some song too low for her to make out.

Daniel seemed mostly oblivious to the travel, but at a particularly long red light, he looked up and frowned.

"Your office is far away."

"Yes, it is," she agreed. "It's a hell of a commute."

"Where do you live?"

"Bethesda."

"That's a nice place. Columbia Heights is not so nice. My part of it, at least."

The cab started moving again. She was pleased; the plan was going very well. Even if they'd clocked her getting on and off the last train, they'd be hard-pressed to keep track of one cab in a sea of identical cabs twisting together through rush hour. Preparation felt like a magic spell sometimes. Like you could force events into the shape you wanted just by planning them *thoroughly* enough.

Daniel wasn't as talkative now. This was the second phase of the drug's action, and he would be getting more tired. She needed him to stay awake just a little bit longer.

"Why did you give me your number?" she asked when his lids started to droop.

He smiled dreamily. "I've never done that before."

"Me either."

"I'll probably be embarrassed about it later."

"Not if I call you, though, right?"

"Maybe. I don't know, it was out of character."

"So why did you do it?"

His soft eyes never left hers. "I like your face."

"You mentioned that."

"I really wanted to see it again. That made me brave."

She frowned, guilt pulsing.

"Does that sound weird?" He seemed worried.

"No, it sounds very sweet. Not many men would tell a woman something like that."

He blinked owlishly. "I wouldn't usually. Too . . . cowardly."

"You seem pretty brave to me."

"I feel different. I think it's you. I felt different as soon as I saw you smile."

As soon as I roofied you, she amended in her head.

"Well, that's quite a compliment," she said. "And here we go, can you get up?"

"Sure. This is the airport."

"Yes, that's where my car is."

His brow furrowed, then cleared. "Did you just get back from a trip?"

"I just got into town, yes."

"I go on trips sometimes. I like to go to Mexico."

She glanced up sharply. He was staring ahead, watching where he was walking. There was no sign of distress on his face. If she pushed him toward a secret, anything that was a pressure point, his docility would turn to suspicion. He might latch on to another stranger as his leader and try to escape. He might get agitated and call attention to her.

"What do you like about Mexico?" she asked carefully.

"The weather is hot and dry. I enjoy that. I've never lived in a really hot place, but I think I would like it. I get burned, though. I've never been able to tan. You look like you've spent some time in the sun."

"No, just born this way." She got her coloring from her absentee father. Genetic testing had informed her that he was a mix of many things, predominantly Korean, Hispanic, and Welsh. She'd always wondered what he'd looked like. The combination with her mother's Scottish background had created in her an oddly ordinary face — she could have been from almost anywhere.

"That must be nice. I have to use sunblock, a *lot* of sunblock. Or I peel. It's disgusting. I shouldn't tell you that."

She laughed. "I promise to forget it. What else do you like?"

"Working with my hands. I help build houses. Not in a skilled way; I just hammer where they tell me to. But the people are so kind and generous. I love that part."

It was all very convincing, and she felt a thrill of fear. How could he stick to the story so well, so effortlessly, with the chemicals moving through his system right now? Unless he'd built up a resistance somehow. Unless her department had created an antidote, unless they'd prepped him and he was playing her. The goose bumps stood up on the back of her neck. It didn't have to be the department that had prepared him. It could be his interactions with de la Fuentes. Who knew what kind of results strange drugs interacting with her own would have? She touched her tongue to the false cap on her back tooth. The department would have just killed her if that were the goal. De la Fuentes would probably want to punish her for attempting to interrupt his plans. But how would he know in advance? How could Daniel have made her as an opposing agent so quickly? She didn't even actually work for anyone anymore.

Stick to the plan, she told herself. *Get him in the car and you're in the clear. Sort of.*

"I like the houses there, too," he was saying. "You never close the windows, just let the air blow through. Some don't even have glass. It's a lot nicer than Columbia Heights, I can tell you. Maybe not nicer than Bethesda. I bet doctors live in nice houses."

"Not me. Boring vanilla apartment. I don't spend much time there, so it doesn't matter."

He nodded sagely. "You're out saving lives."

"Well, not really. I'm not an ER doctor or anything."

"You're saving *my* life." Wide gray-green eyes, total trust. She knew that if this behavior was genuine, it was the drug talking. But it still made her uneasy.

She could only keep playing her role.

"I'm just checking up on you. You're not dying." That much was true. The boys back at the department might have ended up killing this man. At least she could spare him that. Though . . . after she prevented the catastrophe, Daniel Beach would never see the outside of a prison cell again. Which made her feel . . .

A million dead. Innocent tiny babies. Sweet elderly grandmas. The First Horseman of the Apocalypse on a white steed.

"Oh, a bus too," he said mildly.

"This one takes us to my car. Then you won't have to walk anymore."

"I don't mind. I like walking with you." He smiled down at her and his feet tangled on his way up the steps. She steadied him before he could fall, then maneuvered him into the closest seat on the mostly empty bus.

"Do you like foreign films?" he asked, apropos of nothing.

"Um, some of them, I guess."

"There's a good theater at the university. Maybe if the dinner goes well, we could try some subtitles the next time."

"I'll make a deal with you," she said. "If you still like me after one evening together, I will definitely see a movie I can't understand with you."

He smiled, his lids drooping. "I'll still like you."

This was totally ridiculous. There should have been some way to direct this conversation away from *flirting*. Why was she the one feeling like the monster here? Okay, she *was* a monster, but she'd come to terms with that, mostly, and she knew she was the kind of monster that needed to exist for the sake of the common good. In some ways, she was like a normal physician — she had to cause pain to save lives. Like cutting off a gangrenous limb to save the rest of the body, just disassociated. Pain here, savior elsewhere. And elsewhere was much more deserving of the save.

Rationalizing, as she always had, so that she could live with herself. She never outright lied to herself, though. She knew she didn't exist in some moral gray area; she existed entirely in the black. But the only thing worse than Alex doing her job well was someone else doing it badly. Or no one doing it at all.

But even if she fully embraced the label *monster,* she was never the kind of monster who killed innocent people. She wasn't even going to kill this very guilty one... who was still looking up at her from under his long curls with big hazel puppy-dog eyes.

Dead babies, she chanted to herself. *Dead babies, dead babies, dead babies.*

She'd never wanted to be a spy or work undercover, but now she saw that she was also emotionally unsuited for the job. Apparently she had too much gratuitous sympathy floating around inside her body, which was more than ironic. This is why you never talked to your subject before you *talked* to him.

"Okay, Daniel, off we go. Can you stand up?"

"Mm-hmm. Oh, here, let me take your bag."

He lifted a hand weakly toward her briefcase.

"I got it." Though in truth her fingers were pins and needles around the handle. "You need to focus on your balance right now."

"I'm really tired."

"I know, look, my car is right there. The silver one."

"There are a lot of silver ones."

Exactly the point. "It's right here. Okay, let's put you in the back so you can lie down. Why don't you take off your coat, I don't want you to get too warm. And the shoes, there we go." Less for her to manage later. "Bend your knees up so your legs will fit. Perfect."

He had his head pillowed on the backpack now, which surely wasn't that comfortable, but he was past caring.

"You're so nice, Alex," he murmured, his eyes closed now. "You're the nicest woman I ever met."

"I think you're nice, too, Daniel," she admitted.

"Thanks," he half articulated, and then he was asleep.

Quickly, she pulled the beige throw out of the trunk. It was the same color as the seats. She covered him with it. She pulled a syringe from her bag and inserted it into a vein in his ankle, hunching her body so it blocked any outside view of what she was doing. *Follow the Leader* would wear off in an hour or so, and she needed him to sleep longer than that.

Not an agent, she decided. An agent might have played along with her kidnap drug, but he would never have let himself get knocked out like this. Just a mass murderer for hire, then.

• • •

THE TEMPORARY LAB she had created was in rural West Virginia. She'd rented a nice little farmhouse with a milking barn that had been a very long time without cows. The exterior of the barn was a white composite siding that matched the house; inside, the walls and ceiling were lined in aluminum. The floors were sealed concrete with conveniently spaced drains. There was a little bunk room in the back; it had been advertised as extra space for visiting guests, *delightfully rustic*. She was sure there were many naive travelers who would find the rusticity charming, but all she cared about was that the electricity and water were hooked up and running. The farmhouse and barn were situated in the middle of a 240-acre apple orchard, which was in turn surrounded by more acres of farmland. The closest neighbor was over a mile away. The owners of this orchard were making money during the off-season by renting out the space to city dwellers who wanted to pretend they were roughing it.

It was very expensive. She frowned every time she thought about the price, but it couldn't be helped. She needed a secluded facility with a usable space.

She'd been working nights to get everything ready. During the day she had followed Daniel from a good distance, then caught up on what sleep she could in the car during school hours. She was completely exhausted at the moment, but she still had a lot to do before her workday was over.

First stop, a minor freeway exit more than an hour out of the city. A narrow dirt road that looked as if no one had used it in a decade took her deeper into the trees. It must have led somewhere, but she didn't drive far enough to see where. She stopped under a thick patch of shade, cut the engine, and went to work.

If Daniel was employed by the department or, more likely, one of the organizations that worked closely with it—the CIA, a few military sections, some other black ops floaters that, like the department, didn't have official names—he would have an electronic tracker on him. Just like she'd once had. Absently, she rubbed her finger across the small raised scar on the nape of her neck, covered by her short hair. They liked to tag the head. If only one part of a body could be recovered, the head was best for identification purposes.

She opened the back passenger-side door and knelt on the damp ground beside Daniel's head. She started with the place both she and Barnaby had been tagged, brushing her fingers lightly along his skin, then again, pressing harder. Nothing. She'd seen a few foreign subjects whose trackers had been freshly removed from behind their ears, so she checked there next. Then she ran her fingers through his hair, probing the scalp for any bumps or hard spots that shouldn't be there. His curls were very soft and smelled nice, citrusy. Not that she cared about his hair, but at least she didn't have to put her hands into some greasy, malodorous nest. She appreciated that.

Now for the heavy lifting. If it was de la Fuentes keeping tabs on this man, the tracker would probably be external. She threw the shoes into the woods beside the road first—they seemed the most likely culprit of his clothes; lots of men would wear the same pair every day. Then she stripped off his shirt, grateful for the button-down, though it was still hard to get it out from under the weight of his body. She didn't bother trying to get the undershirt over his head; she pulled a blade from her pocket, untaped it, and cut the fabric into three easily removable pieces. She scanned his chest—no suspicious scars or lumps. The skin on his torso was fairer than his arms; he had a faint farmer's tan, no doubt from building houses in Mexico with a T-shirt on. Or from acquiring superviruses in Egypt—also very sunny.

He had what she thought of as sports muscles rather than gym muscles. No hard-cut edges, just a nice smooth alignment that showed he was active without being obsessive.

Rolling him onto his stomach was hard, and he fell into the foot space, draped over the hump between seats. He had two light scars on his left shoulder blade, parallel and even in length. She explored them carefully, prodding the skin all around, but she couldn't feel anything besides the normal fibrous, hypertrophic tissue that should be there.

It didn't take her long to realize she should have removed his jeans before rolling him over. She had to climb on top of his awkwardly positioned form and reach both arms around his torso to get the button fly open. So very thankful that he was not wearing skinny jeans, she then climbed out the other passenger-side door and yanked the pants off over his feet. She was unsurprised to see that he wore boxers rather than briefs. It fit his clothing profile. She stripped the boxers off, then the socks, and then she grabbed up the rest of the clothes, walked them a few feet off the road, and stuffed them behind a fallen log. She made another trip for the backpack. The laptop would be a very good hiding place for any electronic device someone wanted him to carry around unknowingly.

This wasn't the first time she'd had to strip a target down herself. In the laboratory environment, she'd had people who prepped a subject for her — Barnaby called them the underlings — but she hadn't always been in the lab, and during her first field trip to Herat, Afghanistan, she'd learned to be deeply grateful to the underlings. Stripping down a man who hadn't bathed in months was not pleasant — especially when she didn't have a shower available for herself afterward. At least Daniel was clean. She was the only one working up a sweat today.

She found the screwdriver in the trunk and quickly changed the DC license plate for one she'd pulled off a similar car in a West Virginia scrap yard.

Just to be thorough, she did a cursory examination of the backs of his legs, the bottom of his feet, and his hands. She'd never seen a tracker on the extremities, probably because extremities sometimes got cut off to make a point. She didn't see any scars. She also didn't see any calluses that suggested he trained with guns or used them frequently. He had soft teacher hands, with just a few hard spots that spoke of blisters from inexperienced labor.

She tried to roll him back up onto the seat but quickly realized it was a vain effort. It wasn't a comfortable sleeping position, but he wouldn't wake up regardless. He would be sore later. Though it was completely ridiculous to even think of that.

As she repositioned the blanket and tucked it around his body as best she could, she was constructing a story about him from the documents she'd read and the evidence in front of her.

She believed Daniel Beach was mostly the man she saw now, the pleasant all-around good guy. The attraction for the avaricious ex was understandable. He was probably easy to fall in love with. After some time had passed, enough time for the ex to take love for granted, she would have been able to shift her focus to the things she didn't have — the nice apartment, the big ring, the cars. She probably missed this side of Daniel now, the grass always being greener and whatnot.

But there was also darkness in Daniel, buried deep, perhaps born from the pain and unfairness of losing his parents, aggravated by his wife's betrayal, and then ignited by the loss of his final family member. That darkness would not surface easily. He would compartmentalize it, keep it away from this gentle life, pack it into the dark spaces where it fit. No wonder he could speak of Mexico so blithely. He would have two Mexicos: the happy one the teacher loved, and the dangerous one the monster thrived in. They probably weren't anything close to the same place in his head.

Not a true psychotic, she hoped. Just a fractured man who didn't want to give up the person he thought of as himself but who needed the release the darkness gave him.

She felt comfortable with this assessment, and it changed her plan a little. There was a great deal of performance to what she did. For some subjects, the very clinical and emotionless persona worked best—white coat, surgical mask, and shiny stainless steel; for others, it was the threat of the crazed sadist (though Barnaby was always more successful with that play; he had the face and hair for it—unruly spikes of white, I've-just-been-electrocuted hair). Every situation was slightly different—some feared the darkness, some the light. She'd been planning to go clinical—it was the most comfortable role in her wheelhouse—but she decided now that Daniel would need to be surrounded by darkness to let that side come to the surface. And Dark Daniel was the one she needed to talk to.

She did a little evasive driving on the way in. If someone had been tracking Daniel's clothes or possessions, she didn't want that person coming along any farther on this trip.

She considered the possibilities again for the millionth time. Column one, this was a very elaborate trap. Column two, this was for real and a million lives were on the line. Not to mention her own.

During her long drive, the balance finally shifted to rest solidly on one side. This wasn't a government agent in her car, she was sure of that. And if he was an innocent citizen, picked at random to draw her out, then they'd already missed their best opportunities to bag her. There hadn't been one attack, not one attempt to follow her . . . that she'd seen.

She thought of the mountains of incriminating information on Daniel Beach, and she couldn't help herself. She was a believer. So she'd better get to work saving lives.

She pulled into the farmhouse drive around eleven, dead tired and starving but 95 percent sure that there was no trail that could lead either the department or de la Fuentes to her doorstep. She looked the house over quickly, checking to see if anyone had broken in (and died, as he or she would have upon opening the door), and then, after disarming her safeguards, she drove the car into the barn.

As soon as she'd pulled the barn door shut and reset the "alarm," she went to work getting Daniel prepped.

All the other tasks were done. She'd bought timers from a Home Depot in Philly and plugged lamps into them in several rooms of the farmhouse; like a traveler leaving for a few weeks, she made certain that the place looked occupied. A radio was plugged into one of the timers, so there would be noise, too. The house was good bait. Most people would clear that before progressing to the dark barn.

The barn would stay dark. She'd constructed a kind of tent in the middle of the barn space that would hide light and muffle sound, while also keeping Daniel completely ignorant of his surroundings. The rectangular structure was about seven feet high, ten feet wide, and fifteen feet long. It was constructed of PVC pipe, black tarps, and bungee cords, and lined inside with two layers of egg foam duct-taped into place. Rough, yes, but more functional than a cave, and she'd handled that in the past.

In the center of the tent was an oversize metal slab with black accordion legs that could be adjusted for height. It had been on display in the barn—for authenticity, no doubt—and was some kind of veterinarian's operating table. It was bigger than she needed—this vet had been dealing with cows, not kittens—but still quite a find. It was one of the items that had pushed her over the edge into renting this extortionate tourist trap. There was another metal-topped table that she'd set up as a desk with her computer, the monitors, and a tray of things that would hopefully only be props. The IV pole was next to the head of the table, a bag of saline already hanging. A wheeled metal cart from the kitchen was positioned beside the pole; a mass of tiny but ominous-looking syringes were lined up in easy view on a stainless-steel tray. There was a gas mask and a pressure cuff on the wire rack below the syringes.

And of course, the restraints she'd bought on eBay, prison-medical-facility grade, which she'd chained into place through holes she'd laboriously drilled into the stainless-steel slab.

No one was escaping from those restraints without outside help. And that helper might need a blowtorch.

She'd left herself two exits, just openings in the tarp like the partings in a curtain. Outside the tent she had a cot, her sleeping bag, a hot plate, a small refrigerator, and all the other things she would need. There was a little three-piece bathroom attached to the bunkhouse, but it was too far away for her to sleep in, and there was no tub anyway, just a shower. She'd have to forgo her usual arrangements this weekend.

She used movers' straps to haul Daniel's inert form out of the car and onto a refrigerator dolly, bumping his head a few times in the process. *Probably* not hard enough to cause a concussion. Then she wheeled him to the table, set it to its lowest height, and rolled him onto it. He was still deeply under. She positioned him on his back, arms and legs extended about forty-five degrees from his body, then raised the table. One by one, she locked the restraints into place. He would not be moving out of this pose for a while. The IV was next; luckily he was fairly well hydrated, or maybe he just had really great veins. She got the line placed easily and started the drip. She added a parenteral nutrition bag next to the saline. This was all the sustenance he would get for the next three days, if it took that long. He'd be hungry, but his mind would be sharp when she wanted it to be. She put the pulse oximeter on his toe—he'd be able to pull it off a finger—and the dry electrodes on his back, one under each lung, to monitor his respiration. A quick swipe of the electric thermometer across his forehead told her that his current temperature was normal.

She wasn't as practiced with the bladder catheter, but it was a fairly simple procedure and he wasn't in any state to protest if she did something wrong. There would be enough cleaning up without urine to deal with, too.

Thinking of that, she placed the absorbent, plastic-lined squares—made for house-training puppies—on the floor all around the operating table. There would definitely be vomit if they needed to go past phase one. Whether there would be blood depended on how he responded to her normal methods. At least she had working plumbing here.

It was turning chilly in the barn, so she covered him with the blanket. She needed him to stay under for a while longer, and cold against his bare skin wouldn't help with that. After a moment of hesitation, she got one of the pillows off a bunk-room bed, brought it back, and placed it under his head. *It's just because I don't want him to wake up,* she assured herself. *Not because he looked uncomfortable.*

She inserted a small syringe into the IV port and gave him another dose of the sleeping agent. He should be good for at least four hours.

Daniel's unconscious face was unsettling. Too... peaceful somehow. She couldn't remember ever having seen an alignment of features that was so intrinsically innocent. It was hard to imagine that kind of peace and innocence even existing in the same world that she did. For a moment she worried again that she was dealing with a mental flaw beyond any of her previous experience. Then again, if de la Fuentes had been looking for someone who others would instinctively trust, this was exactly the kind of face he would have wanted. It might explain why the drug lord had chosen the schoolteacher in the first place.

She slipped the gas mask over his mouth and nose and screwed a canister onto it. If her safety precautions killed Daniel, she couldn't get the information she needed.

She did a final patrol around the perimeter. Through the windows, she could see that all the correct lights were on in the farmhouse. In the dead stillness of the night, she thought she could hear the faint strains of Top 40 pop.

Once she was sure that every point of ingress was secured, she ate a protein bar, brushed her teeth in the little bathroom, set her alarm for three, touched her gun under the cot, hugged her canister to her chest, and then sank into the folds of her sleeping bag. Her body was already asleep, and her brain wasn't far behind. She just had time to slip on her own gas mask before she was totally unconscious.

CHAPTER 6

By three thirty in the morning, she was up, dressed, and fed, still exhausted but ready to start. Daniel slept on, oblivious and peaceful. He would feel well rested when he woke up, but disoriented. He would have no idea what time or even what day it was. Discomfort was an important tool in her line of work.

She took his pillow and blanket away, acknowledging the regret this made her feel. But this was important; regardless of training, every subject felt great discomfort being naked and helpless in front of the enemy. Regret would be the last feeling she would allow herself for a few days. She closed off the rest. It had been more than three years, but she could feel things shutting down inside of her. Her body remembered how to do this. She knew she had the strength she would need.

Her hair was still wet from the quick color job, and the makeup felt thick on her face, though she wore very little, really. She didn't know how to do anything complicated, so she'd just smeared on dark shadow, thick mascara, and oxblood-red lipstick. She hadn't planned to adjust her hair color this soon, but black hair and the camouflage on her face were part of the new strategy. The white lab jacket and pale blue scrubs she'd brought lay crisply folded in her bag. Instead, she was in the tight black shirt again with black jeans. It was a good thing the farmhouse had a washer and dryer. The shirt was going to need a wash soon. Well, it needed one yesterday, actually.

It was strange how a little colored powder and grease could change an observer's perception of you. She checked herself in the bathroom mirror and was pleased by how hard her face looked, how cold. She ran a comb through her hair, slicking it straight back, then walked through the barn to her interrogation room.

She'd set up floodlights that hung from the PVC structure overhead, but she left them off now, just turning on two portable work lights that stood waist-high. The black duct tape and gray egg foam looked the same color in the shadows. The air temperature had dropped as the night progressed. There were goose bumps on the subject's arms and stomach. She ran the thermometer across his forehead again. Still within the normal range.

Finally, she turned on her computer and set up the protocols. It would go to screen saver after twenty minutes of inactivity. On the other side of her computer was a small black box with a keypad on top and a tiny red light on the side, but she ignored that now and went to work.

There was a feeling that struggled to break through to the surface as she injected the IV port with the chemical that would bring the subject around, but she suppressed it easily. Daniel Beach had two sides, and so did she. She was her other self now, the one the department called the Chemist, and the Chemist was a machine. Pitiless and relentless. *Her* monster was free now.

Hopefully his would come out to play.

The new drug trickled into his veins, and his breathing became less even. One long-fingered hand fisted and pulled against the restraint. Although he was still mostly unconscious, a frown touched his features as he tried to roll onto his side. His knees twisted, tugging against the fetters on his ankles, and suddenly his eyes flew open.

She stood quietly at the head of the table and watched him panic; his breathing spiked, his heart rate increased, his body thrashed against his bonds. He stared wildly into the darkness, trying to understand where he was, to find something familiar. He stopped suddenly, tense and listening.

"Hello?" he whispered.

She stood still, waiting for the right moment.

For ten minutes, he alternated between wildly yanking against the restraints and trying to listen around the harsh noise of his breathing.

"Help!" he finally called out loudly. "Is anyone there?"

"Hello, Daniel," she answered in a quiet voice.

His head jerked back, stretching his throat, as he looked for where the voice was coming from. It wasn't the instinct of a professional soldier, she noted, to expose the throat that way.

"Who's there? Who is that?"

"It doesn't really matter who I am, Daniel."

"Where am I?"

"Also not relevant."

"What do you *want?*" he half shouted.

"There you go—you got it. *That's* the question that matters."

She walked around the table so he could focus on her, though she was still lit from behind and her face would be mostly shadows.

"I don't have anything," he protested. "No money, no drugs. I can't help you."

"I don't want things, Daniel. I want—no, I *need* information. And the only way you're getting out of here is if you give it to me."

"I don't know anything—nothing important! Please—"

"Stop it," she snapped loudly, and he sucked in a shocked breath.

"Are you listening to me now, Daniel? This part is really crucial."

He nodded, blinking fast.

"I have to have this information. There is no other option. And if I have to, Daniel, I will hurt you until you tell me what I need to know. I will hurt you badly. I don't necessarily *want* to do this, but it doesn't bother me to do it, either. I'm telling you this so that you can decide now, before I begin. Tell me what I want to know, and I will free you. It's that simple. I promise I will not harm you. It will save me time and yourself a lot of suffering. I know you don't want to tell me, but please realize that you *are* going to tell me anyway. It may take a while, but eventually you won't be able to stop yourself. Everyone breaks. So make the easy choice now. You'll be sorry if you don't. Do you understand?"

She had given this same speech to many, many subjects in her career, and it was usually quite effective. About 40 percent of the time, this was when the subject would start confessing. Not often *finish* confessing, of course, and there was always some exploratory work to do, but there was a decent chance the first admission of guilt and some partial information might be surrendered now. The statistic varied depending on who she was giving the speech to; roughly half the time with most military men, the first divulgence would happen before any pain was administered. Only 5 to 10 percent of the actual spies would say anything without some physical distress. Same numbers for religious zealots. For the low-level toadies, the speech worked 100 percent of the time. The man in charge had never once confessed a single detail without pain.

She really hoped Daniel was just a glorified toady.

He stared back at her while she spoke, his face frozen in fear. But then, as she was concluding, confusion narrowed his eyes and pulled his brows together. It wasn't an expression she'd expected.

"Do you understand me, Daniel?"

His voice bewildered: "Alex? Alex, is that you?"

This was exactly why one didn't make contact with a mark beforehand. Now she was off script.

"Of course that's not my real name, Daniel. You know that."

"What?"

"My name isn't Alex."

"But . . . you're a doctor. You helped me."

"I am not that kind of doctor, Daniel. And I didn't help you. I drugged you and I kidnapped you."

His face was sober. "You were kind to me."

She had to control a sigh.

"I did what I had to do to get you here. Now, I need you to focus, Daniel. I need you to answer my question. Are you going to tell me what I want to know?"

She saw doubt in his expression again. Disbelief that she would actually hurt him, that this was really happening.

"I'll tell you anything you want to know. But like I said, I don't know anything important. I don't have any bank account numbers or, I don't know, treasure maps or anything. Certainly not anything worth all this."

He tried to gesture with his trussed hand. Looking at himself as he did, he seemed to realize for the first time that he was naked. His skin flushed—face, neck, and a line down the center of his chest—and he pulled automatically against the restraints as if trying to cover himself. His breathing and heart rate started spiking again.

Nudity; whether black ops agents or just low-level terrorist gofers, they all hated it.

"I don't want a treasure map. I'm not doing this for personal gain, Daniel. I'm doing this to protect innocent lives. Let's talk about that."

"I don't understand. How can I help with that? Why wouldn't I want to?"

She didn't like the way this was going. The ones who clung to the claim of ignorance and innocence often took longer to break than the ones who owned their guilt but were determined not to sell out their government, or their jihad, or their comrades.

She walked to the desk and picked up the first picture. It was one of the very clear surveillance shots of de la Fuentes, a close-up.

"Let's start with this man," she said, holding the photo at his eye level and using one of the work lights as a spot.

Perfectly blank, absolutely no reaction. A bad sign.

"Who is that?"

She allowed her sigh to be audible this time.

"You're making the wrong choice, Daniel. Please think about what you're doing."

"But I don't know who that is!"

She fixed him with a resigned stare.

"I'm being completely honest, Alex. I don't know that man."

She sighed again. "Then I suppose we'll get started."

The disbelief was there again. She'd never dealt with that in an interrogation before. All the others who'd been on her table had known what they were there for. She'd faced terror and pleading and, occasionally, stoic defiance, but never this strange, trusting, almost-challenge: *You won't hurt me.*

"Um, is this some kind of fetish fantasy thing?" he asked in a low voice, somehow finding a way to sound embarrassed despite the bizarreness of his circumstances. "I don't really know the rules for that stuff…"

She turned away to hide an inappropriate smile. *Get a grip,* she ordered herself. Trying to keep the movement smooth, as if she'd meant to walk away at that exact moment, she went to her desk. She clicked one key on her computer, keeping it awake. Then she picked up the prop tray. It was heavy, and some of the props clanked against each other as she moved it. She brought the tray to his side, rested the edge of it beside the syringes, and angled the light so the metallic implements shone brightly.

"I'm sorry you find this confusing," she said in an even voice. "I am in deadly earnest, I assure you. I want you to look at my tools."

He did, and his eyes grew very wide. She watched for some hint of the other side to break through, the Dark Daniel, but there was nothing. His eyes were somehow still gentle even in abject fear. Innocent. Lines spoken by Hitchcock's Norman Bates flashed through her head. *I think I must have one of those faces you can't help believing.*

She shuddered, but he didn't notice, his eyes fixed on her props.

"I don't have to use these very often," she told him, touching the pliers lightly, then stroking her finger along the extra-large scalpel.

"They call me in when they would like to have the subject left more or less ... intact." She brushed the bolt cutters on the hard syllable of the last word. "But I don't really need these tools anyway." She flicked her fingernail against the canister of the welding torch, producing a high-pitched pinging sound. "Can you guess why?"

He didn't respond, frozen in horror. He was starting to see now. Yes, this was real.

Only Dark Daniel must already have known that. So why wasn't he surfacing? Did he think she could be fooled? Or that his charm on the train had melted her weak, womanly heart?

"I'll tell you why," she said in a voice so low it was almost a whisper. She leaned in conspiratorially and held her face in a sweet, regretful half smile that didn't touch her eyes. "Because what I do hurts ... *so ... much ... worse.*"

His eyes looked like they were going to bug out of his head. This, at least, was a familiar reaction.

She took the tray away, letting his focus move naturally to the long line of syringes left behind, glinting in the light.

"The first time will last only ten minutes," she told him, still facing away as she set the tools back on the desk. She spun around. "But it will feel like a lot longer. This will just be a taste—you could look at it as a warning shot. When it's done, we'll try talking again."

She picked up the syringe on the far end of the tray, pushed the plunger till a drop of liquid dewed at the top, then flicked it away theatrically like a nurse in a movie.

"Please?" he whispered. "Please, I don't know what this is about. I can't help you. I swear I would if I could."

"You will," she promised, and she stabbed the needle into his left triceps brachii.

The reaction was nearly instantaneous. His left arm spasmed and jerked against the restraint. While he stared in horror at his convulsing muscles, she quietly picked up another syringe and crossed to his right side. He saw her approach.

"Alex, please!" he yelled.

She ignored him and his attempt to somehow evade her, as if he were strong enough to rip free of his cuffs, and injected this dose of lactic acid into his right quad. His knee wrenched flat, the muscles pulling his foot off the table. He gasped, and then groaned.

She moved deliberately, not in any hurry, but not slowly, either. Another syringe. His left arm was already too incapacitated for him to try to resist her. This time she injected the acid into his left biceps brachii. Immediately, the opposing triceps muscle group began tearing against the biceps, battling for contraction dominance.

The air burst out of his mouth like he'd just been punched in the gut, but she knew the pain was much, much worse than any blow.

One more injection, this time into his right biceps femoris. The same ripping struggle that was happening in his arm started in his leg. And the screaming started with it.

She went to stand by his head, watching dispassionately while the tendons in his neck strained into white ropes. When he opened his mouth to scream again, she shoved a gag in. If he bit off his tongue, he wouldn't be able to tell her anything.

She walked slowly to her desk chair while his muffled shrieks were absorbed into the double layer of foam, sat down, and crossed her legs. She looked at the monitors — everything elevated but nothing in the danger zone. A healthy body could experience a lot more pain than most people would think before its important organs were really in any serious peril. She brushed the touch pad on her computer, keeping the screen brightly lit. Then she pulled her wristwatch out of her pocket and laid it across her knee. This was mostly for theatrics; she could have watched the clock on her computer or the monitors just as easily.

She faced him while she waited, her face composed and the silver watch bright against her black clothing. Subjects tended to find this disconcerting — that she could watch her handiwork so dispassionately. So she stared at him, expression polite, an audience member at a mediocre play, while his body thrashed and distorted on the table and his screams choked past the gag. Sometimes his eyes were on her, pleading and agonized, and other times they whirled crazily around the room.

Ten minutes could be a very long time. His muscles started to spasm independently of each other, some locking into knots and others seeming to want to jerk themselves off the bone. Sweat ran off his face, darkening his hair. The skin over his cheekbones looked ready to split. The screams lowered in pitch, turned hoarse, sounding more like an animal's than a man's.

Six more minutes.

And these weren't even the good drugs.

Anyone who was sick enough to want to could duplicate the pain she was inflicting now. The acid she was using wasn't a controlled substance; it was fairly easy to acquire online, even if one happened to be on the run from the dark underbelly of the U.S. government. Back in her interrogating prime, when she had her beautiful lab and her beautiful budget, her sequencer and her reactor, she'd been able to create some truly unique and ultra-specific preparations.

The Chemist really wasn't the proper code name for her at all. However, the Molecular Biologist was probably too big a mouthful. Barnaby had been the chemistry expert, and the things he'd taught her had kept her alive after she'd lost her lab; she had become her code name in the end. But in the beginning, it had been her theoretical research with monoclonal antibodies that had brought her to the department's attention. It was a shame she couldn't risk taking Daniel to the lab. This operation would have produced results much more quickly.

And she'd been *so close* to actually removing pain from the equation. That had been her Holy Grail, though no one else seemed eager for it. She was sure that if she'd been working in the lab for the past three years instead of running for her life, by now she would have created the key that would unlock whatever one needed from the human mind. No torture, no horror. Just quick answers, given pleasantly, and then an equally pleasant trip to either a cell or the execution wall.

They should have let her work.

Still four minutes to go.

She and Barnaby had discussed different strategies for dealing with these periods of the interrogation. Barnaby had told himself stories. He would remember the fairy tales from his childhood and think of modern versions or alternative endings or what would happen if the characters switched places. He'd said some of the ideas he came up with were pretty good, and when he had time he was going to write them down. She, however, felt like she was wasting time if she wasn't doing something practical. She would plan things. In the beginning, she planned new versions of the monoclonal antibody that would control brain response and block neural receptors. Later, she planned her life on the run, thinking of everything that could possibly go wrong, every worst-case scenario, and what she could do to keep herself from falling into each trap. Then how to escape the trap halfway in. Then after it was sprung. She tried to envision every possibility.

Barnaby said she needed to take a mental break now and then. Have some fun, or what was the point of living?

Just living, she had decided. Just living was all she asked. And so she put in the mental effort needed to make that possible.

Today she thought about the next step. Tonight, tomorrow night, or, heaven help him, the night after that, Daniel was going to tell her everything. Everyone broke. It was just a simple fact that a human being could resist pain for only so long. Some people could deal better with one kind or another, but that meant she would just switch to another type of pain. At some point, if he didn't talk, she would roll Daniel onto his stomach — so he wouldn't choke on his own vomit — and administer what she called the green needle, though the serum was actually clear, just like all the others. If that didn't work, she'd try one of the hallucinogens. There was always a new way to feel pain. The body had so many different ways to experience stimuli.

Once she had what she needed, she would stop his pain, put him under, and then e-mail Carston from this IP address and tell him everything she'd learned. Then she would drive away and keep going for a very long time. Maybe Carston and company wouldn't come after her. Maybe they would. And she might never know, because she would most likely keep hiding until she died — hopefully of natural causes.

Before nine minutes were over, the dose started to wear off. It was different for everyone, and Daniel was on the larger side. His screams turned to groans as his body slowly melted into a pile of exhausted flesh on the table, and then he was quiet. She removed the gag and he gasped for air. He stared at her with awed horror for one long moment, and then he started to cry.

"I'll give you a few minutes," she said. "Collect your thoughts."

She left through the exit he couldn't see, then sat quietly on the cot and listened to him choke back his sobs.

Crying was normal, and usually it boded well. But it was obvious that this crying was Daniel the Teacher. There was still no sign of Dark Daniel, not one knowing glance or defensive tic. What would reach him? If this was truly dissociative identity disorder, could she *force* an appearance of the personality she wanted? She needed an actual shrink on her team today. If she'd gone docilely into the lab as they'd wanted, they probably would have been able to find her one almost the moment she asked. Well, there was nothing she could do about it now.

She quietly ate a soft breakfast bar while she waited for his breathing to even out, and then she ate a second. She washed it down with a box of apple juice out of the minifridge.

When she reentered the tent, Daniel was gazing despairingly at the egg-foam ceiling. She walked quietly to the computer and touched a key.

"I'm sorry you had to go through that, Daniel."

He hadn't heard her enter. He cringed as far away from the sound of her voice as he could.

"Let's not do it again, okay?" she said. She settled back into her chair. "I want to go home, too." Kind of a lie, but also mostly true, if impossible. "And, though you might not believe me, I'm not actually a sadist. I don't enjoy watching you suffer. I just don't have another choice. I'm not going to let all those people die."

His voice was raw. "I don't . . . know what . . . you're talking about."

"You'd be surprised how many people say that — and keep saying it for round after round of what you just went through, and worse! And then on the tenth round for one, on the seventeenth for another, suddenly the truth comes pouring out. And I get to tell the good guys where to find the warhead or the chemical bomb or the disease agent. And people stay alive, Daniel."

"I haven't killed anyone," he rasped.

"But you're planning to, and I'm going to change your mind."

"I would never do that."

She sighed. "This is going to take a long time, isn't it?"

"I can't tell you anything I don't know. You've got the wrong person."

"I've heard that one a lot, too," she said lightly, but it touched a nerve. If she couldn't get the other Daniel to appear, then wasn't she truly torturing the wrong person?

She made a snap decision to go off script again, though she was out of her depth when it came to mental illness.

"Daniel, do you ever have blackouts?"

A long pause. "What?"

"Have you, for example, woken up somewhere and not known how you got there? Has anyone ever told you that you did or said something that you can't remember doing or saying?"

"Um. No. Well, today. I mean, that's what you're saying, right? That I'm planning to do something awful, but I don't know what it is?"

"Have you ever been diagnosed with dissociative identity disorder?"

"No! Alex, *I'm* not the crazy person in this room."

That didn't help at all.

"Tell me about Egypt."

He turned his head toward her. His expression made the words he was thinking as clear as if he'd spoken them out loud: *Are you kidding me, lady?*

She just waited.

He sighed a pained little gasp. "Well, Egypt has one of the longest histories of any modern civilization. There is evidence that Egyptians were living along the Nile as early as the tenth millennium BC. By about 6000 BC—"

"That's hilarious, Daniel. Can we be serious now?"

"I don't know what you want! Are you testing to see if I'm really a history teacher? I can't even tell!"

She could hear the strength coming back into his voice. The nice thing about her drugs was that they wore off quickly. She could have a focused conversation between rounds. And she'd found that the subjects had a greater fear of pain when they weren't feeling any. The high-ups and deep-downs seemed to speed things along.

She touched a key on her computer.

"Tell me about your trip to Egypt."

"I have never been to Egypt."

"You didn't go there with Habitat for Humanity two years ago?"

"No. I've been in Mexico for the past three summers."

"You do know people keep track of these things, right? That your passport number is logged into a computer and there's a record of where you've gone?"

"Which is why you should know I was in Mexico!"

"Where you met Enrique de la Fuentes."

"Who?"

She blinked her eyes slowly, her face very bored.

"Hold on," he said, staring up like an explanation might be posted on the ceiling. "I know that name. It was on the news a while ago . . . with those DEA officers that went missing. He's a drug dealer, right?"

She held up the picture of de la Fuentes again.

"That's him?"

She nodded.

"Why do you think I know him?"

She answered slowly. "Because I also have pictures of you together. And because he's given you ten million dollars in the past three years."

His mouth dropped open and the word came out as a gasp. "Wha...ut?"

"Ten million dollars, in your name, scattered around the Cayman Islands and Swiss banks."

He stared at her for another second, and then anger suddenly twisted his face, and his voice turned harsh. "If I've got ten million dollars, then why do I live in a roach-infested walk-up studio in Columbia Heights? Why are we using the same patched volleyball uniforms that the school's had since 1973? Why do I ride the Metro while my ex-wife's new husband drives around town in a Mercedes? And why am I getting *rickets* from eating a steady diet of ramen?"

She let him vent. The desire to talk was a small step in the right direction. Unfortunately, this angry Daniel was still the schoolteacher version, just not a very happy schoolteacher.

"Wait a minute—what do you mean you have pictures of me with the drug guy?"

She walked to her desk and pulled the appropriate photo.

"In El Minya, Egypt, with de la Fuentes," she announced as she held the photo in front of his face.

Finally, a reaction.

His head jerked back; his eyes narrowed, then opened wide. She could almost watch his thoughts move as they ran through his brain and settled in his face. He was analyzing what he was looking at and making a plan.

Still no sign of the other Daniel, but at least he seemed to recognize that other part of himself.

"Do you want to tell me about Egypt *now*, Daniel?"

Tight lips. "I've never been there. That's not me."

"I don't believe you." She sighed. "Which is really too bad, because we've got to move this party along."

The fear came back, fast and hard.

"Alex, please, I swear that isn't me. Please don't."

"This is my job, Daniel. I have to find out how to save those people."

All the reticence disappeared. "I don't want to hurt anyone. I want you to save them, too."

It was harder not to believe his sincerity now.

"That picture meant something to you."

He shook his head once, expression closing up. "It wasn't me."

She had to admit, she was more than a little fascinated. This was really something new. How she wished she had Barnaby to consult! Oh well, she was on the clock. She didn't have time for wishing. She stacked the syringes one by one onto her left palm. Eight this time.

He stared at her with terror and...sadness. He started to say something, but no sound came out. She paused with the first needle ready in her right hand.

"Daniel, if you want to say something, do it quick."

Dejected. "It won't help."

She waited another second, and he looked straight at her.

"It's just your face," he said. "It's the same as before...exactly the same."

She flinched, then pivoted and moved up the table to stand beside his head. He tried to strain away from her, but that just better exposed his sternocleidomastoid. Usually she'd save this particular muscle for later in the interrogation; it was one of the very most painful things she could do to a subject under her current limitations. But she wanted to leave quickly, so she stabbed the needle into the side of his neck and pushed the plunger down. Without really looking at him, she replaced the gag as soon as his mouth opened. Then, dropping the other syringes, she escaped the room.

CHAPTER 7

She was rusty, that was all. It *had* been three years. That's why she was feeling things. That's why this subject was affecting her. It was nothing except her having been out of the game so long. She could still get her groove back.

She entered the room once during this session to keep the computer alive but didn't stay to watch. She came back only after the dose was waning, about fifteen minutes later.

He lay there gasping again, but this time he didn't cry, though she knew the pain had been much worse than before. Blood from his chafed skin now stained all the restraints and dripped onto the table. She might need to paralyze him for the next round so his injuries didn't get any worse. That was a frightening feeling, too; it might help.

He started to shiver. She actually turned toward the exit one millisecond before she realized that she was heading out to get him a blanket. What was wrong with her?

Focus.

"Do you have anything to say?" she asked gently when his breathing was more even.

His answer came out in exhausted, breathy gasps. "It's not me. Swear. I'm not—planning—anything. Don't know the drug guy. Wish I could help. Really, really, really—wish I could help. Really."

"Hmm. You're showing some resistance to this method, so maybe we'll try something new."

"Re . . . sistance?" he croaked in disbelief. "You think . . . I'm resist . . . ing?"

"Honestly, I'm a little worried about messing up your head with hallucinogens — seems like there's already enough trouble up there." She tapped her fingers against his sweaty scalp as she spoke. "Maybe we have no choice but to try old-school . . ." She continued to absently tap his head as she glanced at the tray of tools on her desk. "Are you squeamish?"

"Why. Is this — happening to me." Totally rhetorical, he wasn't looking for an answer to his broken whisper. She gave him one anyway.

"Because this is exactly what happens when you plan to release a lethal influenza virus in four American states, potentially killing a *million* citizens. The government takes exception to that kind of behavior. And they send me to make you talk."

His eyes focused on her, horror suddenly overtaken by shock.

"What. The. *Actual. Hell!*"

"Yes, it's horrific and appalling and evil, I know."

"Alex, really, this is nuts! I think you have a problem."

She got in his face. "My problem is that you aren't telling me where the virus is. Do you have it already? Is it with de la Fuentes still? When's the drop? Where is it?"

"This is insane. *You're* insane!"

"I'd probably enjoy life a lot more if that were true. But I'm beginning to think they sent the wrong doctor. We *need* the doctor for crazies here. I don't know how to get the other Daniel to show up!"

"Other Daniel?"

"The one I can see in these pictures!"

She whirled and grabbed a handful from the desk, jabbing the computer once angrily in passing.

"Look," she said, shoving them toward his face, peeling off one

after the other and dropping them to the floor. "It's your body"—
she smacked one photo against his shoulder before letting it fall—
"your face, see? But not the right expression. There's someone else
looking out of your eyes, Daniel, and I'm not sure if you're aware of
him or not."

But there it was again, the recognition. He was aware of
something.

"Look, for right now, I'd settle for you just telling me what you
see in this picture." She held up the top photo, Other Daniel skulk-
ing in the back door of a Mexican bar.

He looked at her, torn.

"I can't...explain it...it doesn't make any sense."

"You see something I don't. What is it?"

"He..." Daniel tried to shake his head, but it barely moved, his
muscles were so fatigued. "He looks like..."

"Like you."

"No," he whispered. "I mean, yes, of course he looks like me, but
I can see the differences."

The way he said it. *Of course he looks like me.* The transparent
honesty again, but something still withheld...

"Daniel, do you know who this is?" A real question this time,
not snark, not rhetoric. She wasn't playing psychiatrist—badly—
now. She felt for the first time since the interrogation started that she
was actually onto something.

"It can't be," he breathed, closing his eyes less out of exhaustion
and more to block out the picture, she thought. "It's impossible."

She leaned forward. "Tell me," she murmured.

He opened his eyes and stared at her searchingly. "You're sure?
He's going to *kill* people?"

So natural, his use of the third person.

"Hundreds of thousands of people, Daniel," she promised, earnest as he was. She used the third person, too: "He's got access to a
deadly virus and he's going to spread it for a psychopathic drug lord.

He already has hotel reservations — in your name. He's doing this in three weeks."

A whisper. "I don't believe it."

"I don't want to either. This virus . . . it's a bad one, Daniel. It's going to kill a lot more people than a bomb. There'll be no way to control how it spreads."

"But *how* could he do this? *Why?*"

At this point, she was nearly 65 percent convinced that they were not talking about one of Daniel's multiple personalities.

"It's too late for that. All that matters now is stopping him. Who is he, Daniel? Help me save those innocent people."

A different kind of agony twisted his features. She'd seen this before. With another subject, she would know that his desire to be loyal was warring with his desire to avoid more torture. With Daniel, she rather thought the war was between loyalty and wanting to do the right thing.

In the perfect stillness of the night, as she waited for his answer, through the weak sound barrier of the foam, she clearly heard a small prop plane overhead. Very close overhead.

Daniel looked up.

Time slowed down while she analyzed.

Daniel didn't look surprised or relieved. The noise did not seem to signal rescue or attack to him. He just noticed it the way someone might notice a car alarm going off. Not relevant to himself, but distracting from the moment.

It felt like she was moving in slow motion as she jumped up and raced to the desk for the syringe she needed.

"You don't have to do that, Alex," Daniel said, resigned. "I'll tell you."

"Shh," she whispered, leaning over his head while she injected the drug — into the IV port this time. "I'm just putting you to sleep for now." She patted his cheek. "No pain, I promise."

Understanding lit his eyes as he connected the sound to her behavior. "Are we in danger?" he whispered back.

We. Huh. Another interesting pronoun choice. She'd never had a subject anything like this before.

"I don't know if *you* are," she said as his eyes drooped closed. "But I sure as hell am."

There was a heavy concussion, not immediately outside the barn but too close for her liking.

She put the gas mask securely on his face, then donned hers and screwed in the canister. This time was no drill. She glanced at her computer—she had about ten minutes left there. She wasn't sure it was enough, so she tapped the space bar. Then she jabbed a button on the little black box, and the light on the side started blinking rapidly. Almost as a reflex, she covered Daniel with the blanket again.

She shut the lights off, so the room was lit only by the white gleam of her computer screen, and exited the tent. Inside the barn, everything was black. She searched, hands out in front of her, until she found the bag beside her cot and, with years of practice guiding her, blindly put on all of her easily accessible armor. She shoved the gun into the front of her belt. She took a syringe from her bag, jabbed it into her thigh, and depressed the plunger. Ready as she could make herself, she crept into the back corner of the tent and hid where she knew the darkest shadow would be if someone came in with a flashlight. She pulled out the gun, removed the safety, and gripped it with both hands. Then she put her ear to the seam of the tent and listened, waiting for someone to open the door or a window into the barn, and die.

While she waited through the slow seconds, her mind raced through more analysis.

This wasn't a big operation coming for her. No way any extraction team or elimination team worth its salt would announce its arrival with a noisy plane. There were better ways, quieter ways. And if it was a big, SWAT-style team sent after her without any briefing, just busting their way in by sheer might, they would have come in a copter. The plane had sounded very small—a three-seater at most, but probably two-.

If a lone assassin was coming for her again, as had always been the case in the past, she didn't know what this guy thought he was doing. Why would he give himself away? The noisy plane was the move of someone who was lacking resources and in a very big hurry, someone to whom time was much more important than stealth.

Who was it? Not de la Fuentes.

First of all, a small prop plane didn't seem like a drug lord's MO. She imagined that with de la Fuentes, there would be a fleet of black SUVs and a bunch of thugs with machine guns.

Second, she had a gut feeling about this one.

No, she wasn't a lie detector. Good liars, professional liars, could fool anyone, human or machine. Her job had never been about guessing the truth from the subject's shifty eyes or tangled contradictions. Her job was breaking down the subject until there was nothing left but compliant flesh and one story. She wasn't the best because she could separate the truth from the lie; she was the best because she had a natural affinity for the capabilities of the human body and was a genius with a beaker. She knew exactly what a body could handle and exactly how to push it to that point.

So gut feelings were not her forte, and she couldn't remember the last time she'd really felt something like this.

She believed Daniel was telling the truth. That's why this exercise with Daniel had bothered her so much — because he wasn't lying. It wasn't going to be de la Fuentes coming after him. No one was coming after Daniel, because he wasn't anything more than what he said he was — an English teacher, a history teacher, a volleyball coach. Whoever was coming was coming for her.

Why now? Had the department been tracking her all day and only just discovered her? Were they trying to save Daniel's life, having realized too late that he wasn't the guy?

No way. They would have known that before they set her up. They had access to too much information to be fooled in this. The file wasn't entirely make-believe, but it *was* manipulated. They had *wanted* her to get the wrong person.

For a moment she felt a wave of nausea. She'd tortured an innocent man. She put that away quickly. Time for regret later, if she
didn't die now.

The columns reversed again. Elaborate trap, not real crisis.
Though she did believe the situation with de la Fuentes was genu-
ine, she no longer believed it was quite so urgent as she'd been told.
Time was the easiest small change to make to a file; the tight deadline
was a distortion. Low stakes again—just her own life to save. And
Daniel's, too, if she could.

She tried to shake the thought—it felt almost like an omen—
that her stakes had somehow doubled. She didn't need the extra
burden.

Maybe someone else—that brilliant and unsuspecting kid who
had taken her place at the department—was working on the real terrorist now. Maybe they didn't think she still had the ability to get what
they wanted. But why bring her in at all, then? Maybe the terrorist was
dead, and they wanted a fall guy. Maybe they'd discovered this doppel-
gänger weeks ago and held him in reserve. Get the Chemist to make
somebody confess to *something,* and tie a bow on a bad situation?

That wouldn't explain the visitor, though.

It had to be near five in the morning. Maybe it was just a farmer
who liked to start the day early and knew the area so well that he
didn't mind flying without radar through a bunch of tall trees in the
pitch-black night and then enjoyed a good crash landing for the
adrenaline kick...

She could hear Daniel's breath rasp through the gas mask's filter.
She wondered if she had done the right thing putting him under. He
was just so...exposed. Helpless. The department had already
exhibited exactly how much concern they had for Daniel Beach's
well-being. And she'd left him trussed and defenseless in the middle
of the room, a fish in a barrel, a sitting duck. She owed him better
than that. But her first reaction had been to neutralize him. It
wouldn't have been safe to free him, she knew. Of course he would
have attacked her, tried to exact revenge. If it came to brute strength,

he'd have the advantage. And she didn't want to have to poison him or shoot him. At least this way, his death wouldn't be on her hands.

She still felt guilty, his vulnerable presence in the darkness worrying at the edges of her mind like sandpaper against cotton, pulling threads of concentration away from her.

Too late for second thoughts.

She heard the faint sound of movement outside. The barn was surrounded by bushes with stiff, rustling leaves. Someone was in them now, looking into the windows. What if he just let loose with an Uzi through the side of the barn? He obviously wasn't worried about noise.

Should she lower the table, get Daniel down in case the tent was sprayed with bullets? She had oiled the accordion base well, but she wasn't positive it wouldn't squeak.

She scuttled over to the table and cranked it lower as fast as she could. It did make some low, bass groans, but she didn't think they would carry outside the barn, especially through the foam barrier. She scooted back to her corner and listened again.

More rustling. He was at another window, on the other side of the barn. Her booby trap's wires were inconspicuous, but not invisible. Hopefully he was only looking for a target inside. Had he gone to the house first? Why hadn't he gone in?

Sounds outside another window.

Just open it, she thought to herself. *Just crawl inside.*

A sound she didn't understand—a hissing, followed by a heavy clank from above. Then a *thump, thump, thump* so loud that the barn seemed to shake. Her first thought was small explosives, and she hunkered down into a protective position automatically, but in the next second she realized it wasn't *that* loud, it was just the contrast with the silence before. There was no sound of anything breaking—no glass shattering or metal tearing. Was the reverberation enough to break the connections around the windows or door? She didn't think so.

Then she realized the thumps against the wall were moving *up,* just as they stopped. Above her.

Major hitch—he was coming through the roof.

She was on her feet in a second, one eye to the seam in the tent. It was still too dark to see anything. Above her, the sound of a welding torch. Her intruder had one, too.

All her preparation was falling apart. She glanced back once at Daniel. His gas mask was on. He would be fine. Then she darted out into the larger space of the barn, bent low with her hands stretched out in front of her to find the objects in her way, and moved as quickly as she could toward the faint moonlight filtering through the closest window. There were milking stalls to maneuver around, but she thought she remembered the clearest route. She broke into the open space between the tent and the stalls, half running, and one hand found the milking apparatus. She dodged that and reached out for the window—

Something tremendously hard and heavy threw her to the ground face-first, knocking the wind out of her and pinning her to the floor. The gun flew away into the darkness. Her head thudded resoundingly against the concrete. Bright pops of light skittered across her eyes.

Someone grabbed her wrists and pulled her arms behind her, then wrenched them higher until she guessed her shoulders were close to dislocating. A grunt escaped her lungs as the new position forced the air out. Her thumbs quickly twisted the rings on her left and right hands, exposing the barbs.

"What's this?" a man's voice said directly above her—generic American accent. He changed his grip so he was holding both her wrists in one hand. With the other, he yanked off her gas mask. "So maybe not a suicide bomber after all," he mused. "Let me guess, those hot wires aren't connected to charges, are they?"

She squirmed under him, twisting her wrists, trying to get her rings in contact with his skin.

"Stop that," he ordered. He clocked the back of her head with something hard—probably the gas mask—and her face smacked the floor. She felt her lip split, and tasted blood.

She braced for it. In such close quarters, it would probably be a blade across her carotid artery. Or a wire around her throat. She hoped for the blade. She wouldn't feel the slice as pain — not with the specially designed dextroamphetamine she had racing through her veins right now — but she'd probably feel the strangulation.

"Get up."

The weight lifted off her back and she was drawn up by her wrists. She got her feet under her as quickly as possible to take the pressure off her shoulder joints. She needed to keep her arms usable.

He stood behind her, but she could tell by where his breathing came from that he was tall. He pulled her wrists until she was on her tiptoes, struggling to maintain contact with the floor.

"Okay, shorty, now you're going to do something for me."

She didn't have the training to beat him in a fight, and she didn't have the strength to wrest herself free. She could only try to make use of the options she'd prepared.

She let her weight sag precariously against her stressed shoulders for one second as she kicked the toe of her left shoe down with enough pressure to pop the stiletto blade out of the heel (the front-facing blade was in her right shoe). Then she slashed awkwardly back toward where his legs had to be. He jumped out of the way, loosening his grip enough for her to rip free and spin around, her left hand flying out for an open-handed slap. He was too tall; she missed his face, and her barb scraped against something hard on his chest — body armor. She danced backward, away from the blow she could hear coming but could not see, her hands extended, trying to make contact with unprotected skin.

Something cut her legs out from under her. She hit the ground and rolled away, but he was on top of her at once. He grabbed her hair and bounced her face against the concrete again. Her nose popped and blood flooded her lips and chin.

He bent down to speak directly in her ear. "Playtime is over, honey."

She tried to head-butt him. The back of her head connected with something, but not a face — uneven spires, metallic . . .

Night-vision goggles. No wonder he'd been able to control the fight so well.

He slapped the back of her head.

If only she'd put her earrings on.

"Seriously, stop it. Look, I'm going to get off you. I can see you, and you can't see me. I've got a gun, and I will shoot you in the knee-cap if you try one more stupid trick, okay?"

While he was talking, he reached back with one hand and ripped her shoes off, one after the other. He didn't check her pockets, so she still had the scalpel blades and the needles in her belt. He jumped off her. She heard him move away and click the safety off his gun.

"What do you...want me to do?" she asked in her best frightened-little-girl voice. The split lip helped. She imagined her face was a sight. It was going to hurt like hell when the drugs wore off.

"Disarm your booby traps and open the door."

"I'll need" —sniff, sniff— "the light on."

"No problem. I'm switching my night-vision goggles for your gas mask anyway."

She dropped her head, hoping to hide her expression. Once he had the mask on, 90 percent of her defenses were rendered obsolete.

She limped—too theatrical?—to the panel by the door and turned the light on. She couldn't think of any other option right now. He hadn't killed her immediately; that meant he wasn't under direct orders from the department. He must have an agenda here. She had to figure out what it was he wanted and then keep it from him long enough to gain the advantage.

The bad news was that if he needed the door open, it was probably not just to have an easy escape route. It meant he had backup, which didn't help her odds. *Or Daniel's,* a voice in her head added. Like she needed more pressure. But Daniel was here because of her. She felt responsible for him. She owed him.

When she turned, blinking against the brilliance of the overhead lights, the man was twenty feet from where she stood. He had to be six foot three or four, and the skin on his neck and jaw was definitely white, but that was all she could be sure about. His body was covered with a black one-piece suit—almost like a wet suit, but rough, with jutting plates of Kevlar. Torso, arms, and legs all armored. He looked pretty muscular, but some of that could be the Kevlar. He wore heavy all-terrain boots, also black, and a black watch cap on his head. His face was hidden by her gas mask. Over one shoulder was slung an assault rifle—a McMillan .50-caliber sniper. She'd done her homework; it wasn't hard to become an expert on just about anything when you spent all your free time studying. Knowing gun makes and models could tell her a lot about an assailant, or any suspicious man on the street who might be planning to become an assailant. This assailant had more than one gun; a high-standard HDS was holstered on his hip, and a SIG Sauer P220 was in his right hand, pointed at her knee. *Right-handed,* she noted. She had no doubt he could hit her kneecap from this distance. Given that particular rifle, she figured, he could probably hit her wherever he wanted from however far away he wanted to.

He reminded her of Batman, but without the cape. Also, she thought she remembered something about Batman not ever using guns. Though if he did, assuming taste and skill, he would probably choose these.

If she couldn't get this assassin out of the gas mask, it wouldn't matter how many super-soldier friends were waiting for him outside. He would have no trouble killing her once he had what he wanted.

"Disarm your leads."

She feigned a brief dizzy spell as she limped over to the barn door, trying to get as much time for thinking as possible. Who would want her alive? Was he a kind of bounty hunter? Did he think he could sell her back to the department? If they'd put out a contract on her, she was sure that all they would have asked for was her head. So a blackmailer–slash–bounty hunter? *I have what you want, but I'll release it alive, back into the wild, unless you double the reward.* Smart. The department would definitely pay.

That was the best guess she could come up with by the time she was to the back edge of the door.

The system wasn't complicated. There were three sets of leads for each area of ingress. The first was outside in the bushes to the left of the barn door, hidden under a thin layer of dirt. Then there was the trigger line that ran across the seam where the door opened, connected loosely enough to pull apart with the slightest breach. The third was the safety, tucked under the wood paneling beside the door; its exposed wires were separated by an inch of space. The current was only stable if at least two of the connections were linked. She wondered if she should make the process look more convoluted than it actually was, but then decided there was no point. All he'd have to do was examine the setup for a few seconds to understand it.

She wrapped the ends of the third lead tightly together and then stood back.

"It's...off." She made her voice crack in the middle of the words. Hopefully he would buy that he'd knocked the fight out of her.

"If you would do the honors?" he suggested.

She gimped her way to the other side of the door and then pulled it back, her eyes already on the spot in the darkness where she assumed the dark heads of his companions would be. There was nothing but the farmhouse in the distance. And then her eyes dropped, and she froze.

"What is *that?*" she whispered.

It wasn't actually a question for him, it was just shock breaking through her façade.

"That," he answered in a tone that could only be described as obnoxiously smug, "is one hundred and twenty pounds of muscles, claws, and teeth."

He must have made some kind of signal—she didn't see it, her eyes were locked on his "backup" — because the animal darted forward to his side. It looked like a German shepherd, a very big one, but it didn't have the coloring she associated with Alsatians. This one was pure black. Could it be a wolf?

"Einstein," he said to the animal. It looked up, alert. He pointed to her, and his next word was obviously a command. "Control!"

The dog — wolf? — rushed her with its hackles rising. She backed up until the barn door was against her spine, her hands in the air. The dog braced itself, snout just inches from her stomach, its muzzle pulled back to expose long, sharp white fangs. A low, rumbling growl began deep in its throat.

Intimidate would have been a better name for the command.

She thought about trying to get one of her barbs into the dog's skin but doubted they were long enough to make it past its thick fur. And it wasn't like the thing was going to sit there and let her pet it.

The Batman wannabe relaxed a bit, or she thought he did. It was hard to be positive about what his muscles were doing under the armor.

"All right, now that we've broken the ice, let's talk."

She waited.

"Where is Daniel Beach?"

She could feel the shock on her face even as she tried to suppress it. All her theories whirled around again and turned upside down.

"Answer me!"

She didn't know what to say. Did the department want Daniel dead first? Make sure the loose ends were all tied up neatly? She thought of Daniel, exposed and unconscious in the center of the tent — not exactly a strong hiding place — and felt sick.

Batman stalked angrily toward her. The dog reacted, moving to the side to allow the man through even as its snarl grew in volume. The man shoved the barrel of his SIG Sauer under her jaw roughly, knocking her head against the barn door.

"If he's dead," the man hissed, "you're going to wish you were, too. I'll make you *beg* me to kill you."

She almost snorted. This thug would probably hit her a few times—maybe, if he had any creativity, he would cut her up a bit—and then he'd shoot her. He had no idea how to generate and maintain real pain.

But his threats did tell her something—he apparently wanted Daniel alive. So they had that one thing in common.

Resistance was counterproductive at this point anyway. She needed him to think she was out of the game. She needed him to relax his guard. And she needed to get back to her computer.

"Daniel is in the tent." She pointed with her chin, keeping her hands raised. "He's fine."

Batman seemed to consider this for a moment.

"Okay, ladies first. Einstein," he barked. "Herd." He pointed to the tent.

The dog barked in response, and moved around to her side. It poked her thigh with its nose, then nipped her.

"Ow!" she complained, jumping away. The dog got behind her and poked her again.

"Just walk, slow and steady, to your tent thing, and he won't hurt you."

She really didn't like the dog behind her, but she kept her pace to the injured hobble she'd been faking. She glanced back at the animal to see what it was doing.

"Don't worry," Batman said, amused. "People don't taste very good. He doesn't *want* to eat you. He'll only do that if I tell him to."

She ignored the taunt and moved slowly to the curtained access point.

"Hold that open so I can see in," he instructed.

The tarp was stiff with the layers of egg foam. She rolled it back as far as she could. It was mostly black inside. Her computer screen glowed white in the darkness, the monitors dull green. Because she knew the shapes, she could make out Daniel under the blanket, just a foot off the ground, his chest rising and falling evenly.

There was a long moment of silence.

"Do you want...me to turn on...the lights?" she asked.

"Hold it there."

She felt him come up behind her and then the cold circle of the gun barrel pressing into the nape of her neck, just at her hairline.

"What's this?" he murmured.

She held perfectly still while his gloved fingers touched the skin next to the gun. At first she was confused, but then she realized he had noticed the scar there.

"Huh," he grunted, and his hand dropped. "Okay, where is the switch?"

"On the desk."

"Where is the desk?"

"About ten feet in, on the right side. Where you can see the computer screen."

Would he take off the gas mask and put on the goggles again?

The pressure of the gun disappeared. She felt him move back from her, though the dog's nose was still pressed against her butt.

A slithering noise hissed across the floor. She looked down and watched the thick black cord for the closest work light whip past her foot. She heard the bang when it fell over but no crunch of glass.

He dragged the light past her, then flipped the switch. For a fraction of a second she allowed herself to hope that he'd broken the light, but then it flickered to life.

"Control," he commanded the dog. The snarling started again, and she held herself very still.

Aiming the light in front of him, he stepped into the tent. She watched the wide beam sweep the walls, then settle on the form in the middle.

He moved into the room, sliding into a sinuous gait that was totally silent. Obviously a man of many skills. He walked around the body on the floor, checking the corners and probably looking for weapons before he focused on Daniel. He crouched, removed the blanket, examined the bloody restraints and the IV, followed the sensors to the monitors, and then watched those for a moment. He put the light down, angling it at the ceiling to get the widest spread of illumination. Finally, he reached down, carefully removed the gas mask from Daniel's face, and set it on the floor.

"Danny," she heard him whisper.

CHAPTER 8

Batman ripped the black glove off his right hand and pressed two fingers to Daniel's carotid. He bent down to listen to Daniel's breathing. She examined her attacker's hand—pale skin, fingers so long they almost looked like they had an extra joint. They looked...familiar.

Batman shook Daniel's shoulder lightly and asked, louder, "Danny?"

"He's sedated," she volunteered.

His face jerked up toward her, and though she couldn't see it, she could feel his glare. Suddenly he was on his feet, launching himself at her. He grabbed her arms and yanked them over her head again as he shoved his masked face into hers.

"What did you do to him?" he shouted.

Her concern for Daniel's safety evaporated. *Danny* was going to be just fine. The one she needed to worry about was herself.

"There is nothing wrong with him," she said calmly, dropping the injured-damsel routine. "He'll wake up from the sedation in about two hours, feeling fine. I can bring him around sooner if you want."

"Not likely," he growled.

They had a staring contest for a few seconds, one she wasn't sure if she'd won or lost. She could see only her own face in the reflective mask.

"Okay," he said. "Let's get you situated."

In a smooth move, he had her hands behind her back, wrists held tight in his gloveless right hand, probably holding the gun in his left. He marched her into the room, toward the folding chair by the desk, and she went along docilely. The dog's hot, heavy breath was close, following right behind.

She was almost 70 percent sure she could twist her hand into a position that would put the left barbed ring against his skin, but she didn't try. It was a risk, but she wanted Batman alive. There was a large hole in her picture of what was going on, and Batman would have at least some of the answers she needed. She carefully nudged the covers over the barbs again.

She didn't resist as he sat her — none too gently — in the chair. He pulled her hands in front of her and zip-tied them together.

"I feel like you're the kind of person whose hands I want to keep an eye on," he muttered as he bent down to secure her ankles to the chair legs. All the while, the dog's face was directly in front of her own, eyes unblinking. A few drips of warm drool fell onto her sleeve and soaked through. *Gross.*

He zip-tied her elbows to the chair back and stood up, towering over her now, dark and menacing. The long, silenced barrel of his HDS was just a few inches from her forehead.

"The switch for the overhead lights is right there." She jerked her chin toward the power strip on the back edge of the desk. Two standard outdoor extension cords were plugged into it.

He stared in that direction, and she imagined he was eyeing the switches warily.

"Look, anything that can kill you is going to kill me first," she pointed out.

He grunted and then leaned away and punched the power button.

The lights flared overhead.

Suddenly the tent looked less threatening. With all the medical equipment, it could have been a medic's tent in a war zone. Except for the torture implements on the tray, of course. She saw his face orient toward them now.

"Props," she explained.

She felt the glare again. He whipped a look back at Daniel, naked and clearly intact on the table. His focus swung back to her.

"What's the flashing light?" he demanded, gesturing to the little black box with the keypad.

"It's telling me the door is unarmed," she lied evenly. In fact, the box wasn't hooked up to anything. It was just a nice red herring to distract from the real trap.

He nodded, accepting that, then leaned over to look at her computer. There were no open documents, no files on the desktop. Her background was just a pale geometric design, little white squares on a faintly darker gray field.

"Where are the keys?" He jerked his head toward Daniel.

"Taped to the bottom of the desk."

He seemed to be eyeing her again through the mask.

She willed herself to look calm and compliant. *Take it off, take it off, take it off,* she prayed silently.

He kicked her chair over.

She held her neck tight as her left arm and thigh smashed into the ground with bruising force. She was just able to keep her head from hitting the concrete again. She wasn't sure if she was already concussed, and she really needed her brain working right.

He grabbed the back of the chair and yanked her upright. In his right hand he held the keys.

"That wasn't necessary," she said.

"Einstein, control."

Growling in her face, more drool on her chest.

Batman turned away and quickly unlocked Daniel's shackles.

"What's in the IV?"

"Saline in the top one, nutrients in the lower."

"Really." Sarcastic. "What happens if I pull the tubing out?"

"He'll need a drink when he wakes up. But don't use the water bottles on the left side of the minifridge outside the tent. Those are poisoned."

He turned, pulling the mask off his head so he could glare at her more effectively, yanking the sweaty watch cap off at the same time.

Yessssssssss!

She kept the relief off her face as he dropped the mask on the floor.

"You've changed your tactics," he noted sourly, running his free hand through his short, damp hair. "Or are the ones on the right really the poisoned bottles?"

She looked up at him calmly. "I thought you were someone else."

And then she really *looked* at him.

She didn't have the resources to keep her face from reacting now. All the theories spun around again, and a bunch of things fell into place.

He smirked, realizing what she was seeing.

So many clues she'd missed.

The pictures that *were* Daniel but at the same time *weren't*.

The holes in the file on Daniel's history, the missing photos.

Time, dates, *birth dates* — the easiest small changes to make if you wanted to hide something.

Daniel's strange reluctance to believe what he was seeing when he looked at the spy images.

His struggles with loyalty.

Those long, long fingers.

"Other Daniel," she whispered.

The smirk vanished. "Huh?"

She blew out a breath and rolled her eyes — she couldn't help it. It was all too much like one of her mom's ridiculous soap operas. She remembered the frustration of every holiday she and her mother had spent together, the afternoons lost to the incredibly slow-moving, implausible dramas. No one was ever really dead; everyone came back. And then there were the twins. Always with the twins.

115

Batman actually didn't look that much like Daniel, as far as identical twins went. Daniel's features were refined, his aspect gentle. Batman was all hard angles and tightly gripped expressions. His hazel eyes seemed darker, maybe just because his brows were pulled down, putting them in shadow. His hair had the same color and curl but was cropped close, the way she would expect in an agent. Judging from his thicker neck, she would guess Batman had the gym musculature to Daniel's sports build. Not immensely bulky or he wouldn't have been able to pass for his brother in the pictures. Just harder, more defined.

"Kevin Beach," she said in a flat voice. "You're alive."

He sat on the edge of her desk. As her eyes followed him, she didn't let them rest for even a second on her computer's clock right by his elbow.

"Who were you expecting?"

"There were a few options. All of whom would want both me and your brother dead." She shook her head. "I can't believe I fell for this."

"For what?"

"Daniel's never even met de la Fuentes, has he? It was always you."

His face, which had begun to relax, was suddenly guarded again. "What?"

She nodded to the photographs scattered on the floor. He seemed to notice them for the first time. He leaned over to examine one, then bent down to grab it. Then the one underneath, and the next. He crumpled them in his fist.

"Where did you get these?"

"Compliments of a small department working for the American government—entirely off the books. I used to be in their employ. They asked me to freelance."

His face contorted in outrage. "This is highly classified!"

"You wouldn't believe my clearance level."

Back in her face, he grabbed the front of her T-shirt and lifted her and the chair a few inches off the ground. "Who are you?"

She kept herself calm. "I'll tell you everything I know. I got played and I'm about as happy about it as you."

He set her down. She wanted to count in her head, mark the time, but she was afraid he would notice her distraction. He stood over her, arms folded.

"What's your name?"

She spoke as slowly as she thought she could get away with. "It used to be Dr. Juliana Fortis, but there's a death certificate with that name now." She watched his face to see if any of this information meant something to him; it didn't, as far as she could tell. "I operated under the direction of the department—it doesn't have another name. It doesn't exist officially. They worked with the CIA and some other black ops programs. Interrogation specialists."

He sat back down on the edge of the desk.

"Three years ago, someone decided to dissolve the department's two key assets. Namely, me and my mentor, Dr. Joseph Barnaby." Still no recognition. "I don't know why, although we had access to incredibly sensitive information, and I'm guessing something we knew was the motive. They murdered Dr. Barnaby and tried to murder me. I've been running ever since. They've found me four times. Three times they tried to have me assassinated. The last time, they apologized."

His eyes were narrowed, evaluating.

"They told me they had a problem, and they needed me. They gave me a stack of files on the de la Fuentes situation and named your brother as his collaborator. They said that in three weeks Daniel would be spreading the supervirus across the American Southwest. They told me I had three days to find out where the virus was and how to stop de la Fuentes from implementing his plan."

He was shaking his head now.

"They told you that much?" he asked in disbelief.

"Counterterrorism was always the main component of my job. I know where all the warheads and the dirty bombs are buried."

He pursed his lips, making a decision. "Well, since you already know the details, I guess it's not a huge breach of policy for me to tell you that I shut down the de la Fuentes situation six months ago. De la Fuentes's death is not common knowledge. What's left of the cartel is keeping this quiet so they don't appear vulnerable to the competition."

She was surprised at the relief she felt. The weight of knowing that so many people were doomed to painful execution had been heavier than she'd realized.

"Yes," she breathed. "That makes sense."

The department wasn't *that* cold-blooded, apparently. They'd used a nightmare catastrophe to motivate her, but they weren't messing around with civilians still in danger.

"And the Serpent?"

He looked at her blankly.

"Sorry, department nickname. The domestic terrorists?"

"My associates bagged two of the three ringleaders and took out the entire southern chapter. No survivors."

She smiled tightly.

"You're an interrogator," he said in a suddenly icy voice. "A torturer."

She lifted her chin. "Yes."

"And you tortured my brother for information he didn't have."

"Yes. The very initial phases, at least."

He backhanded her. Her head snapped to the side; the chair bobbled, and he shoved it down with one foot.

"You're going to pay for that," he promised.

She worked her jaw for a second to see if anything was broken. When she was satisfied that nothing was seriously compromised, she responded. "I'm not positive," she said, "but I think that's why they did this to him. Why they fed me this whole elaborate story."

Through his teeth. "What reason?"

"They haven't had the greatest success in killing me. I guess they thought you would get the job done."

He clenched his jaw.

"What I don't understand, though," she continued, "is why they didn't just *ask* you to do it. Or order you, I suppose. Unless...you're no longer with the CIA?" she guessed.

The gun had been the giveaway. From her research, she was pretty certain that the HDS was the gun most commonly carried by CIA agents.

"If you didn't know about me, how do you know where I work?" he demanded.

About halfway through his question, she saw the bright white rectangle in her peripheral vision go black. Trying to be inconspicuous, she sucked in the deepest breath through her nose she could manage.

"Answer me," he growled, raising his hand again.

She just stared at him, not breathing.

He hesitated, brow furrowed, then his eyes went wide. He dove for the mask on the floor.

He was out before he hit the ground.

Another thump—the dog collapsed into a puddle of fur beside her chair.

Under testing circumstances, she'd once held her breath for one minute and forty-two seconds, but she'd never been able to repeat the feat. Usually she ran out of air at about one fifteen, still way above average—lung capacity had become a priority in her life. This time, of course, she hadn't been able to hyperventilate beforehand. But she wouldn't need a full minute.

She hopped her chair over to Batman's inert form and pushed herself forward, bracing her knees against his back. With her hands secured in front of her, it was easy...ish. Kevin Beach had left Daniel's gas mask on the floor; she hooked it with one finger and then tilted the chair back until all four legs were on the ground. She leaned her face as close to her hands as she could and slipped the mask over her head, pressing the rubber rim tight to her face to create a seal. She blew out her air in a big whoosh, clearing the chamber, and then took a hesitant breath.

If some of the chemical had lingered, she figured she still would have been okay. She'd built up a decent resistance and would not have been out as long as the others. But it was especially nice to have such a big head start.

She scooted to the desk and rubbed the zip tie around her wrists against the edge of the scalpel on her props tray. It popped quickly against the pressure she was generating. It was easy work to slice the rest of the ties, and then she was free.

First things first. She reset the screen saver on her computer to come on after fifteen minutes of inactivity.

She couldn't lift Batman, sprawled facedown on the floor beside his brother, but his arms and legs were close enough to Daniel's that she could use the restraints that had been around Daniel's left wrist and left ankle to secure Kevin's. He'd thrown the key carelessly on the table by Daniel's side; she pocketed it.

She didn't resecure Daniel. Maybe it was a mistake, but she'd already done so much to him, it just felt unfair. And underneath it all, she wasn't afraid of him. Another potential mistake.

She stripped Batman of his guns and removed the cartridges and firing pins from the rifle and the HDS. She put the safety on the SIG Sauer and tucked it into the back of her belt. She liked it—it looked more serious than her PPK. She went out to the barn stalls to find her PPK and then shoved it in beside the SIG Sauer. She was more familiar with her own. Better to keep it handy, too.

She found her shoes, stashed the other guns, and then grabbed the movers' straps on her way back into the tent. The dog was too heavy to move easily, so she wrapped the straps around it and hauled it back to the bunk room. At first she simply closed the door and walked away—dogs didn't have opposable thumbs. A moment later, though, she changed her mind. The dog's name *was* Einstein; who knew what it was capable of? She looked for something to drag in front of the door. Most of the heavy machinery was bolted down. After a few seconds of thought, she walked around to the silver sedan. It just fit between the tent and the stalls. She pulled it right up to the bunk-room door, wedged the front bumper tight against the wood, and then put it in park. She threw the parking brake on for good measure.

She closed the barn door and rearmed it. A quick look outside told her that it was almost dawn.

Back to Other Daniel. The Batsuit was a chore to remove. The fabric between the Kevlar panels was thick and ribbed with fine cables, almost like gristle. She snapped two blades on it before finally quitting at his waist. She settled for peeling back the top half and patting down his legs, which didn't have as much Kevlar to disguise them. She found a knife holstered in the small of his back and one shoved into each boot. She pulled his socks off. He was missing the pinkie toe on his left foot, but he had no other weapons that she could find. Not that he'd need any if he got his hands on her again. His whole body was roped with lean, hard bands of muscle. His back was a mess of scars—some from bullets, some blades, and one bad burn—with one more telling scar under the edge of his hairline. He'd removed his tracker, too. Definitely no longer with the CIA. A defector? A double agent?

But how had he found his brother?

She remembered the droning of the noisy prop plane, the booming thud of the improvised crash landing—someone in a hurry, she'd thought. Someone for whom time was the biggest problem.

She turned to look at Daniel; it seemed another examination was in order. She'd done a more thorough job going over his back, so she looked closely now at his stomach, groin, and thighs. Something she should have done before, but she'd misread the situation badly.

It was the idea of time—the hurried way Batman had arrived and attacked—that pointed her toward what she was looking for. An ordinary tracker would indicate only where the subject was, and Daniel wasn't really that far from home, not far enough to cause his dead brother to panic and run in guns blazing. So this tracker must monitor something more than just location, and it would have to be placed in the right spot.

She wanted to kick herself when she saw it—the little red tail of a scar sticking out from the edge of the tape she had used to secure the catheter tube against his leg. She pulled the tape now—always better to do that when the subject was still under anyway—and then removed the catheter. He'd be getting up soon.

The scar was tiny, with nothing raised under the skin. She figured the device must be more deeply implanted, next to the femoral artery, no doubt. When his blood pressure had gone crazy with the first round of interrogation, or maybe even from his fear when he'd first woken up, it must have tipped off his brother. And whoever else was monitoring him. The tracker would have to come out.

She had enough time before he woke up, so she got her first-aid kit. After snapping on some gloves, she numbed the site and sterilized the scalpel—good thing she hadn't broken all of them on the Batsuit. She scrubbed the skin with iodine, then made a quick, neat incision on top of the old one, though a bit longer. She didn't have forceps or tweezers, so she just poked around carefully with one finger on the inside and one on the outside. When she found the device—a little capsule about the size of a throat lozenge—she was able to pressure it out fairly easily.

She cleaned up the site and then superglued the edges together.

After that, she treated the raw skin on his wrists and ankles, cleaning and bandaging everything. Finally, she put the blanket over him and got him the pillow.

The capsule she left to cool on the steel table. To anyone watching the tracker on a monitor, it would appear that Daniel Beach had just died. She had a feeling that his death wouldn't bother anyone in the department. She had a better sense of the other side's plan now, and she was pretty sure it wasn't all about her.

She exited the tent to attend to her own face, first wiping off the blood and then trying to determine the extent of the damage. The lip was swollen, and the tear needed a stitch; she applied a drop of superglue. Her cheek was missing a few layers of skin and she was going to have a matched set of very pronounced black eyes. Her nose was swollen and crooked, so she took advantage of her current pain-less state to push it back into shape as well as she could.

The pain would return fairly soon, though she'd given herself the maximum dose of the drug she'd privately named *Survive*. It wasn't meant to work long term; it was just for making it through an attack like the one she'd just endured. Kind of like the adrenaline her body naturally generated, just much more powerful, and with some opiates to block the pain. *Survive* wasn't on the books; her list of duties had not included creating *anti*-torture concoctions, but she'd thought it might be something she'd need someday, and she'd been right. This wasn't the first time she'd used it — she'd overre-acted to those earlier assassination attempts — but it *was* the first time she'd actually suffered through a decent beating with *Survive* in her system. She was pleased with its performance.

She didn't have anything to stabilize her nose with, so she would have to try to be more careful with her face for a while. Luckily she was a back sleeper.

The face was going to be a problem. A big problem. She couldn't exactly walk into a grocery store right now and escape notice.

When she had done everything she could think of to do, she lay on the cot for ten minutes, just gathering her strength — or what was left of it. The drug still made her feel strong, but she knew she'd sustained some damage. There would be repercussions to deal with. She needed time to rest and heal — time no one was going to give her.

CHAPTER 9

She decided to wake Daniel up. Once Batman came around—which he probably would in about fifteen minutes or so—the conversation was not going to be very genteel. She wanted a chance to explain—and apologize—before the shrieking and the death threats started.

She reset the protocols on the computer.

The chemical mixture in the air had long since dispersed, so she didn't need the gas mask inside the tent anymore. She grabbed the other mask, then tucked both sets of straps through her belt, keeping them close.

She pulled Daniel's IV first. She didn't want him tethered to anything at all when he woke up. He'd had enough of that. His veins were still looking good. It was easy to inject the solution into the antecubital fossa of his other elbow. She sat on the edge of the table, lowered so that it nearly rested on the floor. She wrapped her arms around her knees and waited.

He came to slowly, blinking against the overhead lights. He raised one hand to shade his eyes, then awareness hit. He stared at his hand—free, bandaged—and then his eyes darted around the bright room.

"Alex?" he asked quietly.

"Right here."

He turned toward her gingerly, moving his legs under the blanket, checking to see if he was still bound.

"What is happening now?" he asked cautiously, his eyes still struggling to focus.

"I believe you. And I'm very sorry for what I did to you."

She watched him process that. Carefully, he raised himself up on one elbow, then clutched at the blanket, realizing again that he was naked. It was funny how nonmedical people reacted to that; physicians were fairly relaxed about nudity in general. She felt exactly the same about nudity as any other doctor, but he wouldn't assume that. She should have put on her lab coat.

"You do believe me?" he asked.

"Yes. I know you're not the person I thought you were. I was . . . misled."

He sat up a little farther, moving warily, waiting for something to hurt. He should feel fine, though — just tired from the muscle spasms. And his upper thigh would be a little sore when the local wore off.

"I —" he started, and then froze. *"What happened to your face?"*

"It's a long story. Can I say something before I get into it?"

His expression was full of concern. For her? No, that couldn't be right.

"Okay," he agreed hesitantly.

"Look, Daniel, what I told you before was true. I don't like hurting people. I didn't like hurting you. I only do that when I think the other option is much more horrible. I have never in my life done this before — hurt a totally innocent person. Never. Not every person I've been asked to interrogate was as depraved as the rest, but all of them were at least part of the plot. I've long since realized that my old bosses will stoop to almost anything, but I still can't believe that they set me up to interrogate someone entirely guiltless."

He thought about it for a few seconds.

"Are you asking me to forgive you?"

"No, I'm not asking for that. I would never ask for that. But I wanted you to know. I never would have hurt you if I hadn't truly believed it would save lives. I am so sorry."

"And what about the drug dealer? The virus?" he asked anxiously.

She frowned. "I've received some new information. Apparently, de la Fuentes was taken care of."

"No one is going to die?"

"Not because of a weaponized virus spread by a drug czar, no."

"So that's good, right?"

She sighed. "Yeah, I guess that's the silver lining of what happened here."

"Now will you tell me what happened to your face? Did you have an accident?" Again with the concern.

"No. My injures are related to that new information I mentioned." She wasn't sure how to break it to him.

Sudden indignation. His shoulders tensed. "Somebody *did* that to you—on purpose? For hurting me?"

His mind certainly didn't work like someone in her line of business. Things that would be obvious to anyone who had ever worked on any facet of a mission were totally foreign to him.

"Essentially," she answered.

"Let me talk to him," he insisted. "I believe you, too. I know you didn't want to do it. You were trying to help."

"That's not really the issue. Um, Daniel, you know when I was showing you those pictures before and you recognized the person in them but you didn't want to tell me who it was?"

His face closed up. He nodded.

"You can relax. I'm not asking you to confess anything; this isn't a trick. I didn't know you had a twin. They covered that up in the file so I wouldn't—"

"No, but it wasn't Kevin," he interrupted. "That's what I didn't understand. It looked just like him, but it's impossible. Kevin is dead. He died in prison last year. I don't know who it could be unless we were actually triplets, and I think Mom might have noticed that..."

He trailed off, watching her expression change.

"What?" he asked.

"I'm not sure how to tell you this."

"Tell me what?"

She hesitated for a moment, then stood up and walked around the table. His eyes tracked her, then he sat up, bunching the blanket carefully around his waist. She stopped and looked down. His eyes followed hers.

Kevin Beach's face was turned toward the table where Daniel sat. It was curious how much more he looked like Daniel when he was unconscious, all the tension in his expression erased.

"Kevin," Daniel whispered, face going white, then flushing bright red.

"Did you know your brother worked for the CIA?" she asked quietly.

He looked up, aghast. "No, no, he was in prison. He'd been dealing drugs." He shook his head. "Things got bad after our parents died. Kev went off the deep end. He self-destructed. I mean, after West Point—"

"*West Point?*"

"Yes," he said, face blank. Obviously the significance was lost on him. "Before the drugs, he was a different person. Graduated near the top of his class. He was accepted to Ranger school..." Daniel trailed off, assessing her frown.

Of course. Alex suppressed a sigh, upset with herself for not worrying more about the file's gaps in information, for not taking the time to find a faraway library where she could have safely searched all Daniel's family connections.

Daniel looked down at his brother again. "He's not dead now, is he?"

"Just sleeping. He'll wake up in a few minutes."

Daniel's brow furrowed. "What is he *wearing?*"

"Some kind of military armored suit, I guess. Not my specialty."

"The CIA," he whispered.

"Black ops, I would imagine. Your brother didn't self-destruct, he just switched divisions. That's why he was involved with the drug lord."

His wide eyes turned sober. "He was helping the drug lord with the virus?" he whispered.

"No. Shutting him down, actually. We're basically on the same side, though you wouldn't know it to look at us." She nudged his supine form with her toe.

Daniel's head whipped back up to hers. "Did Kevin do that to your face?" Funny, but he sounded more upset about that than the idea that his brother was a murderous criminal.

"Yes, and I did this to him." Another nudge.

"But he's going to wake up?"

Alex nodded. She was a little conflicted about Batman waking up. It wasn't going to be pretty. And Daniel was being so nice about everything, about her. That would probably change once his brother started talking.

He smiled just a little, staring at his brother's exposed back. "So you won?"

She laughed. "Temporarily."

"He's a *lot* bigger than you are."

"I would say I was smarter, but I made some pretty huge mistakes in my security here. I think I was just luckier this time."

Daniel started to get to his feet, then paused. "Are my clothes around here anywhere?"

"Sorry, no. I thought there might be tracking devices in them. I had to cut them off you and ditch them."

He blushed again, all the way down to that small spot on his chest. He cleared his throat. "Why would someone track *me?*"

"Well, at the time, I thought the drug lord might be monitoring you. Or that you were a trap, and my department would use you to track *me*. Which is a little bit closer to the truth, actually."

He frowned. "I am so confused."

She gave him the bullet-points version as succinctly as possible. While she was talking, he got to his feet, wrapping the blanket around his waist like an oversize towel, and started pacing back and forth in front of his brother's body.

"They tried to kill you *four* times?" he asked when she was finished.

"Five now, I think," she said, looking pointedly at Batman.

"I can't believe Kevin is alive." He sighed. He folded his long legs under the blanket and settled to the floor beside his brother's head. "I can't believe he lied to me. I can't believe he let me think he was a criminal...I can't believe he let me think he *died*...I can't believe how many times I visited him—do you know how *long* it takes to drive from DC to Milwaukee?"

He stared in silence at his brother. She let him have a moment. She couldn't imagine how she would feel if Barnaby walked back into her life without warning. How did you process something like that?

"When he wakes up," Daniel murmured gently, "I'm going to punch him in the throat."

Well, that was one way to process it.

"Why did you handcuff him?" Daniel wondered.

"Because as soon as he's conscious, he's going to try to kill me."

Wide eyes again. *"What?"*

"It's not hard to understand. All he knew when he came through the roof was that someone was hurting you. He let me live only because he wasn't sure if you were really okay. For example, maybe I would have to give you an antidote or something. I'm pretty sure if I hadn't gotten the upper hand for a second, the minute you woke up, he would have shot me."

She could see Daniel didn't believe her. He shook his head, eyebrows pulling down, upset. A thatch of curls flopped onto his forehead, still a little damp with sweat. It was amazing how short a time had actually passed, but everything had changed. And she needed a new plan.

Was it safe to go back to her most recent home, the place she'd been living when Carston had contacted her? It would certainly be easiest. There was food there, and no one would have to see her face for as long as it took to look normal again. She didn't think she'd compromised the house...

But then what? How much of her nest egg had she blown through for this stupid trap? How long would she be able to keep going on what she had?

Carston knew about her online presence, so it would be a risk to go looking for a real job on the Internet. The department didn't have to know where she was to tie her hands.

Something touched her leg and she jumped. It was just Daniel's hand.

"I didn't mean to scare you, sorry."

"Don't apologize."

"You just look so worried. Don't. I can talk to Kevin."

She smiled humorlessly. "Thanks, but I'm not worrying about Lazarus at the moment."

"You're worried about your department."

She turned away, walked to her computer, and rested her hand against the space bar. Hopefully it didn't appear deliberate.

"Yeah," she said without looking at him. "You could say that."

Out of the corner of her eye, she saw a short hitch in Kevin's breathing before it evened out again. Good thing she'd moved away. She definitely didn't want to be within reach now.

"Is there...I don't know...is there anything I can do to help?" Daniel asked seriously.

She stared at him, surprised to feel actual tears pricking her eyes.

"I don't think I deserve your help, Daniel."

He made an exasperated noise in the back of his throat.

"And, really," she continued, "you've got enough problems of your own."

It was clear he hadn't thought through the long-term implications of what had happened.

"What do you mean?"

"You're a target now, too. You've just learned a lot of things that you're not supposed to know. If you go home, if you go back to your normal life, they'll end it."

"Not...go...back?"

He was totally stunned. Pity welled up inside her. Again she remembered how far away his kind of life was from hers. He probably thought he could fix everything by hiring a lawyer or writing to his congressman.

"But Alex, I *have* to go back. My team is in the championship tournament!"

She couldn't help it. She started laughing, and the pricking tears turned into real drops. She saw his expression and waved her hand in apology.

"Sorry," she said, gasping. "It's not funny at all. I'm sorry. I think my painkillers are beginning to wear off."

He got quickly to his feet. "Do you need something? Aspirin?"

"No, I'm good. I just have to come down from the high."

He walked over and rested one hand lightly on her arm. She felt the sting, the bruising there just beginning to grow sensitive. It was going to be a very rough day.

"Are you sure?" he asked. "Can't I get you something?"

"*Why* are you being so nice to me?"

He looked at her in surprise. "Oh. I guess I see your point."

Finally, she thought. She'd been starting to worry that maybe the drug she'd used to kidnap him — *Follow the Leader* — had some permanent neurological effects they'd missed in the trials.

"Look," she said. "After I have a little chat with Kevin, I'll get my stuff together, and then I'll give you the key so you can unlock your brother once I'm in my car."

"But where will you go? What about your injuries?"

"You're being nice again, Daniel."

"Sorry."

She laughed once more. The sound hitched on the end, like a sob.

"Seriously, though," he said, "you don't have to leave right away. You look like you could use some sleep and some medical attention."

"Not on the agenda." She eased herself into the desk chair, hoping he couldn't see just how stiff and weary she felt.

"I wish we could talk some more, Alex. I don't know what I'm supposed to do now. If you really mean it, that I can't go back...I don't even know how to begin to think about that."

"I do mean it. And I'm sorry. But I think your brother can probably fill you in on the details. I imagine he's better at hiding than I am."

He looked at his brother — wearing half of a Batsuit — doubtfully. "You think?"

"Don't you agree, Kevin?" she asked. She was fairly sure he'd been awake for at least a few minutes.

Daniel fell to his blanketed knees next to his brother. "Kev?"

Slowly, with a sigh, Kevin turned his head to look at his brother. "Hey, Danny."

Daniel leaned in and embraced him awkwardly. Kevin patted Daniel's arm with his free hand.

"Why, Kev, why?" Daniel asked, his voice muffled in Kevin's hair.

"Trying to keep you safe, kid. Safe from people like that —" And he added several quite unflattering descriptions of her; she knew all the individual words, but the combinations were fairly unusual.

Daniel jerked away and cuffed Kevin's head.

"Don't talk like that."

"Are you kidding me? That psychopath *tortured* you."

"Not for very long. And she only did it because—"

"Are you *defending* that—" More creativity.

Daniel smacked him again. Not hard, but Kevin wasn't in a mood to play. He grabbed Daniel's hand and twisted it into an unpleasant position. He got his right knee pulled up under his body and tried to yank away from the table. The locked wheels whined against the floor as the metal slab shifted a few inches.

Her eyes widened. The table had to weigh at least four hundred pounds. She scooted her chair back.

Daniel wrestled with his free hand, trying to break his brother's hold.

"I'll gas you again if you don't let go of him," she promised Kevin. "The bad news is, the chemical I'm using does have a few negative side effects. It kills only a small percentage of your brain cells with each use, but it adds up over time."

Kevin dropped Daniel's hand, glared once at her, and then focused on his brother.

"Danny, listen to me," he hissed. "You're bigger than her. Get the keys and get me out of these—" Suddenly his face froze, went beet red, and the vessels in his forehead pulsed in time with his words. *"Where is my dog?"* he shouted at her. The table squealed another inch across the floor.

"Sleeping in the back room." She had to work to keep her voice even. "It weighs less than you; the gas will take longer to wear off."

Daniel was rubbing his wrist and looking confused. "Dog?"

"If he's not one hundred percent—" Kevin threatened.

"Your dog will be fine. Now, I need to ask you a few questions."

Daniel looked up at her, wild-eyed. "What?"

She glanced at him and shook her head. "Not like that. Just a normal exchange of information." She turned back to Kevin. "Can we talk calmly for just a few minutes, please? Then I'll get out of your hair."

"In your dreams, psycho. We've got unfinished business."

She raised her eyebrows over her blooming black eyes. "Can we talk for a few minutes before I put you into a medically induced coma, then?"

"Why would I do anything for you?"

"Because your brother's safety is involved, and I can tell that's something that matters to you."

"You're the one who pulled Danny into this—"

"That's not entirely accurate. This is as much about you as it is about me, Kevin Beach."

He glowered at her. "I already don't like you, lady. You really don't want to make that feeling stronger."

"Relax, black ops. Hear me out."

Daniel's eyes were flashing back and forth like he was a spectator at a tennis match.

Kevin glared.

"The CIA thinks you're dead?" she asked.

He grunted.

"I'll take that as a yes."

"Yeah, that's a yes, you—"

Daniel backhanded the top of Kevin's head and then scooted out of the way as Kevin made a grab for him. Then Kevin refocused on her.

"And I'm going to keep it that way. I'm retired."

She nodded, considering. She opened a blank document on her computer and typed a line of random medical terms.

"What are you typing?"

"Notes. Typing helps me think." Actually, she was sure he would notice if she kept "accidentally" touching the computer to keep it awake, and she might need that trap again today.

"So what does it matter? I died. Danny shouldn't be a target anymore."

"I was a target?" Daniel asked.

Kevin propped himself up on his right elbow and leaned toward his brother. "I worked deep undercover, kid. Anyone who connected me to you would have used you as leverage. It's one of the downsides of the job. That's why I went through the whole prison charade. As long as on paper Kevin Beach was away, the bad guys wouldn't know about you. I haven't been Kevin in a long time."

"But when I visited—"

"The Agency hooked me up with the warden. When you were on your way, if I could, I'd fly in and do the meeting. If I was unavailable—"

"That's why you were in isolation. Or they said you were. Not for fighting."

"Yep."

"I can't believe you lied to my face for so many years."

"It was the only thing I could do to keep you safe."

"What about maybe picking a different job?"

She broke in when the vessels in Kevin's head started to swell again. "Um, could we put the reunion drama on hold for the moment? I think I've got it pieced together. Listen, please. And you'll tell me if I'm wrong, I'm sure."

Two nearly identical faces regarded her with nearly opposite expressions.

"Okay," she continued. "So, Kevin, you faked your death—after the de la Fuentes job, right?" Kevin didn't respond in any way, so she went on. "That was six months ago, you said. I can only conclude that the Agency was concerned about the lack of a body—"

"Oh, there was a body."

"Then they were concerned about the inconsistencies with that body," she snapped. "And they thought of a plan to draw you out, just in case."

He frowned. He knew his former bosses, just like she knew hers.

"Daniel's your weak spot—like you said, their leverage against you. They know this. They decide to take him, see what happens.

But they know what you're capable of, and no one wants to be the one left holding the bag if you do turn up alive."

"But—" Kevin started to say. He stopped himself, probably realizing whatever argument he'd been about to make wouldn't hold up.

"You're a problem for the CIA. I'm a problem for my department. At the top, the people involved in both our former workplaces are pretty tight. So they offer me a deal: 'Do a job for us, and we'll call off the hunt.' They must have had it worked out pretty solidly before they contacted me. Fixed the files, got ready to feed me the crisis story I can't turn my back on. None of them make a move on me because they've already sacrificed three assets trying and they don't want any more losses. They knew I'd come in prepared for anything like that. But, if you were *really* good, maybe I wouldn't be prepared enough for you."

Kevin's face had changed while she was working it out. "And either way," he concluded, "one problem gets solved."

"It's elaborate. Sounds more like your agency than mine, if I had to guess."

"Yeah, it does sound like them, actually," he agreed grudgingly.

"So they put us together like two scorpions in a jar and shake it up," she said. "One way or another, they get a win on the books. Maybe, if they're really, really lucky, we take each other out. Or at least weaken the winner. No chance of any losses on their side."

And they *had* weakened her—reduced her assets and damaged her physically. A partial success for them.

"And it doesn't bother them that my brother is also stuck in the jar," he said furiously. "Only he's an ant, not a scorpion. They just throw him into the mix, don't even care that he's completely defenseless."

"Hey," Daniel protested.

"No offense, Danny, but you're about as dangerous as hand-knitted socks."

Daniel opened his mouth to respond, but a loud whine from the bunk room interrupted. The whine was quickly followed by angry snarls and a few sharp barks, then a strident clawing at the wooden door.

She was glad she'd gone the extra mile in securing the wolf.

"He's upset," Kevin accused.

"The dog is fine. There's a toilet back there, it won't even get dehydrated."

Kevin just raised his eyebrows, not as concerned about the animal as she would have expected. The clawing and snarling didn't let up.

"You really brought a dog?" Daniel asked.

"More of a partner." He looked at her. "Well, what now? Their plan failed."

"Narrowly."

He grinned. "We could go another round."

"As much as I would dearly love to inject a few things into *your* system, I'd rather not give them the satisfaction."

"Fair enough."

The dog was scratching and growling in an unbroken stream through all of this. It was getting on her nerves.

"I do have a plan."

Kevin rolled his eyes. "I bet you always have a plan, don't you, shorty?"

She regarded him with flat eyes. "I can't rely on muscle, so I rely on brains. It appears you have the opposite problem."

He laughed derisively.

"Um, Kev," Daniel interjected. "I'd like to point out that you *are* chained up on the floor."

"Shut up, Danny."

"Please, boys, if I could get one more second of your time?" She waited till they looked at her. "Here's the plan: I write an e-mail to my ex-boss. I tell him I got the truth, the real truth, and both of you are out of the picture. I really don't appreciate the manipulation. If he tries to contact me in any way again, I'm making a personal visit to his kitchen pantry."

"You claim the win?" Kevin asked in a disbelieving voice. "Please!"

"Chained on the floor," Daniel murmured under his breath.

"It's a gift," she snapped back. "You get to be dead again. No one is looking for either of you."

Kevin's cynical expression dissolved. For a second, the twin thing was a lot more evident.

The sound of the dog was like a howling wood chipper in the next room. She hadn't really planned to stick around for her security deposit, but it clearly was not an option now.

"Why would you do that for us?" Kevin asked.

"I'm doing it for Daniel. I owe him. I should have been smarter. I shouldn't have taken the bait."

It was all so completely obvious now: How easily she'd slipped through their surveillance—because there hadn't been any. How simple it had been to snatch Daniel—because no one was trying to stop her. The heavy-handed way they'd given her a deadline with plenty of time for her to act. It was embarrassing.

"Then what happens to you?" Daniel asked quietly. She almost had to read his lips over the noise of the dog.

"I haven't decided yet."

She had learned a few things from this exercise in gullibility, maybe things they didn't want her to know.

There weren't going to be any helicopters or elimination teams. Carston—the one name she could be absolutely certain of at this point—and whoever else wanted her dead had sent only the occa-sional lone assassin because that was all they had. Her enemies had been driven to this wild collaboration, and she knew it wasn't because the department didn't have the resources. It could only be because she wasn't common knowledge. And Carston—and who-ever his confederates were—couldn't afford to have her become so.

She'd assumed, when she'd seen the obituary for Juliana Fortis and read about the cremation, that everyone involved was in on the scam. But what if it was just a few key people? What if Carston had promised his superiors that the job would be done and then was afraid to admit he'd missed on the first swat?

Or—revolutionary idea—what if most people at the department thought it *was* a lab accident? That she and Barnaby had mixed the wrong test tubes and punched out together? What if Carston's superiors *hadn't* wanted her dead? What if only those few key individuals had wanted that, and now they had to keep their attempts to finish the job under the radar? That would change everything.

It played. It fit with the facts.

It made her feel stronger.

The ones who had arranged her death had been afraid of what she knew, but they had never been afraid of *her*. Maybe it was time for that to change.

There was a sudden earsplitting noise—an explosive fragmenting of wood. And then the enraged snarling got a lot closer.

CHAPTER 10

It took her one second to realize what had happened, and by that time the rabid wolf was bounding into the tent.

There was still a little bit of extra adrenaline in her system, apparently. She was on top of the desk before the animal was all the way inside, and her nervous system, not satisfied with that distance, launched her toward the PVC framework overhead before she had time to realize what she was doing. She caught hold with both hands, flipped her legs up and crossed her ankles around the pipe, then wrapped her elbows tightly around as well. She turned her head to the side to see that the creature was right below her, big paws on the desk as it strained to get its teeth into her. One paw mashed down on the keyboard, which was too bad. A little gassing would help a lot right now, and she already had both masks.

The dog snarled and slavered under her while she tried to maintain her hold. She'd used the heavy-duty five-inch-diameter, class 200 pipe, but it was still shaking from her sudden attachment to it. She was sure it would bear her weight... unless someone attacked the base. Hopefully Kevin wouldn't think of that.

Kevin started laughing. She could imagine how she looked.

"Who's chained to the floor now?" he asked.

"Still you," Daniel muttered.

At the sound of his master's voice, the dog gave a little whine and looked around. It dropped off the desk and went to examine Kevin, with one parting growl in her direction. Kevin patted its face while the dog leaned down to lick him, still whining anxiously.

"I'm okay, buddy. I'm good."

"He looks just like Einstein," Daniel said, wonder in his tone. The dog looked up, on guard at the sound of a new voice.

Kevin patted Daniel's foot. "Good boy, he's cool. He's cool." It sounded like another command.

And sure enough, dropping the whine, the huge beast went to Daniel with its tail wagging furiously. Daniel stroked the gigantic head like that was the most natural thing in the world.

"That's Einstein the Third," Kevin explained.

Daniel scratched his fingers through the thick coat appreciatively. "He's beautiful."

Her arms were getting tired. She tried to readjust while still watching, and the dog bounded right back to the desk, snarling again.

"Any hope of your calling the dog off?" she asked, trying to keep her voice composed.

"Possibly. If you throw me the keys."

"And if I give you the keys, you won't kill me?"

"I already said I'd call the dog off. Don't get greedy."

"I think I'll just stay up here, then, until the gas knocks you all out. Daniel's probably got enough brain cells to spare."

"See, I think I'll be okay. Because even though Einstein can't reach you, Daniel *can*. And if the gas hits you after he relieves you of those masks ... well, the unconscious fall to the floor won't kill you, obviously, but it won't do you any favors."

"Why would I do that?" Daniel asked.

"What?" Kevin demanded.

"She's on our side, Kev."

"Whoa there. Are you insane? There are two very different sides here, kid. Your brother is on one, and the sadist who tortured you is on the other. Which side are you on?"

"The side of reason, I guess."

"Good," Kevin grunted.

"Um, that's not your side, Kev."

"*What?*"

"Calm down. Listen, let me broker a truce here."

"I can't believe you aren't reaching up there to throttle her yourself."

"She was only doing what you would have done in her place. Be honest—if you knew some stranger was going to kill millions of people and you needed to find out how to stop him, what would you do?"

"Find another solution. Like I *did*. Listen to me, Danny—you're out of your league here. I know people like her. They're sick. They get some twisted high off other people's pain. They're like venomous snakes; you can't turn your back on them."

"She isn't like that. And what's the big deal to you, anyway? *I'm* the one who got tortured. What do you even know about that?"

Kevin just stared at him, deadpan, for one moment, then pointed with his secured left hand to his secured left foot. He wiggled his four toes.

It took a few seconds for comprehension to hit, and then Daniel sucked in a horrified gasp.

"Amateurs," she scoffed from the ceiling.

"I don't know," Kevin said coolly. "They seemed pretty good to me."

"Did they get what they were after?"

He made a disbelieving noise in the back of his throat. "Are you kidding?"

She raised one eyebrow. "Like I said."

"And you could have made me talk?"

Her lips pulled into a bleak smile. "Oh, *yes*."

Out of the corner of her eye, she saw Daniel shudder convulsively.

The dog was quiet now but still alert underneath her. It seemed unsure of the situation, with its master talking so calmly to its target.

"Hey, I know who you are," Kevin said suddenly. "Yeah, the girl. I heard rumors about you. Exaggerations. They said you'd never had a miss. You were batting a thousand."

"Not an exaggeration."

His expression was skeptical. "You worked with the old guy, the Mad Scientist, they called him. The Agency called you the Oleander. Honestly, I didn't put it together at first because I heard you both died in some lab accident. And also, I always imagined the Oleander was pretty."

Daniel started to say something, but she interrupted.

"Oleander? That's just awful."

"Huh?"

"A flower?" she growled to herself. "That's so *passive*. A poison doesn't do the poisoning, it's just an inert agent."

"What did your unit call you?"

"The Chemist. And Dr. Barnaby was not a mad scientist. He was a genius."

"Tomato, tomahto," Kevin said.

"Back to the truce I was speaking of," Daniel interjected. The way he looked at her hands and arms, she thought he might have guessed how much they were hurting her. "Alex will give me the keys, and Kevin, you will call off Einstein. When I think everything is under control, I'll let you out. Alex, do you trust me?"

He looked up at her with his wide, clear hazel eyes while Kevin spluttered in inarticulate fury.

"The keys are in the left front pocket of my jeans. I'd hand them to you, but if I loosen my hands, I'll fall."

"Be careful, she'll stab you!"

Daniel didn't even seem to have heard his brother's warning. When he climbed onto the chair, his head was actually higher up than hers. He had to stoop, his head pressed against the foam roof. He put one hand under her back, supporting some of her weight, while he fished gently in her pocket for the key.

"I'm sorry my brother is so socially inept," he whispered. "He's always been that way."

"Don't you apologize for me, you moron!" Kevin yelled.

Daniel smiled at her, then took the key and stepped down. She was actually in agreement with Kevin. How could Daniel be like this with her? Where was the totally natural resentment? Where was the human desire for retribution?

"I've got the keys, Kev. Do you have a lead for the dog?"

"A *lead?* Einstein doesn't need a leash!"

"What's your suggestion, then?"

Kevin glared at him balefully. "Fine. I'd rather kill her myself anyway." He whistled at the dog. "At ease, Einstein."

The dog, who had followed Daniel anxiously as he approached Alex, now went calmly to its master's head and sat down, his tongue lolling out in what appeared to be a smile. A very toothy smile.

"Let me out."

"Ladies first." Daniel climbed up on the chair again and offered her his hand. "Need some help?"

"Er, I think I've got it." She dropped her legs toward the desk, her arms extending as she tried to touch down with her toes. How had she gotten up here? Her tired hands started to slip.

"Here you go." Daniel caught her by the waist as she fell and set her carefully on her feet, one on the desk, the other with a clang in the middle of the prop tray. His blanket skirt loosened; he quickly grabbed the fabric and tightened it.

"I can't believe this," Kevin muttered.

Alex stood cautiously, watching the dog.

"If he tries anything," Daniel murmured to her, "I'll distract him. Dogs love me."

"Einstein isn't stupid," Kevin growled.

"Let's not find out. Now your turn." He climbed down from the chair and crouched beside Kevin.

Alex slithered off the desk as quietly as she could, one hand reaching out for the keyboard. The dog didn't respond; it was watching Daniel release its master. She opened the system preferences. Screen saver wasn't the only way to release the sleeping gas, and she still had both masks.

But she knew that would just make things difficult. She would have to trust that Daniel could handle Kevin for now. She eased herself into the chair.

Daniel had started with the ankle and it was going slowly—he was keeping one hand on his blanket.

"Just give it to me, I'll do it," Kevin said.

"Be patient."

Kevin huffed loudly.

The key turned and Kevin was immediately on his feet, crouching beside his tethered arm. He snatched the key from Daniel's hand and had his wrist free in less than a second. He stood tall, stretching his neck and rolling his back muscles. The torso pieces of his Batsuit hung down like an avant-garde skirt. The dog kept still at his feet. Kevin turned to Alex.

"Where are my guns?"

"Backseat of the car."

Kevin stalked out of the tent without another word, the dog at his heels.

"Don't open any doors or windows!" she called after him. "Everything's armed again."

"Is the car booby-trapped?" he called back.

"No."

A second later. "Where are the magazines? Hey, where are the firing pins?!"

"Pins in the fridge, bullets in the toilet."

"Oh, come on!"

"Sorry."

"I want my SIG Sauer back."

She frowned and didn't answer. She got up stiffly. She might as well disarm the traps. It was time to go.

Daniel was standing in the middle of the tent, staring down at the silver table; he had one hand wrapped around the IV pole as if for support. He seemed to be in a daze. She went hesitantly to stand beside him.

"Are you going to be okay?" she asked.

"I have no idea. I can't understand what I'm supposed to do next."

"Your brother will have a plan. He's been living somewhere, he'll have a place for you."

He looked down at her. "Is it hard?"

"What?"

"Running? Hiding?"

She opened her mouth to say something soothing, then thought better of it. "Yeah, it's pretty hard. You get used to it. The worst part is the loneliness, and you won't have to deal with that. So that's one minor plus." She kept to herself the thought that loneliness might be a better companion than Kevin Beach.

"Are *you* lonely a lot?"

She tried to laugh it off. "Only when I'm not scared. So, no, not too often."

"Have you decided yet what you're going to do next?"

"No . . . The face is a problem. I can't walk around like this. People will remember me, and that's not safe. I'll have to hide somewhere until the swelling goes down and the bruises fade enough to cover with makeup."

"*Where* do you hide? I don't understand how this works."

"I may have to camp out for a while. I've got a bunch of subsistence food and plenty of water—by the way, don't drink the water in the fridge without checking with me first, the left side is poisoned.

Anyway, I may just find someplace remote and sleep in the car until I've recuperated enough."

He blinked a couple of times, probably thrown by the poison thing.

"Maybe we can do something about *your* problem with conspicuousness," she said more lightly, touching his blanket with one finger. "I think there might be some clothes up at the house. I doubt they'll fit you, but they're better than what you've got."

A wave of relief passed over his face. "I know it's a small thing, but I think that would actually help quite a bit."

"Okay. Let me go turn off the lethal-gas trap."

• • •

IN THE END, she did surrender the SIG Sauer, although with some regret. She liked its weight. She'd have to find her own.

The farmhouse owners' belongings were stashed in the attic, in a set of dressers from six or seven decades back. The man was obviously a lot shorter and wider than Daniel. She left Daniel to sort that out while she went back to the barn to pack up the car.

Kevin was there when she entered, tightly rolling a big swath of black fabric into a manageable armload; it took her a moment to realize the fabric was a parachute. She kept her distance as he worked, but the truce felt solid. For some reason, Daniel had put himself between her and his brother's animosity. Neither she nor Kevin understood *why* he was doing it, but Kevin cared too much about Daniel to violate his trust today. Not when he was still reeling over years of lies.

Or that's what she told herself to muster up the courage needed to walk past the dog to her car.

She was an old hand at packing, and it didn't take her very long. When she'd come out to meet Carston, she'd stowed her things and dismantled the security at the rental house, just in case she didn't make it back. (One of her nightmares was that the department would get her while she was out, and then some innocent, unsuspecting landlord would enter the premises and die.) She'd stashed everything outside DC, then come back for it when she'd started setting up for Project Interrogate the Schoolteacher. Now she fitted it all into the worn black duffels—the pressurized canisters, the miles of lead wires, the battery packs, the rubber-encased vials of components, the syringes, the goggles, the heavy gloves, her pillow, and her sleeping bag. She packed her props and some of the new things she'd picked up. The restraints were a good find, and the cot was decently comfortable and folded down into a small rectangle. She put her computer in its case, grabbed the little black box that was just a red herring, like her locket, pulled down the long cables, and rolled up the extension cords. She was going to have to leave the lights, which was a bummer. They hadn't been cheap. She dismantled the tent, leaving just a pile of meaningless foam and PVC pipe, and shoved the table back to where she'd found it. There wasn't anything to do about the holes she'd drilled.

She could only hope that she'd obfuscated things enough that the owners would only be confused and angry at the destruction rather than suspicious that something nefarious had happened here. There was a chance they'd report their destructive tenant to the authorities, but local police wouldn't be able to construe anything from the mess either. As long as certain words didn't go into the report, there was no reason for anyone in the government to notice. She was sure there were Airbnb stories of destruction much more interesting than this one.

She shook her head at the door to the bunk room. The dog had chewed or clawed a hole two feet high and a foot wide right through the center of the solid wood door. At least it had only jumped over the car rather than eating it on its way out.

She was finished loading the trunk when Daniel came back in.

"Nice capris," Kevin commented, winding the cable of his grappling hook into a neat coil. Alex wondered if he'd climbed back up onto the roof to retrieve it and, if he had, how she'd missed that.

It was true that Daniel's pants made it only halfway down his shins. The cotton shirt was a few sizes wide, and the sleeves were probably too short as well—he had them rolled to the elbows.

"If only I had half a wet suit." Daniel sighed. "Then I would feel ready to face the world."

Kevin grunted. "I'd have a whole wet suit if the psycho wasn't such a perv."

"Don't flatter yourself, I was looking for weapons."

Daniel watched her close the trunk.

"Are you leaving?"

"Yes. I need to get somewhere safe so I can sleep." She imagined she looked haggard enough that the explanation was a little redundant.

"I was thinking..." Daniel said, and then hesitated.

Kevin looked up from his rifle, alerted by Daniel's tone.

"What were you thinking?" Kevin asked suspiciously.

"Well, I was thinking about the scorpions in the jar. Alex said there were only two outcomes—one kills the other, or both die. And I imagine that the people who wanted to kill you thought the same thing."

"So?" Kevin said.

"So, there was a third option," she said, guessing the direction Daniel was headed. "The scorpions walk away. They won't be expecting that. That's what will make you safe, Daniel."

"But there's a fourth option, too," Daniel answered. "That's what I've been thinking about."

Kevin cocked his head. He clearly didn't get it. She did, just before Daniel said the words out loud.

"What if the scorpions joined forces?"

She pursed her lips, then relaxed them when that pulled at the split.

Kevin groaned. "Stop messing around, Danny."

"I'm serious. They'd never expect that. And then we're twice as safe, because we've got both dangerous creatures on the same team."

"Not happening."

She walked closer to him. "It's a clever idea, Daniel, but I think some of the personnel issues might be too big to overcome."

"Kev's not so bad. You'll get used to him."

"*I'm* not bad?" Kevin snorted, peering through his sights.

Daniel looked straight at her. "You're thinking about going back, aren't you? What you said about visiting the pantry."

Insightful for a civilian.

"I'm considering it."

Kevin was giving them his full attention now. "Counterstrike?"

"It might work," she said. "There's a pattern . . . and after looking at it, I think that maybe not so many people know about me. That's why they're going to such lengths to have a fifty-fifty chance at taking me out. I think I'm a secret, so if I can get rid of the people in on that secret . . . well, then nobody's looking for me anymore."

"Does that hold true for me?" Kevin wanted to know. "If they're relying on this to get to me, do you think I might be a secret, too?"

"It's logical."

"How will you know who's in on it?"

"If I could be in DC when I send my little note to Carston, I could watch to see who he goes running to. If it's really a secret, they won't be able to do it in the office."

"They'll know you're close—the IP will give you away."

"Maybe we could work together in a limited way. One of you could send the e-mail for me from a distance."

"What's your experience in surveillance?" Kevin demanded abruptly.

"Er . . . I've had a lot of practice in the last few years—"

"Do you have any *formal* training?"

"I'm a scientist, not a field agent."

He nodded. "I'll do it."

She shook her head. "You're dead again, remember? You and Daniel get to disappear now. Don't look a gift horse in the mouth."

"That's a stupid saying. If the Trojans *had* looked in the horse's mouth, they might have won that war."

"Forget the saying. I'm trying to make things up to Daniel."

Daniel was quietly watching the back-and-forth again.

"Look, Oleander, I *have* had training. A lot. *No one* is going to catch me watching and I will see more than you will. I have a place to stash Daniel where he'll be totally safe, so that's not an issue. And if you're right, and this Carston guy goes running to his coconspirators, he'll show me who in the Agency thought this up. I'll see who put Danny in danger to get to me. Then I can clean up my problem and you can clean up yours."

She thought it through, trying to be objective. It was hard to keep her dislike for Daniel's brother from coloring her analysis. That dislike wasn't fair. Wouldn't she have felt the same way as Kevin if it were her sibling shackled to a table? Done the same things, insofar as she was capable?

But she still really wished she could inject him with something agonizing, just once.

"First of all, don't call me Oleander," she said.

He smirked.

"Second, I see what you're saying. But how do we coordinate? I've got to go under for a while." She pointed to her face.

"You owe her for that," Daniel said. "If you have a safe place for me, maybe she should go there, too. At least until her injuries have healed."

"I don't owe her anything—except maybe another punch in the face," Kevin growled. Daniel bridled and took a step toward his brother; Kevin held up his hands in an *I surrender* motion and sighed. "But we're going to want to move quick, so that might be the easiest arrangement. Besides, then she can give us a ride. The plane's a loss—I had to bail out on the way down. I had us hiking out of here."

Daniel opened his eyes wide in disbelief. Kevin laughed at his expression, then turned to her with a smile. He looked at the dog, then back to her, and his smile got bigger. "I think I might enjoy having you at the ranch, Oleander."

She gritted her teeth. If Kevin had a safe house, that would solve a lot of her problems. And she could spike his food with a violent laxative before she left.

"Her name is Alex," Daniel corrected. "I mean, I know it's not, but that's what she goes by." He looked at her. "Alex is okay, right?"

"It's as good as any other name. I'll stick with it for now." She looked at Kevin. "You and the dog are in the back."

CHAPTER 11

O nce upon a time, when she was a young girl named Juliana, Alex used to fantasize about family road trips.

She and her mother had always flown on the few vacations they took — if duty visits to ancient grandparents in Little Rock actually qualified as *vacations*. Her mother, Judy, didn't like to drive long distances; it made her nervous. Judy had often said that far more people were killed in car accidents than in plane crashes, though she was a white-knuckle flyer, too. Juliana had grown up unfazed by the dangers associated with travel, or germs, or rodents, or tight spaces, or any of the many other things that upset Judy. By default, she had to be the levelheaded one.

Like most only children, Juliana thought siblings would be the cure to the loneliness of her long afternoons doing homework at the kitchen table while she waited for Judy to get home from the dentist's office she managed. Juliana looked forward to college and dormitories and roommates as a dream of companionship. Except, when she got there, she found that her life of relative solitude and adult responsibility had rendered her unsuited to cohabitation with normal eighteen-year-olds. So the sibling fantasy took a beating, and by her junior year she had her own small studio apartment.

The fantasy about a big, warm family road trip, however, had survived. Until today.

To be fair, she would probably have been in a better mood if her entire body hadn't felt like one huge, throbbing bruise. Also, she *had* instigated the first argument, though quite unintentionally.

When she drove across the county line, she'd rolled the window down and tossed out the small tracker she'd removed from Daniel's leg. She hadn't wanted to carry it with her for long, just in case, but she also didn't want to leave it right in the middle of her last base of operations. She thought she'd removed most of the evidence, but one could never be sure. Whenever she could muddy the trail, she took the time to do so.

In the rearview mirror, she saw Kevin sit forward.

He'd been able to retrieve a backpack he'd thrown from the plane when he jumped; now he and Daniel looked fairly normal in jeans and long-sleeved T-shirts — one black, one gray — and Kevin had two new handguns.

"What was that?" Kevin asked.

"Daniel's tracker."

"What?" Kevin and Daniel said together.

They spoke over each other.

"I *did* have a tracker?" Daniel asked.

"What did you do that for?" Kevin demanded.

The dog looked up at Kevin's tone but then seemed to decide everything was fine and stuck his face out the window again.

She turned to Daniel first, looking up at him from under the ball cap that was supposed to be keeping her mangled face in shadow. "How did you think your brother found you?"

"He tracked me? But...where was it?"

"Sore spot on your inner right thigh. Keep the incision clean, try not to let it get infected."

"Do you know what a pain it was to get that in place?" Kevin grumbled.

"If you can track it, so can someone else. I didn't want to take chances with our position."

Daniel turned around in the passenger seat to stare at his brother. "How did you...How could I not know about this?"

"Do you remember, about two years after the tramp left you, a hot leggy blonde at that bar you go to when you're depressed, what's it called..."

"Lou's. How do you even know about that? I never told you... wait, did you have me *followed?*"

"I was worried about you after the tramp—"

"Her name is Lainey."

"Whatever. I never liked her for you."

"When did you ever like a girl for me? As far as I can recall, you only ever liked girls who wanted you. You took it as an insult if someone preferred me."

"The point is, you weren't yourself. But having you followed was unrelated to the—"

"*Who* followed me?"

"It was just for a few months."

"Who?"

"Some buddies of mine—not in the Agency. A few cops I had a relationship with, a PI for a little while."

"What were they looking for?"

"Just making sure you were okay, that you weren't going to jump off a bridge or anything."

"I can't believe you. Of all the—wait a minute. The blonde? You mean that girl, what was her name, Kate? The one who bought me a drink and...she was a spy?"

She saw Kevin grinning in the rearview mirror.

"No, she was actually a hooker. Kate isn't her real name."

"Apparently no one on the entire planet besides me uses his or her real name. I am living in a world of lies. I don't even know Alex's given name."

"Juliana," she said at the same time Kevin did. They cast irritated looks at each other.

"*He* knew?" Daniel asked her, offended.

"It came up while you were unconscious. It's the name I was given at birth, but it's really not me anymore. It doesn't mean much to me. I'm Alex for now."

Daniel frowned, not entirely mollified.

"Anyway," Kevin went on in the tone of someone who was telling a joke he really enjoyed, "the blonde was supposed to get you back to your place, but you told her that your divorce wasn't finalized yet and it *didn't feel right.*" Kevin laughed raucously. "I couldn't believe it when I heard. But it was so *you.* I don't even know why I was surprised."

"Hilarious. But I don't see how that little exchange got a tracking device into my leg."

"It didn't. I just really like that story. Anyway, that's what was such a pain. The hooker was easy to set up. And if you'd taken her home, having the tracker placed would have been enjoyable for you, at least. Getting you into your GP's office was a lot more work. But eventually I got a temp in the front office to call you in for checkup. When you got there, you saw one of the new partners. A guy you'd never seen before."

Daniel's mouth popped open in disbelief. "He told me *I had a tumor!*"

"A *benign* tumor. Which he took out right there in the office with a local anesthetic and immediately assured you was nothing. He didn't even charge you. Don't make it into a bigger thing than it was."

"Are you serious? How could you—" Daniel was shouting at full volume now. "How do you *justify* these things to yourself? All these years you've been manipulating me! Treating me like some laboratory animal who exists for your own amusement!"

"Hardly, Danny. I've been putting myself out trying to keep you safe. The Agency wanted me to play dead from the very start, but I couldn't do that to you, not after Mom and Dad. So I made a lot of promises and spent all my free weekends flying to Milwaukee to be a criminal."

Daniel's voice was calmer when he answered. "I *drove*. And was all that really necessary?"

"Ask the poison girl. These kinds of jobs aren't for family people."

Daniel looked at her. "Is that true?"

"Yes. They like to recruit orphans — preferably only children. Like your brother told you before, relationships give the bad guys leverage."

His tone mellowed further. "Are you an orphan?"

"I'm not sure. Never met my father. He could still be alive somewhere."

"But your mother..."

"Uterine cancer. I was nineteen."

"I'm sorry."

She nodded.

There was a brief, very pleasurable moment of silence. Alex held her breath and prayed for it to last.

"When I did finally let you think I was dead..." Kevin began.

Alex turned the radio on and started searching through stations. Kevin did not get the hint. Daniel just stared through the windshield.

"...I was just starting with Enrique de la Fuentes. I could tell in the first few days that it was going to get out of hand. I knew what he'd done to the families of his enemies. It was time to set you free."

"Free yourself from the visitation charade, you mean," Daniel muttered.

Alex found a classical station and turned it up so she could hear it over Kevin's voice.

"That's when I put the tracker in. I needed to know you were okay. No one was watching you anymore, just me."

Daniel grunted in disbelief.

The music's volume was making Alex's head hurt more. She turned it down again.

"It ended... badly with the Agency. The plan was to wait until things died down and I was forgotten, then get the face fixed. Eventually, I was coming back for you, kid. You wouldn't have recognized me at first, but I wasn't going to leave you thinking you were alone your whole life."

Daniel stared straight ahead. She wondered if he believed what his brother was saying. He was staggering under the weight of so many different kinds of betrayal.

"What happened with the Agency?" Alex asked. She really didn't want to get involved with this conversation, but it didn't look like Daniel was going to pursue it. Before joining this unlikely alliance, it hadn't mattered much to her one way or the other how Kevin had left the CIA. Now this information was important. It affected her, too.

"When the job with the virus was done, and de la Fuentes was out of the picture, the Agency wanted to pull me back in, but there were still some loose ends that bugged me. I wanted to nail it all down. It wouldn't have taken too much longer and I was in a very unique position of power with the cartel. It was also a good opportunity to influence what happened there — who took over, what their agenda might be — while also getting solid information on the new structure. I couldn't believe the Agency was calling me in. I refused to leave. I thought I had explained myself clearly, but... I guess they didn't believe me. They must have thought I'd gone rogue, that I'd flipped and was choosing the cartel. It still makes no sense to me." He shook his head. "I thought they knew me better."

"What did they do?" Daniel asked.

"They burned me. Ratted me out as an agent, told people I'd killed de la Fuentes. And those people came for revenge."

"And got that revenge, as far as the CIA knew," she guessed.

"Exactly."

"Did you kill him?" Daniel asked. "De la Fuentes?"

"Part of the job."

"Have you killed a lot of people?"

"Do you really want to know?"

Daniel waited silently, not looking back.

"Okay. Fine. I've killed around, oh, forty-five people, maybe more. I can't be sure about the number—you don't always have time to check for a pulse. Do you understand why I had to keep you separated from my life?"

Daniel looked at Alex now. "Have you ever killed anyone?"

"Three times."

"Three...oh! The people your company sent after you?"

"Yes."

"Don't act like that makes her better than me," Kevin interjected, angry.

"I wasn't—" Daniel started to say.

It was Kevin's turn to shout. "Ask her how many people she tortured before you. Ask her how long for each of them. How many hours—how many days? I just shoot people. Clean and fast. I would never do what she does. To anyone, especially not an innocent civilian like—"

"Shut up," Daniel snapped. "Just stop talking. Don't make this about her. Whatever pain she caused me, remember, you caused me more. It hurt more, and it lasted for much, much longer. You say you had a good reason. So did she. She didn't know she'd been lied to, that she'd been manipulated. I know how *that* feels."

"As if she's just some blameless bystander here."

"I said *shut up!*" Daniel bellowed the last two words at a deafening decibel.

Alex cringed. The dog whined, pulling its face inside and staring at its master.

"Easy," Kevin said, maybe to the dog.

Daniel noticed her reaction.

"Are you okay?"

"Actually, on top of a lot of other uncomfortable injuries, I've got a splitting headache."

"I'm sorry."

"Don't worry about it."

"You look like you're going to crash—figuratively and literally. Want me to drive? You could try to get a nap."

She thought about that for a minute. She'd always had to do things on her own, but that was okay, because then she knew they were done right. She didn't have someone to take turns driving with, but that was also okay, because then she didn't have to trust some-one. Trust was a killer.

Still, she knew her limits. There was something so luxurious about the idea of being able to sleep and travel at the same time.

And she did trust Daniel not to hurt her, not to betray her. Knowing it could be a huge mistake, she still trusted him.

"Thank you," she said. "That would be really nice. I'll pull over at the next exit."

The words sounded odd to her as they came out of her mouth. Like something someone would say on television, lines from one actor to another. But she supposed this was how normal human interactions generally sounded. She just didn't have a lot of those in her life.

The silence was lovely for the two miles it took to get to the next exit. The peace made her even sleepier. Her eyelids were already doing the involuntary slow blink as she pulled off onto the dirt shoulder.

No one spoke while they made the exchange. Kevin's head lolled back on his seat, eyes closed. Daniel touched her shoulder lightly as he passed her.

Tired as she was, she didn't fall asleep immediately. At first she thought it was the weirdness of having the car moving beneath her; her body assumed from long habit that she would be the one at the wheel and knew sleep was not allowed. She peeked at Daniel a few times from under her hat, just as reassurance. He knew how to drive a car. It was okay to relax. Sure, the seat was uncomfortable, but not much worse than her usual nighttime setup. She'd taught herself to get rest where she could. But her head felt ... too unrestrained. As soon as she realized this, she knew it was the gas mask she was missing. It had become part of her sleep ritual.

Understanding the problem helped. She pulled her baseball cap farther down over her sore face and told herself to relax. She'd strung no wires today. No poison gas threatened. Everything was okay, she promised herself.

• • •

IT WAS DARK when she woke up. She felt stiff, incredibly sore, and hungry. She also really had to pee. She wished she could have stayed asleep longer and thus avoided all of these unpleasant feelings, but the brothers were arguing again. She'd been out for a long time, she knew, so she couldn't blame them for forgetting her, but she wished they hadn't been arguing about *her* when she awakened.

"...but she *isn't* pretty," Kevin was saying as she began to surface.

"You don't even know what she looks like," Daniel replied angrily. "You mauled her face before you had a chance to introduce yourself."

"It ain't just about the face, kid. She's built like a skinny ten-year-old boy."

"You are the reason why women think all men are dogs. Also, the term is *sylphid*."

"You read too many books."

"You don't read enough."

"I call it how it is."

"You have limited perception."

"Hey, it's okay," Alex interrupted. There was no graceful way into this conversation, but she didn't want to pretend to be asleep. "No offense taken."

She pulled the hat off her face and wiped away the drool that had leaked from her damaged lip.

"Sorry," Daniel muttered.

"Don't worry about it. I needed to wake up."

"No, I mean *him*."

"Your brother's low opinion of my charms is its own special kind of compliment."

Daniel laughed. "Good point."

Kevin snorted.

Alex stretched, and then groaned. "Let me guess. When you pictured the Mad Scientist's female partner, the mysterious Oleander, you saw a blonde, right?" She glanced at his face—suddenly rigid. "Yes, definitely a blonde. Large breasts, long tan legs, full lips, and huge blue doe eyes? Did I get it all? Or was there a French accent, too?"

Kevin didn't respond. She glanced back at him; he stared out the window as if he weren't listening to her.

"Got it in one." She laughed.

"He was always a fan of the obvious," Daniel said.

"I never saw one of those on the job," Alex told Daniel. "I'm not saying such a creature wouldn't have the brains necessary, but really, why spend decades buried in unglamorous research when there are so many other options?"

"I've seen girls like that on the job," Kevin muttered.

"Sure, agents," Alex allowed. "That's a sexy job. Exciting. But trust me, lab coats really aren't that figure-flattering, despite the slutty Halloween-costume version."

Kevin went back to looking out the window.

"How are you feeling?" Daniel asked.

"Ouch."

"Oh. Sorry."

She shrugged. "We should find a place to pause. I'm not going to be able to eat in a restaurant without someone calling the cops on you two. We'll have to get a motel somewhere, and then somebody's going to have to go out for groceries."

"Room service not an option?" Daniel wondered.

"Those types of hotels notice when you pay cash," Kevin explained before she could. "Sorry, bro. We'll have to rough it for a night."

"Have you been driving all day?" she asked.

"No, Kev and I switched out a couple of times."

"I can't believe I slept through all of that."

"I think you needed it."

"Yeah, I guess I've been burning the candle at both ends for too long."

"So little time," Kevin muttered, "so many people to torture."

"True story," she agreed lightly, just to annoy him.

Daniel laughed.

Daniel seemed so kind and gentle—more so than anyone she'd ever known—but he was definitely weird. Possibly unstable.

They found a small place on the outskirts of Little Rock. Alex thought she ought to recognize the city just a bit, but nothing reminded her of her childhood visits to the grandparents. Maybe the city had grown too much in the years since she'd been here. Maybe she was just in the wrong part. Somewhere nearby, her mother and her grandparents were buried. She wondered if that should make her feel something. But the place didn't really matter. She was no closer to them for being closer to the remains of their genetic material.

Kevin insisted on making the arrangements at the front desk. It was probably for the best that Kevin took the lead now; Alex was out of commission, thanks to her face, and even if she had looked fine, he was still the expert. She knew only what she'd learned through theoretical research and a couple of years of trial and error. Kevin had been taught so much more, and he'd proved it all in the field. Daniel wasn't even an option. Oh, his face was fine, but his instincts were all wrong.

Case in point, the way he argued when he saw that Kevin had gotten them only one room. It hadn't occurred to him that a hotel clerk would be more likely to remember a man who came in alone yet paid cash for two rooms. And when Kevin parked three doors down from their actual room, Daniel didn't understand why. Misdirection, they explained, but it was foreign to everything Daniel had ever known, every habit he'd formed. He thought like a normal person who'd never had anything to hide. There was a lot he was going to have to learn.

He even asked if they should get permission before they brought the dog into the room.

It had only one bed, but Alex had been asleep for twelve hours straight, so she was happy to be the lookout. Kevin went out for a half hour and came back with cellophane-wrapped sandwiches, sodas, and a large bag of dog food. Alex scarfed her sandwich down, and then chased it with a handful of Motrin. Einstein ate just as enthusiastically as she had, straight from the bag, but Daniel and Kevin were more relaxed about the food. Apparently, she'd missed a couple of stops at the drive-through, too.

A quick assessment of herself in the scratched bathroom mirror was not encouraging. Her nose was swollen to twice its normal size, red and bulbous. On the plus side, odds were it would heal up differently than it began, thus changing her appearance a little. Maybe not as aesthetically pleasing a result as she would get from plastic surgery, but probably less painful on the whole, or at least faster. Her black eyes were an impressive contradiction to their name, boasting a rainbow of colors from jaundice yellow to bilious green to sickly purple. Her split lip puffed out from either side of the scabby fissure like flesh balloons, and she hadn't even known you could develop bruises *inside* your mouth. There was one stroke of luck: she still had all her teeth. Getting a bridge would have been tricky.

It was going to be a while before she could do *anything*. She really hoped Kevin's safe house lived up to the name. It worried her to be headed into the unknown. She hadn't prepared anything, and that was 100 percent unnerving.

She showered and brushed her teeth—a more painful ordeal than usual—and slipped into her black leggings and a clean white tee. She'd reached the limits of her wardrobe. Hopefully the safe house had a washing machine.

Daniel was asleep when she came back out, stretched out on his stomach with one hand under the pillow and one arm falling over the edge of the bed, long fingers brushing the faded carpet. His sleeping face was really something else—like before, when he was unconscious, his innocence and serenity didn't seem to belong in the same world that she did.

Kevin wasn't in the room and neither was the dog. Though she assumed the dog had needs, she couldn't bring her alert level down from orange-red until they'd returned.

Kevin didn't acknowledge her, but the dog sniffed her once as it passed. Kevin lay down flat on his back, his arms at his sides, and immediately closed his eyes. He didn't move again for six hours. The dog jumped onto the end of the bed and curled up with its tail over Daniel's legs and its head pillowed on Kevin's feet.

Alex sat in the only chair—the carpet was just too questionable for her to lie on the floor—and bent over her laptop, surfing the news. She wasn't sure when Daniel's disappearance would be noticed or if it would be broadcast when it was. Probably not. Grown men wandered off all the time. For example, her father. That sort of thing was too common to make waves unless there was some sensational detail—like dismembered body parts in his apartment.

There was also no story yet about the crash of a single-prop plane in West Virginia—no fatalities or injured found, still trying to locate the owner — but she doubted the news would merit more than just a note in a local online paper. When it did surface, there would be nothing in the report that would catch anyone's attention in DC.

She exhausted her search for information that might endanger them. It seemed that, for now, they were in the clear on that front, at least. What was Carston thinking right at this moment? What was he planning? She wasn't due to deliver Daniel until Monday before school, and it was still only Saturday — well, almost Sunday. The department knew she wasn't going to crack Daniel — he had nothing to spill. They had to know she would eventually learn of the identical twin's existence. They must have been pretty sure of Kevin's status in the land of the living. They had expected him to be drawn out into the open early in the game, and they'd been right about that. The only thing they hadn't foreseen was that the torturer and the assassin might have a conversation.

It would never have shaken out this way without Daniel's interference. He'd been a ploy for them, just a pawn moved into peril to lure the more critical players into the center of the board. They never would have guessed that he'd be a catalyst for change.

She planned to hold true to her side of the bargain — she would take the role of victor (though that was really the losing role) and let Daniel and Kevin be dead. Dead *again*, in Kevin's case. But oh, how she wished that she could be the one to die. Wouldn't it be easy for the department to believe that someone like Kevin Beach — who'd toppled a cartel — had succeeded where they had failed? Wouldn't it make sense for them to stop looking then? What would it be like to disappear, but this time with no one searching for her?

She sighed. Fantasies only made it harder; there was no point indulging in them. The men were both pretty well under, she was sure, so she dug into her bag and pulled out the pressurized canister she'd selected earlier. She had only the two gas masks, so nothing deadly tonight, just the airborne sleeping agent she'd had hooked up to her computer yesterday. It was enough. It would let her control the outcome if someone discovered them.

After she'd strung the leads—only a double line; she wouldn't have to arm or disarm from outside the room tonight—she settled back into her chair. She glanced at the twins. Both were deep, peaceful sleepers. She wondered if that was a healthy habit for a spy. Maybe Kevin actually trusted her—enough to sound the alarm at the very least, and maybe even to deal with a problem without killing them all. She and the brothers were strange bedfellows indeed.

How odd it was, watching over them. It felt wrong, and she'd expected that. But it also felt good, satisfying some need she'd never known was there, and *that* she *hadn't* expected.

She spent some time thinking about her analysis of the situation, searching for flaws in her theory, but the more she looked at it, the more it made sense. Even the woeful lack of evolution in her would-be-assassins—by the third try, *someone* should have been aware of her system and changed the approach—made sense in this light. There had never been any *operation,* just expendable individuals sent after her with little or no briefing. She thought through every conjecture two or three times and felt more confident than ever that she finally understood the ones hunting her.

And then she was bored.

What she wanted to do was log on to the website of Columbia University's pathology program and read the latest doctoral dissertations, but it wasn't safe to do that while the department was actively trying to locate her, which she was certain they were. The department couldn't trace *every* connection anyone made to her old interests, but this one might be too obvious. With a sigh, she put in earbuds, opened up YouTube, and started watching a tutorial about fieldstripping a rifle. It probably wasn't anything she'd ever need to know, but it couldn't hurt.

Kevin woke up at five thirty on the dot. He just sat up, as alert as if someone had flipped a switch to turn him on. He patted the dog once and headed toward the door. It took him only a second to notice the gas mask she was wearing and jerk to a stop. The dog, right on his heels, paused too and pointed its nose in her direction, looking for whatever had upset its master.

"Give me a sec," Alex said.

She got awkwardly to her feet, still aching and sore—whether more or less than at the beginning of the night, she couldn't tell—and walked stiffly to the door to undo her security precautions.

"I didn't say you could do that," Kevin said.

She didn't look at him. "I didn't ask for your permission."

He grunted.

It took her only a few seconds to clear his path. She removed her mask and used it to gesture to the door.

"Knock yourself out."

"Knock *you* out," she thought she heard him mutter as he passed her, but it was too low for her to be sure. The dog followed him, tail swishing so fast it blurred. She imagined the guy at the front desk probably wasn't paying any attention at this hour, but she still thought Kevin was pressing their luck a little. A screaming match with the management wasn't going to help them stay incognito.

She rummaged through the food Kevin had bought last night. The remaining sandwiches weren't as appetizing as they had been eight hours ago, but there was a box of cherry Pop-Tarts she'd missed before. She was working her way through the second pastry in the sleeve when Kevin and the dog came back.

"You want to catch a few hours?" he asked her.

"If you don't mind driving, I can sleep in the car again. Better to get where we're going."

He nodded once, then went to the bed and lightly kicked his brother.

Daniel moaned and rolled onto his back, covering his head with a pillow.

"Is that necessary?" she asked.

"Like you said, better to get going. Danny's always had a problem with the snooze button."

Kevin yanked the pillow off Daniel's head.

"Let's go, kid."

Daniel blinked owlishly for a few seconds, and then she watched his face change as the memories hit, as he realized where he was and why. It hurt to see the peace of his dreams crumble into the devastation of his new waking reality. His eyes darted around the room until he found her. She tried to make her expression reassuring, but the damage done to her face would probably trump any arrangement of her features. She searched for something to say, something that would make the world a little less dark and scary for him.

"Pop-Tart?" she offered.

He blinked again. "Um, okay."

CHAPTER 12

Alex did not approve of the safe house.

They'd reached it late in the afternoon. She'd kept her nap to just four hours during the drive. She didn't want to be on a nocturnal schedule forever. So she'd been awake as they turned off the highway onto a two-lane surface road, then to an even smaller road, until finally they were on a one-lane dirt *path* — calling it a road was too complimentary.

Sure it was hard to find, but once you did . . . well, there was only one way out. She never would have chosen to live backed into a corner like this.

"Relax, killer," Kevin told her when she complained. "No one is looking for us out here."

"We should have switched plates."

"Took care of it while you were snoring."

"You weren't actually snoring," Daniel said quietly. He was driving now, while Kevin directed. "But it is true that we stopped at a junkyard and stole a few license plates."

"So we're trapped out here on a dead-end lane while Mr. Smith goes to Washington," she muttered.

"It's secure," Kevin snapped in a tone that was clearly intended to close the discussion. "So don't go stringing your death traps through my house."

She didn't answer. She would do what she wanted when he was gone.

At least his setup was far away from neighbors; they drove for at least fifteen minutes down the dirt path without seeing any evidence of other human beings. That would keep the collateral damage low if for some reason she felt the need to burn everything to the ground.

They arrived at a tall gate flanked by a heavy-duty chain-link fence with a crowning line of spiraled razor wire. The fence ran so far off into the distance to both the right and the left that she couldn't see where it turned or ended. Beside the gate, there was a very serious-looking NO TRESPASSING sign with an additional notice below that read ENTER AT YOUR OWN RISK; OWNERS ARE NOT LIABLE FOR INJURIES OR HARM THAT MAY RESULT FROM TRESPASSING.

"Subtle," she said.

"It gets the job done," Kevin responded. He pulled a key fob from his pocket and clicked a button. The gate swung open, and Daniel drove through.

She should have expected that his safe house would be so obvious.

After a few more miles, the house came into view like a mirage, its dull gray second story hovering on a light haze over the dry yellow grass. Here and there, a few dark, scrubby trees studded the grassland with some texture. Over it all, the washed-out blue sky stretched to infinity.

She'd never been totally comfortable with the Great Plains. She'd been a city girl for too long. This felt so exposed, so . . . unanchored. Like a strong wind could just erase everything in sight. Which probably did happen around these parts, biannually. She really hoped it wasn't tornado season.

The rest of the house was revealed as they topped a low rise in the mostly flat road. It was large but dilapidated, two stories high with a rickety porch wrapped around half the ground floor. The coarse, dead grass ended about twenty yards from the house, replaced by sand-colored gravel that covered the dirt up to the cracked lattice that attempted to camouflage the foundation. The only breaks in the monotone vegetation were the house, the stunted trees, the reddish scar of the dirt lane, and then several indistinct shapes that were in motion, roving along the edges of the road. She'd seen a lot of cows on the way in, but these animals looked too small to be cows. They did seem to be furry, ranging in color from black to brown to white to a combination of all three.

The shapes started to converge on the car, moving a lot faster than cows.

Einstein's tail began wagging so ferociously that it sounded like a small helicopter in the backseat.

"What is this place, Kev?"

"My retirement plan."

The animals reached the car—half a dozen dogs of various sizes. *Fantastic,* Alex thought. One could have been Einstein's twin. Another was gargantuan, looking like it was more closely related to equines than canines. She recognized a Doberman, two Rottweilers, and a traditionally colored German shepherd.

On the approach, the dogs had been totally silent and aggressive in their posture, but as soon as they saw Einstein, all the tails started wagging and they shared in a raucous chorus of barks.

"I train dogs for placement as guard dogs—commercial and private ownership. I also sell a few to families who just want a really well-behaved animal."

"How do you keep this under the radar?" she wanted to know.

"You can drive, Danny, they'll get out of the way," Kevin instructed.

Daniel had come to a stop when the dogs surrounded the car. Now he eased carefully forward and, as promised, the dogs moved to flank them and follow them in. Kevin then addressed Alex. "Nothing is in my name. No one ever sees my face. I have a partner for that."

As he spoke, she saw a figure walk out onto the porch—a large man wearing a cowboy hat. She couldn't make out any other details from this distance.

"Everybody knows the dog ranch is out here. Nobody bothers with us. It has no connection to my past life," Kevin was saying, but she wasn't paying much attention. Her eyes were riveted on the man waiting at the top of the porch stairs.

Kevin noticed her preoccupation. "What, Arnie? He's good people. I trust him with my life."

She frowned at that expression. Daniel was looking at her, too. He started to slow.

"Is there a problem, Alex?" he asked in a low voice.

She heard Kevin's teeth grind behind her. It was obvious how much he hated the way Daniel turned to her for guidance.

"It's just..." She frowned, then gestured to Daniel and his brother. "*This* is already a lot for me. The two of you. I don't know how to trust even you, let alone *another* person. Who only *this* one vouches for." She pointed at Kevin and he scowled.

"Well, that's just tough, shorty," Kevin answered. "Because this is your best option, and the guy I vouch for is part of the deal. If you want to execute this plan of yours, you'll have to suck it up."

"It will be okay," Daniel reassured her. He put his right hand lightly over her left.

Stupid how something like that could make you feel better. It wasn't like Daniel comprehended even the most basic elements of the danger they were in. But still, her heartbeat decelerated a tiny bit, and her right hand—unconsciously clenched around the door handle—relaxed.

Daniel drove slowly; the dogs kept up with them pretty easily until they stopped on the gravel. She was able to get a better look at the man waiting for them.

Arnie was a tall, heavyset man, part Latino, maybe part Native American. He could have been forty-five, but he could have been ten years older, too. His face was lined, but it looked like the kind of leathering that was due to wind and sun rather than age. His hair, which hung several inches below the hat, was salt-and-pepper gray. He stared at them without any emotion as they stopped, though there was no way he could have expected a third passenger, even if Kevin had told him about Daniel.

Einstein exploded out of the car as soon as Kevin cracked the door open and immediately set to sniffing and being sniffed. Daniel and Kevin climbed out almost as quickly, eager to stretch their long legs. Alex was more hesitant. There were a lot of dogs, and the brown-spotted horse-dog looked to be taller on all fours than she was standing. They seemed to be occupied with one another at the moment, but who knew how they would react to her?

"Don't be such a coward, Oleander," Kevin called.

Most of the dogs had converged on him now, nearly forcing him to the ground with the combined weight of their greeting.

Daniel came around the car and opened the door for her, then offered his hand. She sighed, irritated, and got out on her own. Her shoes crunched on the gravel, but the dogs didn't seem to notice her.

"Arnie," Kevin called over the sound of the happy dogs. "This is my brother, Danny. He'll be staying here. And, um, a temporary... guest, I suppose. Don't know what else to call her. But *guest* seems kind of over-positive, if you know what I mean."

"Your hospitality takes my breath away," Alex murmured.

Daniel laughed, then climbed the stairs in two quick steps. He offered his hand to the stone-faced man, who didn't look as tall standing next to Daniel, and they shook.

"Nice to meet you, Arnie. My brother's told me nothing at all about you, so I look forward to getting to know you better."

"Ditto, Danny," Arnie said. His voice was a rumbly baritone that sounded as if it wasn't used often enough to keep it running smoothly.

"And that's Alex. Don't listen to my brother; she's staying as long as she wants."

Arnie looked at her, focusing now. She waited for a reaction to the mess of her face, but he just regarded her coolly.

"A pleasure," she said.

He nodded.

"You can move your stuff inside," Kevin told them. He tried to walk toward the stairs, but the dogs were weaving around his legs at high speed. "Hey, boneheads! *Attention!*"

Like a small platoon of soldiers, the dogs immediately backed off a few paces, formed an actual line, and froze with their ears up.

"That's better. At ease."

The dogs sat down in unison, tongues lolling out in sharp-fanged smiles.

Kevin joined them at the door.

"Like I said, you can grab your stuff. Danny, there's a room for you at the top of the stairs on the right. As for you..." He looked down at Alex. "Well, I guess the room at the other end of the hall will work. I wasn't expecting extra company, so it's not fitted up as a bedroom."

"I've got a cot."

"I don't have any stuff," Daniel said, and though she listened for it, she didn't hear any sadness in the words; he was putting up a good front. "Do you need help with yours, Alex?"

She shook her head. "I'll only take a few things in. The rest I'll stash somewhere outside the fence."

Daniel raised his eyebrows in confusion, but Kevin was nodding.

"I've had to run out in the middle of the night before," she explained to Daniel, pitching her voice low, though Arnie could probably still hear. She had no idea how much he knew about Kevin's old job. "Sometimes it's not so easy to get back to pick up your things."

Daniel's brow creased. Some of the sadness she'd been expecting before flickered across his expression. This was a world not many people entered on purpose.

"You don't need to worry about that here," Kevin said. "We're secure."

Kevin was one of those people who *had* chosen this life, which made his every judgment suspect to her.

"Better to keep in practice," she insisted.

Kevin shrugged. "If that's what you want, I know a place that might work."

· · ·

THE HOUSE WAS quite a bit nicer on the inside than the outside. She'd expected moldy wallpaper, 1970s oak paneling, sagging couches, linoleum, and Formica. While there was still an attempt at a rustic theme, the fixtures were new and state of the art. There were even granite countertops on the kitchen island under the elk-horn chandelier.

"Wow," Daniel murmured.

"But how many contractors were inside this place?" she muttered to herself. Too many witnesses.

Kevin heard, though she hadn't meant him to. "None, actually. Arnie used to be in construction. We got all the materials from across the state line and did the work ourselves. Well, mostly Arnie did it. Satisfied?"

Alex pursed her balloon lips.

"How did you two meet?" Daniel asked Arnie politely.

She really ought to study Daniel, Alex thought, practice his ways of interacting. *This* was how to act like a normal person. Either she'd never really known how or she'd forgotten completely. She had her lines down for waitressing, for cubicle jobs; she knew how to respond in a work environment in the least memorable way. She knew how to talk to patients when she was doing her illicit doctor gig. Before that, she'd learned the best ways to pull answers from a subject. But outside of the prescribed roles, she always avoided contact.

It was Kevin who answered Daniel's question. "Arnie was in a little trouble that related tangentially to a project I was working on a while back. He wanted out, and he gave me some very valuable information in exchange for my killing him."

The silent Arnie grinned widely.

"We hit it off," Kevin continued, "and kept in touch. When I decided to start preparing for retirement, I contacted him. Our needs and interests aligned perfectly."

"Match made in heaven," Alex said in a sweet voice. *Great, so people might be looking for* him, *too,* she didn't add aloud.

Kevin and Daniel went to the downstairs master to gather a wardrobe for Daniel and outfit him with toiletries. Alex showed herself upstairs, easily locating the small room Kevin had offered her. It would work. He was using it for storage right now, but there was enough space for her cot and personal things. One of the large plastic storage bins would make a decent substitute for a desktop. The bathroom was down the hall; it connected to both the hallway and what would be Daniel's bedroom.

It had been a very long time since she'd shared a bathroom. At least this one was bigger and posher than she was used to.

The brothers were still busy when she went back to the car to sort through her stuff. There were three dogs on the porch; one she was pretty sure was Einstein, one huge black Rottweiler, and a reddish-brown, sad-faced dog with floppy ears who reminded her of the dog whose leg gets broken at the end of *Lady and the Tramp.* So that probably meant he was a hound dog or a bloodhound or something—she wasn't sure which was which.

The Rottweiler and the hound started toward her with more interest than menace, but it was enough for her to take a huge step back toward the door. Einstein raised his head and gave a low, cough-like bark, and the other two stopped. They sat down where they were, like they had when Kevin had given them the at-ease command.

She wasn't sure if Einstein actually had the authority to give the other dogs orders — did dogs recognize rank? — so she moved cautiously along the porch, waiting for them to attack. They held their relaxed positions, just watching her curiously. As she passed, the hound's tail thumped loudly against the wooden slats of the floor, and she had the odd impression that he was playing up the sad eyes in anticipation of being petted. She hoped he wasn't too disappointed that she wasn't brave enough to try it.

She dug through her things wedged in the trunk, pulling together an emergency kit and fitting it into a backpack; this she would keep with her at all times. She took most of her dirty clothes to wash inside — hopefully there was a washing machine — but left the businessy stuff with the other bags in the trunk. She had to have at least one set of clothes with her off-property stash. She'd run out one memorable night — after assassin two was gassed trying to cut her throat — in just her underwear and had to steal a neighbor's coveralls out of the back of his work van. She'd learned that lesson. And to always sleep in pajamas that could double as daytime clothes.

Even with the cot, it was an easy load to take up the stairs. She went back for one of the duffel bags, this one containing her basic lab gear. She shouldn't waste the downtime when she could be prepping. As she passed the master bedroom, she heard squabbling, and the sound made her happy to be out of the way of it.

The lab setup was a quick process after so much practice. One of her glass flasks was chipped, but it looked like it was still usable. She pieced her rotary evaporator together and then laid out a few condensers and two stainless-steel vessels. She'd used almost all of her *Survive*, and the way this week was going, she would probably need more. She had plenty of D-phenylalanine, but she was disappointed when she checked on her opioid store. Less than she'd thought. Not enough to synthesize more *Survive*, and she had only one dose left.

She was still scowling at her lack of supplies when she heard Kevin calling up the stairs.

"Hey, Oleander. Ticktock."

By the time she got through the front door, Kevin was already in the sedan, Daniel in the passenger seat. When Kevin spotted her hesitating on the porch, he held the horn down for one annoyingly long blast. She walked as slowly as possible to the car and climbed into the backseat with a frown — dog hair was going to get all over her.

They drove along the same slender dirt lane out through the gate and a few miles farther before turning onto an even less pronounced road that headed in a mostly westerly direction. This road was nothing more than two tire tracks worn into the grass. They followed it for about six or seven miles, she guessed. For the first few miles, she caught glimpses of the ranch's fence line, but after that, they were too far west for her to see it anymore.

"Is this your land, too?"

"Yes, after passing through a few other names. This parcel is owned by a corporation that is not affiliated in any way with the parcel the ranch is on. I do know how to do this, you know."

"Of course."

The landscape started to change on her right. The yellow-white grass cut off at a strangely even border and beyond that, the ground turned to level, bare red dirt. When they started to wind back to the north toward that border, she was surprised to see that the red dirt was actually a riverbank. The water was the same color as the red bank, and it moved smoothly west, without rapids or obstacles. It was about forty feet across at the widest point she could see. She watched the flow of the water as they drove roughly parallel to it, fascinated by its existence here in the middle of the dry grassland. For all its smooth progress, the river seemed to be moving fairly quickly.

There was no fence this time. A crumbling-down barn, grayed by the sun, sat about fifty yards from the road, looking as if it had reached the end of its very long life and was only waiting for the right weather system to put it out of its misery. She'd seen hundreds just like it on their quick tour through Arkansas and Oklahoma.

It was nowhere near as nice as her milking barn.

Kevin turned toward it, driving right through the grass now; she couldn't see any official road or pathway.

She waited in the running car while he jumped out to unlock the massive antique padlock and swing the doors open. Outside, in the brilliant light of the open, cloudless sky, it was impossible to see anything inside the murky interior. He was back quickly to drive the car into the darkness.

This time, the inside matched the outside's promise. Dim light filtered through the slats of the barn to illuminate piles of corroded farm equipment, most of a rusted tractor, the shells of a few ancient cars, and a massive stack of dusty hay in the back, half covered with a tarp. Nothing worth stealing, or even examining more closely. If anyone bothered to break in here, the only valuable thing he would find was shade.

When the engine cut off, she thought she could just make out the rush of the river. They couldn't be more than a couple hundred yards away from it.

"This will work," she said. "I'll stick my stuff in a corner and you can use this car when you head back."

"Roger that."

She piled her four rectangular duffels into a shadowy crevice, partially hidden behind a stack of spiderwebbed firewood. The webs were dusty.

Kevin was rummaging near a pile of blackened metal—maybe parts for another tractor—and came back with a tattered old tarp, which he spread over her bags.

"Nice touch," she approved.

"It's all in the presentation."

"I guess you haven't gotten around to fixing this place up yet," Daniel commented, one hand on the closest car shell.

"I kind of like it how it is," Kevin said. "Let me give you a tour. Just in case you need something while I'm gone. Which you won't. But still."

She nodded thoughtfully. "Overpreparation is the key to success. It's kind of my mantra."

"Then you'll love this," Kevin said.

He walked to the half-tractor and bent down to fiddle with the lug nuts in the center of the huge flat tire.

"There's a keypad behind this hubcap." He spoke directly to Daniel. "The code is our birthday. Not too original, but I wanted you to be able to remember it easily. Same combination for the lock on the outside door."

A second later, the entire front face of the tire swung outward—it wasn't made of rubber, it was something stiffer and lighter, and it moved on hinges. Inside, an arsenal.

"Oh, *yes,*" she breathed. "Batcave."

She immediately spotted a SIG Sauer that matched the gun she'd briefly stolen from him. He really didn't need two.

Kevin gave her a puzzled look. "Batman doesn't use guns."

"Whatever."

Daniel was examining the hinges on the hidden door. "This is very clever. Did Arnie make it?"

"No, I did, thanks."

"I didn't know you were handy. And when did you have the chance to do this, what with toppling cartels and all that?"

"Downtime between jobs. I can't sit still or I go crazy."

He closed up the fake tire and then gestured to the car shell near where Daniel had been standing before. "Lift the top of the battery and type in the same code. That one's rifles, the next is rocket launchers and grenades."

Daniel laughed, then caught his brother's expression. "Wait, really?"

"She likes preparation; I like to be extremely well armed. Okay, now, this one I couldn't hide so well, and anyway, it's the kind of thing I might need quickly."

Kevin walked around the side of the massive hay tower, and they followed. The tarp hung to the ground on this side. She was pretty confident she knew at least the category of what he was hiding here, and sure enough, he lifted the tarp to reveal a cozy garage behind the hay with a very large vehicle wedged inside. From the way he stood, it was obviously his pride and joy.

"There's a truck back at the ranch that blends in, but *this* is here in case of emergencies."

Daniel made a small noise like a hiccup. Alex glanced at him and realized he was trying not to laugh. She got the joke immediately.

They had both dealt with DC traffic for years, though he more recently. And despite the congestion and tight parking options that were more suited for a Vespa than a medium-size sedan, there was always that one guy trying to shove his gigantic compensation-mobile into a parallel slot. As if anyone needed a Hummer anywhere, let alone in the city. You might as well just get a vanity plate that read D-BAG and be done with it.

When Daniel saw her mouth twitch, he lost his own control. Suddenly he was snorting with laughter. It was an awkward, infectious *heh-heh-snort-heh-heh* that was much funnier than the military monster truck. She started chortling along, surprised at how out of control the laughter felt almost immediately. She hadn't laughed big like this in so long; she'd forgotten how it grabbed your whole body and wouldn't let go.

Daniel had one hand on the hay while he bent over, the other hand on his side like he had a stitch. It was the funniest thing she'd ever seen.

"What?" Kevin demanded. "*What?*"

Daniel tried to calm himself to answer, but then a sudden burst of giggles from Alex derailed him, and he guffawed again, gasping for air between outbursts.

"This is a state-of-the-art assault vehicle," Kevin complained, half shouting to be heard over their frenzied hilarity. "It has solid rubber tires and missile-proof glass. There are panels through the whole body that a tank can't crush. This thing could save your life."

He was just making it worse. Tears streamed down both their faces. Alex's lip was protesting and her cheeks ached. Daniel was hiccupping for real now, unable to straighten up.

Kevin threw up his hands in disgust and stomped away from them. They busted up again.

Finally, several long minutes after Kevin had disappeared, Alex started to be able to breathe. Daniel's laughter was trailing off as well, though he was still holding his side. She could sympathize; she had a cramp, too. Oddly exhausted, she sat down on the hay-strewn floor and put her head between her knees, working to even out her breathing. After a second, she felt Daniel settle next to her. His hand came to rest lightly on her back.

"Ah, I needed that." He sighed. "It was starting to feel like nothing would ever be really funny again."

"I can't remember the last time I laughed like that. My stomach *hurts*."

"Mine too." And then he laughed another *heh-heh-heh*.

"Don't start," she begged.

"Sorry, I'll try. I might be a little hysterical."

"Huh. Maybe we should slap each other."

He laughed another burst, and she couldn't help but giggle.

"Stop," she moaned.

"Should we talk about sad things?" he wondered.

"Like living a life of isolation and fear, hunted every minute of the day?" she suggested.

It felt like the murky barn got even darker, and she immediately regretted speaking. Even if it hurt, it had felt so nice to laugh.

"That's a good one," Daniel said quietly. "How about letting down all the people who count on you?"

"Doesn't really apply for me, but it's definitely a depressing idea. Though in your case, I doubt anyone will look at it that way. They'll probably think you've been murdered. Everyone will be heartbroken and they'll leave flowers and candles in front of the school marquee."

"Do you think they will?"

"Sure. There will probably even be teddy bears."

"Maybe. Or maybe no one will miss me. Maybe they'll say, 'Finally, we got rid of that joker and now we can hire a real history teacher. The girls' volleyball team might actually have a chance with him out of the way. You know what? Let's just find a chimp to do his job and put his salary into the retirement fund.'"

She nodded with false gravity. "You could be right."

He smiled, then was serious again. "Did anyone burn candles for you?"

"There wasn't really anyone left to care. If Barnaby had been the one to survive, he might have lit a candle for me. I did a few times for him, in cathedrals. I'm not Catholic, but I couldn't figure out another place where I could do it inconspicuously. I know Barnaby's not around to care, but I needed something. Closure, mourning, whatever."

A pause. "Did you love him?"

"Yes. Aside from my work—and you've seen how warm and cuddly *that* was—he was all I had."

Daniel nodded. "Well, I don't feel like laughing anymore."

"We probably needed the release. Now we can get back to our regularly scheduled depression."

"Sounds lovely."

"Hey, Moe and Curly," Kevin called from outside the barn. "Are you ready to get back to work, or do you want to giggle like schoolgirls a little while longer?"

"Um, giggle, I guess?" Daniel called back.

She couldn't help it—she snickered.

Daniel put his hand gently over her bruised mouth. "None of that, now. We'd better go see what work there is to do."

CHAPTER 13

Kevin kept a firing range set up behind the barn, facing the river. Alex eyed it suspiciously, but she had to concede that random gunshots were probably less likely to arouse attention in rural Texas than anywhere else in the world.

"When's the last time you picked up a gun?" he asked Daniel.

"Hmm...with Dad, I guess."

"Seriously?" Kevin heaved a sigh. "Well, I suppose all we can do is hope you remember *something*."

He'd brought out an array of weapons and laid them on a hay bale. Other hay bales, each stacked to a man's height and wearing printed black silhouettes, were arranged at varying distances from their position. Some were so far off she could barely make them out.

"We could start with the handguns, but what I'd like is to try you on some rifles. The best way to stay safe is to be shooting from very, very far away. I'd rather keep you out of the close-up stuff if I can."

"These don't look like any rifles I've ever used," Daniel said.

"They're snipers. This one"—he patted the McMillan he wore slung across his back—"has the record for the longest distance kill at over one mile."

Daniel's eyes widened in disbelief. "How do you even know who you want to kill from that far away?"

"Spotters, but don't worry about that. You don't need to learn that kind of distance. I just want you to be able to sit in a perch and pick people off if it comes to that."

"I don't know if I could actually shoot a person."

It was Kevin's turn to look disbelieving. "You'd better figure that out. Because if you don't shoot, the person coming sure as hell won't hesitate to take advantage."

Daniel seemed about to argue, but Kevin waved the mini-conflict away. "Look, let's just see if you can remember how to shoot a gun."

After Kevin reviewed the basics, it was evident that Daniel did remember plenty. He took to the rifle with much more instinctive ease than Alex had ever felt with firearms. He was clearly a natural, while she never had been.

After enough rounds were fired for her to get over the fear of all the noise, she lifted the SIG Sauer.

"Hey, do you mind if I try this out on the closer targets?"

"Sure," Kevin said, not looking up from his brother's sight line. "Join the party."

The SIG was heavier than her PPK and had a more substantial kick, but in a way that felt good. Powerful. It took her a few rounds to get used to the sight, but then she was about as accurate with it as she was with her own gun. She thought that with time, she would get better. Maybe she'd be able to get in some consistent practice while she was here. It wasn't the kind of thing she usually got to indulge in.

When Kevin put an end to the shooting instruction, the sun was almost all the way down. It colored all the yellow grass deep red, as if it were actually touching down on the horizon and setting all the dried brush ablaze.

Reluctantly, she put the SIG away with the other guns. It wasn't as if she didn't know the code. She might do some stocking up when Kevin's *party* was over.

"Well, Danny, it's good to see you've still got it . . . and that my talent isn't just a fluke. Mom and Dad passed us some solid genes," Kevin said when they were heading back to the house.

"For target practice. I still don't think I could do what you do."

Kevin snorted. "Things change when someone is trying to kill you."

Daniel looked out his side window, clearly unconvinced.

"Okay." Kevin sighed. "Think of it this way. Imagine someone you want to protect—Mom, for example—is standing behind you. Some new recruits need to visualize in order to get themselves in the right frame of mind."

"That doesn't really fit with shooting from a sniper's perch," Daniel pointed out.

"Then picture Mom getting stuffed into the trunk of a car by the guy in your crosshairs. Use your imagination."

Daniel was done. "Fine, fine."

She could tell he still wasn't persuaded, but she had to agree with Kevin on this one topic. When someone came for you, your survival instincts kicked in. In a him-or-you situation, you always chose yourself. Daniel wouldn't know how that felt until the hunters caught up with him. She hoped he'd never have to learn the feeling.

Well, Kevin would do what he could, and so would she. Maybe together they could make the world a safer place for Daniel Beach.

Back at the ranch, the tour continued. Kevin took them to a sleek modern outbuilding, invisible from the front of the house and full of dogs.

Each animal had a climate-controlled stall and access to its own private outdoor run. Kevin explained the exercise schedule to Daniel, which dogs were already spoken for and which were ready to be listed, training him for his future life at the ranch, she assumed. Daniel seemed to love it, petting all the dogs and learning their names. The dogs adored the attention—and asked for it; she wished she could turn down the volume of the barks and whines. The dogs who ran loose were apparently graduates of the program; these followed Kevin on the rounds.

Alex suspected Kevin had let her tag along just to make her uncomfortable. The horse-size spotted one—a Great Dane, she learned—was constantly on her heels, and she was sure the dog hadn't decided to do that on his own. Kevin must have given some unseen command. She could feel the giant's breath on the nape of her neck, and guessed there were probably flecks of saliva on the back of her shirt. The hound dog was tailing her, too, but she thought he might have chosen the assignment for himself. He was still milking those sad eyes every time Alex glanced at him. The other graduates circled Daniel and Kevin, except for Einstein, who stuck close to Kevin only and seemed to take troop inspections very seriously.

They passed stalls with German shepherds, Dobermans, Rottweilers, and several other working-group dogs she didn't know names for. Alex kept to the middle of the long pathway between kennels and didn't touch anything. Always best to minimize the number of fingerprints for wiping down later.

There were two small hound puppies sharing a stall, and Kevin mentioned to Daniel that they were Lola's offspring, gesturing to the bloodhound tailing Alex.

"Oh, Lola, huh? Sorry," Alex murmured, too low for the men to hear. "I shouldn't have assumed."

Lola appeared to know she was being addressed. She stared up at Alex hopefully, and her tail pounded against Alex's leg. Alex leaned down quickly to pat her on the head.

Kevin made a disgusted sound and she straightened up to see him staring at her.

"Lola likes *everyone*," Kevin said to Daniel. "Great nose, poor taste. I'm trying to breed out the lack of discrimination while keeping the olfactory genius."

Daniel shook his head. "Enough already."

"I'm not kidding. I expect better instincts from these animals."

Alex squatted to scrub her fingers along Lola's sides like she'd seen Daniel do, knowing it would drive Kevin crazy. Lola immediately rolled over, offering her belly. Abruptly, the giant dog lay down on Alex's other side, and she was nearly positive he was also looking hopeful. She carefully patted his shoulder with one hand, and he didn't bite it off. His tail beat the ground twice. She took that as encouragement and scratched behind his ears.

"C'mon, Khan, not you, too!"

Both Alex and the Great Dane ignored him. She twisted down so that she was sitting cross-legged with both dogs in view and her back to the brothers. If she was going to be surrounded by furry killing machines, she might as well have a few of them on her side.

Lola licked the back of her hand. It was disgusting, but also kind of sweet.

"Looks like Alex has a fan," Daniel said.

"Whatever. Over here is where we keep the chow. Arnie picks it up every other week in Lawton. We've got most of what we need for..."

The rest of what Kevin said was lost in the yips and grumbles of the dogs left behind.

She stroked the dogs for a few minutes more, not sure how they would take it when she quit. Finally, she rose cautiously to her feet. Both Lola and Khan were quickly on all fours and seemed totally happy to follow her as she walked back to the house. They escorted her right to the door and then made themselves comfortable on the porch.

"Good girl, good boy," she said as she went inside.

Kevin had probably meant to intimidate her, but she liked the way it felt as if the dogs were actually looking out for her, rather than keeping an eye on her. She supposed it was what they were trained for. It was a comfortable feeling. If she had a different lifestyle, it might be nice to add a dog. Except she didn't know where she would get a dog-size gas mask.

Arnie was on the couch in the great room, parked in front of a flat-screen TV that was mounted on the opposite wall. He had a microwave dinner in his lap to which he was assiduously applying himself; he didn't react to her entrance.

The smell of the food—macaroni and Salisbury steak—had her mouth watering. Not a four-star meal, but she was *really* hungry.

"Um, do you mind if I help myself to some food?" she asked.

Arnie grunted without looking away from the baseball game. She hoped it was an affirmative, because she was already en route to the fridge.

The refrigerator — an impressive, double-wide stainless-steel affair — was crushingly bare. Condiments, a few sports drinks, and a supersize jar of pickles. It also needed to be cleaned. She checked the freezer drawer and there found pay dirt: it was stuffed full of dinners like the one Arnie was eating. She heated a cheese pizza in the microwave and ate it on a bar stool scooted up to the island. Arnie seemed completely oblivious to her presence the entire time.

If you *had* to add another person into the equation, Arnie wasn't half bad, really.

She heard the men coming back, so she headed upstairs. They'd all been forced into close quarters on the ride here, but now that there were rooms to retire to, it was possible to give one another some space. She knew Daniel and his brother had a lot to sort through, and there was no reason she needed to hear any of it.

There wasn't a ton to do in her storage room. She refilled her little acid syringes, though she couldn't think of a scenario where she would need them here. She could have worked on harvesting the kernels out of her peach pits, but she'd left them in the barn. It wasn't worth taking the chance to try to connect to the Internet, just in case she was going to be here for a while, and she didn't have any reading material. There was one project she'd been thinking about, but part of her violently rejected the idea of writing any of it down. Though national security hadn't exactly been her friend for a while, she still wasn't going to put the public in danger. Writing her memoirs was not an option.

But she needed to think it all through in an organized way. Maybe if she just wrote some key words to help her remember?

She was sure of one fact: Something she'd overheard in the six years she'd worked with Dr. Barnaby had been the reason for the lab attack and for every assassination attempt that had followed. If she could pinpoint the information involved, she would have a much better idea of who was behind the murder agenda.

The problem was that she'd heard a lot of things, and all of it was insanely sensitive.

She started to make a list. She created a code, designating the biggest issues, the nuclear ones, as A1 through A4. Four big bombs that had been controlled during her tenure. Those were the most serious projects she'd worked on. It would have to have been something of the gravest nature to merit destroying her section.

She hoped. If it was some petty whim by a cheating admiral who thought he might have been mentioned in an investigation, she had no chance of ever figuring it out.

T1 through T49 were all the non-nuclear terrorist actions she could remember. There were minor plans—ones that hadn't come to much—that were slipping through her memory, she knew. The major plans, T1 through T17, ranged from biological attacks to economic destabilization to importing suicide bombers.

She was trying to come up with a system to help her keep all of the different actions separate (the first letter of the city of origin plus the first letter of the target city? Would that differentiate the events enough? Would she forget the meaning of her notations? But listing the full place-names was too much information to commit to writing) when she heard Kevin calling for her.

"Hey, Oleander! Where are you hiding?"

She snapped her computer shut and walked to the top of the stairs. "Did you need something?"

He came around the corner and looked up at her. Both of them held their position, keeping the length of the stairs between them.

"Just a heads-up. I'm taking off. I left a phone with Daniel. I'll call when I'm ready for you to send the e-mail."

"Prepaid disposable?"

"This ain't my first rodeo, sister."

"Well, good luck, I guess."

"Don't turn my house into some death lab while I'm gone."

Too late. She suppressed a grin. "I'll try to rein myself in."

"This is probably it. I'd say it was a pleasure..."

She smiled. "But we've always been so honest with each other. Why start lying now?"

He smiled in return, then was suddenly serious. "You'll keep an eye on him?"

She was slightly taken aback by the request. That Kevin would entrust his brother to her this way. And even more shocked by her own response.

"Of course," she promised immediately. It was disturbing to realize how sincere her answer was, and how involuntary. Of course she would keep Daniel safe to the best of her ability. It wasn't even a question. She remembered again the strange feeling that had first surfaced in the dark of her torture tent—her premonition that the stakes had doubled from one life to two.

Part of her wondered when she would be free from this feeling of responsibility. Maybe this was always how someone felt after interrogating an innocent person. Or maybe it only happened when that person was as...what was the right word? *Honest? Virtuous? Wholesome?* Someone as *good* as Daniel.

He grunted, then turned his back and headed toward the main room of the house. She couldn't see him anymore, but she could still hear him.

"Danny, c'mere. We've got one more thing we need to do."

Curious—and procrastinating; the catalog of nightmares past was beginning to give her a headache—she walked quietly down the stairs to see what was happening. She knew Kevin well enough to be sure he wasn't calling Daniel over for a heartfelt good-bye, complete with hugs and snuggles.

The front room was empty—Arnie had cleared out—but she could hear voices through the screen door. She went out to the porch, where Lola was waiting for her. She absently scratched the dog's head while she took in the scene, lit by the porch lamps and the headlights of the sedan.

Einstein, Khan, and the Rottweiler were all lined up at attention in front of Kevin. He looked to be addressing them while Daniel watched.

Kevin started with his star pupil. "Come, Einstein."

The dog stepped forward. Kevin turned his body to point at Daniel. "That's your honey, Einstein. *Honey.*"

Einstein ran to Daniel, tail wagging, and commenced sniffing up and down his legs. From Daniel's expression, he was just as confused as Alex was.

"Okay," Kevin said to the other dogs. "Khan, Gunther, *watch.*"

He turned back to Einstein and Daniel, dropping into a wrestler's crouch and approaching slowly.

"I'm gonna get your honey," he taunted the dog in a growly voice.

Einstein wheeled around and put himself between Daniel and Kevin's advance. The hackles rose at least six inches off the top of his shoulders, and a menacing snarl slid from between his suddenly exposed fangs. The demon dog she'd first met was back.

Kevin feinted to the right, and Einstein blocked him. He dove left toward Daniel and the dog launched himself at his master, taking him down with a solid-sounding thud. In the same second, Einstein had his jaws wrapped around Kevin's neck. It would have been a frightening picture if it weren't for the smile on Kevin's face.

"Good boy! Smart boy!"

"Kill! Kill!" Alex whispered under her breath.

Einstein released and jumped back, tail wagging again. He pranced a few steps back and forth, ready to play another game.

"Okay, Khan, your turn."

Once again, Kevin identified Daniel as the Great Dane's *honey* and then made as if to attack. Einstein stayed with Khan; supervising, Alex imagined. The big dog simply shoved one massive paw against Kevin's chest as he attacked and toppled him backward. Khan used the same paw to pin him to the ground while Einstein moved in for the jugular.

"Kill!" she said again, louder.

Kevin heard this time and shot her a look that clearly said: *If I weren't in the middle of teaching these dogs something very important, I would have them tear you to shreds.*

Khan sat out the next round, while Einstein supervised again. The barrel-chested Rottweiler took Kevin down even harder than Einstein had. She heard the breath crush out of his chest; that *had* to hurt. She smiled.

"Do you mind if I ask what all that was about?" Daniel asked as Kevin heaved himself to his feet and started brushing the dirt off his dark jeans and black T-shirt.

"It's a command behavior I created for personal-protection dogs. These three dogs will guard you with their lives from here on out. They'll also probably be under your feet a lot."

"Why *honey?*"

"It's just a word. But, to be honest, I was mostly picturing it being used for women and children..."

"Thanks," Daniel retorted.

"Oh, relax. You know I don't mean it that way. Think of a better command and we'll use it with the next generation."

There was an awkward pause. Kevin looked at the car, then back to his brother.

"Look, you're safe here. But stay close to the dogs anyway. And the poison lady. She's tough. Just don't eat anything she tries to feed you."

"I'm sure we'll be fine."

"If anything happens, give Einstein this command." He held out a little piece of paper, about the size of a business card. Daniel took it and stuck it in his pocket without looking at it. Alex thought it was odd that Kevin wouldn't say it out loud. Or maybe he just wrote it down because he didn't trust Daniel's memory.

Kevin looked now as if a hug was actually on his mind, despite what she'd imagined before, but then Daniel's posture stiffened slightly, and Kevin turned away. He kept talking as he walked to the sedan.

"We'll talk more when I get back. Keep the phone on you. I'll call when things are set."

"Be careful."

"Wilco."

Kevin got in the car and revved the engine. He put his right hand on the back of the passenger headrest and watched out the rear window as he maneuvered the car to face the road. He didn't look at his brother again. Then the red taillights were fading into the distance.

A weight seemed to lift off Alex's chest with his leaving.

Daniel watched the car for a minute, the loyal three all sitting close to his feet. Then he turned and walked thoughtfully up the porch steps. The dogs moved with him. Kevin hadn't been kidding about them staying underfoot. Daniel was lucky Khan kept to the rear or he wouldn't have been able to see where he was going.

He stopped next to Alex and turned to face the same way she did, both of them staring out into the featureless black night. The dogs arranged themselves around their feet. Lola got muscled out by the Rottweiler and whined once in protest. Daniel gripped the porch railing in both hands, holding tight like he was expecting a shift in gravity.

"Is it bad that I'm relieved he's gone?" Daniel asked. "He's just . . . a lot, you know? I can't process everything with him always *talking*."

His right hand relaxed its hold, then moved to rest on the small of her back in an almost automatic manner, like he hadn't consciously decided to place it there.

The way he was always touching her reminded Alex of the experiments she and Barnaby had done years back with sensory deprivation tanks. It was an effective means of getting someone to talk without leaving any marks, but on the whole, it took too much time to be the best option.

Anyone who went into the tank, though, no matter his level of resistance, had the same reaction when he was let out: he craved physical contact like a drug fix. She thought of one memorable experience with an army corporal—a volunteer they worked with in the initial testing phase—and the very long and somewhat inappropriate hug she'd received upon his exit. They'd had to have security peel him off her.

Daniel must feel a lot like that soldier. For days he'd been completely out of touch with anything he considered to be normal life. He would need the reassurance that another warm, breathing human being was there next to him.

Of course, this diagnosis also applied to herself; she'd been out of touch with normal life for much longer than Daniel had. While that meant she was used to the lack, it also meant that she'd been starved of human contact for a very long time. Maybe this was why she felt so improbably comforted whenever he touched her.

"I don't think it's a bad thing," she answered him. "It's natural that you'd need space to deal with all of this."

He laughed once, a darker sound than his earlier fit of hysteria. "Except that I don't need space from anyone but him." He sighed. "Kev has always been like that, even when we were kids. Has to be in charge, has to have the spotlight."

"Funny traits for a spy."

"I guess he's figured out a way to suppress those instincts when he's working—and then it all comes surging out when he's not."

"I wouldn't know anything about it. Only child."

"Lucky, lucky you." He sighed again.

"He's probably not so bad." Why was she defending Kevin? she wondered. Just trying to cheer Daniel up, maybe. "If you weren't stuck in this very extreme situation, he'd be easier to deal with."

"That's fair. I should try to be fair. I guess I'm just ... angry. So angry. I know he didn't mean to do it, but *his* life choices have suddenly destroyed all of *mine*. That's so ... *Kevin*."

"It takes a while to accept what has happened to you," Alex said slowly. "You'll probably stay angry, but it gets easier. Most of the time,

I forget how angry I am. It's different for me, though. It was people I didn't know very well who did this to me. It wasn't my family."

"But your enemies actually tried to kill you. That's worse; don't even try to compare what happened to you to what's happening to me. Kevin never meant to hurt me. It's just hard, you know? I feel like I've died, but I have to keep on living anyway. I don't know how."

She patted his left hand on the rail, remembering how that had made her feel better in the car. The skin over his knuckles was stretched tight.

"You'll learn, like I did. It turns into a routine. The life you had before gets...dimmer. And you get philosophical. I mean, disasters happen to people all the time. What's the difference between this and having your nation overrun by guerrilla warfare, right? Or your town destroyed by a tsunami? Everything changes, and nothing is as safe as it was. Only that safety was always just an illusion anyway... Sorry, that might just be the world's crappiest pep talk."

He laughed. "Not the *very* crappiest. I do feel infinitesimally better."

"Well, then I guess my job here is done."

"How did you get started with all this?" The question rolled out lightly, as if it were a simple thing.

She hesitated. "What do you mean?"

"Why did you choose this...profession? Before they tried to kill you, I mean. Were you in the military? Did you volunteer?"

Again, the questions were spoken lightly, like he was inquiring how she had become a financial planner or an interior decorator. The very lack of emotion was its own tell. He kept his face forward, staring out into the darkness.

She didn't evade this time. She would want to know this, too, if fate had saddled her with one of her peers as a companion. It was something she'd asked Barnaby in the early days of their association. His answer wasn't much different from hers.

"I never actually chose it," she explained slowly. "And no, I wasn't military. I was in medical school when they approached me.

I'd first been interested in pathology, but then I shifted focus. I was deep into a particular vein of research—you could call it a kind of chemical mind control, I guess. There weren't many people doing precisely what I was doing, and there were a lot of roadblocks in my way—funding, tools, test subjects…well, most of it came down to funding. The professors I was working under didn't even fully understand my research, so I didn't have a lot of help.

"These mysterious government officials showed up and offered me an opportunity. They picked up the tab for my massive student loans. I got to finish my schooling while focusing my research toward my new handlers' goals. When I graduated, I went to work in their lab, where every technology I could dream of was at my disposal and money was never an object.

"It was obvious what they had me creating. They didn't lie to me. I was aware of the work I was contributing to, but it sounded noble, the way they described it. I was helping my country…"

He waited, still staring ahead.

"I didn't think I would be the one who would actually *use* my creations on a subject. I thought I would just be supplying the tools they needed…" She shook her head back and forth slowly. "It didn't work like that, though. The antibodies I'd created were too specialized—the doctor who administered them had to understand how they worked. So that left exactly one person."

The hand on the small of her back didn't move—it was too still, frozen in place.

"The only person ever inside the interrogation room with me, besides the subject, was Barnaby. At first, he handled the questioning. He frightened me in the beginning, but he turned out to be such a gentle person…We were mostly in the lab, creating and developing. Actual interrogations made up only about five percent of my job." She took a deep breath. "But often, when there was a crisis at hand, they needed to be running multiple interrogations simultaneously; speed was always critical. I had to be able to work alone. I didn't want to do it, but I understood why it needed to be that way.

"It wasn't as difficult as I'd thought it would be. The hard part was realizing how good I was at it. That scared me. It's never really stopped scaring me." Barnaby was the only one she'd confessed this to. He'd told her not to worry; she was just one of those people who were good at anything they tried. An overachiever.

Alex cleared the sudden lump out of her throat. "But I got results. I saved a lot of lives. And I never killed anyone—not while I was working for the government." Now she stared out into the darkness, too. She didn't want to see his reaction. "I've always wondered if that was enough to make me less than a monster."

She was fairly certain, though, that the answer was no.

"Hmmm..." It was just a low, lingering sound in the back of his throat.

She kept staring at the dark nothing in front of her. She'd never tried to explain this choice—the line of dominoes that had made her what she was—to another human being. She didn't think she'd done a very good job.

And then he quietly chuckled.

Now she turned to stare up at him in disbelief.

His lips were puckered in an unwilling half smile. "I was braced for something really disturbing, but that all sounded a lot more reasonable than I expected."

Her brows pulled together. He found her story *reasonable?*

His stomach growled. He laughed again, and the tension of the moment seemed to vanish with the sound.

"Did Kevin not feed you?" she asked. "This is a help-yourself kind of place, I guess."

"I could use some food," he agreed.

She led him to the freezer, trying to hide her surprise that he seemed to be treating her no differently than before. It had felt dangerous, speaking all of that out loud. But then, she supposed he already knew the worst of it, having learned it in the cruelest way possible. Her explanation was really nothing after that.

Hungry Daniel might have been, but he wasn't too thrilled by the available supplies. He unenthusiastically chose a pizza, as she had, grumbling about Kevin's deficiencies in the kitchen, which seemed to be long-standing, from what she heard. The conversation rolled easily, like she was just an ordinary person to him.

"I don't know where he gets all that manic energy," Daniel said. "Eating nothing but this."

"Arnie can't be much of a cook, either. Where'd he go, anyway?"

"He hit the sack before Kev left. Early riser, I infer. I think his room is back that way." Daniel gestured in the opposite direction from the stairs.

"Does he seem a little strange to you?"

"What, with the mute thing? I figure that's just the glue in his relationship with Kevin. You have to be able to stomach listening to someone else talk nonstop if you're going to be friends with Kev. No room for your own words."

She snorted.

"There was ice cream under the pizza. You want some?" he asked.

She did, so the search began for silverware and bowls. Daniel did locate an ice cream scooper and soupspoons, but they had to put the ice cream into coffee mugs. As she watched him ladle the ice cream out of the carton, something occurred to her.

"Are you left-handed?"

"Er, yes."

"Oh. I thought Kevin was right-handed, but if you're identical twins, doesn't that mean —"

"Usually," Daniel said, passing her the first mug. The ice cream was plain vanilla, not her first choice, but she was happy to have any kind of sugar right now. "We're a special case, actually. We're called mirror-image twins. About twenty percent of identical twins — the ones where the egg splits late, they think — develop as opposites. So our faces aren't exactly the same unless you look at one as a reflection. It doesn't mean much, for Kevin especially." He savored his first bite of ice cream, then smiled. "I, on the other hand, will run into a problem if I ever need an organ transplant. All of my insides are reversed, so it's very complicated to replace certain things unless they find an organ from another reversed twin who also just happens to be a genetic match. In other words, I better hope I never need a new liver." He took another bite.

"It would make a lot more sense to me if it was Kevin who had everything backward."

They laughed together, but it was much gentler than it had been earlier in the day. Apparently they'd gotten the hysteria out of their systems.

"What does the paper say—the one with the command for the dog?"

Daniel pulled the card from his jeans pocket, glanced at it, and then handed it to her.

It read, in all caps, ESCAPE PROTOCOL.

"Do you think something bad happens if we say it out loud?" she wondered.

"I suppose it's possible. I'll believe anything after seeing his secret lair."

"Kevin really needs to hire someone to come up with better names for his commands. He's not very good at that part."

"I guess that could be my job now." Daniel sighed. "I *do* like dogs. It might be fun."

"It's still kind of teaching, right?"

"If Kev lets me do any." Daniel scowled. "I wonder if he sees me just mucking out stalls? I wouldn't put it past him." And then he sighed again. "At least the students all appear to be pretty bright. Do you think I could teach them to play volleyball?"

"Well ... actually, yeah. They don't seem to have many limitations."

"I guess it won't be so bad. Right?"

"Right," she said confidently. And then mentally called herself a liar.

CHAPTER 14

When Alex woke up, the first issue was the soreness. Unconsciousness had given her a break from the pain, and that period of relief, though welcome, made the awakening to reality worse.

The room was pitch-black. She assumed there was a window somewhere behind the boxes, but it must be covered with a blackout shade. Kevin wouldn't want too many lighted windows at night. Better to keep the house looking only partially inhabited. As far as any locals knew, Arnie was the sole occupant.

She rolled out of the cot, groaning when her left shoulder and hip hit the wooden edge, and then felt her way to the light switch. She'd cleared a wide path from the cot to the door so that she wouldn't add to her injuries fumbling around in the dark. Once the light was on, she disarmed the leads and then removed her gas mask. Given that there were people here that she didn't want to kill, she'd used a pressurized canister of knockout gas.

The hall was empty, the bathroom door open. There was one damp towel hanging on the rack, so Daniel must already be awake. That was no surprise. She'd been up pretty late with her memory list, despairing, even as she continued typing, at the probability of recalling in a week's time what any of her cryptic notes stood for. As she worked through it, she noted plenty of secrets worth killing over, but none specific to her or Barnaby. There would have been other victims if any of those particular secrets were the root problem. From what she'd been able to track in the news, her death and Barnaby's had not been followed by any other names she recognized. Nothing public, anyway.

While she shampooed her hair, she thought about how she could narrow down the time frame. She usually did her best creative thinking in the shower.

Barnaby had always been paranoid, but he hadn't started *acting* on that paranoia until two years before his death. She remembered that initial conversation, the first time she'd realized she was in actual danger. It had been late fall—around Thanksgiving. If that was not a random change, if there had been some sort of catalyst, maybe Barnaby had been reacting to the case that was the issue. She couldn't be sure of the timing, but she was fairly positive about the interrogations that had taken place *after* that change—in her memory, they were all riddled through with the new stress and distraction. So those could be ruled out. And she knew all the cases from her first year easily, when everything had been horrifically new and awkward; those could be set aside as well. It still left her three years of work to sort through and two of the nuclear scares, but she was happy to have even the slightest measure of containment.

She appreciated the fluffy towels the bathroom was stocked with. Kevin apparently enjoyed his creature comforts. Or maybe it was Arnie who liked things plush. Whoever it was had also stocked the bathroom with all the toiletries a hotel would provide, only in full-size bottles. There had been shampoo and conditioner in the shower. Toothpaste, lotion, and mouthwash were all set out on the counter. Nice touch.

She took a swipe at the mirror with the towel and quickly confirmed that she was still unfit to be seen. The black eyes were mostly a sickly green color now, with some of the darker purple in the inside corners. Her lip was starting to deflate, but that only made the superglue more obvious. The bruises on her cheeks were just barely beginning to yellow around the edges.

She sighed. It would be at least a week before her face could go out in public, even in makeup.

After dressing in her least dirty clothes, Alex gathered the rest, balled them up inside a T-shirt as an improvised laundry bag, and set off in search of the facilities. It was empty and quiet downstairs. She could hear barking in the distance. Daniel and Arnie must be out dealing with the animals.

She found the spacious laundry room tucked away behind the kitchen. She noted the back door—always good to be familiar with the exits—and the large plastic attachment to the bottom half of it. It took her a minute to realize it was a doggie door—a huge doggie door, big enough to let Khan in. She hadn't seen any dogs in the house so far, but it must not always be off-limits. She started her load, then went to find breakfast.

The cupboards weren't much more helpful than the refrigerator had been. Half were full of cans of dog food, and the other half mostly empty. There was some coffee left in the pot on the counter, thank goodness. She also found a stash of Pop-Tarts, which she pilfered. Apparently Kevin and Arnie cared less about food than they did about towels. She found a mug from a Boy Scout camp circa 1983, chipped and faded. The time frame didn't fit either of the men who lived here—must be a secondhand acquisition. It worked just fine, regardless. When she was done, she loaded the mug in the stainless-steel dishwasher and then went to see what was on the day's agenda.

Lola and Khan were on the front porch, along with the Rottweiler whose name she couldn't remember. They all got up like they'd been waiting for her and followed as she headed out to the barn. She patted Lola a few times as they walked; it seemed like the polite thing to do.

North of the modern outbuilding was a big run full of animals,

Arnie in the center of them all, calling out commands to the frolicking dogs. It didn't look like many of them were listening to him, but a few played teacher's pet. She couldn't see Daniel anywhere. She wandered into the outbuilding, went down the length of it to where the supply room was. Kevin and Arnie stocked the place much better for the dogs than for themselves. Daniel wasn't there, either.

She meandered out to the edge of the practice yard, not sure what else to do. It was odd; she was used to being alone all the time. But now Daniel wasn't around to check on, and suddenly she was at loose ends.

Arnie, of course, paid zero attention to her as she came up to the fence and hooked her fingers through the links. She watched him work with a young German shepherd—still all oversize paws and floppy ears—long past the point when her own patience would have run out. Lola's two pups came over to press their bodies against the fence and beg for licks from their mother. She obliged a few times, then yelped at them, a funny sound that made Alex think of her own mother reminding her to study after dinner. Sure enough, the two half-grown puppies ambled back toward the man with the treats.

Maybe Daniel had returned to the practice range. Kevin had said there was a truck around here, but she'd seen no sign of it. She wished Daniel had waited for her. She wanted to play with the SIG some more. And, honestly, she could use some exercise with her PPK, too. Her life had never depended on her aim in the past, but it very well might in the future. She didn't want to waste the unexpected opportunity to improve her skills.

She watched Arnie with the young dogs for another half hour. Finally, she interrupted, more out of boredom than any driving need to know.

"Hey," she called over the dog sounds. "Um, Arnie?"

He looked up, his face betraying no interest.

"Did Daniel take the truck over to the range? What time did he leave?"

He nodded, then shrugged. She tried to guess at a translation, but quickly gave up. She would have to keep the questions simpler.

"He took the truck?" she verified.

Arnie was focused on the dogs again, but she did get an answer. "Guess so. Wasn't there the last time I went to the barn."

"How far is it to the range?" she asked. It had seemed too long a distance to walk, but she might as well ask.

"'Bout five miles, as the crow flies."

Not as far as she'd thought. Daniel was a runner—couldn't he have left the truck? Well, she could use a run herself, but he'd probably be on his way back before she could get there.

"And you don't know what time he left?"

"Didn't see him. It was before nine, though."

It had been more than an hour. Doubtless he'd return soon. She'd wait her turn.

It was good that Daniel was taking an interest in the practice. Maybe some of what she and Kevin had been trying to tell him had sunk in a little. She didn't actually want him to have to live in fear, but it was the best option. Fear would keep him alive.

She waved her thanks to Arnie, then headed back to the house to finish the laundry, furry entourage in tow.

An hour later, she was in clean clothes for the first time in several days, and it felt fantastic. She put the outfit she'd been wearing in the washing machine, happy at the thought of having her whole wardrobe smelling nice again. She put in another thirty minutes on her memory project; at least she remembered her notations twelve hours later. She was trying to do things chronologically as best she could, though her numbering system was based on severity. It might have made things more confusing than they should be, but she didn't want to reorganize it all now.

This morning she worked terrorist events number fifteen and three—an attempted subway bombing and a stolen biological weapon—trying to think of any names that had come up in context.

The terrorist and Russian profiteers on number fifteen had been dealt with, so it was probably nothing to do with them. She noted it down anyway. *NY* was too obvious an abbreviation, so she used *MB* for Manhattan–Bronx; the 1 train had been the target. *TT* for the faction behind it, *KV* for Kalasha Valleys, *VR* for the Russian who sold them the materials. A few outsiders who had aided and abetted: *RP, FD, BB.*

Number three had a few loose ends, as she remembered, but those had been turned over to the CIA. She looked at her letters: *J, I-P* for Jammu, India, on the border of Pakistan. *TP;* the Tacoma Plague, they'd called it. It had been developed by a known terrorist cell from the notes of an American scientist, lifted from a lab near Seattle. The splinter cell, *FA,* was involved in events T10 and T13 as well. The department had still been helping the CIA procure information about the remnants of the cell back when she'd been "fired." She wondered if the CIA had ever shut it down completely. Kevin had been busy enough in Mexico that he probably couldn't give her the answer. She noted down initials for a few connected names. *DH* was the American scientist the formula was stolen from, and *OM* was a member of the terrorist cell whom she'd interrogated. She thought there was another American involved somehow—not a participant in the event. Or had that name been related to number four? She only remembered the name was short, clipped-sounding... did it start with a *P?*

She'd never been allowed to keep any notes, of course, so there was nothing to refer back to. It was frustrating. Enough so that she gave up and decided to look for lunch. The Pop-Tart hadn't exactly been filling.

As she walked into the great room, she could hear the low rumble of an engine pulling up outside, then the grinding sound of heavy tires on the gravel. Finally.

Habit had her checking out the door to make sure it was Daniel. Just as she peeked out, the engine noise cut off. A dusty white older-model Toyota truck with an equally aged and dusty camper shell was parked where they'd left the sedan last night, and Daniel was getting out of the driver's seat. Einstein jumped out the car door after him.

Even as she was admiring the vehicle's ordinary exterior — perfect for blending in — a slow creeping sensation started to inch up her back, raising bumps on her skin as it moved. She froze, wide eyes darting around like a startled rabbit trying to suss out the direction danger was coming from. What had her subconscious noticed that she had not?

She zeroed in on the paper bag cradled in Daniel's left arm. As she watched, he pulled the front seat forward and grabbed another bag. Einstein danced happily around his legs. Khan and the Rottweiler ran down the porch steps to join in.

She felt the blood drain out of her face, leaving a dizzy sensation behind.

And then the second of shock passed, and she was in motion. She charged after the dogs, feeling the blood pulse back into her bruised cheeks.

"Hey, Alex," Daniel called cheerfully. "There are a few more bags in the back, if you're feeling—" He stopped abruptly when he processed her expression. "What's happened? Kevin—"

"Where did you go?" She spit the words through her teeth.

He blinked once. "I just ran out to that town we passed on our way in. Childress."

Her hands balled into fists.

"I took the dog," he offered. "Nothing happened."

She pressed one fist to her mouth, winced, and tried to calm herself. It wasn't his fault. He just didn't understand. She and Kevin should have advised him better. It was her own misstep for assuming some of that guidance had happened while she'd been asleep in the car. But if Kevin hadn't been prepping Daniel for his new life, then what *had* they been talking about for all those hours?

"Did anyone see y—of course they did. You bought things. How many people saw you?"

He blinked again. "Did I do something wrong?"

"You went into town?" A deep voice rumbled behind her.

Daniel shifted his gaze to a point over her head. "Yeah—I mean, you guys were pretty short on groceries. I just wanted to get some nonfrozen stuff, you know? You seemed busy..."

She turned to look at Arnie. His face was impassive, but she knew it well enough now to see little breaks in the façade—stress marks around his eyes, one slightly more prominent vein in his forehead.

"Do you have a way to contact Kevin?" she asked him.

"You mean Joe?"

"Probably. Daniel's brother."

"Nope."

"What did I do?" Daniel asked pleadingly.

She sighed as she turned back to him. "Do you remember when Kevin said that no one around here had ever seen his face? Well... now they have."

Daniel's color started to ebb as he processed that. "But...I used a fake name. I—I said I was just passing through."

"How many people did you talk to?"

"Just the cashier at the grocery store and the one at the—"

"How many places did you go into?"

"Three..."

She and Arnie exchanged a glance—horrified on her part, more inscrutable on his.

"Kevin left me money for things I might need—I assumed he meant stuff like eggs and milk," Daniel offered.

"He meant fake IDs," Alex snapped.

The rest of Daniel's color vanished, and his mouth fell open.

They stared at him for a long moment.

Daniel took a deep breath, visibly centering himself.

"Okay," he said. "I screwed up. Can we take the groceries in before you tell me how bad? It only adds waste to my mistake if the perishables spoil in the truck."

Lips pressed into a tight line — ignoring the irritating glob of superglue — Alex nodded once and went around to the back of the truck to help unload. She saw all the bags inside the camper and felt the blood behind her bruises again.

Of course, on top of going into the closest town, he would have bought enough food to feed an army. And if there was any other thing that would make him more memorable, he'd probably done that, too.

In ominous silence, Alex and Arnie brought all the bags in and put them on the counter. Daniel worked back and forth between the cupboards and the fridge, sorting each item into the right spot. Alex might have thought that he wasn't taking this seriously enough except for the fact that his color kept changing; though his expression was steady, his cheeks and neck would suddenly flush, and then he'd go white again.

The cooling-off period was probably a good idea. It gave Alex a chance to think everything through and be realistic about the danger posed. She'd been about ready to steal Arnie's truck and disappear, but she knew that would be overreacting. Sometimes overreactions saved your life; sometimes they just put you in more danger. She had to remember her face; running now would only cause her more problems.

Daniel placed the last item — some kind of leafy green vegetable — in the fridge and shut the door. He didn't turn, just stood there with his head slightly bowed toward the stainless steel.

"How bad?" he asked quietly.

She looked at Arnie. He didn't seem inclined to speak.

"Tell me you paid cash," she began.

"Yes."

"Well, that's something, at least."

"But not everything," Daniel guessed.

"No. Childress is a very small town."

"Just over six thousand people," Arnie rumbled.

It was worse than she'd thought; she knew of high schools with bigger student bodies.

"So a stranger in town is memorable," she said. "You would have been noticed."

Daniel turned to her. His face was composed, but his eyes were troubled.

"Yes, I can see that," he agreed.

"You were in Arnie's truck, with Arnie's dog," Alex said. "Someone could connect you back to Arnie."

"Einstein stayed in the truck," Daniel said. "I don't think anyone was watching me get in or out."

"There're a hundred similar trucks in town. Five that are the exact same color, year, and model; two of those have campers," Arnie said, not to Daniel, but to Alex. "Half the people there would have a dog with them."

"That's helpful," she told Arnie. "You guys did good here."

"How much does this affect you?" Daniel asked him.

Arnie shrugged. "No way to know. People forget stuff pretty quick when they've got no real reason to remember. We lie low, it'll probably come to nothing."

"Anyway, what's done is done," Alex mused. "We'll just have to be extra careful."

"Kevin's going to be furious." Daniel sighed.

"When *isn't* he furious?" Alex asked, and Arnie actually laughed out one brief chuckle. "Anyway, it's his own fault for not explaining anything to you. A mistake I'm not going to repeat." She gestured toward the couch.

Arnie nodded to himself, then clumped out the front door, back to his work. Kevin had picked a good partner. She found herself wishing that Arnie were Daniel's brother rather than Kevin. Arnie was so much easier to deal with.

"How about I make lunch while you lecture?" Daniel offered. "I'm suffering extreme hunger pangs. I don't know what Arnie survives on around here."

"Sure," she said. She grabbed a bar stool and planted herself.

"I did honestly think that I was helping," Daniel murmured as he went back to the fridge.

"I know, Daniel, I know. And I'm hungry, too," she conceded.

"I'll ask first next time," he promised.

She sighed. "That's a start."

•   •   •

THOUGH SHE DIDN'T want to admit it, the large sandwich Daniel made for her did a lot to mellow her perspective on the incident. She gave him the basics while they ate — there'd be time for more detail when they had a specific task ahead of them — and he listened attentively.

"I don't know how to see the world that way," he confessed. "It all seems so paranoid."

"Yes! Paranoia is exactly what we're shooting for. Paranoia is good."

"That's a little contradictory to how they teach it in the real world, but I'll work on flipping my perspective. I know I can do this much — I will check with you on everything from now on. Before I *breathe*."

"You'll start to get it. It becomes habit after a while. But don't think of what you used to know as the *real* world. The things that happen in *this* world are a whole lot more real, and a whole lot more permanent. It's primitive — survival instincts. I know you have them; you were born with them. You just have to tap into that part of yourself."

"I have to think like the hunted." He tried to keep his face positive, but she could see how much the idea devastated him.

"Yes. You *are* the hunted. And so am I. And so is your brother.

And hell, so is Arnie, apparently. It's a very popular state of being around here."

"But you," he said slowly, "and my brother, and probably even Arnie, are still predators. I'm just prey."

She shook her head. "I started out as prey. I learned. You've got advantages I never had. You share an exact genetic code with your brother, the apex predator. I saw you down at the range—once those instincts kick in, you'll be plenty able to take care of yourself."

"You're just saying that to make me feel better."

"I'm saying that because I'm jealous. If I could be tall, and strong, and a natural shot, it would change this game I'm playing."

"If I could be smart and paranoid, I wouldn't have put us at risk."

She smiled. "There's no comparison. You have the ability to learn; I'll never be able to grow any taller."

He grinned back. "But you're so much stealthier the way you are."

"Ugh," she groaned. "Let's go do something productive and shoot up some hay bales."

"Okay, but I have to be back by"—he glanced at the clock on the range—"six o'clock at the latest."

Alex was confused. "Is your favorite TV show on or something?"

"No. I owe you dinner, and it's not like I can take you out on the town." He smiled apologetically. "That's one of the reasons, beyond starvation, I went shopping."

"Um…"

"I asked you to dinner. You don't remember?"

"Oh, I remember. I just think we're probably quits on anything you might have offered before I kidnapped you."

"I won't feel right if I don't make good. Anyway, someone has to cook, and I'm not half bad at it. I already know that Kevin and Arnie are useless in that department."

Alex sighed. "I'm probably just as bad."

"So it's settled. Now let's go improve our aim."

• • •

DANIEL PICKED THINGS up so quickly, it was no wonder Kevin had been recruited. While they practiced, Daniel told Alex about Kevin's prowess at sports and his particular gift for shooting. Apparently the boys and their father had taken part in many competitions, and Kevin had almost always come away with the first-place trophy.

"I made the mistake of beating him once, when we were nine. *Not* worth it. From then on, I went along to keep Dad happy, but I didn't really compete. I found my own interests, things that Kevin didn't want to bother with. Like books. Community involvement. Distance running. Culinary classes. Girl stuff, as he frequently informed me."

Alex loaded a new magazine. They were really burning through Kevin's ammo, but she didn't much care. He could afford new ammo.

She'd done a thorough search of the barn today and found a few of his cash hoards. It looked like some of the drug money had come home with him. As a general rule, she avoided stealing unless she'd run out of other options, but she was very tempted now to grab as much as she could carry. After all, it was partially Kevin's fault she was so much poorer than she had been last month.

"I wonder what would have happened to me if I'd had a sibling who was better at chemistry and biology in high school?" she asked. "Would I have given it up? Become an accountant?"

She took a shot, then smiled. Right in the heart.

"Maybe you're more competitive than I am. Maybe you would have fought it out for the crown."

He leaned casually into his shooting position and fired a round at a bale a hundred yards farther away than hers.

She fired again. "Maybe I would be happier as an accountant."

Daniel sighed. "You're probably right. I was pretty happy as a teacher. Not a glamorous career, but the mundane can be quite satisfying. In fact, being ordinary in general is highly underrated."

"I wouldn't know. But it sounds nice."

"You were never ordinary." It wasn't a question.

"No," she agreed. "Not really. Unfortunate, as it turned out." Always too smart for her own good, though it had taken her a while to see things that way. She shot her target in the head twice in quick succession.

Daniel straightened up and leaned the long rifle against his shoulder. Einstein got to his feet and stretched out his back. "Well, I had my few areas where I transcended the mundane," he said, and Alex could tell from his tone that he was purposely lightening the mood. "And lucky you," he continued, "tonight you get to see me work in my favorite field."

Alex set the SIG down and stretched, much like the dog had. Her muscles got stiff more quickly with her injuries. She wasn't moving the way she usually did; she was favoring the damaged parts of her body. She needed to force herself to use her limbs equally.

"Sounds exciting. And I'm hungry, so I really hope the field you're talking about is the kitchen."

"It is, indeed. Shall we?" He made a sweeping gesture with his free hand toward the truck.

"As soon as we clean up our toys."

• • •

DANIEL DID SEEM very at home, humming as he diced things and sprinkled spices on things and put other things into saucepans. Of course, she couldn't help but notice that a lot of the tools appeared to be brand-new and hadn't been in the cupboards when she'd dug through them earlier. She would hold off on the lecture about how people who were just passing through town rarely bought things for their kitchens. It was starting to smell kind of amazing and she didn't want to jinx anything.

She sat sideways on the sofa, her legs curled up under her, watching the news and Daniel at the same time. Nothing interesting on TV—just a lot of local stuff and a little bit about the primaries, which were still about nine months away. The whole election process was irritating to Alex. She would probably have to stop watching the news altogether when the real campaigning started. As someone who knew better than most the kind of darkness that went on behind the scenes and how little any of the important decisions had to do with the figurehead spokesperson the people elected, it was hard for her to care much about left or right.

Arnie had eaten another frozen dinner and retired around seven thirty, as seemed to be his habit. Alex had tried to convince him that a home-cooked meal was worth waiting for, but he hadn't even bothered responding to her coaxing. She was surprised that Daniel didn't give it a try, but maybe he was concentrating too hard on the food to notice. She offered to help once or twice only to be told in no uncertain terms that all she was allowed to do was eat.

Daniel grumbled to himself as he set out the unmatched plates, random silverware, and coffee mugs. She would have to remind him that he wasn't to go off on another shopping spree for monogrammed china. He moved all the food to the table, and she got up eagerly, famished and driven half wild by the various fragrances wafting through the room. He held a chair out for her, which reminded her of things she'd seen in old movies. Was this what normal people did? She wasn't sure, but she didn't think so. At least, not in the places she went out to eat.

With a flourish, he pulled out a lighter and lit a blue-and-pink-polka-dotted candle shaped like the number 1 that he'd stuck into a bread roll.

"This was the closest I could find to a taper," he explained as he saw her expression. "And this was the best I could do for wine," he continued, gesturing to the bottle that sat open beside her coffee mug. The words on the label were all unfamiliar to her. "It's the choicest vintage the United Supermarket carries."

He made as if to pour, and she automatically covered the top of her mug with her hand.

"I don't drink."

He hesitated, then poured a small amount for himself. "I got some apple juice this morning. Or I could get you some water?"

"Juice would be great."

He got up and headed for the fridge. "Can I ask? AA or a religious preference?"

"Safety. I haven't touched anything that might cloud my perception in four years."

He returned and poured her a mugful of juice before sitting opposite her. His face was carefully nonchalant.

"Didn't you start running just three years ago?"

"Yes. But once it really sank in that someone might try to kill me at any moment, it was hard to think about much else. I couldn't afford to be distracted. I could miss something. I did miss something, I guess. If I'd really been on my toes, Barnaby might still be alive. We shouldn't have waited."

"You don't feel safe here?"

She looked up at him, surprised by the question. The answer was so obvious. "No."

"Because I was stupid this morning?"

She shook her head. "No, not at all. I never feel safe anywhere."

She heard how blasé the words sounded, the way the words *of course* seemed to be embedded in her answer, and watched his face fall a little in response.

"Hey, but I probably have PTSD. It doesn't have to be like that. I'm sure another person could handle things better."

He raised one eyebrow. "Yes, Kevin seems completely normal."

They laughed again. She hadn't laughed this much in the past three years put together.

He lifted his fork. "Shall we?"

CHAPTER 15

N o, I'm not exaggerating. I am fairly certain this is the best meal I've ever eaten in my entire life. Granted, I'm generally a fast-food girl, so I'm not a very sophisticated judge, but I also mean what I say."

"Well, that's a lovely compliment. Thank you."

"What is this again?" She poked her fork at the dessert on her plate, wishing she had a tiny bit more space in her stomach. She'd eaten herself nearly sick, but still she craved just one more bite.

"Bananas Foster butter cake."

"I *mean*..." She went for it, ignoring her stomach and savoring a small forkful. "Where did you learn to do this?"

"I took a few culinary courses in college. I watch a lot of the Food Network on the weekends, and I practice when I can afford to."

"Time amazingly well spent. I think you might have missed your calling, though."

"I worked in a few restaurants back in the day. It wasn't conducive to a social life. When I was dating my ex... well, she wasn't a big fan of the schedule. My day job gave us more time together."

"Not everyone would make the sacrifice."

"It wasn't one, really. Working with the kids always felt most important. I loved it. And it wasn't like I couldn't cook at home. So I got both for a while."

"Then you stopped?"

He sighed. "Well, when Lainey left ... I didn't want to fight. I let her have whatever she wanted."

Alex could easily picture how that had worked. She'd seen Daniel's postdivorce bank account. "She cleaned you out."

"Pretty much. Hence the ramen diet."

"That is a crime." She looked longingly at what was left of the butter cake.

"Life," he said. "You've had your share of heartbreak."

"Honestly, though it all went down with a little too much terror and tragedy, I was ready to quit anyway. It was never what I wanted to do with my life; it's just what I was really good at." She shrugged. "The job took a toll."

"I can't even begin to imagine. But I meant ... romantically."

She stared at him, uncomprehending. "Romantically?"

"Well, as you said, it ended in tragedy."

"My life, sure. But ... ?"

"I just figured, from the way you talk about him, it must have been devastating to lose ... Dr. Barnaby the way you did. You never said what his first name was?"

"It was Joseph. But I always called him Barnaby."

She took a sip of her juice.

"And were you in love with him ... from the very beginning?"

Her shocked gasp pulled a mouthful of juice into her lungs, and she spluttered and choked. Daniel jumped up and pounded her on the back while she tried to regain control of her breathing. After a minute, she waved him off.

"I'm okay," she coughed out. "Sit."

He stayed by her, one hand half extended. "Are you sure?"

"Just. Caught by surprise. *With Barnaby?*"

"I thought you said yesterday ..."

She took a deep breath, then coughed one more time. "That I loved him." She shuddered. "Sorry, I'm just having some seriously squicky incest reflexes right now. Barnaby was like my father. He was a good father — the only one I ever knew. It was really hard knowing how he died, and I miss him like hell. So, yes, definitely devastating. But not like that."

Daniel returned slowly to his seat. He thought for a moment, and then he asked, "Who else did you have to cut ties with when you disappeared?"

She could imagine the long array of faces parading through his mind right now. "That part wasn't so hard for me. It sounds pretty pathetic, but Barnaby was my only real friend. My work was my entire life, and I wasn't allowed to talk about my work to anyone besides Barnaby. I lived a very isolated existence. There were others around…for example, the underlings who prepped subjects. They knew what was happening in a general sense but had none of the classified details about the information we were trying to retrieve. And, well, they were terrified of me. They knew what my job was. So we didn't chat much. There were a few lab assistants who performed a variety of duties outside the action rooms, but they *didn't* know what we were doing and I had to be careful not to say anything to tip them off. Occasionally, people from the different agencies visited individually to monitor a particular interrogation, but I had very little contact with them except to receive instructions about the angles I should cover. Mostly they watched from behind one-way glass, and Carston gave me the information. I used to think Carston was sort of my friend, but he *did* just try to kill me…So I can't compare it to what you're losing. Obviously, I didn't have that much of a life to lose. Even before I was recruited…I guess I just don't bond with other humans like a normal person. Like I said, pathetic."

He smiled at her. "I haven't noticed any deficiencies."

"Um, thanks. Well, it's getting late. Let me help clear this all up."

"Sure." He stood and stretched, then started stacking plates. She had to move quickly to grab a few things before he had efficiently made off with all of it. "But the night is still young," he continued, "and I'm going to have to bring up the other half of our deal now."

"Huh?"

He laughed. His hands were full so she pulled the dishwasher open. She filled in the bottom rack while he did the top and put the bigger pieces in the sink. The chore moved quickly with both of them working in easy tandem.

"You don't remember? It's only been a few days, really. I'll admit, it does seem a lot longer. It could be weeks."

"I have no idea what you're talking about."

He closed the dishwasher and then leaned back against the counter, folding his arms. She waited.

"Think back. Before things got ... strange. You promised that if I still liked you after we had dinner together ..."

He looked at her with raised eyebrows, waiting for her to fill in the blank.

Oh. He was talking about their conversation on the train. She was shocked he could refer to it so lightly. That was the last moment his life had been normal. The last moment before everything had been stolen from him. And though she hadn't been the architect of that theft, she'd been the hand they used.

"Um. Something about a foreign film theater at the university near you, right?"

"Yes — well, but I didn't mean for you to be *quite* so specific. The university theater is not exactly convenient right now. However ..." He opened the cupboard behind him, reached up, and pulled something off the highest shelf. He turned back to her with a huge grin and presented a DVD case. The faded cover had a picture of a beautiful woman in a red dress and a dark, wide-brimmed hat.

"Ta-da!" he said.

"Where on earth did you get that?"

His smile got a little smaller. "Second store I went to. Thrift store. I got very lucky. This is actually a great movie." He assessed her face. "I can read your thoughts. You're thinking, *Is there any place this idiot* didn't *go? We'll be dead by sunrise.*"

"Not in so many words. And we'd be disappearing into the night in Arnie's stolen truck right now if I thought it was that bad."

"Still, while I'm very, very sorry for my rash behavior, I'm also quite happy I was able to find this gem. You'll love it."

She shook her head—not disagreeing, just wondering how things had gotten so odd in her life. One wrong move and suddenly she was committed to reading subtitles with the most kind and... *uncorrupted* person she'd ever met.

He stepped toward her. "You can't say no. You made a bargain and I intend to hold you to it."

"I'll do it, I'll do it. You just have to explain why exactly it is that you still like me," she said, finishing more glumly than she'd begun.

"I think I can do that."

He took another step forward, backing her against the island. He put his hands on the edge of the counter behind her, one on either side, and as he leaned forward, she could smell the clean, citrusy scent of his hair. He was so close, she could see that he must have shaved recently—his jaw was smooth and there was the hint of razor burn just under his chin.

Daniel's proximity confused her, but it didn't frighten her the way it would have with just about any other person on the planet. He wasn't dangerous to her, she knew that. She didn't understand what he was doing, though, even when he slowly lowered his face toward hers, his eyes starting to close. It never occurred to her that he was about to kiss her until his half-open lips were just a breath away from hers.

That realization startled her. It startled her a lot. And when she was startled, she had ingrained reactions that manifested without her conscious approval.

She ducked under his arm, spinning free. She dashed several feet away, then spun back to face the source of the alarm, sliding into a half crouch. Her hands were automatically at her waist, looking for the belt she wasn't wearing.

As she took in Daniel's horrified expression, Alex realized that her reaction would have fit better if he'd pulled a knife and held it to her throat. She straightened up and dropped her hands, her face burning.

"Uh, sorry. Sorry! You, um, caught me off guard."

Daniel's horror shifted into disbelief. "Wow. I didn't think I was moving that fast, but maybe I should reevaluate."

"I just...I'm sorry, what *was* that?"

A shade of impatience crossed his expression. "Well, I was about to kiss you."

"That's what it looked like, but...*why?* I mean, kiss *me?* I don't...I don't understand."

He shook his head and turned to lean back against the island. "Huh. I really thought we were on the same page, but now I kind of feel like I'm speaking English as a second language. What did *you* think was going on here? With the dinner date? And the sad little candle?" He gestured to the table.

He walked toward her then, and she forced herself not to back away. Confusion aside, she knew her wild overreaction had been rude. She didn't want to hurt his feelings. Even if he was a crazy person.

"Surely..." He sighed. "*Surely* you've been aware of how often I just...touch you." He was close enough at that point to reach out one hand and brush his knuckles along her arm in demonstration. "On the planet I come from, that kind of thing signifies romantic interest." He leaned toward her again, his eyes narrowed. "Please tell me, what does it mean on yours?"

She took a deep breath. "Daniel, what you're processing now is a kind of sensory deprivation reaction," she explained. "It's something I've seen before, in the lab..."

His eyes widened; he backed out of her space. His expression was totally flummoxed.

"This is a valid response to what you've experienced, and it's actually a very mild response, under the circumstances," she continued. "You're doing remarkably well. Many people would have had a complete nervous breakdown by this point. This emotional reaction might seem similar to something you've experienced before, but I can assure you that what you're feeling right now is not romantic interest."

He regained his composure as she explained, but he didn't seem enlightened or reassured by her diagnosis. His eyebrows lowered and his lips tucked in at the corners like he was annoyed.

"And you're sure you know my feelings better than I do because..."

"As I said, I've seen something like this before in the lab."

"'Something like this'?" he quoted back at her. "I imagine you saw many things in your lab, but I'm also sure that I'm still the best qualified to know when I'm experiencing romantic interest." He *sounded* angry, but he was smiling and he was moving closer while he spoke. "So if your only argument is anecdotal..."

"That's not my only argument," she began slowly, unwillingly. These weren't the easiest words to say. "I may have been... absorbed by my work, but I wasn't totally oblivious. I know what men see when they look at me, the ones who know what I am...like you do. And I understand that reaction. I don't disagree with it. Your brother's animosity—that is a normal, rational response. I've seen it many times before—fear, loathing, an eagerness to assert physical dominance. I am the bogeyman in a very dark and scary world. I frighten people who aren't afraid of anything else, not even death. I can take everything they pride themselves on away from them; I can make them betray everything they hold sacred. I am the monster they see in their nightmares." It was a version of herself she'd come to accept, but not without some pain.

She wasn't unaware that outsiders, people who didn't know her, saw her as a woman rather than a demon. When she needed to, she could make use of her ability to appear delicate and feminine, as she had with the walrus-y hotel manager. It was no different from her ability to look like a boy. Both were deceptions. But even those outsiders who saw her as a female didn't look at her with ... *desire*. She wasn't that girl, and that was okay. She'd been born with her own gifts, and you didn't get everything.

He waited patiently while she spoke, his expression neutral. She didn't think he was reacting to her words strongly enough.

"Do you understand what I'm saying?" she asked. "I am intrinsically incompatible with being an object of romantic interest."

"I understand you. I just don't agree."

"I don't understand how you of all people can disagree."

"First, but not entirely to the point, I'm not afraid of you."

She exhaled impatiently. "Why not?"

"Because, now that you know who I am, I am in no danger from you, and I never will be unless I change into the kind of person who should be."

Her lips screwed into a half-pursed frown. He was right ... but that wasn't really the issue.

"Second, still tangential, I think you've been spending all your time with the wrong kind of man. A hazard of your particular work, I'd imagine."

"Maybe. But what is the main point you're dancing around?"

He got into her personal space again. "How I feel. How you feel."

She held her ground. "And how can you be sure what you're feeling? You're in the middle of the most traumatic experience of your life. You've just lost your whole world. All that's left is a brother you don't completely trust, your kidnapper-slash-torturer, and Arnie. So it was probably fifty-fifty on whether you'd attach yourself to me or to Arnie. This is pretty basic Stockholm syndrome stuff, Daniel. I'm the only human female in your life—there aren't any other options. Think about it rationally; think about how inappropriate the timing is. You can't trust feelings born in the midst of severe physical and mental anguish."

"I might consider that, except for one thing."

"And what's that?"

"I wanted you before you were the only human female in my life."

This threw her, and he took advantage, placing both his hands lightly on her shoulders. The warmth from his palms made her realize that she'd been cold without recognizing it. She shivered.

"Remember when I told you that I'd never asked a woman out on a train before? That was kind of an understatement. On average, it takes me about three weeks of fairly regular interaction—along with an embarrassing amount of encouragement from the girl—before I work up the nerve to ask someone to go for a casual coffee. But from the second I saw your face, I was willing to leap miles outside my comfort zone to make sure I saw it again."

She shook her head. "Daniel, I roofied you. You were high on a chemical compound with manifestations similar to Ecstasy."

"Not then, I wasn't. I remember. I felt the difference before and after you 'shocked' me. That was when things got confusing. And before the drug, I was already in neck-deep. I was trying to figure out how I was going to get off at your stop without looking like a stalker."

She had no answer. His physical proximity was becoming disorienting. He still held her loosely, bending in slightly so that his face was closer to hers.

It wasn't until this moment that she began to really consider his words. She'd written off everything he'd said and done since the kidnapping as aftershocks from the trauma. She'd analyzed him like a subject, always separating herself from the equation. Because none of it was *about* her. And all of it was within normal parameters for what he'd been through.

She tried to remember the last time a man had looked at her this way, and she came up empty.

For the past three years, every person she'd met, male or female, had been a potential source of danger. For the six years before that, as she'd just excruciatingly explained, she'd been anathema to every man she'd interacted with. Which took her all the way back to college and medical school and the few brief relationships that had never included much romance. She was a scientist first, even then, and the men she'd formed attachments to had been the same. Their relationships were born from massive amounts of time logged in together and very specific interests that 99.99 percent of the populace couldn't begin to grasp. Each time, they'd settled for each other by default. No wonder it had never amounted to much.

And none of them had ever worn this expression. Wonder and fascination mixed with something electric as he gazed at her face... her battered, swollen face. For the first time, she felt mortified about her mangled appearance for an entirely vain reason. Her hands had been hanging limply at her sides. Now she raised one and covered as much as she could, hiding like a child.

"I've put some thought into this," he said, and she could hear the smile in his voice. "I know what I'm saying."

She just shook her head.

"Of course, all of that is moot if you don't feel a similar way. I've been a little overconfident tonight." He paused. "Given that we haven't been speaking the same language at all, have we? I've been misreading you."

He paused again like he was waiting for an answer, but she had no idea what to say.

"What do you see when you look at me?" he asked.

She lowered her hand an inch and glanced up at him, at the same perplexingly honest face she'd been trying to understand from the beginning. What kind of a question was that? There were too many answers.

"I don't know how to respond to that."

His eyes narrowed for a moment, considering. She wished he would take a step back so that she could think more clearly. Then he seemed to brace himself, squaring his shoulders for some kind of blow.

"Might as well get everything out in the open. Answer this instead: What's the very worst thing you see when you look at me?"

The honest answer popped out before she could think it through. "A liability."

She saw how harshly the word landed. Now he gave her the space she'd just wished for, and she regretted it. Why was the room so cold?

He nodded to himself as he backed away.

"That's fair, that's completely fair. I'm an idiot, clearly. I can't forget I've put you in danger. Also, the fact that—"

"No!" She took a hesitant step toward him, anxious to be clear. "That's not what I meant."

"You don't have to be kind. I know I'm useless in all this." He gestured vaguely toward the door, toward the world outside that was trying to kill them both.

"You're not. Being a normal person is not a bad thing. You'll learn all the rest. I was talking about . . . leverage." She couldn't help herself—his expression was just so openly devastated. She took another step toward him and grabbed one of his big, warm hands with both of her little icy ones. It made her feel better when the word *leverage* replaced the pain in his eyes with confusion. She hurried to explain. "You remember what Kevin and I were saying about leverage? About how you're the leverage the Agency needed to get him to expose himself?"

"Yes, that makes me feel *so* much better than useless."

"Let me finish." She took a deep breath. "They've never had anything on me. Barnaby was my only family. I didn't have some sister with a couple of kids and a house in the suburbs that the department could threaten to blow up. There was no one I cared about. Lonely, yes, but I was also free. It was only myself I had to keep alive."

She watched him think through the words, trying to sort out her meaning. She fumbled for a concrete example.

"See, if . . . if they had you," she explained slowly, "if they grabbed you somehow...I would have to come after you." It was so true it frightened her. She didn't understand why it was true, but that didn't change the fact.

His eyes widened and seemed to freeze that way.

"And they'd win, you know," she said apologetically. "They'd kill us both. But that doesn't mean I wouldn't have to try. See?" She shrugged. "Liability."

He opened his mouth to speak, then shut it again. He paced to the sink, then back to stand right in front of her.

"Why would you come after me? Guilt?"

"Some," she admitted.

"But it wasn't you who involved me, not really. They didn't choose me because of you."

"I know—that's why I said *some*. Maybe thirty-three percent."

He smiled a tiny bit, like she'd said something funny. "And the other sixty-seven percent?"

"Another thirty-three percent...justice? That's not the right word. But someone like you...you deserve more than this. You're a better person than any of them. It's not right that someone like you should have to be a part of this world. It's an evil waste."

She hadn't meant to be quite so vehement. She could tell she'd only confused him again. He didn't realize how unusual he was. He didn't belong down here in the filth of the trenches. Something about him was just...pure.

"And the last thirty-four?" he asked after a moment of thought.

"I don't *know*." She groaned.

She didn't know why or how he had become a central figure in her life. She didn't know why she automatically assumed he would be there in the future when that made no sense at all. She didn't know why, when his brother had asked her to keep an eye on him, her answer had been so earnest and so...*compulsory*.

Daniel was waiting for more. She spread her hands helplessly. She didn't know what else to say.

He smiled a little. "Well, *liability* doesn't seem such an awful word as it did before."

"It does to me."

"You know if they came for you, I would do what I could to stand in their way. So you're a liability for me, too."

"I wouldn't want you to do that."

"Because we'd both end up dead."

"Yes, we would! If they come for me, you *run*."

He laughed. "Agree to disagree."

"Daniel—"

"Let me tell you what else I see when I look at you."

Her shoulders hunched automatically. "Tell me the worst thing you see."

He sighed, then reached out to gently lay his fingertips along her cheekbone. "These bruises. They break my heart. But, in a really twisted and wrong way, I'm sort of grateful for them. How shameful is that?"

"Grateful?"

"Well, if my idiot bully of a brother hadn't beaten you up, you would have disappeared, and I would have had no way to ever find you again. Because of your injuries, you needed our help. You stayed with me."

His expression when he said the last four words was very unsettling. Or maybe it was his fingers lingering on her skin.

"Now can I tell you what else I see?"

She stared at him warily.

"I see a woman who is more . . . *real* than any other woman I've ever met. You make every other person I've known seem insubstantial, somehow incomplete. Like shadows and illusions. I loved my wife, or rather—as you so insightfully pointed out while I was high—I loved my idea of who she was. I truly did. But she was never as *there* to me as you are. I've never been drawn to someone the way I am to you, and I have been from the very first moment I met you.

It's like the difference between . . . between *reading* about gravity and then falling for the first time."

They stared at each other for what felt like hours but could have been minutes or even seconds. His hand, at first just touching her cheekbone with the very tips of his fingers, slowly relaxed down until his palm was cradling her jaw. His thumb brushed across her lower lip with a pressure so light, she wasn't totally sure she hadn't imagined it.

"This is entirely irrational on every level," she whispered.

"Don't kill me, please?"

She might have nodded.

He put his other hand on her face — so softly that despite her bruises there was no hint of pain. It was just live current, like the way a plasma globe must feel from the inside.

She started to remind herself, as his lips pressed gently against hers, that she was not thirteen years old and this was not her first kiss, so really . . . then his hands moved into her hair and held her mouth more firmly against his, his lips opened, and she couldn't even finish the thought. She couldn't think how the words were supposed to string together.

She gasped — just a tiny puff of breath — and he pulled his face an inch back, still holding her head secure in his long hands.

"Did I hurt you?"

She couldn't remember how to say *Just keep kissing me,* so instead she stretched up on her tiptoes to throw her arms around his neck and pull him closer. He was not unwilling to comply.

He must have felt the drag in her arms, or his back was protesting the considerable difference in their heights; he grabbed her waist and swung her up onto the island counter, never breaking the contact between their lips. Reflexively, her legs wrapped around his hips at the same time that his arms pulled tight around her torso, so their bodies were warmly fused together. Her fingers twisted themselves into his hair, and she was finally able to admit to herself that she had always been attracted to these unruly curls, that she'd secretly enjoyed running her fingers through them while he was unconscious in a way that was totally unprofessional.

There was something honest and so *Daniel* about the kiss, as if his personality — along with his scent and taste — was a part of the electricity humming back and forth between them. She started to understand what he'd been saying before, about how she was real to him. He was something new to her, an entirely new experience. It *was* like her first kiss, because no kiss had ever been so vivid, so much stronger than her own analytical mind. She didn't have to think.

It felt amazing not to think.

Everything was just kissing Daniel, like there had never been another purpose for breathing in and out.

He kissed her throat, her temple, the top of her head. He cradled her face against his neck and sighed.

"It feels like I've been waiting a century to do that. It's like time has lost all continuity. Every second with you outweighs days of life before I met you."

"This shouldn't be so easy." Once he'd stopped kissing her, she could think again. She wished she didn't have to.

He tilted her chin up. "What do you mean?"

"Shouldn't there be some...awkwardness? Noses bumping, all that. I mean, it's been a while for me, but that's how I remember it."

He kissed her nose. "Normally, yes. But this hasn't been a normal thing in any facet."

"I don't understand how this could happen. The odds are astronomically against it. You were just the random bait they put in a trap for me. And then, coincidentally, you just happen to be exactly..." She didn't know how to finish.

"Exactly what I want," he said, and he leaned in to kiss her again. He pulled back too soon. "I'll admit," he continued, "it's not a bet I would have taken."

"Your chances at winning the lottery would be better."

"Do you believe in fate?"

"Of course not."

He laughed at her scornful tone. "I guess karma is out, too, then?"

"Neither of those things is real."

"Can you prove that?"

"Well, not conclusively, no. But no one can prove they are real, either."

"Then you'll just have to accept that this is the world's most unlikely coincidence. I, however, think there is some balance in the universe. We've both been treated unfairly. Maybe this is our balance."

"It's irrational—"

He cut her off, his lips making her forget instantly what she had been about to say. He kissed along the skin of her cheekbone till he got to her ear.

"Rationality is overrated," he whispered.

Then his mouth was moving with hers again, and she couldn't help but agree. This was better than logic.

"You're not off the hook for *Indochine,*" he murmured.

"Huh?"

"The movie. I endangered our lives to acquire it, the least you can do is—"

This time, she didn't let him finish.

"Tomorrow," he said when they came up for air.

"Tomorrow," she agreed.

CHAPTER 16

Alex woke up the next day feeling both full of anticipation and also very, very stupid.

Honestly, it was like she couldn't complete a solid paragraph of thought without going back to some piece of Daniel's face, or the texture of his hands, or the way his breath felt against her throat. And of course, that was where the feeling of anticipation was coming from.

But there were so many practical matters that simply had to be considered. Last night, or rather this morning, by the time he'd kissed her good night for the hundredth time at the top of the stairs, she'd been too exhausted to think through any of it. She'd barely had the energy to arm her defenses and slip on her gas mask before she passed out.

It was probably a good thing; she'd been too addled then to grasp exactly what madness she'd just embarked on. Even now, it was hard to focus on anything but the fact that Daniel was probably awake somewhere. She was impatient to see him again, and yet also a little frightened. What if the crazy swell of emotion that had felt so natural and irresistible last night had evaporated? What if they were suddenly strangers again, with nothing to say?

That might be easier than if the feeling continued.

Today or tomorrow, or perhaps the next day, Kevin was going to call—

Ugh, Kevin. She could just imagine his reaction to recent developments.

She shook her head. That was irrelevant. Because today or tomorrow, Kevin was going to call and then she would send the e-mail that would make the rats scurry. Kevin would compile a list of names. He would go after his rats, and if she didn't act simultaneously, her rats would go to ground once they realized the danger. So she would have to leave Daniel here and embark on her retaliatory strike, knowing full well that there was a good chance she wouldn't be coming back. How would she explain that? How long did she have? Two days, at most? What truly hideous timing.

It didn't feel right to go into the day anticipating all the hours together with Daniel. It was dishonest. He'd heard the plan, but she was positive he hadn't thought it through enough to realize what it meant. So soon, she'd be leaving him here alone. Their time would be much better spent training him in the art of hiding. Some more shooting-range practice wouldn't hurt, either.

The feeling of anticipation turned to a sinking dread as her thoughts wound to a conclusion. Her behavior last night had been irresponsible. If she'd had any idea of what Daniel was thinking, she might have been able to work all this through before it had gotten out of hand. She might have been able to keep the appropriate distance between them. But she'd been taken completely by surprise.

Trying to understand a normal person was not her forte. Though, truly, someone who found the real Alex attractive was not a normal person at all.

She heard barking outside—it sounded like the dogs were coming back from the barn. She wondered if it was still morning or already afternoon.

She grabbed a set of clean clothes, disarmed the door, and snuck to the bathroom. She didn't want to see Daniel until her teeth were brushed. Which was stupid. She couldn't be allowed to kiss him again. That wouldn't be kind to either of them.

The hall was dark, the bathroom empty. The door to Daniel's room was open and the room beyond was empty, too. She ran through her ablutions quickly, trying not to spend too long at the mirror, wishing her face were further along the road to healing. Her lips were worse than yesterday, swollen again, but that was her own fault. The superglue had fallen off in her sleep and the darker welt down the center of her bottom lip showed some promise of changing the shape of her mouth permanently.

She heard the TV on as she came down the stairs. When she walked into the big front room, she saw Daniel bending over the console beneath the flat-screen. The front door was open, a warm breeze blowing in through the screen. It ruffled the curls on the back of his head

He was grumbling to himself. "*Why* does anyone need five different input options?" He ran a hand through the hair that was falling into his eyes. "It's a DVD. I'm not trying to launch the space shuttle."

His Danielness stopped her where she stood, and a wave of cowardice made her want to turn around and sneak back upstairs. How would she tell him the things she needed to say? The thought of making him unhappy was suddenly more repugnant than she had been prepared for.

Lola yelped from outside the front door, looking hopefully through the screen at her. Daniel spun around and when he caught sight of Alex, a huge grin lit his face. He was across the room in four long strides, and then he lifted her up in an exuberant bear hug.

"You're up," he said excitedly. "Are you hungry? I've got everything for omelets."

"No," she said, trying to extricate herself. At the same time, her stomach growled.

He put her down and stared at her with raised eyebrows.

"I mean yes," she admitted. "But first can we talk for a second, please?"

He sighed. "I thought you might wake in an analytical mood. Just one thing before you start…"

She wanted to duck away. The guilt was very strong. But it wasn't as strong as her need to kiss him back. She didn't know if she would get another chance. It was a very gentle kiss, soft and slow. He'd noticed the condition of her lips.

When he broke away—him, not her; it was like she had no self-control at all—it was her turn to sigh.

He let his arms fall but took her hand as he led her to the couch. Little zings of electricity buzzed up her arm, and she silently castigated herself for being such a sucker. So what if this was the first time he'd held her hand? She had to get a grip.

Lola yelped again, hopefully, when she saw Alex nearing the door. Alex shot her one apologetic look. Khan and Einstein were both curled up on the porch behind her, Khan creating a massive boulder of fur.

Daniel grabbed the remote out of his way, muting the TV before dropping it onto the ground. He pulled her down next to him, keeping her hand. He was still smiling.

"Let me guess. You think we are being unwise," he said.

"Well…yes."

"Because it's impossible that we could really be compatible, given the genesis of our relationship. I'll concede it wasn't exactly a Hollywood meet-cute."

"It's not that." She looked down at his hand. It entirely engulfed hers.

Maybe she was wrong. Maybe this whole retribution scheme was poorly thought out. There was nothing to stop her from running again. She could make back the money she'd lost. She could go to Chicago, work things out with Joey Giancardi, be a Mob doctor again. Maybe, given what she now knew about the plan to eliminate her, the Family could actually offer her some protection.

Or she could just work a counter at a backwoods diner and live without the extras—like tryptamines and opioids and booby traps. Who knew how long the IDs she already had might last if she kept her head down?

"Alex?" he asked.

"I'm just thinking about the future."

"Our long-term compatibility?" he guessed.

"No, not long term. I was thinking about what happens tonight. Or tomorrow." She finally looked up at him. His soft gray-green eyes were just a little confused, not troubled. Yet.

"Your brother will call soon."

He made a face. "Wow. I hadn't thought about that." He shuddered. "I guess it's better to mention this casually over the phone—by the way, Kev, I've fallen in love with Alex—than in person, right?"

She disapproved entirely of the tingles that snapped through her nervous system when he made his facetious practice announcement. That wasn't a word to bandy around casually. He shouldn't have used it. But still, the tingles.

"That's not the part I was worrying about. You remember the plan."

"Once he's in position, we send the e-mail. He watches who reacts. Then we meet up with him and..." He trailed off, his brow suddenly furrowing. "Then you both are going to—what's the phrase?—*take them out,* right? That's going to be very dangerous, isn't it? Couldn't we just let Kevin handle things alone? It seems like he probably wouldn't mind. I get the sense he liked his job."

"That wasn't our deal. And, Daniel..."

"What?" His voice was harder now, with an edge. He was beginning to understand.

"Neither Kevin nor I will be able to...well, perform at our best if the leverage they have against us is in the same place the bad guys are."

There was almost a physical weight to the meaning of her words as they dropped, an aftershock in the silence that followed.

He stared at her, unblinking, for a long moment. She waited.

"Are you joking?" he finally asked. His voice wasn't much more than a whisper. "Do you think I'm really going to let you leave me here to twiddle my thumbs while you risk your life?"

"No. And yes, you are."

"Alex..."

"I know how to take care of myself."

"I know that, but...I just can't wrap my mind around it. How will I stand it? Waiting here, not knowing? Alex, I'm serious!"

His voice turned impatient at the end. She wasn't looking at him; she was staring straight ahead at the television.

"Alex?"

"Turn up the volume. *Now.*"

He glanced at the TV, froze for one brief second, then jumped up and fumbled on the floor for the remote. He jammed a few wrong keys before the newscaster's voice thundered through the surround-sound speakers.

"—missing since last Thursday, when police believe he was abducted from the high school where he teaches. A substantial reward is being offered for information leading to his recovery. If you've seen this man, please call the number below."

On the large screen, Daniel's face was blown up to four times its actual size. It was a snapshot rather than an official portrait from the yearbook. He was outside somewhere sunny, smiling widely, his hair tousled and damp from sweat. His arms were stretched over the shoulders of two shorter people whose faces were cropped out of the image. It was a very good picture of him, both attractive and engaging; he looked like the kind of person you would want to help. An 800 number was printed in bright red across the bottom of the screen.

The picture disappeared, replaced by a handsomely aging anchorman and a much younger, perky blond anchorwoman.

"That's a shame, Bryan. Let's hope they get him back home to his family soon. Now we'll take a look at the weather with Marceline. How are things looking for the rest of the week, Marcie?"

The picture moved to a sultry brunette standing in front of a digital map of the entire country.

"This is national news," Alex whispered. Her mind started working through the scenarios.

Daniel muted the sound.

"The school must have called the police," Daniel said.

She just looked at him.

"What?"

"Daniel, do you know how many people go missing every day?"

"Oh ... their pictures don't all end up on the news, do they?"

"Especially not full-grown men who've only been missing a few days." She got up and started pacing. "They're trying to flush you out. What does that mean? Where are they going with this? Do they think Kevin killed me? Or do they think I figured out the truth and took off with you? Why would they think I'd take you with me? It has to be about Kevin. It *is* his face, too. They must think I lost. Right? This news spot would be easier for the CIA to arrange than for my department. Of course, if they're working together ..."

"Will Kevin see this?" Daniel worried. "He's right there in DC."

"Kevin's not showing his face, regardless."

She paced for another minute, then went to sit with Daniel again. She curled her legs under her and took his hand.

"Daniel, who did you talk to yesterday?"

His color heightened. "I told you. I didn't speak to anyone but the people at the counter."

"I know, but who were they? Male, female, old, young?"

"Um, the checker at the grocery store was a guy, older, maybe fifty, Hispanic."

"Was the store busy?"

"A little. He was the only checker. There were three people in line behind me."

"That's good."

"The dollar store was small. It was just me. But the woman at the counter had a TV on — she was watching a game show. She didn't look up much."

"How old was she?"

"Older than the first guy. White hair. Why? Older people watch more news, don't they?"

She shrugged. "Possibly. The third?"

"Just graduated, I guess. I remember wondering if school was out before I realized she worked there."

Her stomach felt suddenly heavier. "A young girl? And she was friendly — very friendly." It wasn't a question.

"Yes. How did you know?"

She sighed. "Daniel, you're an attractive man."

"I'm ordinary, at best. And I'm a decade too old for a girl that age," he protested.

"Old enough to be intriguing. Look, it doesn't matter. We'll do the few things we can. You stop shaving as of now, and we lie not just low, but *flat*. Aside from that, all we can do is hope the girl's not a news watcher. And that they don't run any pieces on whatever social media kids are using right now."

"Would they?"

"If they think of it. They're throwing Hail Marys."

He dropped his head into his free hand. "I'm so sorry."

"It's okay. We've all made mistakes on this little endeavor."

"You haven't. You're trying to make me feel better."

"I've made several major errors in the past few weeks."

He looked up, disbelieving.

"One, I didn't just ignore Carston's e-mail in the first place. Two, I fell for the trap. Three, I missed your tracker. Four, I didn't arm the ceiling in the barn. And then Kevin made the mistake of taking off his gas mask...I guess that's the only one I can think of for him, except for not having transport out. Bummer, I guess he wins that round."

"Well, he also did something wrong in the beginning or the CIA would have bought that he was dead."

"Good point. Thanks."

"Arnie, though," he said sadly. "Arnie's still batting a thousand."

"Don't you just hate those insufferable perfectionists?"

Daniel laughed. "So much." The humor left his face. "But I don't think you made so many mistakes. I mean, I guess when it comes to what's best for you, yes. But for me . . . Well, I'm glad you fell for it."

She gave him a sardonic look. "That's taking romance a little too far, don't you think?" She wished she could completely excise the memory of their first night together, with a scalpel if necessary. She wished those images weren't so clear and sharp in her mind — the tendons standing out in his neck, the sound of his muffled screams. She shuddered, wondering how long it would take until they faded.

"I'm serious. If it wasn't you, they would have sent someone else for me. And if that person had gotten the best of Kevin, whoever it was would have killed me right then, wouldn't he?"

She looked into his earnest eyes, and then shuddered again. "You're right."

He stared back for a long moment, then sighed. "So what do we do now?"

Alex frowned. "Well, our options are limited. My face still isn't ready for scrutiny. But it's now better than yours. So we can stay here and keep our heads down, or we could go north. I have a place. It's not as fancy as this one or as well protected. I don't have a Batcave." The jealousy in her voice on the last line was unconcealed.

"So you think it's safer here?"

"It depends. I'd like to get Arnie's thoughts about the town before we decide. Kevin's take wouldn't hurt, either. Hopefully he'll call soon. The plans have changed a little. I think he's going to get his wish. He gets to be the victor after all."

• • •

THE DAY DRAGGED. Alex didn't want to leave the television. It didn't change things much, knowing how many times they aired the piece and how many outlets picked it up, but she still had to watch. Arnie took the new situation with the stoicism she expected, only the tightening of his eyes betraying his worry.

Alex wanted to send Arnie to the Batcave with a list of everything she needed. She'd love to have the SIG for herself, plus extra ammo, and for Daniel the sawed-off shotgun that she'd seen in Kevin's stash. A sniper rifle wasn't as helpful in close quarters as a shotgun would be. It could incapacitate multiple attackers with one load of buckshot.

She also wanted to hunt for gas masks—she couldn't wire up the house if she didn't have a third for Arnie. She doubted Kevin would have overlooked such an obvious safety feature, but then again, maybe it was obvious only to someone like her. In his world, Kevin probably only worried about bullets and bombs.

But though she wanted these things badly, it might already be too late for preparations. If the flirtatious checker had called after the first broadcast—which could have aired earlier in the day than the one they'd seen, or even the day before—it would take a certain amount of time for their enemies to begin the search. Someone had to get here, then ask questions around town, and finally start investigating possible leads. But then, if that someone had good luck, the surveillance would begin. And she had no way of knowing if it already had.

Even though she and Daniel were staying inside with the windows covered, someone could be watching Arnie right now. If Arnie took a field trip to the Batcave, the watcher would follow. At that point, they might as well put up a banner that read CONGRATULATIONS, YOU'VE FOUND THE RIGHT PLACE! HELP YOURSELF TO A FEW ROCKET LAUNCHERS!

They could do nothing that might give away the existence of the Batcave.

Her most essential defenses were in easy reach, everything of importance loaded into her backpack—neatly Ziplocked by category—for a quick retreat. She had Arnie move the truck to the back of the house, close enough to Arnie's bedroom window that they could be in the front cab with one well-hidden step.

She wished Kevin would call or that he'd trusted them enough to give Daniel the number to his own burner phone, in case of emergency. There might be additional safeties he'd built into the place that Arnie wasn't aware of.

Daniel made dinner for the three of them, and though it wasn't as high-spirited an affair as the previous night's, it was still delicious. She told him to slow down with his stock of ingredients. It might be a while before shopping was on the agenda again, even for Arnie.

It surprised her how unaware Daniel seemed to be of Arnie's presence—well, not unaware, exactly, just unaffected. Not that he was rude to Arnie or ignored him, but Daniel made no effort to hide his new closeness with Alex in front of him. Twice he took her hand; once he kissed the top of her head as he passed with the dishes. Arnie, unsurprisingly, showed no reaction to Daniel's exhibition, but she couldn't help but wonder what he thought of it.

Arnie told them he had the dogs on rotation to run the perimeter fence—all six miles of it—while it was light out, the time when scouts would be watching through binoculars. If anyone was perched close enough to watch the house, the dogs would alert him. After that announcement, he went to bed early, keeping his normal routine. Alex and Daniel stayed up to watch the evening news.

He curled around her on the sofa so naturally that it didn't feel out of the ordinary at all. She couldn't remember feeling so physically comfortable with anyone in all her life. Even her mother had been a brittle hugger, someone who rarely expressed affection, in words or actions. Alex's closeness with Barnaby was verbal, never physical. So she thought that she should feel awkward and embarrassed with her legs draped across another person's lap, her head cradled against that person's shoulder while his arms were wrapped around her, but she felt only oddly relaxed. As if his proximity somehow removed a portion of the stress from the situation.

The Daniel piece played again, but it ran later in the program than before, and she could tell the night anchor was bored by the story. The Agency might be able to force this bit into the news for a short time, but they couldn't keep the networks from reacting to what a nonstory it was. Of course, there was the obvious second act.

"I should probably warn you . . . if you haven't thought of it already," she said.

He tried to sound glib, but she could hear the wariness. "I'm sure I haven't."

"Well, if this story doesn't get results quickly, they'll have to up the ante to keep the press working for them."

"What does that mean, up the ante?"

She leaned back so she could see his face, her nose wrinkling in distaste at what she had to say. "They'll make the story more salacious somehow. Say you're suspected of a crime. Invent a student who you abducted or abused. Something along those lines, probably. They could be more creative, though."

His eyes shifted from her face back to the television screen, though the announcer had moved on to early primary predictions. He flushed, then went pale. She let him take his time with the idea. She could imagine how hard it would be for a good man to realize he was about to become a villain.

"There's nothing I can do about it," he said quietly. It was not quite a question.

"No."

"At least my parents aren't around to see it. Maybe . . . I don't think *all* my friends will believe it."

"I wouldn't," she agreed.

He smiled down at her. "At one point in the not too distant past, you thought I was going to murder a couple million people."

"I didn't know you then."

"True."

When the late news was done, they engaged in a more subdued

good-night, then she began the cleanup. They might have to leave quickly. She dismantled and stowed her lab, then changed into leggings and a black T-shirt — things she would be comfortable in if tonight was the night they had to run.

She knew she was tired, but her brain couldn't seem to slow down. She didn't want to miss anything else. Daniel might be right — perhaps her first big mistakes were actually good things in that they might have saved his life. But she couldn't afford any more errors. It wasn't just her own life at stake now. She sighed to herself. There were benefits to having a liability, but the load was definitely much heavier.

A quiet knock interrupted her thoughts.

"Don't open the door," she cautioned quickly, jerking upright. The cot rocked underneath her.

After a short pause, Daniel asked, "Are you wearing a gas mask?"

"Yes."

"I thought so. Your voice sounds muffled."

Another pause.

"Is your security system terribly difficult to disarm?" he wondered.

"Give me a minute."

It took less than that to secure the live wires. She pushed her mask back onto the top of her head and opened the door. He was leaning against the frame. She couldn't see him perfectly in the darkness, but she thought he looked tired... and sad.

"You're very worried," he inferred, reaching to touch her mask lightly.

"Actually, I always sleep with this. It feels weird if I don't have it on. Is something wrong?"

"More than everything? No. I was just... lonely. I couldn't sleep. I wanted to be with you." He hesitated. "Can I come in?"

"Um, okay." She took a step back, switching the light on.

He looked around, a new expression taking over. "*This* is the room Kevin gave you? Why didn't you say something? You should have my room!"

"I'm fine here," she assured him. "I'm not much for beds, anyway. It's safer to sleep light."

"I don't know what to say. I can't sleep in a king-size bed knowing you're stuck in a storage box."

"Really, I like it."

He gave her a doubtful look, which turned suddenly sheepish. "I was going to invite myself in, but there's barely room for you."

"We could shift some crates..."

"I have a better idea. Come with me." He offered his hand.

She took it without considering what she was doing. He pulled her down the dark hall, past the bathroom door, to his own room. The only light came from a small lamp on the bedside table.

It was a very nice room, more in line with Kevin's usual aesthetic than her own storage space. There was a massive bed in the middle of the room, covered in a white comforter, with a rustic four-poster frame made of artfully unfinished logs. A gold blanket that matched the tone of the wood was draped over the foot of the bed.

"You see?" he said. "There's no way I could sleep in here again after seeing your sad situation. I'd feel like a horrible excuse for a man."

"Well, I'm not trading. I already have my room wired."

They stood awkwardly in the doorway for a moment.

"I didn't really have anything specific in mind to talk about. I just wanted to be where you were."

"It's okay. I wasn't sleeping, either."

"Let's not sleep together," he said, then he flushed and laughed embarrassedly. "That didn't sound right at all." He pulled her hand again, toward the big bed. "Look, I promise to be a perfect gentleman," he said. "I'll just feel less anxious if I can see you."

She climbed up on the thick white comforter next to him, laughing with him at his awkwardness and wondering privately if she *wanted* him to be a perfect gentleman. She reminded herself sternly that this was not the appropriate time for those kinds of thoughts. Maybe someday in the future when their lives weren't in danger. If that day ever came.

He took her hand but otherwise gave her space. They both lay back on the stacks of feather pillows. He put his free hand behind his head and looked over at her.

"Yes, see, this is better."

And it was. It didn't make sense — she was out of her secured room and farther from her other weapons — but, paradoxically, she felt safer.

"Yes," she agreed. She slipped the gas mask off her head and laid it beside her.

"Your hand is cold."

Before she could respond, he sat up and grabbed the blanket from the foot of the bed. He shook it out, then settled it over them. When he lay back, he was closer to her. His shoulder touched hers, and his arm lay over hers as he took her hand again.

Why was she so vividly aware of things that, in the grand scheme of survival, didn't really matter?

"Thanks," she said.

"Don't take this the wrong way — I mean it as the highest compliment and not as a slight to your company — but I think I might actually be able to sleep with you here."

"I know what you mean. It's been a long day."

"Yes," he agreed fervently. "Are you comfortable?"

"I am. Don't take *this* the wrong way, but I might put my mask back on at some point. It's just a weird sleep habit."

He smiled. "Like hugging a teddy bear."

"Exactly like that, only not adorable."

He rolled toward her and leaned his forehead against her temple. She could feel his eyelashes brush against her cheek as he closed his eyes. His right arm snaked around her waist.

"*I* think you're adorable," he breathed. His voice sounded like he was already half asleep. "And terrifyingly lethal, too, of course." He yawned.

"Very sweet," she said, but she wasn't sure if he heard her. He was breathing so evenly she thought he might already be out.

She waited a few moments and then, carefully, she reached up with her free hand to touch his curls. They were so soft. Her fingers traced his features, totally calm in unconsciousness. It was that same innocent, serene face that had never belonged in her world. She didn't think she'd ever seen anything quite so beautiful.

She fell asleep like that, with her hand tucked possessively around the nape of his neck, the gas mask forgotten behind her back.

CHAPTER 17

Kevin didn't call.

Daniel didn't seem to think this was odd, but Alex thought she detected some extra strain in Arnie's shoulders.

It was too long.

As she'd understood things, Kevin only had to get into a position from which he could follow the one person they knew for certain was involved—Carston. He could have made the drive to DC in two days, even taking it easy. She'd told him exactly where to find her old boss once he was there. It was only a few hours' work, at most. If Carston wasn't where he was supposed to be, Kevin should have called. What was he doing?

Or had something happened to him? How long should she wait before suggesting that possibility to Daniel?

The new worry added to her paranoia. She strung an extra lead outside the door to her room so that it could be armed while she was in another part of the house. It was so frustrating, not being able to wire the whole first floor. Just one gas mask short.

On the plus side, every hour hidden helped her face. Under low-wattage lighting and with a lot of makeup, she might be able to escape notice for three or even four seconds.

The wait was an odd mix of boredom, stress, and the strangest kind of happiness. Doomed happiness, happiness with a deadline, but that didn't make it less...all-encompassing. She should be in a very dark place right now, the pulsing beat of the hunt filling her ears, but she found herself smiling as a default expression. It didn't help that Daniel was just as inappropriately giddy as she was. They talked about it the next afternoon while watching the news.

Alex had snuck Lola inside when Arnie left to go train with the other animals—she felt bad that they had to keep the door closed on the dogs; it seemed rude—and Einstein and Khan had come with her. Which made the room awkwardly full of dog. She hoped Arnie wouldn't be upset. The dogs must come in sometimes or there wouldn't be the doggie door in the laundry room. She didn't know if the dogs were usually kept outside as part of their training or as an early alarm system or because Arnie had allergies—though if it was the last option, he'd chosen the wrong lifestyle.

Lola parked her floppy jowls and ears on Alex's thigh, where there would shortly be a drool situation, Alex was sure. Einstein jumped right up on the couch beside Daniel, tail waving enthusiastically at the rule breaking. Khan turned himself into a long ottoman in front of the couch. After the program's dull opening story—focused on politics, naturally, as if there weren't almost a year to go before anything actually happened—Daniel stretched his long legs out across Khan's back. Khan didn't seem to mind. Alex stroked Lola's ears, and Lola's tail thumped against the floor.

It all felt comfortable and *familiar,* though she'd never been in a position like this in her entire life. She'd never been so closely surrounded by living things—touching them, hearing their breathing—let alone holding hands with a man who thought she was adorable... and lethal. That he could know her full story and still be able to look at her the way he did...

Her eyes moved automatically to his face while the thought ran through her mind, and she found him looking at her, too. He smiled his wide, bright grin—the two days' stubble making him look unexpectedly rugged—and she smiled back without thinking about it. All kinds of bubbly emotions percolated through her chest, and she realized it was probably the best feeling she'd ever known.

She sighed, then groaned.

He glanced at the TV, looking for a reason, but it was just a commercial. "What is it?"

"I feel goofy," she admitted. "Stupid. Bubbly. Why does everything seem so positive? I can't string logical thoughts together. I try to worry, and I end up smiling. I might be losing my mind, and I don't care about that nearly as much as I should. I want to punch myself, but my face is finally just starting to heal."

Daniel laughed. "That's one of the drawbacks of falling in love, I think."

Stomach tingles again. "Is that what you think we're doing?"

"Feels like it to me."

She frowned. "I don't have any comparisons. What if I'm actually going insane?"

"You are most definitely sane."

"But I don't believe people can fall in love so quickly." Truthfully, she didn't entirely believe in *love,* romantic love, at all. Chemical responses, sure; sexual attraction, yes. Compatibility, yes. Friendship. Loyalty and responsibility. But *love* just seemed a little too much of a fairy tale.

"I . . . well, I never used to. I mean, I always believed in *attraction* at first sight. I've experienced that. And that's definitely a part of what's happening for me now." He grinned again. "But love at first sight? Just fantasy, I was sure."

"Of course it is."

"Except . . ."

"There's no except, Daniel."

"Except that something happened to me on that train, something totally outside of my experience or ability to explain."

She didn't know what to say. She glanced at the TV just as the newscast's ending theme began to play.

That caught Daniel's attention, too. "Did we miss it?"

"No, it didn't run."

"And that's not a good thing," he assumed, an edge creeping into his voice.

"I can think of a couple different things it could mean. One, they pushed the story out, and when it didn't get results, they had to let it die. Two, the story is about to change."

Daniel's shoulders squared defensively. "How soon do you think we'll see the next version?"

"Very soon, if that's what's happening."

There was a third possibility, but she wasn't ready to say it aloud. The story would definitely disappear if they'd gotten what they needed from it. If they had Kevin now.

She thought she understood enough about Kevin's character to be fairly certain that he wouldn't give them up easily. He was smart enough to go with the most believable version of the story if the department caught him: He'd been too late to save Daniel, and—after killing the Oleander—he'd gone to DC for revenge. He'd be able to stick to that story for a while . . . she hoped. She didn't know who they had doing interrogations now. If that person was any good—well, eventually Kevin would tell the truth. As much as she wasn't Kevin's biggest fan, she felt sick for him now.

Of course, he could have been prepared for capture, the way she would have been. He could be dead already.

Batcave or no Batcave, if Kevin didn't call by midnight, it would be time to leave. She could feel when she was pushing her luck.

Well, all the happy feelings had subsided. At least that was a sign that she wasn't totally crazy. Yet.

They shooed the dogs out onto the porch before Arnie was due to come back, though the animal smell would probably give them away regardless. Daniel started a meat sauce for spaghetti, and she helped with the simple parts—opening cans, measuring spices. It was effortless and companionable working side by side, like they'd been doing this for years. Was that the feeling Daniel was talking about? The strange ease of their togetherness? Though she didn't believe his theory, she had to admit to herself that she had no explanation of her own.

Daniel hummed as he worked, a familiar-sounding tune that she couldn't place at first. She caught herself humming along a few minutes later. Without seeming to realize he was doing it, Daniel started to sing the words.

" 'Guilty feet have got no rhythm,' " he sang.

"Isn't that song older than you are?" she asked after a moment.

He seemed surprised. "Oh, was I singing that out loud? Sorry, I tend to do that when I cook if I don't keep a strict hold on myself."

"How do you even know the words?"

"I'll have you know that to this day, 'Careless Whisper' remains a very popular song on the karaoke circuit. I kill it on eighties night."

"You're into karaoke?"

"Hey, who says schoolteachers don't know how to party?" He stepped away from the stove, sauce-covered spoon still in his right hand, and pulled her into a loose embrace with his left. He danced her once around a small circle, pressing his rough cheek against hers, while singing, " 'Pain is *ah-all* you'll find...' " Then he turned back to the stove, dancing in place while he sang cheerfully about how he was never going to dance again.

Don't be an idiot, her mind told her as the goofy smile stretched across her face again.

Shut up, her body responded.

Daniel didn't have a voice that belonged on the air, but it was a pleasant, light tenor, and he made up for any deficiencies with his enthusiasm. By the time they heard the dogs greet Arnie at the door, they were in the middle of a passionate duet of "Total Eclipse of the Heart." Alex quit singing immediately, her face flushing, but Daniel seemed oblivious both to her cowardice and to Arnie's entrance.

" 'I really need you tonight!' " he belted out as Arnie came through the door, shaking his head. It made Alex wonder if Kevin was ever any fun or if it was just business all the time when he and Arnie were here alone.

Arnie didn't comment, just shut the screen door behind him, letting the fresh warm air mix with the smells of garlic, onion, and tomato. Now that it was dark outside and light inside, she'd have to make sure he closed the exterior door before she or Daniel went into the part of the room that would be visible to anyone watching.

"Anything from the dogs?" she asked Arnie.

"Nope. You would have heard them if they'd found anything."

She frowned. "The story didn't run."

Alex and Arnie exchanged a look. Arnie's eyes cut to Daniel's back, then returned to her. She knew what he was asking, and she shook her head no. No, she hadn't talked to Daniel about Kevin and what his silence could mean. Arnie's eyes did that subtle tightening thing that seemed to be his only physical tell for stress.

For Arnie's sake, they'd have to get out as soon as possible. If anyone connected Daniel and Alex to this house, it would put Arnie in danger. She hoped he would understand about the truck.

Dinner was subdued. Even Daniel seemed to catch the mood. She decided she would tell him her fears about Kevin as soon as they were alone. It would be nice to allow him one more night of decent sleep, but they should probably leave before first light.

After they were finished — and not a noodle had survived; Arnie would miss this part of having houseguests, at least — she helped clear while Arnie went to turn on the news. The story lineup was repetitively familiar. She felt like she could recite along with the anchorwoman word for word. Arnie hadn't already watched three rounds today; he settled into the couch.

Alex rinsed the plates and handed them to Daniel to load. One of the dogs whined through the screen door; probably Lola. Alex hoped she hadn't spoiled them too much this afternoon. She'd never thought she was a dog person, but she realized she was going to miss the warm and friendly inclusion of the pack. Maybe someday — if Kevin was somehow still alive and well and the plan was operable after all — she might get herself a dog. If all the happy thoughts were real, maybe Kevin would even sell her Lola. It probably wasn't a practical —

A low, fast *thud* interrupted her thoughts—it was a sound that didn't belong. Even as her eyes were moving toward Daniel, looking for a dropped utensil or a slammed cupboard that would explain the noise, her mind was leaping ahead. Before her body had realigned with her brain, a huge baying cry erupted from the porch, along with a vicious growling. Another *thud,* quieter beside the hullabaloo of the dogs, and the baying broke off into a shocked and pained yelp.

She tackled Daniel to the ground while he was still turning toward the door. He outweighed her by a lot, but he was off balance and went down easy.

"*Shhh,*" she hissed fiercely in his ear, then she crawled over him to the edge of the island and peered around. She couldn't see Arnie. She looked at the screen door—a small round hole was torn through the center of the top panel. She tried to listen over the sound of the dogs and the TV, but she couldn't hear any sound from where Arnie should be.

It had to be a distance shot or the dogs would have seen it coming.

"Arnie!" she hoarsely whisper-shouted.

There was no response.

She slithered to the dining-room table, where her backpack was propped against the leg of the chair she'd used. She ripped her PPK out of its Ziploc bag, then slid it across the floor to Daniel. She needed both hands.

Daniel snagged the gun when it was halfway to the island and leaned around the edge. He hadn't practiced with a handgun, but at this distance that wouldn't matter terribly much.

She shoved her rings on and flung the belt around her waist.

Daniel was on his feet in a fraction of a second, bracing his elbows on top of the counter. He didn't look at all conflicted about his ability to fire. She scuttled to the nearby wall where the dining room jutted out from the great room. As she moved, she saw a hand shoving the handle down—but it wasn't a hand. It was a black furry paw.

So Kevin had chosen not to go with the standard round door-knob for more reasons than aesthetics.

She breathed again as Einstein burst into the room, Khan and the Rottweiler close on his heels. She could hear Lola panting pained cries outside, and her teeth ground together.

While the dogs congregated silently around Daniel, forming a furry shield, she got her fighting shoes on and shoved the garrote wire into one pocket, the wooden handles into the other.

"Give the command," she whispered to Daniel.

The shooter would be running in now, though he would have to be on the lookout for the dogs. If he had the option, he'd switch the distance rifle for something that made bigger holes. Dogs like these would keep coming through a lot of hurt.

"Escape protocol?" Daniel whispered uncertainly.

Einstein's ears quivered. He gave a quiet cough of a bark, then trotted to the far end of the kitchen and whined.

"Follow him," Alex instructed Daniel. She darted across the space between the wall and the island, keeping herself in a low crouch.

Daniel started to straighten, but before she could say anything, Einstein hurtled over and caught Daniel's hand in his mouth. He yanked Daniel back to the ground.

"Keep low," she translated in a whisper.

Einstein led them toward the laundry room, as Alex had expected, with Khan and the Rottweiler bringing up the rear. As she ducked from the great room to the darkened hallway, she tried to see Arnie. She could see only one hand at first, unmoving, but then she spied splatter against the far wall. It was obvious that there was brain matter mixed in with the blood. So there was no point in trying to drag him with them. It was too late for Arnie. And the shooter was obviously a marksman. The good news just kept coming.

Alex was surprised when Einstein stopped short of the laundry room and pawed at a closet in the hall. Daniel pulled the door open, and Einstein jumped past him and tugged at something inside. Alex crept closer just as a weighty pile of fur fell out on top of her.

"What is this?" Daniel breathed in her ear.

She felt her way through the pile. "I think it's a fur coat—but there's something else. It's too heavy..." She ran her hands quickly over the coat, along the sleeves; there was something stiff and rectangular under the fur. She stuck her hand inside the sleeve, trying to understand what she was examining. Finally, her fingers made sense of it. She wasn't sure she would have put it together if she hadn't recently cut Kevin out of a Batsuit.

Einstein pulled another dense bulk of fur down on them.

"They're lined in Kevlar," she whispered.

"We should put them on."

Alex struggled into hers as she worked through it in her head. The Kevlar made sense, but why the cumbersome fur? Had Kevin trained the dogs during cold weather? Was this just preparation for the elements? Did it even get that cold here? But as she yanked up the arms—too long, of course—to free her hands, she saw how Daniel's coat was blending into Einstein's fur so that she couldn't see where one stopped and the other began. Camouflage.

The coat even had a Kevlar-lined hood, which she pulled over her head. Now she and Daniel were just two more furry shapes in the darkness.

Einstein went directly through the doggie door at the far end of the laundry room, and Daniel went right after. She could feel Khan's heat close behind her. She got through the door and saw Einstein pulling Daniel back down as he tried to rise into a crouch.

"Crawl," she explained.

It was frustratingly slow; the coat got heavier and hotter with every foot she gained, and the gravel was like knifepoints under her palms and knees. Once they got onto the stubbly grass, it was a little less painful, but she was so impatient with the pace that she barely noticed. She worried, as Einstein led them toward the outbuilding where the dogs lived, that he was trying to take them to the truck that she'd instructed Arnie to move. But the truck wasn't such a great escape. The shooter might be holding his position, just waiting for someone to try to drive out on the only road. Or this could be a new variation, where the shooter had friends to sweep the house and flush his victims out while he waited.

She could hear the restive dogs penned in the outbuilding ahead, none of them happy with what was happening. They'd made it three-fourths of the way when another sharp *thud* kicked a cloud of dirt into her face. Einstein barked sharply, and Alex heard one of the dogs behind her thunder off from their little pack, growling in a low bass. The heavy sound of his paws combined with his compact stride made her sure it must be the Rottweiler. Another *thud,* farther out, but the growling didn't change tempo. She heard something, maybe a muffled curse, and then a hail of bullets rattled out from what was most definitely *not* a sniper rifle. Her muscles tensed, even as she crawled as quickly as she could in Daniel's wake, waiting for the inevitable sound of the Rottweiler's yelps. The sound didn't come, but the growling vanished. Tears pricked her eyes.

Khan moved into position at her side—the shooter's side—and she saw Einstein was providing the same protection to Daniel. Kevin had said the dogs would give their lives for Daniel, and they were proving it. It would probably irk Kevin to know they were doing the same for her.

Kevin. Well, the odds were now better that he was alive. The news broadcasts hadn't cut off because the Agency had found Kevin but because they'd successfully located Daniel.

They made the outbuilding. She crawled gratefully into the obscuring dark. The dogs inside were whining and barking anxiously. Fighting the heavy mass of the lined coat, she struggled to her feet, still bent over but able to move faster. Daniel copied her, keeping an eye on Einstein to see if he would insist they get back down. Einstein wasn't paying attention to Daniel at the moment, though.

Both he and Khan were doing a stuttering race down the line of kennels, stopping at each door and then bounding to the next. At first she wasn't sure if she was supposed to run, too, but then she realized what they were doing. The closest kennels swung open, then the following set. Kevin had taught his prize pupils how to open the kennels from the outside.

The freed dogs were immediately silent. The first pair was a matched set of standard German shepherds. The two dogs raced out the barn door, heading north. Before they were out of sight, three Rottweilers sprinted past her toward the south. A lone Doberman followed, then a quartet of German shepherds, each group heading in a different direction. The dogs started flooding out of the building so quickly that she lost count entirely. Easily more than thirty animals, though some of them were still very young. Part of her wanted to cheer, *Tear 'em up, boys!* while the other part wanted to tell them, *Be careful!* She saw Lola's pups run past, and her eyes teared again.

In the dark night, someone shouted in panic. Gunfire, then screaming. A tight, mirthless smile stretched her lips.

But it wasn't entirely good news. She heard shots from another direction. Definitely multiple attackers.

"Gun?" she whispered to Daniel. He nodded and pulled it out from the waist of his jeans. He offered it to her. She shook her head. She'd just wanted to know he hadn't dropped it. She was dripping sweat inside the thick fur. She pushed back the hood and wiped her forearm across her forehead.

"What now?" he murmured. "Are we supposed to wait here?"

She was just about to say that as an *escape,* this didn't quite answer, when Einstein was back, tugging Daniel down again. She got on her hands and knees and followed as Einstein led them out the door they'd come in. Khan was still there, bringing up the rear again. This time Einstein led them due north, though she didn't know of any additional structure that way. It was probably going to be a long crawl, she realized, and her hands were already deeply scratched from the dry stalks of grass. She tried to protect her palms with the cuffs of the coat's sleeves, but that part wasn't lined, so it only helped a little. At least there were too many furry shapes in the night for a shooter to bother with four that weren't attacking. She looked back toward the house in the distance. She didn't see any new lights on. They hadn't started clearing the house yet. The dog sounds continued, faraway growling, the baying of Lola's pups, and random staccato barks.

She lost track of time, only aware of the amount of sweat she was producing, the rasping sound of her panting, the fact that they'd been going slightly uphill the whole way and now Daniel was slowing some, and that her palms were being pierced again and again, despite the coat. But she didn't think they'd gone very far when Daniel gasped quietly and stopped. She crawled up beside him.

It was the fence. They'd reached the northern boundary of the ranch. She looked for Einstein, wondering what they were supposed to do next, and then she realized that Einstein was already on the other side. He looked at her, then pointed his nose down to the bottom edge of the fence. She felt her way along the place he indicated and found that the earth dropped away from the line of chain link; what she'd thought was a shadow was actually a narrow gorge of dark rock. The space was easily big enough for her to slip through. She felt Daniel grab her ankle, using her for guidance. After they were both through, she turned to watch Khan struggle his way into the gorge. She winced, knowing the bottom edge of the chain link must be gouging into his skin. He didn't make any audible complaint.

They came out on top of a shallow, rocky ravine. It had been invisible from the house, hidden in the lee of the slight rise of land; she'd never guessed that there was any end to the flat plains stretching north toward Oklahoma. Einstein was already scrambling down the rocks. It looked like he might be on a faint, narrow path. Khan nudged her from behind.

"Let's go," she whispered.

She lifted herself into a low crouch and, when Einstein didn't object, started carefully down the slope. She could feel Daniel following closely. There did appear to be a path, though it could have been a game trail, too. There was a new sound in the darkness, a gentle whooshing that it took her a few seconds to place. She hadn't realized the river came so close to the house.

It was only about fifteen feet to the bottom of the ravine, and when they reached it, Alex felt it was safe to straighten up. The water coursed quietly past them in the dark. She thought she could make out the far side; the river was much narrower here than it was by the barn. Einstein was yanking at something under a ledge, a place where the water had cut away the bank, leaving an overhanging shelf of stone. She went to help and was thrilled to see that it was a small rowboat. She thought she understood the protocol now.

"I will never say another bad word about your brother," she muttered rashly as she helped tow the boat from its hiding place. If Kevin was still alive — and if she and Daniel lived through the night — she would no doubt break that promise, but for now she was filled with gratitude.

Daniel caught the other side of the boat and pushed. They had it in the water in seconds, the eddies swirling around their calves. Her coat trailed so much lower to the ground than his that the bottom edge was already in the river. The fur soaked up the water, getting heavier with each step. The current ran faster than the smooth surface implied, and they had their hands full hanging on to the boat while the dogs jumped in. Khan's weight lowered the stern of the boat dangerously close to the rippling water, so they both piled into the prow next to Einstein; first Alex while Daniel held the boat, and then he leaped in next to her. The boat took off like an arrow shot from a bow.

She threw off the hot, heavy coat. She'd never be able to swim in it, if that became necessary. Daniel followed suit quickly, whether because he'd thought of the same danger or just because he trusted her to do the right thing.

The strong current pushed them swiftly westward. Alex had to assume that this was part of the plan; Kevin hadn't left any oars. About ten minutes later, the water began to slow as it widened out around a broad bend. Her eyes had adjusted enough for her to make out what she thought was the far edge of the water. The current was pushing them toward the south bank — the same bank they'd started off from. Einstein was anxious in the prow, his ears pointed sharply upward, his muscles stretched taut. She wasn't sure what he was watching for, but when they'd passed some invisible boundary, he suddenly launched from the boat and into the water. It was deep enough that he had to swim, but she couldn't guess how far beneath his churning legs the bottom lay. He looked back at them and yelped.

Realizing it was probably a good idea to get out before Khan did, Alex jumped just a second later. The cool water closed briefly over her head before she surged back to the surface. She heard two splashes behind her — first a small one, then a huge one that sent a wave rolling over her head again. Khan swam past her, the water foaming white around his legs, and found his footing just a second before her toes scuffed against the sandy bottom. She turned to see Daniel fighting with the current as he tried to drag the wooden boat toward the bank. She knew she couldn't help him if she was in too deep, so she waded downriver and met him when he reached the shallows. She grabbed the prow, and he pulled from the middle, his hand wrapped around the bench. It didn't take long to get to the shore, where the dogs were shaking themselves off. They lugged the boat ten feet out of the water, then Daniel dropped it and looked at his hands. She did the same; the rough wood hadn't been kind to her already torn palms. They were bleeding freely now, drops of red trickling from the tips of her fingers.

Daniel wiped his right hand against his jeans, leaving a bloody streak, then reached back into the boat and retrieved the gun and something smaller—a phone; it must have been Kevin's. Daniel had had the good sense to keep both out of the water—impressive, given the shock and pressure they were both under. Luckily everything in her backpack was carefully Ziplocked.

She examined his face quickly. He didn't *look* like he was going to break down, but there might not be much warning.

Daniel grabbed the coats and held them awkwardly bundled in both arms. She was about to tell him to leave them, but then she realized that there was going to be a murder investigation in the near future. Better to hide what evidence they could.

"Put them in the river—the boat, too," she whispered. "We don't want anyone to find either."

Without hesitation, he hurried back to the edge of the water and dropped the coats into the current. Heavy as they were, it didn't take long for them to saturate and disappear under the surface. Alex started shoving the boat, and Daniel joined her, pulling it downhill. In seconds, it was racing off across the dark water. She knew it was marked with their blood and prints, but hopefully it would travel far enough tonight that no one would connect it with Kevin's house in the morning. The boat looked old and weathered, certainly not valuable. Perhaps the people who found it would consider it trash and treat it accordingly.

Alex imagined Kevin and Einstein on the red water in the daylight, running the route for practice. They must have tried it many times. Kevin would probably be upset about her losing his boat, regardless of the value.

She and Daniel turned back toward land together. The barn was easy to see, the only tall shape in the flat darkness. As they ran toward it, a solid square being suddenly reared up. Alex startled, expecting the dogs to react. Then her eyes made sense of the shape—it was one of the firing-range haystacks. She took a deep breath to settle herself and ran on.

They reached the barn and then raced around to the front doors. Daniel's longer legs got him there first, and he already had the lock free when she caught up to him. He yanked the door out of the way, waited for her and the dogs to get inside, then shut it behind them.

It was pitch-black.

"Gimme a sec," Daniel whispered.

She could barely hear his movement over the sound of her own heartbeat and the panting of the dogs. There was a tinny creak, and then a quiet metallic groan. A faint green light glowed to her right. She could just make out Daniel's shape—his hand lit up as he touched a glowing keypad. Suddenly, brighter white light burst through a long line beside him. As he yanked the crevice open and more light flooded the space, she saw what he was doing. He was at one of the old cars on blocks. He'd opened the fake battery, entered his birthday code, and the false engine had opened. It was the stash of rifles, illuminated from the inside.

"Put some of those in the Humvee," she whispered to Daniel. The low volume was probably unnecessary, but she couldn't make herself speak louder.

The light was enough to brighten a space about fifteen feet around him in every direction. The two dogs stood by the door, facing out as if expecting intruders, waiting and panting.

Alex sprinted to her duffels and threw off the old tarp. She unzipped the side of the bottom bag and grabbed a pair of latex gloves. She pulled them over her bleeding hands. She took a second pair and stuffed them halfway into her front jeans pocket.

When she turned, Daniel had already moved on to the hollow tractor tire. He had two rifles slung over his back, and cradled in his arm were two Glocks and the shotgun she'd been wishing for. As she watched, he reached for the SIG Sauer he'd seen her practice with. He might be new to her world, but his instincts seemed up to the task.

It took her two trips to get her bags into the vehicle hidden behind the hay bales. On the first trip, she gave Daniel the gloves as they passed each other. He put them on without asking for an explanation. She was happy to see the Humvee's interior lights had been disengaged. After her stuff was in, she loaded the grenades but chose to leave the rocket launchers behind—she wasn't sure she could figure out how to use them without blowing herself up.

"The cash?" Daniel asked when she passed him.

"Yes, all of it."

He moved quickly in response, and for one crazy second she had a sense of déjà vu. They worked well together—just like doing dishes.

There was a supply of Kevlar. She put a vest on and tightened the straps as far as they would go, but it still hung a little loose. It wasn't unbearably heavy, so she guessed it had ceramic plates. She pulled another for Daniel. There were a couple of Batman wet suits, but they were too big for her and would probably take too long for Daniel to struggle into. She smiled when she found two thick baseball caps. She'd heard about these but thought only the Secret Service used them. She stuck one on her head and took the other to Daniel along with the vest.

He put both on silently, his face determined and pale. She wondered how long he could hold it together. Hopefully, the natural adrenaline would last until they got out of this.

She strapped a long, thin blade to her thigh, wrapped a holster belt under her usual leather utility, then slung another over her shoulders. She went to the back of the Humvee. She took one of the Glocks and put it on her right hip. She put the SIG under one arm and her PPK under the other. Then she holstered the sawed-off shotgun on her left hip.

"Ammo?"

He nodded. He'd left his favorite rifle slung over one shoulder. She jerked her chin toward it.

"Keep that on you, and take a handgun, too."

He picked up the other Glock and gripped it in his gloved hand. "We need to wipe down everything you touched."

Before she was finished speaking, he was in motion. He grabbed the tarp that had hidden her bags and tore off two long strips. He threw her one and went out to the lock, Einstein shadowing him. She started on the first car he'd opened. It didn't take them long to get everything. There was blood on the pieces of tarp, so she stuffed them into the back of the Humvee, too.

She stopped to listen for a moment. Nothing but four nervous animals breathing.

"Where do we go now?" Daniel asked. His voice was strained and more inflectionless than usual, but he sounded in control. "Your place up north?"

She knew her expression was hard—and possibly frightening—as she told him, "Not yet."

CHAPTER 18

"Y ou're going back," he said in a hollow whisper.

She nodded.

"Do you think Arnie might still be—"

"No. He's dead."

Daniel's body swayed ever so slightly in reaction to the cold certainty of her words. "Then shouldn't we be running? You told me if they come for us, we run."

He was right, and it was also her nature to run.

She wondered if this was the feeling those mothers had—the ones you read about in the news who lifted the minivan off their child. Desperate, terrified, but also as powerful as a superhero.

Alex had her way of doing things: plan, plan, plan, plan for every possibility, and then, when disaster hit, execute the plan that was the best fit. She did not do spur-of-the-moment. She did not do instinct. She did not do fight; she did flight.

But she didn't just have herself to protect tonight. She had a minivan to lift.

There was no plan, only instinct.

Her instinct was that a serious attack was happening, a well-coordinated one organized by people who had more intel than they should have. She and Daniel could run, but who knew what else the hunters had set up? There could be another trap.

If she could find out who they were and what they knew, her escape with Daniel had a much better chance of success.

Finding things out was her specialty, after all.

Attacking was not, but that just meant it would not be expected. Hell, she was more than a little surprised herself.

The hunters didn't know about the Batcave, or they would have been waiting for her here. They didn't know about the resources she had access to.

If she thought this through at all, she would probably change her mind. But she was high on her own adrenaline now, and trying to make the smart choices. Not just the ones that would save them tonight, but that would save them tomorrow and the next day. She couldn't make the right choices if she didn't have the right information.

"Running would probably be safest in the short term," she answered.

"Then?"

"I haven't had this chance before — to interrogate one of the assassins sent for me. The more I know about who they are, the safer we'll be in the future."

A second passed.

"You're not leaving me behind," he stated evenly.

"No, I need your help. But only on one condition."

He nodded.

"You have to do *exactly* what I say. I don't care if you like it or not."

"I can do that."

"You have to stay in the car."

His head jerked back just a little, then his lips tightened.

"Exactly what I say," she repeated.

He nodded again, not pleased. She was not convinced he meant it.

"I'll need you to cover me," she explained, "and the Humvee is the best place for that. You can't watch my back if someone shoots you. Okay. This is going to get ugly. Can you handle that?"

"I've handled ugly."

"Not like this." She paused for a second. "My best guess is that these guys think they're here for Kevin and you. There's a chance I'm already dead, as far as the people who matter are concerned. That means I have to do things differently than I usually would. I can do only those things that Kevin could do. It's going to be old school, and we won't be able to leave any survivors."

He swallowed, but nodded once more.

"All right, take the night-vision goggles, you're driving."

She truly wished he didn't have to see what was coming — to see her the way she was going to have to be — but there was no help for it now.

As they drove carefully through the barn door, the dogs silent in the back of the Humvee except for some heavy breathing, she could feel herself changing, getting ready. It was going to be both ugly and very, very messy. That was, if they didn't get her first.

She pulled a small syringe from a bag in her pack. Her last, but then, if she didn't use it now, she might not live to need it another night.

"Do you trust me?" she asked him.

"Yes." The way he said it gave unusual weight to the simple affirmative.

"I've got only this one dose left, so we're going to have to share a needle, like junkies. My blood's clean, I promise."

She stabbed herself in the leg and depressed the plunger a little less than halfway. Daniel was bigger than she was.

"What is it?" he asked nervously.

She'd forgotten. He didn't like needles. "A synthesis of dextro-amphetamine and an opioid — kind of like . . . adrenaline and pain-killers. It will help you keep going if you get shot." *Anywhere but the head or heart,* she didn't add.

He nodded, and then very carefully kept his eyes forward as she stabbed him through his jeans and into his thigh. He didn't wince. She pushed the rest of the solution into his body. It was enough to last for thirty minutes at most.

"How well can you see?"

"Surprisingly well."

"Can we go faster?"

He stepped on the gas as his answer.

"When you're in place," she instructed, "get in the backseat and crack open these little side windows. Shoot anything human that isn't me. I shouldn't be hard to pick out—I'll be a lot smaller than anyone else you'll see."

His lips tightened again.

"You stay in here no matter what, you got that?"

He nodded.

"Are you going to have a problem shooting these people?"

"No." He said it forcefully, then clenched his teeth.

"Good. Anything goes wrong—your gun jams, someone gets into the Humvee somehow, whatever, you throw a grenade out the window. That's the signal that you need help. Do you know how to use a grenade?"

"What's your signal?"

"Huh?"

"If you need my help, what's your signal?"

"My signal is *stay in the car, Daniel*. The grenade?"

"I think so," he grumbled.

"This might take a little while, so don't get antsy. I won't start an interrogation until I have everything secured. Oh, pull the goggles off before you throw a grenade, or close your eyes. Look out for flares—they'll blind you."

"Got it."

Suddenly, a phone rang.

Daniel jumped a foot, hitting his head on the low ceiling.

"The hell?" Alex shouted.

"It's Kevin's phone," Daniel said, patting his vest frantically with his right hand. He dug the phone out of a snap pocket meant for ammo. She took it from him as he fumbled with it.

An unfamiliar number glowed on the display. She jabbed the answer button.

"Danny?" Kevin barked in her ear.

"Rotten timing, Beach! He'll call you back!"

"Put him on, you—"

She hung up and powered the phone off.

"Stay focused. You can call him back when we're finished."

"No problem."

Well, Kevin was alive. She supposed that was good news. Except someone was going to have to tell him his retirement arrangements were gone and his friend was dead.

"What are you going to do?" Daniel asked. "Tell me the plan so I know what to watch for."

"You're going to ram through the gate, if they closed it. That will get their attention. We'll tweak the plan if there are more than four waiting. You accelerate up to the house, then turn right so that your side of the vehicle is exposed. Four or less, you slow down, but don't stop. I'll slide out. Hopefully, they'll stay focused on you. Keep going a few yards, then stop driving and start shooting. I'll hit them from the side. You shoot to kill. I will try to get someone down that I can still talk to. I'm hoping that somebody is passed out in my room upstairs, too. I'll take Einstein to keep the other dogs off me. Khan stays with you. If they hole up in the house, I'll get back in and we'll come in through the wall."

"I can see the gate. It's open."

"Punch it up to the house."

He accelerated.

"Lights!" he told her in the same moment she saw them. Headlights coming up the road toward them, moving closer fast.

"Goggles off! New plan. Hit them. Hard. Roll right over them if you can. Brace yourself, don't lose control of the car."

She grabbed the dash with one hand, her seat with the other. Daniel shoved the goggles to his forehead and floored the gas pedal. She wished there was a way to secure the dogs. They were going to feel this.

The other car didn't react to their charge until the last second, like maybe its occupants had been watching behind them rather than out front. Or maybe, with the headlights and running lights off and the matte-black paint, the Humvee was mostly invisible in the night.

It was a midsize SUV, white. Once he saw them, the driver veered off to Alex's right. Daniel jerked the wheel right and the Humvee plowed into the passenger side of the SUV with a deafening shriek of tearing metal and the explosive pop of safety glass crumpling. The dogs flew forward; a shower of metallic clanks and jangles sounded while Khan's body crashed heavily into the back of both the driver's and the passenger's seats. Alex's head whipped forward but missed the dashboard by inches when the seat belt yanked her back. The SUV flew a few feet away, tottered on two wheels for a second, then smashed, driver-side-first, into the ground. The passenger-side headlight burst with another explosion of glass. Khan and Einstein whimpered, falling back to the floor.

"Again!" she yelled.

Daniel slammed the front of the Humvee into the undercarriage of the SUV. Metal protested and squealed. The SUV slid across the flat yard like it weighed no more than a cardboard box. She could see they weren't going to be able to roll it. There was nothing to push it against, just the endless grass.

"Cover me." She snagged the goggles off his head. "Use the nightscope on the rifle. Einstein, come!"

Alex didn't wait for a response. She was out of the Humvee before it was totally stopped. Einstein's toenails scrabbled against the back of her wet jeans as he hurried to join her. She had to move fast, before the men in the car could recover from the impact. Before they could get their automatic weapons back into play.

She ran straight for the windshield, Glock held tight in both hands. She was better with the SIG Sauer, but this was going to be extremely close up and she would probably want to ditch the gun afterward.

Everything was incredibly clear through the lenses, bright green with vibrant contrasts. The driver-side headlight was still on but buried in the ground so it emitted only a low hazy glow in the dust they'd churned up. The windshield frame was entirely empty, and she could see two men in the front seats, two deflated airbags from the initial impact hanging across the hood. The driver was a bloody mess, the top of his head pressing tight against the side-door frame, his thick neck bent at an impossible angle. She could see one eye open, staring sightlessly at her. He looked young, early twenties, with ruddy skin, light hair, and the kind of over-built anatomy that screamed *steroids*. He *might* have been an agent, except the rest of his look was wrong. His hair was about eight inches long and there was an ostentatious diamond stud in the one earlobe she could see. She would bet he was hired muscle. He didn't look like he'd been a decision maker.

The passenger was moving, his head wobbling confusedly as if he were just coming around. He was older than the other, maybe midthirties, and swarthy, with a thick three-day growth on his cheeks, burly through the middle in the way that men who lifted the really heavy weights sometimes were. She'd bet he was a bull on his feet. He was wearing a well-fitting shiny suit that seemed inappropriate for this kind of operation but rang a few bells for her. Still strapped in his seat, he was right about at her eye level. She approached swiftly and jammed the barrel of her gun into his forehead, glancing down to see what his hands were doing. They were currently empty and limp.

"Are you in charge?" she demanded.

"Huh?" he moaned.

"Who is your boss?"

"Accident. We've been in an accident, Officer," he told her, blinking into the dark. His eyes seemed to be moving just slightly out of sync with each other.

She modified her approach, pulling the gun back and softening her voice. "Help is coming. I need to know how many of you there are."

"Uh, six..."

That meant there were four more, possibly heading out toward the sound of the crash right now. At least the dogs were beginning to congregate around her, all of them on silent mode thanks to Einstein's presence. She wondered if they would have remembered her if she were alone.

"Sir?" she asked, trying to imagine how a cop would speak to someone in a car accident. "Where are the others?"

"Hitchhikers," he said, his rolling eyes starting to move more purposefully. "The others are hitchhikers. We picked up four men and dropped them off here. Then there were dogs — crazy dogs attacking us. I thought they were going to chew through the tires."

He was gaining more control, spinning the story carefully. He made a fist, then released it. She raised the gun again and kept her eyes on his hands.

"Were these...hitchhikers hurt in the attack?"

"I think so. I think maybe two of them. The others went in the house."

So hopefully there were only two others. But was this the guy in charge? The age was right; however, she'd picked up a few things during her time in Chicago. In an orchestrated hit, usually the guys left in the car were lower on the totem pole. The driver was secondary. The star of the show would be the one the contract was made with. The one with the skills.

"I think I need a doctor," he complained.

"An ambulance is on the way."

The light from the SUV's one surviving headlight was almost entirely blocked by thick grass and settling dirt, but there was enough that his eyes were beginning to adjust. She saw them widen when he abruptly realized there was a gun in his face.

He made a grab inside his jacket. She fired a round into his right shoulder; she didn't want to aim for the hand and take the chance of the bullet passing through and into a vital organ. She wasn't done with him yet.

He screamed, and his right arm jerked out in a pained spasm, flinging blood across her neck and chin. The gun he'd been reaching for slipped from his fingers, dropped onto his dead companion's face, then bounced out of the car and against her shoe. She knew it wouldn't be his only weapon, so she aimed down and shot him through the palm of his left hand.

He howled again and struggled against the seat belt as if he were trying to hurl himself through the empty windshield frame at her. Something was wrong with his legs—he couldn't get the purchase he was looking for.

The action had roused the dogs, who were all snarling now. Einstein launched himself at the passenger side of the car, which was currently the top side. Bracing his paws against the frame of the missing window, he stretched his neck into the SUV and locked his massive jaws around the man's right shoulder—the one she'd just shot.

"Get it off me! Get it off me!" the man shrieked in abject terror.

She took advantage of his total distraction to grab the gun at her foot. It was a cheap .38, safety off.

"Einstein, control!" Alex ordered as she straightened. It was the only command she remembered besides *escape protocol* and *at ease,* and *control* seemed closest to what she wanted. Einstein let go of the shoulder but kept his teeth right in the man's face, slavering spots of bloody saliva onto his skin.

"Who are you?" the man screamed.

"I'm the person who is going to have this animal chew your face off if you don't tell me what I want to know in the next thirty seconds."

"Keep it away!"

"Who's in charge?"

"Hector! He brought us in!"

"Where is he?"

"In the house! He went in and didn't come out. Angel went in after him and didn't come out. The dogs were going to rip the doors off the car! We bailed!"

"Who was on the sniper rifle? Hector?"

Einstein snapped his teeth inches from the terrified man's nose.

"Yes! Yes!"

She'd never thought of using animals in an interrogation, but Einstein was an unexpectedly effective asset.

"Hector was going to make the hit?"

"Yes!"

"Who was the target?"

"I don't know! We're just supposed to drive and shoot anyone who tried to leave."

"Einstein, *get him!*" It wasn't the best improv; Einstein's eyes cut over to her, clearly confused. It didn't matter to the man in the SUV.

"No, no!" he screamed. "I swear! Hector didn't tell us. Those Puerto Rican hitters don't tell outsiders anything!"

"How did you find this place?"

"Hector gave us the addresses!"

Plural? "More than one?"

"There were three houses on the list! We did the first one earlier. Hector said it was the wrong place!"

"What did you do there?"

"Hector went in. Five minutes later, he came out. Told us to move on to the next."

"That's all you know?"

"Yes! Yes! Everything!"

She shot him in the head twice with his own gun.

There was a countdown running in her mind. She had no idea how long it had actually taken to release the dogs, float downstream, and load the Humvee. She didn't know when Hector had entered the house or how long it had taken him to get to her room. What she did know was that the pressurized canister of gas she'd left armed there would continue to quietly exude the chemicals it was packed with for about fifteen minutes after someone opened the door. Once the contents ran out, she had maybe thirty minutes more — dependent on the size of the person involved — before the quarry was back on his feet. It was going to be close.

She jumped into the Humvee, holding the door open so Einstein could climb over her. She threw the goggles back to Daniel, getting only one glimpse of his face before she was blind again. All she could see was that his expression was tense.

"Get us to the house. Same plan as before if anyone comes out. Stop far enough back that you can see the sides of the house; watch for someone coming around."

"The dogs will let me know if they see something."

"Right," she agreed. The advantages of the pack were more extensive than she could have anticipated.

She removed her PPK and holstered the Glock in its place. She stuck the .38 in her belt, shoved the PPK into the bag at her feet, then dug through that bag, pulling the things she needed by feel. She switched the bulletproof hat for the gas mask, quickly tightened it into place over her mouth and nose, screwed in the filter, then grabbed two more pressurized canisters, zip ties, thin tactical gloves, and her earring box; she stowed them in the pockets of her vest. She extracted the heavy bolt cutters last and stuck them through the belt by the empty holster, one handle inside, one out. Though the cutters were compact for their abilities, the handles still reached nearly to her knee. They would impede her movement a little, but if things went the way she wanted, she would need them.

She didn't have time to think about what Daniel might be processing right now—how he might feel about her killing a helpless man.

The house came into view, all the visible windows downstairs lit. The windows upstairs were blacked out too well for her to be able to tell if the lights were on or not.

"Do you see anyone?"

"A body—over there." Daniel pointed toward the outbuilding.

"We need to make sure he's dead." There were still three men unaccounted for. The fewer breathing, the better her chances.

"I'm pretty sure he is. It looks like he's . . . in more than one piece." His voice sounded a little hollow.

Hers didn't. "Good."

She couldn't see anyone near the house. They weren't dumb enough to run out and see what was going on, apparently. No silhouettes appeared in the windows. Surely they would have shut off the lights if they were going to shoot from one of them. Maybe upstairs . . . the windows were so completely covered that she couldn't even tell exactly where they were. Or the blackout treatments had been pulled back and someone was watching from a darkened room.

"Can you see the upstairs windows?"

"They all look covered," Daniel told her.

"Okay, start slowing. Two seconds after we're out, stop and get ready to shoot."

He nodded. "Got it."

"Einstein, come here. Get ready."

Daniel angled the car so that his side was facing into the lights of the house. She hoped she would be invisible on the dark side of the vehicle. She opened the door and slid down toward the slowly moving grass below. She tried to re-create the move she'd seen in a hundred movies: she fell to her knees, then rolled onto her side as Einstein leaped over her. She was sure she'd done it wrong, but she wouldn't know *how* wrong until the *Survive* wore off.

She'd forgotten to tell Daniel to close the door and lock everything down, but it was common sense and he seemed to be thinking quickly tonight. Maybe it was genetics again—he was wired for this kind of situation, just like his brother. Anyway, if someone tried to get into the car, Khan would be waiting. She could imagine what it would feel like if someone who'd already been harried by dozens of attack dogs came face to face with Khan on higher ground in the dark. There was no way this wouldn't affect his aim and reaction time.

Even though she had gloves on, crawling across the gravel would have been excruciating if she hadn't drugged herself up. As she hurried away from the Humvee, she heard the rush of her pack's paws approaching in the dry brush—not just Einstein, but the dozens of other survivors. She'd never had backup like this before. A sniper above would have trouble separating her from the mass.

She moved into a crouch next to the porch. The Humvee was stopped now. She heard the door slam. A low whimper, quite near her head, made her freeze. The quiet whine happened again. It wasn't a human sound.

She heaved herself up onto the porch, rolled under the banister, and then stayed down, lower than the windows. Lola was there, curled up in the far corner. Alex knew that even injured, Lola would sound the alarm if someone else were close by. She crawled to the dog, her gloved hands slipping against a trail of blood. Lola raised her head half an inch, and her tail lifted for one limp wag.

"It's going to be okay, Lola. I'm coming right back. You hold on, all right?" She caressed the dog's ears once, and Lola panted softly.

Einstein waited in the shadows by the door. Alex crawled to him.

"Stay with Lola, Einstein."

She couldn't interpret the look he gave her. Hopefully he understood. She had to go in alone this time.

If she got through this night alive, she was going to track down a gas mask made for dogs.

Alex crouched beside the door and carefully inserted her earrings. They were out of place—delicate and fussy—next to the rest of her serious gear, but she didn't have time to be worried about appearances and this could very well get physical. She grabbed the bigger canister from the front pocket of her vest, twisted the top off, pulled the door open, and threw it inside.

There was no reaction. No shout or sound of footsteps retreating as the gas filled the room. She waited two seconds, then half stood and ran crouched through the doorway with the Glock in her right hand and the shotgun in her left. She would be clumsy with her left hand, but you didn't need good aim with a gun like this, not in close quarters.

She didn't bother searching the first floor. If someone tried to come after her in the next five minutes and he didn't have a gas mask, he'd be down quick. She played it out in her head as she moved to the stairs. Hector had come inside, searching for Daniel or Kevin or both of them. Because he'd come in alone, she suspected he'd been looking for only two people. With Arnie down, he'd think it was one on one. Still, he must have been very confident in his abilities to go in solo.

He would have had to check all the rooms downstairs. Then he would have tried the doors upstairs.

She was halfway up the steps now. The mist spilling from the canister below was heavy; it wasn't climbing with her. Looking up, she could see that Daniel's door was open, as was the bathroom's. Light spilled down from the far right. That could only be her storage room.

She holstered the shotgun, crept to the top, put her elbows on the first step down, and leaned around the edge of the banister.

A man was down in the hallway, dressed in rugged black pants and combat boots. His head and shoulders rested on another set of legs, coming out of her room, these in similar pants but wearing black sneakers rather than boots.

Hector would be the one on the floor in her room, if the man in the suit had described events correctly. He would have opened the door, flipped on the light, and dropped. After a few minutes, Angel would have come looking to see if he needed help, seen his legs, and slid along the wall with gun in hand until the gas overpowered him.

She had no idea how long they'd been down.

So far, the man in the suit had been pretty honest with her. It made her feel safe enough to holster the Glock and get started. First, she took the gun she found in the first man's hands and tossed it over the railing to the floor below. There was another gun tucked into the back of his pants—that went over the railing, too. She didn't have time for a better search. She wished she could inject him with something that would keep him quiet, but unlike the gas, which would disappear from his system in the next half hour, the longer-term sedation would linger in his bloodstream and be a dead giveaway to anyone who suspected she might be here. She zip-tied his hands behind his back and then zip-tied his ankles together.

Hector was smaller than Angel, who looked similar to the dead blond in the SUV except for his coloring; both Hector and Angel were dark-haired, as she'd expected from the suit guy's description. Hector was no more than medium height and lean, fit, but not in a way that would stand out on the street. He was clean-shaven and his skin was unmarked, at least the parts she could see; he wore a long-sleeved black athletic shirt. Angel had tattoos on three of his fingers and one on the side of his neck. Hector was smarter. If you were going to do wet work for a living, it was better to blend in, avoid features that any witness could easily describe to the police sketch artist.

A huge suppressed Magnum lay inches from Hector's right hand. The sniper rifle was holstered across his back. She pulled the magazine from the rifle, took the massive handgun, and carried them back to the hallway to dump them over the stair railing. She heard them thud against the hard wood below; one of them made a metallic *chink* when it hit the previously discarded weapons.

She turned back to secure Hector.

The body lying in her storage room was gone.

She ripped the shotgun out of its holster and pressed her back against the wall beside the door. There was no sound. He would have to come through the door. When he did, she would shoot him. Even the most experienced assassin would be incapacitated with his legs blown off.

When the movement came, it was not through the door. Angel began to writhe, moaning in Spanish. In the split second that Alex was distracted, a shadow peeled off from Angel's body and flew straight at her, knocking the shotgun from her hands and sending them both crashing toward the ground. She braced for the impact even while wrestling with the hands that were trying to strip the gun from her waist. His hands were stronger than hers, but then the crash came, and with it the shattering of tiny glass bulbs.

She could feel the scalding gas sear her neck, the exposed skin around the base of her mask, and she knew she would probably look sunburned there for a few hours, but her eyes and lungs were protected.

Her attacker was not prepared. He choked, his hands flying of their own accord to his throat, his blinded eyes. She whirled, .38 already drawn, and shot, aiming for his kneecap. She hit him in the left thigh instead.

He crumpled to that side and rolled into Angel, who was thrashing in earnest now, straining to pop the zip ties from his wrists. They were heavy-duty restraints, but he was a strong man.

She couldn't handle them both. She was going to have to make a choice. Quickly.

Angel's head was the closest thing to her. She fired twice into the top of it. He went limp.

Hector was gasping and scrubbing at his eyes at the same time as he was trying to roll away from her toward the stairs. She sprinted after him, hugging the wall to avoid his reach. He wasn't in control enough to make a grab for her yet. She pulled the bolt cutters from her waist and clubbed the back of his head. His convulsing jerked to a stop.

This was all going to be a wasted effort if she'd killed him, but she had to secure him before she could even check for a pulse.

To be safe, she put an additional bullet through his left kneecap, then threw the .38 over the banister to the floor below. It had only one bullet left anyway. She used another zip tie to attach his uninjured right leg to the railing at the ankle and the knee, then his right arm at the wrist and the elbow. He wouldn't be able to do much with his left leg. For lack of a better option, she zip-tied his left hand to Angel's big black boot. Angel's inert form had to weigh two seventy, at least. It was better than nothing. She touched Hector's wrist, marginally satisfied to locate a steady pulse. He was alive; whether or not his brain function was preserved, she would have to wait to see.

She decided to double the cables, just in case. While she was tightening the second tie around Angel's boot, she heard the change in Hector's breathing as he came to. He didn't cry out, though he had to be in tremendous pain. That wasn't a good thing. She'd interrogated other hardened soldiers with good control over their reactions to pain. It took a long time to break them.

But those men had loyalty to their companions or their missions. She was confident this was a hit for hire. Hector would owe nothing to the people who'd given him the job.

She scooted a few feet away with the Glock gripped tight in her hands, watching to see how well her containment system would perform. It was too dark. She got up and backed toward the bathroom doorway, keeping her eyes on the figure on the ground. She felt behind her until she found the light switch and flipped it on.

Hector's face was turned toward her; his dark eyes, although still tearing, were intensely focused. His face showed no evidence of the pain he was in. It was a disconcerting gaze, though his face was in other ways one of the most ordinary she had ever seen. His features were even and nondescript. He wasn't attractive, but he wasn't ugly, either. It was the kind of face that would be extremely hard to pick out of a lineup.

"Why haven't you killed me?" he asked, his voice hoarse from the chemicals. Other than that, his voice was unremarkable. He had no accent at all. He could have been a network news anchor—no hint of where he came from in his inflections.

"I want to know who hired you." Her voice rasped through the mask, slightly distorted. It sounded a little less human. She hoped that would throw him.

He nodded once, as if to himself. She saw minute shifts in his hands as he tested his bonds.

"Why would I tell you anything?" He didn't say it angrily or as a challenge. He just sounded curious.

"Do you have any idea who I am?"

He didn't answer, his face neutral.

"That's the first reason why you should tell me what you know— because whoever sent you out here didn't give you the information you needed to be successful. They didn't prepare you for what you were facing. You don't owe them anything."

"I don't owe *you* anything," he pointed out, still in a polite, conversational voice. His fingers stretched downward, trying to reach the zip tie.

"No, you don't. But if you don't talk to me, I'll hurt you. That's the second reason."

He weighed that. "And the third reason... if I talk, you'll let me live."

"Would you believe me if I promised you that?"

"Hmm." He sighed. He thought for a moment and then asked, "But how will you know whether to believe what I tell you?"

"I know most of it. I just want you to fill in a few details."

"I'm afraid I can't help you much. I have a manager; he works as the middleman. I never saw the person who paid for this."

"Just tell me what your manager told you."

He considered that, then twitched his shoulders as if to shrug. "I don't like your offer. I think you could do better."

"Then I'll have to persuade you."

CHAPTER 19

He watched with a poker face as she stuck the Glock in its holster and retrieved the bolt cutters from the floor by Angel's leg.

She'd considered bringing the welding iron. Fire could be more painful than almost anything else, and many people had related phobias. But Hector was a professional. She didn't have the time to break him down with pain; his resistance would be too high. What would frighten him more than agony would be losing his physical edge. If he didn't have a trigger finger, he couldn't do his job. She'd start with something less vital to him, but he would be able to see the inevitable coming. If he could survive tonight, he would want to do it with functional hands. So he would have to talk to delay her.

Hector's left hand was most convenient. As she fit the metal blades around his pinkie finger, he curled the rest into a fist and fought harder against the ties. She kept a tight hold on the handles, knowing what she would be thinking in his position—if he could get control of the cutters, he would have a chance to free himself. Sure enough, he tried to kick out with his left leg, despite the excruciating pain it must have caused him. She dodged the blow, moved a few feet higher, then refit the cutters to the base of his folded finger.

These were made for cutting through rebar, and she kept the

blades sharp. It didn't take too much muscle on her part to snap those blades together.

She watched his reaction. He thrashed against the ties ineffectually. His face turned dark red and the vessels pulsed in his forehead. He gasped and panted, but he didn't scream.

"Sometimes people don't think I'm serious," she told him. "It's good to get that misconception out of the way."

Right now, Hector would be thinking about the amount of time that could pass before it was too late to reattach a finger. He could live without a pinkie, but he needed his hands, and he must know she wasn't going to stop there.

She would emphasize her point.

She snagged the warm, bloody finger off the floor and backed to the bathroom, keeping her eyes on him as he writhed in his bonds; even the best zip ties weren't foolproof. She made sure he was watching as she dropped the finger into the toilet and flushed. Now he knew that she wasn't going to leave him options. Hopefully it would encourage him to give her what she wanted quickly.

"Hector," she told him as he stared, gritting his teeth, fighting to control the pain. "Don't be stupid. It's not going to hurt you to tell me what I want to know. It *is* going to hurt you if you don't. Your trigger fingers are next, then the rest of them. This is what I do, and I can keep it up for as long as I need to. Don't you see? They sent you after the wrong people, Hector. They told you nothing about what you were up against. They just *handed* you to me. Why protect them?"

"You're going after them next?" he grunted through his teeth.

"Of course."

His eyes were full of venom and hatred. She'd seen the look before, but in the past, she'd viewed it from a much better protected position. If he somehow got his hands on her, if their roles were reversed, she would do what she had to in order to die immediately.

"I didn't come for you," he spit out unwillingly. "I was sent for a man. I was given a picture. I was told there would be a second man, but that the second would be easy. The first would be hard. I never saw that one."

"When were you hired?"

"Last night."

"Then you rounded up some extra help and came in today," she guessed. "From where?"

"Miami."

"How did you know where to come?"

"They gave me three addresses. This was the second try."

"I guess I don't need to ask what happened at the first place."

His seething fury twisted into a ghoulish smile. "They were old. A man and a woman. They didn't fit the description, but I was paid well. It doesn't hurt to be thorough, and all it cost me was two bullets."

She nodded. He could see nothing of her expression behind the gas mask, but she kept her features smooth out of habit.

"How far away was the other house?"

"Fifteen minutes south of the little town."

"Where did the addresses come from?"

"No one told me that. I didn't ask."

She hefted the bolt cutters. "No guesses?"

"The other place was nothing like this. I saw nothing in common."

It could be a lie, but it would make more sense for it to be the truth. Why would Carston or whoever was calling the shots at the Agency need to give the hit man more than this location?

She puzzled over it for a moment, trying to think of another avenue to explore. Her eyes never left his hands. What kinds of things might link Arnie's home to random others? What similarity would generate a list of otherwise unconnected addresses?

With a sinking feeling, she thought of a possibility. One she did not like much.

"What kind of car was in the driveway of the first place?"

He seemed surprised by her question. "An old truck."

"White?"

"With a black camper."

Her jaw clenched.

So they'd gotten a very good look at Arnie's truck—the one he'd said had two perfect matches around town. They must have gotten Daniel on camera or they wouldn't be so certain of the make and model. Daniel would have had to drive down the main drag, passing the bank; that was probably how they'd done it. Why bother questioning the girl who called in about the missing teacher? Just take the CC camera footage from town and get something solid, then call the DMV. They didn't get everything—if the plates had been clear, that couple across town wouldn't be dead. But they knew Daniel was alive because Kevin wouldn't have made that mistake. Also, even in a grainy black-and-white video, Daniel didn't look exactly like Kevin if you knew what to look for.

She needed Arnie's truck. She needed it badly. It was inconspicuous. They couldn't exactly roll through town in the Batmobile and escape notice. Where was she going to get another vehicle out here?

She took a step back, feeling tired. She'd had a good resting place, but now the hunt was on again. It didn't even matter that, most likely, the bad guys thought she was dead. Because they knew Daniel was alive.

Liability.

Hector's right hand was busy. He was scratching at the zip tie with the tips of his fingers, almost dislocating his wrist in the process. It didn't look like he was trying to break it or even get to the locking tab. What was he doing? She reached for the Glock; it would probably be safest to put a round through that hand—

A single, concussive shot exploded in the silence, much louder than she would have expected it to sound from outside the house. Daniel—

Her eyes had darted to the direction of the shot though she knew better. In the fourth of a second it took her to recall them while simultaneously ripping her Glock from the holster, Hector's fingers found what they were searching for. He extracted a five-inch serrated blade from the cuff of his sleeve. It sawed across the taut zip tie with a twanging snap. The same motion turned into a cast. She fired into his central mass as the blade flew at her face. She tried to dodge while she kept shooting, ignoring the sudden pressure that wasn't quite pain as it slashed across her jaw—wasn't pain yet, but would be soon, when the drug wore off. She could feel the heat of the blood coating her neck as she continued firing into Hector's chest until the clip was empty.

Hector lay still, his open eyes still pointed in her direction, but no longer focused.

Moving in swift, jerky bursts, she wiped down the Glock and threw it over the banister, wiped and holstered the cutters, and retrieved her shotgun from the end of the hall, trying to concentrate on what to do next. She didn't know what was waiting for her outside. As she crept down the stairs, her fingers worked quickly to make sense of the new damage. The assassin's blade had just missed her carotid artery, hitting the bottom corner of her jaw and slicing halfway through her earlobe. The loose piece dangled against her neck. *Beautiful.*

She fished the remains of her left earring from the damaged lobe—just the hook was left, with a few tiny fragments of thin glass still stuck in the twist of wire—then removed the right. She stowed them in a pocket on the tactical vest. It would be unwise to leave such evidence behind. Even something so small could tip her enemies off, give them a reason to believe she was alive.

On the ground floor, she spared a second to take one quick look at Arnie. His face was turned to the floor. She could see only what was left of the back of his head. It was obvious that he hadn't suffered, but that was weak comfort.

She'd planned to gather evidence on her way out, but she wasn't sure she had time for that now. The dogs were quiet—did that mean everything was okay?

Well, after the volley of shots upstairs, it wasn't like anyone outside was unaware of her presence. She sidled over to the door and crouched beside it, lower, she thought, than anyone would aim to shoot through the drywall. She reached over and pulled the door open a crack. No one shot at her.

"Daniel?" she called loudly.

"Alex!" he shouted back—he sounded as relieved as she suddenly felt.

"You're okay?" she checked.

"Yes. Are you?"

"I'm coming out. Don't shoot."

She walked through the front door with her hands raised above her head, just in case. Einstein popped off the floor beside Lola and was at her heels.

She dropped her arms and jogged toward the Humvee. It was lit only by the lamps shining through the front door and windows, but from this vantage it appeared to be totally unharmed by their intentional accident.

Daniel slid out of the front seat.

"The shot?" she asked, her voice quieter as she approached. The dogs around the Humvee seemed relaxed enough, but...

"The last man. He must have climbed the side of the house to get away from the dogs. He was trying to edge around to the roof of the porch."

Daniel gestured with the rifle to a dark mass crumpled on the gravel close to the east corner of the house. She pushed the gas mask back on her forehead, carefully moving the straps on the left side over her ear without touching it. She adjusted her trajectory, edging closer to the broken figure. Einstein shadowed her. A large standard German shepherd was pacing not too far off, seeming uninterested in the body.

Einstein suddenly sped up and passed her. He sniffed the body a few times while she cautiously picked her way forward, and then he turned to her with his tail wagging.

"Is that the all clear?" she muttered.

He kept wagging.

She leaned in for a closer look. It didn't take long to see all there was to see. Impressed, she turned and walked back to the Humvee. Daniel was standing beside the open driver-side door, looking unsure what to do. He still didn't appear to be having any kind of shock reaction.

"Nice shot," she said. One bullet, literally right between the eyes. It couldn't have been more perfect.

"I wasn't very far away."

He stepped toward her, closing the distance, and his gloved hands wrapped tightly around the tops of her arms. Then he gasped and spun to the side, wheeling her around so that the light was no longer behind her.

"How much of this blood is yours?"

"Not much," she said. "I'm good."

"Your ear!"

"Yeah, that's not going to help anything, is it? You handy with a needle and thread?"

His head jerked back in surprise. "What?"

"It's not hard. I can talk you through it."

"Um..."

"One thing first." She shook out of his grasp and ran back up the porch stairs. Lola was still curled in the same spot. She raised her head and thumped her tail limply when she saw Alex.

"Hey, Lola, good girl. Let me take a look at you."

Alex sat cross-legged in front of her. She stroked Lola's side with one hand while searching for the wound with the other.

"Is she okay?" Daniel asked softly. He was on the other side of the porch banister, his elbows resting on the edge of the floorboards. He seemed unwilling to get any closer to the house. She didn't blame him. Lola whimpered as Alex felt along her legs.

"She's lost some blood. It looks like the bullet went through her back left leg. I can't tell if it hit bone, but the bullet definitely passed through. She was lucky."

He reached through the slats to rub Lola's nose. "Poor girl."

"The stuff in the back of the Humvee must be in total chaos. I'm going to hunt up the first-aid kit. Keep her calm, will you?"

"Sure."

Einstein followed Alex back to the vehicle, just as he'd trailed her to the porch. It surprised her how the silent support buoyed her, made her feel safe despite all the evidence to the contrary.

She opened the back of the Humvee, and an impatient Khan almost knocked her down. She dodged out of his way just in time as he sprang over her. She imagined the cargo hold was tight for him, though she had plenty of space as she crawled inside.

Guns and ammo were strewn haphazardly, loose bullets rolling under her knees. There wasn't time to organize. Her conversation with Hector had been cut short; she hadn't been able to ask one last vital question. *What happens when the job is done?* Who was expecting a call, and when? At least there was the third house still waiting. Unless Hector had made a call between the first and second stops.

Had he called his manager, told him which address had been cleared and which he was heading to next? Was the manager waiting for another call? Would he have realized that the call was overdue?

She located the duffel that held her first-aid kit. There was nothing she could do now except move fast and make the right decisions. The only problem was she still didn't know exactly what those right decisions were.

"Okay," she huffed as she and Einstein arrived back at Lola's side.

She knelt beside Lola's legs and quickly realized it was too dark for her to see what she was doing.

"I need you to bring the Humvee around and give me some light," she said.

Daniel lurched away from the porch, a massive shadow hulking beside him: Khan still on duty. She wondered how Khan and Einstein had decided to switch assignments. She pulled off her tactical gloves and replaced her bloody latex gloves with a fresh pair. She was just injecting Lola with a mild sedative when the brilliant lights of the Humvee came shooting through the banister slats. She adjusted her position so the glare was out of her face and on the wound. It looked like a clean through-and-through. She waited for Lola's eyes to droop before she started cleaning the wound. Lola's leg twitched a few times, but she didn't cry out. Antiseptic, then ointment, then gauze, then a splint and more gauze. It should heal well, if she could keep Lola off it.

She blew out a sigh. What were they going to do about all these dogs?

"What's next?" Daniel asked when she was done. He was on the ground beside the porch, rifle in hands, scanning the dark plains around them.

"Can you throw a couple of stitches in my ear while I've got the stuff out?"

He balked. "I won't get it right."

"It'll be easy," she assured him. "Haven't you ever sewn on a button?"

"Not through human flesh," he muttered, but he slung his rifle over his shoulder and started up the stairs as he spoke.

She lit a match from the kit and sterilized the needle. It wasn't the highest standard of medical technique, but it was the best she could do under the circumstances. She waved the needle quickly back and forth to cool it, then poked the suture thread through the eye and knotted one end.

She held it out to him along with a fresh pair of gloves. He put the gloves on and then reached slowly for the needle. He didn't seem to want to touch it. She tilted her head back and poured antiseptic across the wound, waiting for the scorching sting to run the course of the cut all the way to her ear. Then she angled her jaw toward him, making sure she was in the brightest beam of light.

"Probably just needs three little ones. Start at the back and pull through."

"What about a local anesthetic?"

"I've got enough painkiller in me already," she lied. She could feel the slash across her jaw like a brand. But she was out of *Survive*, and anything else she could use would incapacitate her at least partially. This wasn't an emergency, it was only pain.

He knelt down beside her. He put his fingers gently under the edge of her chin.

"This was very close to your jugular!" He gasped, horrified.

"Yeah, he was good."

His face was out of her sight, so she couldn't interpret the little hitching sound in his breath.

"Do it, Daniel. We have to hurry."

He sucked in a deep breath, and then she felt the needle pierce her earlobe. She was braced for it — she kept it off her face and didn't let her hands clutch into fists; she'd learned to localize her reactions. She clenched the muscles in her abdomen, letting the pressure vent there.

"Good," she said as soon as she was sure she could keep her voice even. "You're doing great. Now just fit the pieces together, and stitch them in place."

While she spoke, his fingers moved quickly through the task. She couldn't feel the needle in the severed bottom portion of her earlobe, so she only had to deal with the pain when he perforated the top half. Just three little stabs. It wasn't too bad after the first.

"Do I . . . tie a knot or something?" he asked.

"Yes, in the back, please."

She could feel the pull of the thread tightening as he worked.

"It's done."

She looked up at him and smiled. It tugged at her slashed jaw. "Thank you. I would have had a hard time managing that on my own."

He touched her cheek. "Here, let me bandage this for you."

She held still while he covered the wound with ointment, then taped a strip of gauze to her cheek. He wrapped her ear front and back.

"Probably should have cleaned it first," he muttered.

"It will do for now. Let's put Lola in the Humvee."

"I'll get her."

Daniel gently lifted the sleeping Lola into his arms. Her long front paws and ears dangled out from his arms and wiggled with every step he took. Alex felt a bubble of inappropriate humor rising in her chest, and swallowed against it. There was no time for hysteria. Daniel laid Lola in the space behind the passenger seat. There were only the two front seats in the Humvee. Kevin had removed the rest to leave room for cargo, she guessed.

"What now?" Daniel asked as he walked back to where she was still sitting on the porch. He was probably wondering why she wasn't doing something proactive. He didn't know she was procrastinating.

She took a deep breath and steadied her shoulders. "Give me the phone. It's time to talk to your brother."

"Should we be moving?"

"There's one thing more I need to do, but I want to tell him first."

"What?"

"We really ought to burn the house down."

His eyes widened as he stared at her. Slowly, he pulled the phone from his vest pocket.

"I should make the call," he said.

"He already hates me," she countered.

"But this was my fault."

"You weren't the one who hired a team of hit men."

He shook his head and pressed the button to power up the phone.

"Fine," she muttered.

As she packed up her first-aid supplies, she watched Daniel from the corner of her eye. He pulled up the only number that had ever called, but before he could touch it, the phone rang again.

Daniel sucked in a deep breath, the same way he had before

making the first pass on her ear. She imagined this conversation would be the harder of the tasks.

He hit the screen. She could hear Kevin shrieking so loudly that at first she thought the phone was on speaker mode.

"YOU DON'T HANG UP ON ME, YOU—"

"Kev, it's me. Kev! It's Danny!"

"WHAT THE HELL IS HAPPENING?"

"It's my fault, Kev. I was an idiot. I ruined everything. I'm so sorry!"

"WHAT ARE YOU BABBLING ABOUT?"

"Arnie's dead, Kev. I'm so sorry. And some of the dogs, I'm not sure how many. It's all my fault. I wish I could tell you how—"

"PUT THE POISON LADY ON THE PHONE!"

"This is on me, Kev. I messed up—"

Kevin's voice was calmer when he interrupted now. "There's no *time* for this, Danny. Give her the phone. I need someone who can talk sense."

She stood up and reached for the phone. Daniel watched anxiously as she held it a few inches away from her ear.

"Are you secure?" Kevin asked.

Surprised by his businesslike detachment, she answered in the same tone. "For the moment, but we've got to move."

"Have you torched the house?"

"I was just about to."

"There's kerosene in the closet under the stairs."

"Thanks."

"Call me when you're on the road."

He hung up.

Well, *that* had gone better than she'd hoped. She handed the phone back to Daniel. His expression was blank with surprise. The gas in the house would long since have dissipated, so she didn't bother with the mask. Daniel followed her inside, but she made Einstein keep watch at the door.

"Get some clothes out of Kevin's room," she instructed. She could have sent him upstairs for the first set he'd borrowed, but that would take more time, and she didn't know how he would react to the bodies. She could see his eyes cutting away to the sofa that obscured Arnie, and then back to her. They both had to keep it together. They still had a long night ahead of them if they were going to be alive tomorrow. "When you have enough for a few days, get to the kitchen and grab anything that's nonperishable. Water, too, as much as we've got."

He nodded and headed down the hall to Kevin's room. She darted up the stairs.

"Do you want these guns?" he called up after her.

She dodged around the bodies, careful not to slip in the blood slick. "No, those've killed people. If we get caught, I don't want to be linked to anything. Kevin's guns will be clean."

In her room, she stripped off her blood-spattered clothes and pulled on clean jeans and a T-shirt. She gathered up her sleeping bag, wrapping the rest of her clothes in it, then grabbed her lab kit in her open hand and kicked the bloody clothes into the hallway. She hurried back down the stairs and out to the car with her awkward load. While Daniel foraged in the kitchen, she located the kerosene. Kevin had three five-gallon gas cans stashed together. He could only have intended them for lighting up the house. She was glad that he was so prepared and businesslike. It meant his reaction—once Daniel was safe—was likely to be more pragmatic than violent. She hoped.

She started upstairs, making sure her clothes and the bodies were well saturated with the kerosene. The wooden floors wouldn't need as much help. She splashed the baseboards in all three rooms, then trailed the rest down the stairs. She grabbed another can and hurried through the ground floor. It was the first time she'd seen the other bedrooms. They were both large and well appointed with luxurious attached baths. She was glad Arnie had had a comfortable life here. She wished she could have done something to spare him this. But even if she and Daniel had left the first day the missing-person trap had run on the news, Arnie would still have ended up like this. It was a depressing thought.

Daniel's fingerprints were in the dogs' outbuilding, but there was no way to fool Carston's counterpart at the CIA into thinking Daniel—or Kevin—had died here, so it didn't really matter. They would know Daniel was on the run. She didn't want to torch the outbuilding and endanger the animals. It didn't have a wide gravel skirt like the house did, which would hopefully prevent a wildfire. No doubt Kevin had laid the gravel for exactly this reason.

Daniel was waiting for her in front of the Humvee.

"Back this up," she said, waving toward the Humvee. "See if you can get the dogs to move, too."

He got to work. She had the pack of matches from her first-aid kit. She'd left a nice thick trail of kerosene down the middle of the porch steps, so it was easy to set that trail alight and then get out of the way before the blaze really got going. When she turned, the dogs were automatically backing away from the flames. That was good.

Alex opened the driver-side door and called for Einstein. He jumped over the seat in one bound and then positioned himself next to Lola. His ears were up and his tongue out. He still looked eager; Alex envied his energy and positivity.

Daniel was walking through the crowd of surviving animals, giving each one an emphatic "At ease." She hoped that would help when the fire trucks started rolling up. The noise of the shootout wouldn't have carried to any of the distant neighbors, but the orange light of the fire against the black night sky was another matter. They had to run now. She couldn't think of anything else she could do for the dogs. It felt like failure—these animals had saved her and Daniel's lives.

A rumble just behind her head startled Alex. She spun and found herself face to face with Khan. He was staring at her in what seemed like an impatient way, as if he were waiting for her to move. His nose pointed over her shoulder toward Einstein.

"Oh," she said as she realized he was trying to get into the car. "Sorry, Khan, I need you to stay."

She'd never seen an animal look so offended in her life. He didn't move, just stared into her face as if demanding an explanation. She was the more surprised of the two of them when she suddenly threw her arms around his neck and buried her face against his shoulder.

"I'm sorry, big guy," she whispered into his fur. "I wish I could take you with me. I owe you huge. Take care of the others for me. You're in charge, okay?"

She leaned away, stroking the sides of his thick neck. He looked slightly mollified and took an unwilling step back.

"At ease," she said quietly; she patted him once more, then turned to the Humvee. Daniel was already belted into the passenger's seat.

"Are you all right?" Daniel asked quietly as she climbed in. It was obvious he wasn't talking about physical injuries.

"Not really." She laughed once, and there was an edge of the hysteria she was fighting in the sound. Khan was still watching as she pulled away from the house.

Once through the gate, she donned the goggles and turned the headlights off. It was safer to drive the Humvee across the open plains rather than stay on the only road that led to the ranch. Eventually, they reached another road—it was even paved. She ditched the goggles and put the headlights on as she turned northwest. She didn't have a destination in mind, only distance. She needed to get as far away from Kevin's ranch as possible before the sun rose.

CHAPTER 20

K evin picked up on the first ring.

"Okay, Oleander, where do we stand?" was his greeting.

"We're headed north in the Humvee. I've got Daniel, Einstein, and Lola with me. We managed to scavenge some of what we need, but not much."

She heard him blow out a relieved breath when she said Einstein's name, but the edge was still there in his voice when he asked, "The Humvee? The truck is blown?"

"Yes."

He thought for a second. "So, only night driving until you can find something new."

"Easier said than done. We've both got major face problems."

"Yeah, I saw Daniel on the news. But yours can't be that bad anymore. Throw some makeup on."

"It's gotten *slightly* worse over the course of the evening."

"Ah." He clicked his tongue a few times. "Danny?" he asked, and she could hear the tension he was trying to hide.

"Not a scratch." The hands didn't count; they'd done that to themselves.

"She made me stay in the car," Daniel yelled loud enough for his brother to hear.

"Good job," Kevin responded. "How many were there?"

"Six."

He sucked a breath in. "Agents?"

"No, actually. Get this—they put a hit out with the *Mob*."

"*What?*"

"It was mostly muscle, but they had at least one authentic professional in the group."

"You took out *all* of them?"

"The dogs did most of the work. They were magnificent, by the way."

He grunted in acknowledgment. "Why'd you bring Lola?"

"Shot in the leg. I was afraid that if someone found her, they would put her down. Speaking of, should I call Animal Control?" she asked. "I worry that when the firemen get there..."

"I'll take care of it. I've got a contingency plan in place for them."

"Good." She would never think of herself as the most prepared again. Kevin was the king of prepared.

"What's your plan now?"

She laughed—and there was the sound of hysteria again. "No idea, actually. I'm thinking we camp out of the Humvee for a few days. After that..." She trailed off.

"You don't have a place?"

"Not one where I can park this beast or hide two large dogs. I've never felt so conspicuous in my life."

"I'll think of something."

"What took you so long to call?" she asked. "I thought you were dead."

Daniel gasped. He stared at her, shocked.

"Getting set up. These things take time. I can't be everywhere at once—I had to plant a lot of cameras."

"A call would have been nice."

"I didn't know you guys were going to blow everything." His voice got suddenly much lower. "What did the idiot do? No, don't answer. I don't want him to hear. Just yes or no. Did he call someone?"

"No," she snapped, irritated.

"Wait — the truck is blown . . . he didn't leave the house, did he?"

She wanted to say, *No one told him not to,* but Daniel would know they were discussing him. She didn't respond, keeping her eyes straight ahead, though she wanted to sneak a look at Daniel to see if he'd heard any of it.

Kevin sighed. "Not an ounce of common sense."

So many things she wanted to say to that, but she couldn't think of a discreet way to phrase any of them.

He changed the subject. "Arnie . . . Was it bad?"

"No. He didn't see it coming. He wouldn't have felt anything."

"His real name was Ernesto," Kevin said, but it felt like he was saying it to himself rather than to her. "He was a good partner. We had a good run. A short run, but a good one." He cleared his throat. "Okay, now tell me everything that happened." Then lower: "Except whatever he did to set it off. He's probably traumatized enough."

Alex ran through the events of the evening, keeping it clinical and glossing over the gruesome parts. When she said simply, "I questioned him," Kevin would have a pretty clear picture of what that meant.

"So what happened to your face?"

"He was very flexible. And he had some kind of throwing blade in the lining of his sleeve."

"Hm, that's rough," he said gloomily, and she knew what he was thinking. Facial scars were bad news when you wanted to keep a low profile. They were too easy to remember and recognize. Suddenly the search changed from *Have you seen a short, nondescript female, unknown hair length or color, or a man fitting that same description?* to *Have you seen a person with this scar?*

"Well," she concluded, "it appears the people in charge pegged you for the win. I won't pretend I'm not insulted. We'll have to tweak the plan. The bait has to come from you, and it needs to go to the right person. Do you have any idea who that would be yet?"

Kevin was quiet for a minute. "When word gets back to my guy about what happened tonight . . . well, we might not need the e-mail. He's going to have to talk to your guy about this. I'm ready—I'll see them do it. Then we can decide if we need more."

"Sounds good."

"By the way," he said in his covert voice, "I know you sanitized the story for the kid. I want the whole thing when I see you again."

She rolled her eyes. "Right."

"Look, Ollie, don't let this go to your head, but . . . you did good. Real good. You saved Danny's life. Thank you."

She was so surprised, it took her a minute to respond. "I think we're quits. Without your dogs or your Batcave, we wouldn't have made it out. So . . . thank you."

"You could have taken off as soon as you saw that first newscast. You knew they thought you were dead, but you stayed to keep a virtual stranger safe, though I'm sure you'd love nothing better than to be rid of both of us. That's honor, right there. I owe you."

"Mmm," she said noncommittally. They didn't need to discuss *everything* tonight.

"Let me talk to him before you hang up," Daniel whispered.

"Daniel wants to talk."

"Put him on."

She handed the phone over.

"Kev—"

"Don't beat yourself up, Danny," she heard Kevin tell him. She wondered if Daniel had been able to hear just as clearly.

"Yeah," Daniel responded, morose, "I'm only responsible for getting Arnie murdered tonight, not to mention the dogs. Why should I suffer?"

"Look, what's done is done—"

"Funny, Alex said that, too."

"Poison girl knows the score. This is a new world, kid. It's got a higher body count. Now, I'm not saying that things like this won't affect you. You just can't let them cloud your vision."

304

Kevin's voice dropped into a lower register, and Alex was glad to know that Daniel probably hadn't been able to make out the quieter part of their conversation. But she also wanted to know what Kevin didn't want her to hear.

"I think so," Daniel said. A pause. "Maybe not...I will. Yes. Okay. What are you going to do about the dogs? We had to leave Khan."

"Yeah." Kevin's voice was back to normal volume. "I love that monster, but he's not exactly travel-size, is he? There's a breeder not too far away that Arnie's worked with in the past. He's more a competitor than a friend, but he knows the value of my dogs. Arnie made a deal with him that if we ever wanted out, we'd sell him our stock. Arnie also sort of implied that we might decide to do that suddenly, without any warning and in the middle of the night. I'll call him and he'll meet up with Animal Control before they do anything stupid."

"Won't the cops wonder—"

"I'll coach him. He'll say Arnie called when he heard shots or something. Don't worry, the dogs will be okay."

Daniel sighed, relieved.

"It does piss me off that he's getting his hands on Khan, free of charge. He's been trying to buy him for years."

"I'm sorry—"

"Seriously, kid, don't sweat it. You don't last in this life by getting attached. I know how to start over. Now, be good and do whatever the Oleander says, okay?"

"Wait, Kev, I had an idea. That's why I wanted to talk to you."

"You've got an idea?"

Alex could hear the skepticism from three feet away.

"Yes, actually. I was thinking about the McKinleys' cabin by the lake."

Kevin was silent for a second. "Um, now's not really the time for a trip down memory lane, kid."

"I'm actually two minutes older than you, *kid,* which I'm sure you haven't forgotten. And I don't want to reminisce. I was thinking that the McKinleys only ever used the cabin in the winter. And that your CIA people probably wouldn't know *that* much detail about our childhood. And that I know where Mr. McKinley always kept the key."

"Hey, that's not bad, Danny."

"Thanks."

"That would be about, what? Eighteen hours from the ranch? Just two nights' driving. And that'll bring you closer to my position. Didn't the McKinleys used to keep a Suburban out there?"

"We can't *steal their car,* Kevin."

In the darkness, though more than a thousand miles apart, Alex felt like she was exchanging a loaded glance with Kevin. And maybe an eye roll—on his part, at least.

"We'll talk about finding a car later. Tell the Oleander to take better care of her face next time. We're going to need it."

"Yes, because I'm sure she *so* enjoys having people beat it bloody that it will be hard for her to quit."

"Yeah, yeah. Call me if you have any troubles. I'll make contact when I know more about our friends in Washington."

Kevin disconnected. Daniel stared at the phone for a minute before putting it away. He took a deep breath and let it out slowly.

"How are you holding up?" she asked.

"Nothing feels real."

"Let me see your hand."

He stretched his left arm out to her, and she took his hand with her right. His temperature was warmer than hers. She felt his wrist, and the pulse seemed even. The scratches and punctures on his palm were shallow; they'd already stopped bleeding on their own. She glanced over at him and then looked back to the road. It was too dark to be able to assess his coloring with any degree of certainty.

"What was that?" he asked as she released his hand.

"Looking for signs of shock. Do you feel nauseated?"

"No. But then, I kind of feel as if I *should,* if you know what I mean. Like I will when I can process everything."

"Let me know if you start to feel dizzy, faint, or cold."

"*You* feel cold. Are you sure you're not going into shock?"

"Not entirely, I suppose. If I feel dizzy, I'll pull over and you can drive."

He reached over, took her gloved hand off the wheel, and held it loosely, letting their arms dangle in the space between seats. He took another deep breath. "I heard all those shots, so close together, and I thought—"

"I know. Thanks for staying in the car like I asked. It's good to know I can trust you."

He didn't say anything.

"What?" she asked.

"Well, when you put it like that," he said, sounding ashamed, "I don't really want to admit this...but I did get out for a few minutes. I was about to go into the house, but Einstein stopped me. And then I realized that one way or another, things were decided inside, and if they *had* got you, my best bet to kill the bastards would be from the Humvee. I wasn't going to let them walk away, Alex. Not a chance."

She squeezed his hand lightly.

"Do you remember what Kevin told me before, about visualization?"

She shook her head. It sounded only vaguely familiar.

"We were at the shooting range for the first time, and I said I didn't think I could shoot another person." He laughed a dark little chuckle. "He told me to visualize someone I cared about in danger."

As he spoke, it came back clearly. "Ah."

"Well, I get it now. And he was right. The second I realized someone had killed Arnie and that he was coming for *you* next..." He shook his head. "I didn't realize I was capable of feeling so...primal."

"I told you that you would get in touch with your instincts," she said lightly. The joking tone, recalled from that day at the range, felt all kinds of wrong the instant the words were out. Her voice was somber when she added, "I wish it hadn't happened like this."

He squeezed her hand this time. "It's going to be okay."

She made an effort to focus. "So, where exactly are we headed?"

"Tallahassee. We did a couple of Christmases there when we were kids. Some family friends kept a place there so they could get out of the snow. They must have liked their privacy, because the cabin is in the middle of nowhere. It's not actually on the lake, but it's swampy, and the mosquitoes will be murder this time of year."

"You should be in real estate. You're sure no one will be there?"

"I haven't seen the McKinleys since my parents' funeral, but they never went south in the summertime during all the years I knew them. It was always just their winter spot."

"Well, we might as well head that way as any other. If that cabin won't work, maybe we can find something else that's empty."

She saw a sign for State Highway 70, heading north.

"We'll have to turn east, go through Oklahoma City, then down through Dallas. It'll be good, if anyone's looking, to be headed back into Texas. Makes us look innocent."

"We only defended ourselves."

"That won't matter. If we got picked up for what just happened, the police would have to take us in. Even if we explained every detail and they believed every word—which is unlikely, to put it mildly— they'd still have to put us in a cell for a while. It wouldn't take long. The people who hired the hit men would have no trouble getting to us in jail. We'd be sitting ducks."

He felt the tremble in her fingers and rubbed his thumb soothingly across the back of her hand.

"So you're saying a crime spree is a bad idea right now?"

She couldn't believe he was the one trying to cheer her up. "Probably," she agreed, "but it might come to that." She glanced down at the gas gauge, then hissed. "This thing is burning through gas like it *wants* to piss me off."

"What can we do?"

"I'm going to have to go into a gas station, pay with cash."

"But your face."

"There's no help for it. I'll just pretend I was in a car accident . . . which, actually, is not pretend at all, is it? Anyway, there's nothing else I can do."

The gas-guzzling monster forced Alex to stop much earlier than she would have liked. She followed the signs in Oklahoma City to the airport, guessing that the gas stations around it would be some-what busy even late at night. Also, if anyone noticed them there, he might assume they were planning to fly out. Any ensuing search would be concentrated on the airport.

She'd had Daniel find her oversize hoodie while she was driving. She slipped into it now, wishing it were cooler out so that she would look more normal. There were two other vehicles — one taxi and one work truck. Both male drivers eyed the Humvee, of course. She moved in her boy-slouch as she got out and stuck the nozzle into the tank. While it was filling, she slouched her way into the store. She grabbed a box of granola bars and a six-pack of bottled water and took them to the fifty-something woman at the counter. The woman had bleached-blond hair with an inch of dark roots, nicotine-stained teeth, and a name tag that said BEVERLY. At first she didn't pay much attention to Alex, just rang up the goods. But then Alex had to speak.

"Pump six," she said in the lowest register that wouldn't sound put on.

Beverly looked up, and her mascara-smeared eyes opened round.

"Aw, sweet hell, honey! What happened to your face?"

"Car accident," Alex muttered.

"Everyone okay?"

"Yeah." Alex looked pointedly down at the cash in her hand, waiting to count it out. From the corner of her eye, she saw the taxi drive away.

"Well, I hope you feel better soon."

"Um, thanks. What's the total?"

"Oh, is this right? Seems high. One-oh-three fifty-five?"

Alex handed Beverly six twenties and waited for the change. Another truck—a big, black F-250—pulled into the pump behind the Humvee. She watched as three tall thin men got out. As two of them walked into the minimart, she revised her assessment. They were very tall teenage boys; half of a basketball team, maybe. Like her, they wore dark hoodies. At least that made her unseasonable getup look more normal.

"That sure is a big truck you got out there," Beverly commented.

"Yeah."

"Must be a pain to keep that thing full."

"Yeah." Alex held her hand out impatiently.

The boys came in, noisy and boisterous. The smell of beer and marijuana drifted in through the door with them. Outside, the work truck pulled out of the lot.

"Oh, here you go," Beverly said, her voice suddenly impersonal. "Sixteen forty-five."

"Thanks."

Beverly was distracted by the newcomers. She stared over Alex's head, her eyes narrowed. The big boys were headed for the liquor aisle. Hopefully they would be a huge pain as they tried to get fake IDs past Beverly. Anything that would make Alex fade in her memory.

Alex headed for the automatic door with her head down. She didn't need more than one witness.

With a thud, her head knocked into the chest of the third boy. The first thing she registered was the smell; his sweatshirt reeked of whiskey. She looked up automatically when he grabbed her by the shoulders.

"Watch yourself, little playa."

He was a thick white kid, not as tall as the others. She tried to shake him off. He held on tighter with one hand, yanking her hood back with the other.

"Hey, it's a girl." Then louder, toward the boys by the refrigerated cases, "Looky what I found."

Alex's voice was ice. She was not in the mood for this nonsense. "Get your hands off me."

"You leave that gal alone or I'm calling the police," Beverly called shrilly. "I've got the phone in my hand."

Alex wanted to scream. This was all she needed.

"Relax, old bag, we got plenty to go around."

The other two, one black, one Hispanic, were already in place to back their friend up. Alex slid a thin syringe from her belt. This wouldn't help her stay under the radar, but she had to put this kid down and get out of here before Beverly called the cops.

"I've dialed the nine and the first one," Beverly warned them. "You all get out now."

Alex tried to yank herself out of the boy's grip, but the grinning idiot had both hands locked around her upper arms now. She angled the needle.

"Is there a problem, son?"

Nooooo, Alex moaned internally.

"What?" the white kid said aggressively, dropping her and pivoting to face the newcomer. He then took a quick step back, and she had to duck out of his way.

She'd spent so much time around Daniel that she'd forgotten how tall he really was. He had an inch on even the tallest kid, and he stood with wider shoulders and much more assurance. At least he'd put a ball cap on, hiding his hair and shading his face a little. The beginnings of his beard were dark enough to slightly camouflage the contours of his face. That was good. But it was not good that he'd stuck a Glock—in a very obvious way—into the waistband of his jeans.

"No, no problem, man," the black kid said. He grabbed the white kid's shoulder and tugged him back a step.

"Good. Why don't you head on out, then?"

The white kid thrust his chest forward. "When we get what we came for."

Daniel did something different with the way he held his jaw. Alex couldn't quite put her finger on it, but suddenly his face was the opposite of friendly. He leaned in toward the troublemaker.

"Now."

There was no bluster in how he spoke, just absolute authority.

"C'mon," the black kid insisted. He shoved the white kid past Daniel while tugging on the sleeve of the third boy. They walked quickly to the truck, elbowing each other and scuffling a little. Alex kept her back to Beverly, nudging Daniel so he would turn that way, too. The boys got in the truck and the driver punched the gas, swerving around the Humvee with tires squealing.

"Hey, thanks, buddy," Beverly cooed at him. "I appreciate your help."

"Sure thing," he responded, holding one arm out courteously for Alex to exit first.

Alex hurried back to the Humvee. She could feel Daniel close behind her and just hoped he had the sense to keep his head down and not turn around.

"Well, I don't know how that could have gone worse," Alex said disgustedly when they were back on the road. "That woman will remember us for the rest of her natural life."

"Sorry."

"You just had to go in there like some cowboy, with a gun in your pants."

"We *do* have Texas plates," he pointed out. "And what was I supposed to do? That kid was—"

"Was about to have a violent and prolonged episode of projectile vomiting. It would have incapacitated him totally and perhaps made enough of a mess that Beverly would have forgotten all about me."

"Oh."

"Yeah. *Oh,* indeed. I can take care of myself, Daniel."

His jaw suddenly got hard again, like it had in the gas station store. "I know that, Alex, but there might actually come a time when you need help. When that happens, I'm not going to be waiting in the car again. You should probably wrap your head around that now."

"I'll tell you when I need backup."

"And I'll be there," he snapped.

She let the quarrel drop, and for a moment there was no sound but the roar of the oversize engine burning through the new gas. Then he sighed.

"I should have known you were one step ahead," he said.

She nodded her acceptance of the implied apology, though she had mixed feelings about his declarations.

"Where did you learn how to do that?" she asked after another short lull.

"What?"

"Intimidate people."

"My school isn't exactly an exclusive private prep. Anyway, most kids just want someone to take control. It makes them feel more secure."

She laughed. "Then those boys will sleep sound tonight."

• • •

THE REST OF the night was less fraught. Daniel dozed against the window, snoring lightly, until the next gas stop, about twenty miles east of Dallas. The sleepy man in the booth showed no interest in Alex's face. When they were away from the gas station's cameras, she pulled off on a dark shoulder and traded seats with Daniel. He claimed to be wide awake and ready. She napped as best she could until the next stop, south of Shreveport, where they switched seats again.

Dawn was coming. Alex searched the fancy GPS for a close-by national park or wildlife reserve and found they were not far from the huge expanse of the Kisatchie National Forest. She headed for the corner of the park that came closest to the I-49, then wandered through back roads until she found an area isolated and overgrown enough that she felt comfortable pulling over into the thick shade of some tightly grouped trees. She backed into a barely wide enough space between the tree trunks and then reversed until there was just room for the rear hatch to open. When she cracked her door, the humid heat outside quickly overpowered the cooler air inside the vehicle.

Einstein was thrilled to get out of the car and relieve himself. It was harder for Lola. Alex had to redress Lola's wound when she was done. Daniel had food and water out for them before Alex was finished. Then Daniel had the easier job of relieving himself, and Alex got the more complicated version. She'd lived out of a car before, though, and while it wasn't her favorite thing, she was prepared.

She took a look at the front of the Humvee and had to admit she was impressed. To the naked eye, there was no evidence that they'd been in even a minor fender-bender.

The breakfast options were minimal. Alex found herself with the same box of Pop-Tarts that she'd started with her first morning at the ranch. Daniel took a packet, too.

"What are we going to do about food?" he asked.

Alex wiped her arm across her forehead, drying the sweat before it could drip into her eyes. "Tonight I'll stock up a little at each gas station. It will get us through a few days. Let me know if you have any requests." Alex yawned, then hissed when the motion pulled at the cut on her face.

"Do you have aspirin?"

She nodded tiredly. "That might be a good idea. We both need to get some sleep. The dogs will be fine if we just leave them outside, right? I don't want them to have to be cooped up all night and all day, too."

Alex dug up a couple of Motrin while Daniel shoved the mess in the back of the Humvee to the sides of the bed, leaving a narrow flat space in the middle for them. Satisfied that she'd done everything she could, Alex spread out her sleeping bag and rolled down the top edge for a pillow.

It felt normal in an abnormal way to have Daniel lie down beside her, instinctive and comfortable for him to wrap one arm around her waist and bury his face in the hollow of her neck. The scratch of his short beard tickled her skin, but she didn't mind.

She was starting to drift off when she became conscious of his movement beside her. At first she thought he was beginning to snore, but the shuddering didn't pause. She grabbed his fingers at her waist, and found them trembling. She jerked up and twisted to face him. His eyes flew wide when she moved so suddenly, and he started to sit up. She pushed him down with one hand on his chest.

"What's wrong?" he whispered.

She looked at his face. It was hard to tell in the shade, but he looked paler than before. She should have been watching for this. Now that they had the chance to figuratively lay their weapons down for a moment, of course the severe strain of the night before would catch up to them. Probably not authentic shock; more likely just a traditional panic attack.

"Nothing. Except maybe with you." She touched his forehead; it felt clammy. "Do you feel sick?"

"No, I'm fine."

"You were shaking."

He shook his head and took a deep breath. "Sorry, I was just thinking about . . . how close it was."

"Don't. It's over. You're safe."

"I know, I know."

"I won't let anything happen to you."

He laughed once, and she could hear the same sound of hysteria that had been in her own laugh last night. "I *know*," he repeated. "*I'll* be fine. But what about you? Are *you* safe?" He pulled her down onto his chest, cradling the damaged side of her face carefully in his long fingers, and whispered into her hair, "I could have lost you, just like that. Everything that means anything to me is gone— I've lost my home, my job, my life . . . I've lost *myself*. I'm hanging on by my fingernails, Alex, and it's you I'm hanging on to. If something happens to you . . . I don't know what that means for me. I don't know how I keep going. I'm dealing with the rest, Alex, but I can't lose you, too, I can't."

Another shudder ran through his body.

"It's okay," she murmured uncertainly, reaching up to rest her fingers against his lips. "I'm here."

Was that the right thing to say? She didn't have any experience comforting someone. Even when her mother had been in the last stages of the illness that had killed her, Judy didn't want sympathy and she didn't want lies. If Juliana were to say something like *You look great today, Mom,* Judy's response was always along the lines of *Don't bother with that nonsense, I have a mirror.* It never seemed to occur to Judy that Juliana might need comfort; after all, Juliana wasn't the one who was dying.

She'd learned early not to seek sympathy for herself; she'd never really known how to show it to someone else. She would be more comfortable with the clinical, explaining that what he was feeling now was just a natural response to the specter of a violent death, but she'd said things like that to him before and she knew they didn't help. So she found herself mimicking things she'd seen on television, speaking softly, stroking the side of his face.

"We're okay . . . it's over."

She wondered if she should put the sleeping bag over him, just in case, though it was already sweltering and he didn't feel cold. Still, she'd already come to the conclusion that he ran at a warmer temperature than she did. Both physically and metaphorically.

His breathing still sounded rough. She pulled her head free and then propped herself up so she could examine his face.

He was no longer just pale. His soft eyes were haunted, tormented, his jaw tight against the panic he was trying to control. A raised line pulsed in his forehead. He stared at her like he was pleading for a release from pain.

His expression ignited a nightmare of a memory, the memory of his interrogation, and she impulsively threw her arms around his neck, pulling his head up off the floor of the Humvee and hugging it tight to her chest to hide that face. She felt her own convulsive shiver, and the clinical side of her brain let her know that she was every bit as traumatized as he was. Her nonclinical side didn't care what the reason was. A wave of panic was washing through her and she felt as if she couldn't hold him close enough to reassure herself that he was actually alive and safe and here. As if she might suddenly blink and be back inside her black tent with Daniel screaming in agony. Or, worse, she would open her eyes to the dark upstairs hallway only to find Daniel's bleeding body at her feet instead of the hit man's. Her pulse spiked and she couldn't breathe.

Daniel rolled their bodies so he was at her side, and his hands peeled hers free from his head. For a second she thought he was about to take the comforter's role at which she had failed so spectacularly, but then their eyes met and she was looking into a mirror of all the turmoil and fear in her own head. Fear of loss, fear of *having* because that made the loss possible. Rather than comfort, the depth of his fear multiplied hers. She could lose him, and she didn't know how to live with that.

CHAPTER 21

Their lips crushed together so suddenly she wasn't sure who had moved first.

And then their bodies were tangling together with a kind of desperate fury, lips and fingers, tongues and teeth. Breathing was secondary and she managed it only in broken pants that left her still dizzy. She wanted nothing but to be closer, and then closer, to be *inside* his skin somehow so that he could never be ripped away from her. She felt the scald as the wound along her jaw reopened, and all the bruises, old and new, flared to life, but the pain did nothing to distract from that acute need. They grappled almost like adversaries, turning and twisting together in the limits of the small space, slamming against the duffel bags and then back to the floor. She was amazed at how electrifying his brute strength was—strength in a man had always been something to fear, but now she thrilled to it. Fabric tore, and she couldn't guess who it belonged to. She remembered the texture of his skin, the shape of his muscles under her hands, but she had not imagined they could feel like this against her own.

Closer, her blood pulsed. *Closer.*

And then he suddenly jerked away, his mouth sliding from hers with a choked gasp. An anxious whine sounded at her feet. She leaned over and saw Einstein with his jaws locked on Daniel's ankle. Einstein whimpered again.

"Einstein, *at ease,*" he growled, kicking to free his foot. "Get *off.*"

Einstein let him go, looking to her nervously.

"At ease!" Her voice was husky. "It's okay."

With a hesitant huff, Einstein dropped out of the open hatch.

Daniel rolled up and slammed the door shut. He turned toward her on his knees, his pupils dilated and his eyes wild. He gritted his teeth as if he were fighting for some kind of control.

She reached up for him, her fingers stretching to hook into the waistband of his jeans, and he collapsed into her with a low groan.

"Alex, Alex," he breathed against her neck. "Stay with me. Don't leave."

Even in the frenzy of the moment, she was aware what he was asking. And she meant what she said when she answered, knowing it could be the worst kind of mistake.

"I will," she promised roughly. "I won't."

Their mouths locked together again, and she could feel his heart drumming a syncopated rhythm against her own, aligned beneath their skin because his mirrored hers.

The shrill peal of the phone pierced through the lower register sounds — the double heartbeat, the gasping breaths — and had her pushing away from him in a different kind of panic.

He shook his head quickly once, eyes closed, as if trying to remember where he was.

She sat up, looking for the source of the sound.

"I've got it," Daniel said, gasping. He shoved his hand in his jeans pocket as the phone pealed again.

He looked at the number, then hit Answer with his thumb. With his left hand, he pulled her back against his chest.

"Kev?" Daniel answered between pants.

"Danny — hey, are you guys safe?"

"Yeah."

"What are you doing?"

"Trying to get some sleep."

"Sounds like you're running a marathon."

"The phone scared me. Nerves a little frayed, you know." He lied so smoothly that she almost smiled in spite of the tumult inside her.

"Oh, right, sorry. Let me talk to Oleander."

"You mean Alex?"

"Whatever. Give her the phone."

She tried to slow her breathing, to sound normal. "Yes?"

"What? Don't tell me the phone scared you, too."

"I am not a black ops agent. And it's been a very long night."

"I'll keep it quick. I found my guy. Does the name Deavers mean anything to you?"

She thought for a second, working to pull her mind back to the things that mattered. "Yes, I know the name. It was on some of the files when information was being extracted for the CIA. He never came in to monitor an interrogation, though. Is he a supervisor over there?"

"He's more than a supervisor. He's second in command these days, with an eye to moving up. He was one of several potentials I was monitoring. Early this morning, Deavers gets a call, punches a few walls, then makes his own call. I know this guy—he loves to make the peons scurry. He doesn't leave his office; he sends an aide to bring the person he wants to him. Always the power play. But after that second call, he goes running out to see your man Carston like a gofer. They met up at a random little residential park miles away from both their offices and then went for a leisurely and sweaty walk, looking like they wanted to murder each other the whole time. It's Deavers, for sure."

"What are you thinking?"

"Hmm. I think I still want the e-mail. I need to see who else knows about this. Taking out Deavers won't be too hard, but it just tips the other guys off if he's not alone. Have you got a pen?"

"Gimme a sec."

She crawled to the front seat and located her backpack. She dug for a pen, then scribbled the e-mail address he gave her onto the back of a gas receipt.

"When?" she asked.

"Tonight," he decided. "After you've gotten some sleep and have your nerve back."

"I'll send it from Baton Rouge. Do you have a script or do you want me to wing it?"

"You know the gist. Don't make it sound too cerebral."

"I think I could channel some caveman."

"Perfect. Once you trade cars with the McKinleys, start heading up here." He switched to his library voice, but Daniel was so close it was a wasted effort. "Danny going to give you trouble about staying behind?"

She tilted her face up toward Daniel's. It was easy to read his reaction.

"Yeah. I'm not so sure it's a good idea anyway. Call me paranoid, but I don't believe in safe houses anymore."

Daniel bent down to press his lips hard against her forehead, which made it difficult to pay attention to what Kevin was saying.

"... figure a place for Lola. How bad is your face? Oleander?"

"Huh?"

"Your face. What does it look like?"

"Big bandage across my left jaw and ear." As she spoke, Daniel leaned closer to examine her wounds and then drew in a sharp breath. "Plus all the original fun."

"That could play," Kevin said. "Lola's injured, too. I'll feed them a story that will keep them satisfied."

"Who?"

"The dog-boarding place for Lola. Damn, Ollie, you need some sleep. You're getting dumber by the second."

"Maybe I'll write your e-mail now, while I'm in the right frame of mind."

"Call me when you're on the road again." Kevin hung up.

"You're bleeding through the bandage," Daniel said anxiously.

She handed him the phone. "It's fine. I should have glued it last night."

"Let's take care of it now."

She looked up at his face—the panic and ferocity in his eyes had dimmed to simple concern. His chest was still slick with sweat, but his breathing was regular. She wasn't sure she had reached a similar state of calm.

"*Right* now?" she asked.

He gave her a measured look. "Yes, right now."

"Is it bleeding that much?" She touched the gauze gingerly but felt only a bit of warm wet. From his expression, she'd expected blood to be gushing out in a torrent.

"It's *bleeding;* that's enough. Where is the first-aid kit?"

With a sigh, she turned to the piled duffels. The wrong one was on top, so she had to readjust. While she dug, she felt his fingers cautiously brushing along her left shoulder blade.

"You're all over bruises," he murmured. His fingers followed the line of her arm. "These look fresh."

"I got tackled," she admitted as she pulled out the kit and turned around.

"You never told me what happened in the house," he commented.

"You don't want to know."

"Maybe I do."

"Okay. *I* don't want you to know."

Daniel took the first-aid kit from her hands and then crossed his legs and set it between them. She followed suit with a heavy sigh, angling the left side of her face toward him.

Gently, he started easing the tape from her skin.

"You can do that faster," she told him.

"I'll do it my way."

They sat in silence for a moment while he worked. The stillness allowed her body to remind her how exhausted she was.

"Why don't you want me to know?" he asked as he dabbed a medicated wipe against her skin. "Do you think I can't handle it?"

"No, I just..."

"What?"

"The way you look at me now. I don't want that to change."

From the corner of her eye, she saw him smile. "You don't have to worry about that."

She shrugged in response.

"How do I do this?" he asked, pulling her superglue from the case.

"Push the edges of the cut together, draw a line of glue across the top, then hold it till the glue dries. About a minute."

She suppressed a wince as he pressed his fingertips firmly against her skin. The familiar smell of the adhesive filled the space between them.

"Does this hurt?"

"It's fine."

"Do you ever get tired of being tough?"

She rolled her eyes. "The pain is manageable, thank you."

He leaned away to examine his work. "It looks messy," he told her. "You should have saved the life of an EMT."

She took the glue from him and screwed the cap back on. She didn't want it to dry out. Who knew how soon she might need it again, the way this trip was going.

"I'm sure it will do the job," she said. "Just hold it for a little longer."

"Alex, I'm sorry about just now." His voice was quiet, apologetic.

She wished she could turn her head and look at him straight on.

"I don't know what that was," he continued. "I can't believe I was so rough with you."

"I wasn't exactly pulling my punches."

"But I'm not injured," he reminded her sourly. "Not a scratch on me, as you put it."

"I don't think that's entirely true anymore," she told him, brushing her fingers against the skin of his chest. She could feel the faint welts her nails had left.

He inhaled sharply, both of them caught for one second in the memory, and her stomach contracted. She tried to turn her head, but he held her face still.

"Wait," he cautioned.

They sat motionless in the charged silence while she counted to sixty in her head twice.

"It's dry," she insisted.

Slowly, he lifted his fingers from her jaw. She turned to him, but his face was down as he searched the kit. He found the antibacterial spray and applied it liberally to her wound. Then he pulled out the roll of gauze and tape. Gently — and without looking her in the eye — he took her chin between his thumb and forefinger and repositioned her head. He taped the gauze in place.

"We should sleep now," he said as he pressed the last piece tight to her skin. "We're both overwrought and not thinking clearly. We can reopen this . . . discussion when we're rational."

She wanted to argue, but she knew he was right. They weren't acting like themselves. They were acting like animals — responding to a near-death experience with a subconscious imperative to continue the species. It was primitive biology rather than responsible adult behavior.

She still wanted to argue.

His fingers rested against the side of her neck, and she could feel her pulse begin to jump under his touch. He could, too.

"Sleep," he repeated.

"You're right, you're right," she grumbled, flopping back against the rumpled sleeping bag. She really was bone-weary.

"Here." He handed her his T-shirt.

"Where's mine?"

"In pieces. Sorry."

It was already too warm and stuffy inside the Humvee. She tossed his shirt aside and grinned remorsefully, feeling the glue pull. "For people with quite limited resources, we are not being very careful with our things."

He must have noticed the lack of air circulation as well. He leaned over and opened the back hatch again. "Like I said — we're overwrought."

He lay down next to her, and she curled into his chest, wondering if it would really be possible to sleep with him half naked beside her. She closed her eyes, trying to will herself into unconsciousness. His arms wrapped around her, tentatively at first and then, after a few seconds, more securely, almost like he was testing his resolve.

If she'd been any less tired, she might have made the test harder for him. But despite her heightened awareness of his body and all the little volts of electricity that sparked where her nerve endings met his bare skin, she quickly drifted. As she surrendered to oblivion, one strange word circled through her head.

Mine, her brain insisted as her thoughts faded to black. *Mine.*

• • •

WHEN ALEX WOKE, the sun was still bright in the west, and the sleeping bag underneath her was damp with sweat. The shadows had shifted, and a shaft of light was hitting her full in the face, albeit through the tinted window. She blinked sleepily for a minute, waiting for her brain to wake up.

Then she came to with a jolt as she realized she was alone. She sat up too quickly, making her head ache and spin. The back hatch of the Humvee was still open, and the warm, humid air sat heavily on her skin. Daniel was nowhere in sight. Neither was his T-shirt, so she had to swiftly and silently dig into her things to find something to wear before she could look for him. It was stupid, but if she was about to run into another team of assassins, she didn't want to do it in no more than a worn tan bra. She threw on her thin, oversize gray sweater because it was the first thing her fingers touched, not because it was weather-appropriate. She pulled the PPK out of her bag and tucked it into the small of her back. As she was climbing out the open hatch, she heard the crinkle of paper under her knee.

It was the receipt she'd written the e-mail address on. Underneath that was another neatly printed note.

Taking Einstein for a walk. Back soon.

She shoved the note in her pocket. Still moving quietly, she climbed out of the Humvee. Lola was sprawled out in a patch of shade beside the water and food Daniel had left. Her tail started thumping against the grass when she saw Alex.

Well, at least with Lola there, Alex knew that there was no one else around. Alex gulped down some water, wiped the sweat from her face with the sleeves of the sweater, then shoved them up as high as they could go.

"I don't even know which direction they went," she complained to Lola, scratching her ears. "And you're in no shape to track them down, are you, girl? Though I bet you could pretty fast if you were on your feet."

Lola licked her hand.

Alex was very hungry. She explored the small stash of food Daniel had brought and settled for a bag of pretzels. She would definitely need to replenish their stores tonight, but she so hated leaving a trail. Of course, there were hundreds of possible routes they could have taken to any number of destinations. But if someone were persistent enough and had a little luck on his side, he might be able to put together a pattern. She was out of carefully prepared traps and well-thought-out plans, let alone Batcaves. Her assets were money, guns, ammo, grenades, knives, a variety of venoms and chemical incapacitators, an assault vehicle, and one brilliant attack dog. Her physical liabilities included that same attention-demanding assault vehicle, one lame dog, her own somewhat lame body, one conspicuous face, one face off a wanted poster — more or less — and a lack of food, shelter, and options. Her emotional liabilities were even worse. She couldn't believe how much trouble she'd brought on herself in such a limited time. Part of her wanted nothing more than to rewind, to go back to her cozy little bathtub, her unbroken face, and her safety nets. To choose differently in that distant library and delete the e-mail.

But if she could turn back the clock, would she? Was that life of daily terror and loneliness really such a better option? She'd been safer, yes, but still hunted. In so many ways, wasn't her new, more endangered life a fuller existence?

She was sitting next to Lola, slowly stroking her back, when she heard Daniel's voice approaching. After the first shock of alarm, she didn't panic that he was talking to someone else. There was a special edge in his voice that appeared only when he was speaking with Kevin.

Einstein arrived first. He ran excitedly to Alex and touched his wet nose to her hand. He exchanged a snuffly greeting with Lola, then went to get a drink.

Daniel walked into view, striding quickly down the center of the unkempt dirt road. He had the bulletproof hat on. Beneath it, his brows were furrowed. He held the phone half an inch from his ear.

"I'm back now," he was saying. "I'll see if she's awake . . . No, I will not wake her if she's still sleeping."

Alex got to her feet, brushing debris from her backside and stretching. The movement caught Daniel's eye, and his expression shifted from annoyance to a slow, wide smile. Though she was a little exasperated, she couldn't help grinning back.

"She's right here. Just one more second of patience, brother dear."

Rather than hand her the phone, Daniel pulled her close for a lingering hug. With her face hidden in his chest, breathing in his smell, she smiled. But when he finally leaned away, she was shaking her head, her eyebrows raised in disbelief.

"Sorry," he said. "Wasn't thinking."

She blew out a frustrated breath, then held her hand out for the phone. He gave it to her with a sheepish grin, his other arm still loosely around her.

"Don't mind me, I'm just trying to keep us alive," she muttered, then spoke into the phone. "Hello."

"Good morning. I see my idiot brother hasn't learned anything from his mistakes."

"What's happened?"

"Not much. A flurry of phone calls, but no one else has implicated himself at this point."

"Then why are you calling?"

"Because it feels like you and Daniel have an infinite capacity to screw things up. It's making me a nervous wreck."

"Well, it's been *lovely* chatting—"

"Don't get mad, Oleander, you know I mean Daniel. I just wish you could somehow put a leash on him."

"He's new. He'll get it."

"Before he kills himself?"

"You know I can hear you, right?" Daniel asked.

"No one likes an eavesdropper," Kevin said loudly. "Give the girl some space."

"Here, just talk to him yourself. I'm going to sort our things out so we'll be ready to go when the sun sets."

She handed the phone back to Daniel and freed herself. He didn't stay on much longer with his brother. They just exchanged a few insults while she walked back to the Humvee and surveyed the damage. The cargo hold was still total chaos. Well, she had plenty of time on her hands now and not much else productive to do. She pulled the PPK from the small of her back and put it away inside a Ziploc bag in her backpack. Next, she rolled up the sleeping bag and stashed it out of the way on the passenger's seat so she could locate all the stray ammo.

She heard Daniel climb in beside her. He went to work combing the space for loose objects.

"I *am* sorry," he said while he worked, not looking in her direction. "It's just, you were sleeping and Einstein was restless, and we seem so alone here. It felt normal. I guess that should have been my first clue that I was committing a crime."

She kept her eyes on her work, too. "Imagine if *you* had woken up here alone."

"I should have thought of that."

"I remember someone recently promising me that he would ask if it was okay before he *breathed*."

He sighed. "Kevin's right, isn't he? I'm terrible at this."

She started organizing the different magazines into Ziploc bags and then sliding each into an outside duffel pocket.

"I see what you're doing there," she told him. "You're making it so I have to either agree with Kevin or forgive you."

"Is it working?"

"Depends. Did anyone see you?"

"No. We saw no signs of life aside from a few birds and squirrels. You know how most dogs chase squirrels? Einstein *catches* them."

"That might come in handy if we have to live out of this Humvee any longer. I'm not much of a hunter."

"One more night, right? We'll survive."

"I truly hope so."

"Er...do you want to save these?" Daniel asked, sounding confused. "Are they...walnuts?"

Alex glanced up to see which Ziploc he was referring to.

"Peach pits," she said.

"Trash?"

She took the bag from his hand and tucked it into the duffel she was reorganizing.

"Not trash," she said. "I use them for the sodium cyanide that occurs naturally in the inner kernel of the pit. There's not much in each—I have to collect hundreds of pits to get a usable amount." She sighed. "You know, I used to like peaches. Now I can't stand them."

She looked over and saw that Daniel was frozen in place, eyes wide. "Cyanide?" He sounded startled.

"One of my security systems. When it reacts with the right liquid acid, it creates hydrocyanic acid. Colorless gas. I make ampoules large enough to saturate a ten-by-ten room. Pretty basic stuff. I don't have access to high-end materials anymore. It's a lot of bathtub chemistry for me these days."

Daniel's expression evened out and he nodded like everything she'd just said was perfectly sane and normal. He turned back to collecting stray ammo. She smiled to herself.

Alex had to admit she felt a little calmer when their gear was all organized and neatly stowed; the best thing about obsessive-compulsive disorder was the cozy high you got from a tidy space. She took stock of all the weapons that remained to her and was comforted by that as well. The earrings could not be replaced, and she was low on several compounds, but the majority of her arms were still in working order.

For dinner they had granola bars, Oreos, and a bottle of water they shared as they sat on the back edge of the open Humvee; her legs dangled a good foot off the ground, but his toes touched. At his insistence, she took more Motrin. At least the over-the-counter pills were easily replaceable. She didn't need to be such a hoarder with those.

"When do we leave?" Daniel asked when they'd cleaned everything up.

She judged the position of the sun. "Soon. Fifteen more minutes, and I think it will be dark by the time we meet the main road."

"I know I'm in terrible trouble and probably deserve, I don't know, to be in solitary confinement or something, but do you think I could kiss you until it's time? I'll be more careful with your face and your clothes, I promise."

"Careful? That's not very tempting."

"Sorry. It's my best offer currently."

She sighed with mock reluctance. "I guess I haven't really got anything else to do."

He took her face in his hands, placing his fingertips delicately again to avoid her injuries, and when his lips touched hers this time, they were so soft there was barely any weight to them at all. She still felt the buzz, the electricity under her skin, but there was an odd kind of comfort to the very gentleness of it. It was like before, like back in the kitchen at the ranch, only a little more cautious. Still, she remembered the morning vividly, and that shifted things. She considered changing the tempo, twisting into his lap and wrapping her legs around him, but she hesitated. It felt so nice just as it was. Her fingers found their way to his curls, as was rapidly becoming her habit.

He kissed her neck, lightly tasting the places where her pulse beat beneath her skin.

He whispered into her good ear, "One thing concerns me."

"Just *one* thing?" she breathed.

"Well, aside from the obvious."

His mouth returned to hers, still careful, but this time more exploratory. It had been a decade, nearly, since anyone had kissed her, but it felt longer. No one had ever kissed her like *this,* with time slowing down and her brain stopping and all the electricity...

"Do you want to know what it is?" he asked a few minutes later.

"Hmm?"

"The thing that concerns me."

"Oh, right. Sure."

"Well," he said, pausing to kiss her eyelids, "I know exactly how I feel about you." Her lips again, her throat. "But I'm not entirely sure how you feel about me."

"It's not obvious?"

He leaned away from her, still holding her face, and stared at her, curious. "We seem to share a level of attraction."

"I'll say."

"But is there anything more for you?"

She stared, not sure what he was looking for.

He sighed. "You see, Alex, I'm in love with you." He searched her face, analyzing her reaction, then frowned and let his hands drop to her shoulders. "And I can tell that you're not buying that, but there it is. Despite what my recent behavior may have implied, sex is not my end goal here. And...I guess I'd like to know what your goals are."

"My *goals?*" She looked at him incredulously. "Are you serious?"

He nodded gravely.

Her voice sounded sharper than she'd meant it to when she answered. "I have only one goal, and that's to keep both you and me alive. Maybe, if I can do that long enough, we'll actually have a reasonable expectation of life beyond the next twenty-four to forty-eight hours. Should we ever be in that happy position, I can think about having other goals. Goals imply a future."

His frown spread from his mouth to his eyes. His brows pushed down and together. "Are things really that bad?"

"Yes!" she exploded, her hands clenching into fists. She took a deep breath. "I thought that was obvious, too."

The sun was setting. They should have been on the move five minutes ago. She jumped down from the Humvee and whistled for the dogs. Einstein bounded past her eagerly, ready to be back on the road. She went to pick up Lola, but Daniel was there first.

Alex stretched and tried to focus. She felt decently rested and would probably be fine driving all night. That was all that mattered. Just making it through the night without garnering any more attention than she had to. Sending Kevin's e-mail, and then getting her little traveling circus into a less flamboyant vehicle. That was the limit of her ambition.

They drove in silence for a while. It got dark while they were still on back roads. When they eased onto I-49, Alex relaxed a little.

There hadn't been very many cars, and everything they had seen was old and fit the countryside. For now, she was fairly certain that no one knew exactly where they were.

She knew she should be concentrating, but the dark road with the steady flow of anonymous traffic was monotonous, and she couldn't help wondering what Daniel was thinking. It wasn't like him to be so quiet. She thought about turning on the radio, but that felt sort of cowardly. She probably owed him an apology.

"Um, I'm sorry if I was rough back there," she said, the words sounding very loud after the long lull. "I'm not good at this people stuff. There's really no excuse for me. I'm a full-grown adult—I should be able to hold a normal conversation. Sorry."

His sigh didn't sound exasperated; it was more like relief. "No, I'm the one who's sorry. I shouldn't have pushed. My lack of focus landed us in this position. I will get it together."

She shook her head. "You can't think of it that way. You're not responsible for this. Look, someone has decided to kill you. It happened to Kevin six months ago and it happened to me a few years before that. You'll make mistakes, because it's impossible to know what is or isn't a mistake until it's made. But mistakes don't mean you're guilty for what is happening. Never forget that there is a real human being who decided to put his agenda ahead of your existence."

He thought about that for a minute. "I know what you're saying. I believe it. But I need to listen to you more closely—act like you, keep my mind on what matters. It doesn't help us to have me mooning around like a teenager, worrying about whether or not you *like*-like me."

"Honestly, Daniel, I—"

"No, no," he interrupted immediately. "I did not mean to hijack this conversation with that comment."

"I just want to explain. If you're a teenager, I'm a toddler. I'm emotionally backward. Defective, even. I don't know how to do any of this, and while survival is obviously the priority, I'm also using it to deflect questions I should be able to answer. I mean...love? I don't even know what that is, or if it's real. Sorry, it's just...foreign to me. I evaluate things based on needs and wants. I can't deal with anything...*fluffier*."

Daniel laughed his funny *heh-heh-heh* laugh and all the tension bled right out of her. She laughed with him, and then sighed. Everything felt less awful when she could laugh along with Daniel.

He released one final chuckle, then said lightly, "So tell me what you need."

She thought it through. "I need...you to be alive. And I would like to be alive, too. That is my baseline. If I get more than that, I would prefer to have you close by. After that, anything else is just frosting."

"Call me an optimist, but I think we may just be dealing with nothing more than some semantic issues here."

"You could be right. If we get a few more weeks together, maybe we'll figure out how to speak the same language."

He took her hand. "I've always been a quick study with linguistics."

CHAPTER 22

Alex chose the gas station outside Baton Rouge based on the age of the cashier. He was eighty if he was a day and she had high hopes that his vision and hearing were past their prime.

Once she ascertained that he was paying her absolutely no attention at all, despite the fact that her thick makeup was far from convincing, she did some thorough shopping. More water, lots of nuts and jerky—any kind of nonperishable protein she could find. She grabbed some cans of V8, though she wasn't a fan, as the convenience store didn't have a fresh produce section. She acknowledged to herself that she would have to go to an actual grocery store at some point, but she hoped they could wait it out a bit longer. Every day her bruises faded a little more.

There was no drama at the twenty-four-hour Internet coffee place, either. It was near the university, so it had no shortage of late-night seat fillers. She kept her hood up and her face down, sat in a secluded corner, and asked for a plain black coffee without looking at the barista who came for her order. She wished she had time to do this from somewhere not on the trail to their destination, but the first priority had to be exchanging the Batmobile. It was currently her biggest disadvantage.

She created a brand-new e-mail account registered to a name that was no more than a random combination of letters and numbers. Then she tried to channel Kevin.

You should have left it alone, Deavers. You shouldn't
have involved a civilian. I'm not here to do your dirty
work, but I took care of the little interrogator for you.
Texas was a nice way to say *you're welcome*. Enough
is enough.

Not a specific threat, but plenty implied. She hesitated for a second with her finger over the mouse, the little arrow touching the Send button. Was she giving them anything they didn't have? They would know by now that Daniel wasn't among the dead back at the ranch. She couldn't try to fool Deavers on that point. Was there some way she wasn't seeing for this to come back at them? Could this make things worse?

She hit the button. Things couldn't get that much worse, anyway.

As soon as it was sent, she was on her feet. The Humvee was parked in the alley around the back, behind a couple of dumpsters. She walked quickly with her head down, hood up, and a syringe in hand. The side street was mostly empty, just one small knot of people huddled close together in the darkness of a recessed emergency door. She studied the trio for a second before she climbed into the dark vehicle.

Einstein touched his nose to her shoulder. Daniel took her hand.

"Do you know where the night-vision goggles are?" she murmured.

He dropped her hand. "Is something wrong?" he whispered back. He turned to rummage between the seats.

"Nothing new," she promised. "Maybe something helpful."

He handed her the goggles. She switched them on and took a better look at the little conference.

It was just breaking up. This wasn't a particularly rough area of town, and all three participants were expensively dressed, though their clothes were casual. A dark-haired man was holding hands with a blond girl who had so many showy labels on the different pieces of clothing she wore that she looked like a NASCAR driver sponsored by midlevel luxury brands. These two were walking off now, their path angling away from the Humvee. The blonde bobbled and swayed a little as she walked. The man with her was stuffing something into the pocket of his hoodie.

The third person stayed in the dark door frame, leaning against it casually like he was expecting more guests soon. His clothing was what she would describe as *upmarket frat boy*.

She thought about what she'd just been feeling inside the café before she pushed Send—that things couldn't get much worse. She supposed there were ways this spontaneous idea of hers could go south, but she couldn't think of any that she wouldn't be able to handle quietly. And it would be a big help if the frat boy was what she thought he was.

She pulled the goggles off.

"Where's the cash?" she whispered.

Thirty seconds later, syringe in one hand and roll of fifties in the other, she slid quietly from the Humvee and walked toward the man, who was still relaxed against the wall, like there was no place he'd rather be. She couldn't see very clearly without the goggles, but she thought she caught his minimal reaction when he realized she was approaching him. His body stiffened just slightly, but he didn't move.

"Hello," she said when she was close enough that she could speak quietly and still be sure he could hear.

"Evening," he responded in a lazy southern drawl.

"I was wondering if you could help me. I'm looking for ... a specific product." Her inflection went up on the end, like it was a question. She didn't know how to buy drugs off the street. She'd never had to do it before. This was the first time the supply she'd been able to amass during her time in Chicago had run dry. Joey G never minded paying in product.

She expected that the frat boy would accuse her of being a cop, like dealers always did on TV, but he just nodded.

"I might be able to help. What are you looking for?"

It was unlikely *he* was a cop, unless the sale she'd just watched had been faked to draw a real customer in. If he tried to arrest her, she'd knock him out and escape. A manhunt in Baton Rouge would hardly be her biggest problem, and she knew he couldn't see her face well—he hadn't reacted to the damage.

"Opioids—opium or heroin or morphine."

There was a pause as he peered into the darkness under her hood. She didn't think he was successful in seeing much.

"Well—that's an exotic list. Opium? Huh. I have no idea where you could get that around here."

"Heroin will do just as well. I'd prefer the powdered form, if possible. I don't suppose it's likely you'd have anything uncut?" It was all but impossible that he would have pure heroin. Whatever he had would have been modified two or three times before it reached his hands. Not that he would tell her the truth. Purification was a bit of a pain, but she'd make the time.

He laughed once, and she guessed her shopping style was probably not the norm.

"I've got some upscale stuff. It's not cheap, though."

"You get what you pay for," Alex said. "I'm not looking for a deal."

"Two hundred a gram. Pure white powder."

Sure it is, she thought to herself. But corrupted heroin was better than no heroin. "Three grams, please."

He paused. Though it was too dark to really read his expression, she could tell what he wanted from the way he cocked his head to the side. She pulled the cash from her pocket and counted out twelve bills. She wondered for a second if he would try to steal the rest from her. But he seemed to be a businessman. He'd want an apparently affluent customer like her to become a regular client.

He took the money she offered, looked it over quickly, then stowed it in the back pocket of his cargo shorts. She tensed when he crouched down, but he was just pulling a backpack out from behind a pile of garbage bags dumped against the wall. He didn't have to search for what he wanted. He was standing again a second later, holding out three small plastic bags. In the dark she couldn't be positive about the color, but it *looked* close to white. She held out her hand and he laid the bags on her palm.

"Thank you," she said.

"My pleasure, ma'am." He did a funny little nod, almost a bow.

Alex hurried back to the Humvee, glad that it was hard to make out from this angle. The dealer would see a large, dark-colored vehicle, and not much more than that.

Einstein whined quietly as she climbed into the passenger seat.

"Let's go," she said.

Daniel started the engine.

"Turn left down that side street so that guy won't get a good look at the Humvee."

"What just happened?" Daniel whispered as he followed her instructions. Even in a whisper, the tension was easy to hear. No wonder the dog was anxious.

"Just picking up some ingredients I needed."

"Ingredients?"

"I was out of opioids."

As they moved out onto a wider road, Alex could feel his tension easing, probably due to her nonchalance.

"Was that a drug deal, then?"

"Yes. Remember what I said about bathtub chemistry? Getting my raw materials is a little more complicated than it used to be. I didn't want to pass up the opportunity."

It was quiet for a moment.

"I hope that was the right move," she muttered.

"You think he'll tell someone about us?"

She blinked for a second. "What? Oh, no. I'm not worried about the dealer. I was just thinking about sending that e-mail."

"The e-mail was Kevin's call," Daniel responded.

She nodded. "And he has a better batting average than I do."

"No, I just meant that if it goes south, it was *his* call."

She laughed once. It was a heavy sound.

"You don't like it?"

"I don't know. I want to finish this . . . but I'm tired, Daniel. I also want to run away and hide."

"That doesn't sound so bad," he agreed. "Oh, um, if I was invited?"

She glanced at him, surprised. "Of course."

"Good."

There it was again, that automatic *of course*. That crazy assumption that he would be present for whatever future she was allowed.

She didn't know if it was the wearying strain or something more, but an annoying feeling of presentiment haunted her for the rest of the night. Maybe it was just the jitters from finally getting her hands on some coffee for the first time in two days.

She was almost shocked when, seven hours later and with the sun already well above the horizon, they reached the secluded cabin without incident.

Daniel had taken them down only two wrong turns — impressive, considering he hadn't been to the cabin since he was ten years old — and all the roads they'd traveled after sunrise were empty. That meant no one could report seeing an armored vehicle in the vicinity.

She parked the Humvee behind the detached garage for the present. Daniel kicked a few rocks around the base of the stairs until he found the plastic one. He removed the concealed key and then walked up the porch steps with Einstein at his heels.

Alex stood in front of the log cabin — it was a red cedar A-frame, charming despite some evidence that it had been built in the seventies — so tired she couldn't move those last few steps. Though the night had been blessedly uneventful, it had still been a long time on the road. She'd traded seats with Daniel outside Baton Rouge and then been too wired by the sense of apprehension that had troubled her since sending the e-mail to relinquish control again. Daniel had napped off and on, and he seemed almost chipper now. He passed her to go retrieve Lola from the back of the Humvee.

"You look like you might need to be carried, too," he commented as he passed her again, this time with the dog. He set Lola beside the door and then came back for Alex.

"Give me a second," she mumbled. "Brain sleeping."

"Just a few more steps," he encouraged. He put an arm around her waist and pulled her gently forward.

Once she started moving, it was easier. Momentum got her up the stairs and through the front door. She only partially took in a high wall of triangular windows looking out over a swampy forest, aged but comfortable-looking couches, an old-fashioned wood-burning stove, and a short open stairway as he steered her past it all and down a compact hallway.

"The master is over here...I think—Kev and I always got the loft. I'll unload and get the dogs settled, then I'll crash, too."

She nodded as he showed her into a dim room with a large iron bedstead. That was all she noticed before her head hit the pillow.

"Poor darling," she heard Daniel chuckle as she sank into the dark.

. . .

SHE CAME BACK to consciousness slowly, drifting up through layers of dreamy nonreality. She was comfortable and calm; nothing had startled her awake, and even before she was fully lucid she was aware of Daniel's body warm beside her. A low, close thrumming caught her attention, but before the sound could frighten her, she felt the breeze of the oscillating fan move gently down the length of her body. She opened her eyes.

It was still dim, but the light was a different color than it had been when she'd collapsed. It leaked in around the lined floral curtains that covered the big window on the opposite wall. Early evening, not as hot as before. She must have been sweating earlier, but it was dried now, a film that felt stiff against the skin of her face.

The room was made of long red logs, just like the outside. More light came from behind her. She rolled over and saw the skylight above the open vanity. Her backpack, her gas mask, and the first-aid kit were by the sink.

Daniel might not be a natural fugitive, but he was more thoughtful than anyone else she'd ever known.

She tiptoed out to the hall and did some quick surveillance. The rest of the cabin was small, just a kitchen with an attached nook for a dining room, the living room with all the windows, the open loft above it, and a small second bedroom with a hall bath. She used that bath to take a quick, much-needed shower. There were shampoo and conditioner in the little blue shower-tub combo, but no soap, so she used the shampoo as body wash. She was glad the soap was missing, just like she was glad the refrigerator was empty and that there was a fine layer of dust on all the counters. No one had been in these rooms for a while.

After she quickly applied new bandages to her face and examined her hands, which looked much better than she'd thought they would, she peeked through the long windows beside the front door to check on the dogs. They were snoozing contentedly on the porch. She was getting used to the comfort of having an early alarm system.

She was a little hungry but felt too lazy to do anything about it right away. She remembered how it felt yesterday to wake up alone, and she didn't want Daniel to experience the same panic. She wasn't really *sleepy* anymore, but she was tired, and the bed still looked pretty good. It was probably avoidance. As long as she kept her eyes closed and her head on the pillow, she didn't have to start planning what needed to happen next.

She returned to her earlier position, curled up against Daniel's chest, and let herself relax. There wasn't anything that she had to do immediately. Twenty minutes of unthinking rest wasn't so much to ask. Or even an hour. She'd gotten them here alive; she'd earned it.

Unfortunately, not thinking was easier said than done. She found herself dwelling on the promise she'd made to Daniel—that she wouldn't leave him behind. On the one hand, she knew she would never be satisfied with any long-distance arrangement for his safety. Even if she could stockpile a year's worth of food, even if she could be positive that the owners wouldn't come back, even if she could arm this place to vaporize any intruder, and even if she could lock Daniel inside like a prisoner so he couldn't wander off and find trouble, she would not be satisfied. Because *what if?* The hunters had found him before, and she'd left a trail, albeit a faint one, to this place. She could take him north to her rental, but the department had contacted her while she was living there. She didn't think they knew her address, but what if? As long as Daniel stayed near her, she could do what was necessary to protect him, things he wouldn't think of himself. She could see the traps he wouldn't see.

On the other hand, was that just her own wants talking? She wanted to be with Daniel. Was her mind coming up with proofs for that necessity? Was her logic flawed—twisting to accommodate her personal wishes? How could she be sure? When she'd told him before that it wasn't a good idea to have her liability close beside her while she went on the attack, she knew that was sound logic. Of course, if they got to him while she was far away, that distance wouldn't remove the hold they'd have on her.

She sighed. How could she see clearly? Her emotions had tangled this whole situation into a knot of Gordian complexity.

Still unconscious, Daniel shifted to wrap his arm around her. She knew what he would say about her dilemma, and she also knew that his perspective would not help her to see more clearly.

He sighed, starting to stir. His fingers traced down the length of her spine, then slowly back up. They played with the wet fringes of hair on the back of her neck.

He stretched with a groan, and then his hands were back in her hair.

"You've been up," he murmured.

His eyes opened slowly, blinking as they worked to focus. In the dusky room, they were dark gray.

"It didn't stick," she answered.

He laughed as his eyes slid shut again. He tucked her more tightly into his chest. "Good. What time is it?"

"Around four, I think."

"Anything to worry about?"

"No. Not for right now, at least."

"That's nice."

"Yeah, it really is."

"*This* is nice," he said.

His hand traced back up her spine again, then trailed over her right shoulder, traced lightly across her collarbone, and finally curved around the good side of her face. He tilted it up until their noses touched.

"Yes, this, too," Alex agreed.

"More than nice," he murmured, and she would have agreed, but he was kissing her. His hand on her face was soft, his lips soft, but the arm around her waist strained her tight against his chest. She wrapped her arms around his neck and held herself closer still.

It wasn't like the car, where the pulse of the hunt had been loud in their ears, when they were still shocked and panicking. There was no horror. Just the rhythm of her heart and his, speeding without fear.

She supposed it was inevitable, the way they'd been carrying on, that given a quiet place far away, for the moment, from any danger, with just the two of them together and no interruptions, there would be nothing to keep them apart any longer.

The strange thing, then, was how it didn't feel at all inevitable. Somehow, it was the biggest surprise of her life. It was all a jumble of opposites tumbling together in a way that left her helpless to analyze any of them. Comfortable, familiar... but also electric and new. Gentle at the same time it was extreme, both soothing and overwhelming. It was like every nerve ending in her body was lit up with dozens of conflicting stimuli simultaneously.

All she was really sure of was the Danielness of him, that core of something pure, something better than anything she'd known before. He belonged to a more excellent world than the one where she resided, and while they were part of each other, she felt like she was allowed to be there with him.

She knew her past experience with relationships was quite limited by most people's standards, so she didn't have much to compare this to. She'd always thought of sex as a single event that had a defined end, an effort at physical gratification that sometimes satisfied and sometimes did not.

This experience didn't fit into the same category on any level. It was less an event and more an ongoing exploration of each other, a satisfaction of curiosity, a fascination over each little detail discovered. It wasn't *about* gratification, but there was no need that wasn't met, whether it was physical or something less definable.

She searched for the right word as they lay kissing quietly, patiently now, with the light turning red around the edges of the curtain. She wasn't sure what to label this emotion that filled her so entirely that she thought it might stretch her skin. It was a little like that bubbly feeling that had left her smiling at the thought of him but multiplied by thousands, millions, and then fired in a crucible until every impurity, every lesser sensation, was burned out, leaving only *this* behind. She didn't have a name for it. The closest she could think of was *joy*.

"I love you," he whispered against her lips. "I love you."

Maybe that was the word. She'd just never thought its definition could be so... huge.

"Daniel," she murmured.

"You don't have to say anything back. I just needed to say that out loud. I might have exploded had I tried to keep it in. I will probably have to say it again soon. You are forewarned." He laughed.

She smiled. "I never want to go back to having nothing to lose. I'm glad I have you as my liability. I'm grateful. I'd have you as *anything*."

She laid her head against his chest and listened to his breath moving in and out. For so long now, breathing had been her priority. If she could have spoken to the woman she was even just a month ago, she knew that woman would have been terrified of expanding that priority to include another set of lungs. That woman would have run away from needing anything more than her own life. But what she would have missed! Alex couldn't even remember what she'd been holding on to back then. *This* was the kind of life worth fighting to keep.

"I think I was probably twelve, maybe thirteen, when I sort of gave up on living an extraordinary life," he mused thoughtfully, running his fingers in aimless patterns through her hair. "That's probably about the age that everyone starts to grow up and leave fantasy behind. You realize you're never going to discover that you're actually an alien, adopted by those prosaic human parents, with amazing superpowers that will save the world." He chuckled. "I mean, you *know* that much earlier, but you can't quite let go, not for years. And then the world beats you down a little, and some of the color goes out of life, and you settle for reality . . . I think I did a decent job of it. I found plenty of happiness in the drab, everyday world. But I want you to know—this time with you has been extraordinary. There has been terror, yes, but along with it, there's been a kind of joy I didn't know existed. And it's because *you* are extraordinary. I'm so glad you found me. My life was destined to change drastically, it seems, in one way or another. I'm just so grateful that it got to be with you."

Her throat was tight, and she marveled as she blinked furiously to keep the moisture in her eyes from pooling. She'd cried in grief, in pain, in loneliness, and even in fear, but this was the first time in her life she'd had tears of joy in her eyes. It seemed a strange response, something she'd never truly taken at face value when she'd read about it. This was the first time she'd understood that joy could be even more severe than pain.

She would happily have never left the bed, but eventually they had to eat. Daniel didn't complain, but she could tell he would be pleased when he had access to real food again. It was strange, as they sat at the little table in the alcove eating jerky, peanuts, and chocolate chip cookies, laughing and scratching the dogs' ears—of course they'd caved quickly and brought Einstein and Lola inside; if you were going to break and enter, you might as well do it in style—to think that they didn't have to get back into the Batmobile and drive tensely through the night again. They had a dozen empty hours ahead of them, open to fill in any way they wanted. She had a fairly good idea of what they would probably choose to do, but the point was the freedom. It felt too good to be true.

So, naturally, Kevin had to call.

"Hey, Danny, you guys good?" she heard him say. His voice was, as always, penetrating.

"I'm excellent," Daniel said. Alex shook her head at him. No need to elaborate.

"Uh, great. You got to the McKinleys', I presume."

"Yeah. The place hasn't changed."

"Good. That means it still belongs to them. Did you get enough rest?"

"Er, yes. Thanks for inquiring."

Alex sighed, knowing Kevin would never ask just to be polite. Too good to be true, indeed. She held out her hand at the same time that she heard Kevin say, "Let me talk to Oleander."

Daniel looked confused, clearly not following, but he handed her the phone.

"Let me guess," Alex said. "You need us to join you as soon as possible."

"Yes."

The corners of Daniel's lips turned down.

"What did Deavers do?" Alex asked.

"Nothing...and I don't like it. Because of course he's doing something, but he's being more cautious now. He's not letting me see anything, because he guesses that I'm watching. He must be making calls from other people's offices so I can't hear. What did the e-mail say?"

She recited it to him word perfect; she'd known he would want the details, so she'd memorized it.

"Not bad, Ollie, not bad. Maybe a little smart for me, but that's okay."

"So what are you thinking?"

"I want to strike within the week, which means you need to get here and get set to move at the same time."

She sighed heavily. "Agreed."

"Is the Suburban still there?"

"Um, I haven't checked yet."

"Why not?" he demanded.

"I slept in."

"You need to toughen up, sweetheart. The beauty sleep can wait for a few weeks."

"I'd like to be in top form for this."

"Yeah, yeah. When can you move?"

"Where are we going exactly?"

"I've got a place for us to crash. Do you have something to write with?"

He gave her an address. It was in a part of DC she wasn't familiar with. She thought the area he was sending them to was in a rather posh part of town, but that didn't fit with her idea of a bolt-hole. She must be picturing the wrong neighborhood. She'd been out of the city for a while.

"Okay, let me get our stuff together. We'll leave as soon as we can...*if* we have another car option available."

"You'll need to stop outside Atlanta sometime after nine a.m. I found a place for Lola."

"What did you tell them? About the bullet hole in her leg, I mean?"

"You were in a carjacking. Both you and the dog were injured. You're heading to Atlanta to stay with your mother for a while, but she's allergic. You're very traumatized, and they shouldn't ask about it. Your name is Andy Wells, and they know you'll pay cash. I'm your concerned brother in this scenario, by the way."

"Nice."

"Of course. Now go check the garage and call me back."

"Wilco, sir," she said sarcastically.

He hung up on her.

"Are we really going to steal the McKinleys' car?" Daniel asked.

"If we're lucky, yes."

He sighed.

"Look, we'll leave the Humvee in the garage. It's got to be worth four or five Suburbans at least. If we aren't able to bring their car back, they won't take a loss, right?"

"I suppose. Kevin won't like his favorite plaything being offered as collateral."

"That part's just the gravy."

The house key fit the garage door. Daniel promised that inside and just to the right of the door, next to the light switch, there would be a little hook with two sets of car keys hanging from it. He flipped the switch.

Alex gasped. "I've died and gone to heaven."

"Huh, they got a new car," Daniel said, less excited. "I guess the old Suburban must have finally quit."

Alex moved around the vehicle, stroking its side with her fingertips. "Look at this, Daniel! Have you ever seen anything more beautiful?"

"Um, yes? It's just a silver SUV, Alex. It looks exactly like every third car on the road."

"I know! Isn't that fantastic? And look at this!" She towed him around the car and pointed to a little chrome plaque by the taillight.

He stared at her, totally confused. "It's a hybrid? So?"

"It's a hybrid!" she half sang, throwing her arms around him. "This is like Christmas!"

"I had no idea you were so green."

"Pssh. You know how many times we're going to have to stop for gas in this thing? Twice! Maybe three times, max, all the way to DC. And look—just *look* at those gorgeous plates!" She pointed with both hands, part of her noting that she must look like a game-show hostess.

"Yes, they're Virginia plates. The McKinleys live in Alexandria most of the year, Alex. That's not a huge surprise."

"This car is going to be invisible in DC! It's like a stealth bomber. If anyone manages to follow the trail we left in the Texan Batmobile, they'll hit a dead end now. This is a beautiful thing, Daniel, and I don't think you're fully appreciating what amazing luck this is."

"I don't like stealing from friends," he grumbled.

"The McKinleys are nice people?"

"Very nice. They were lovely to my family."

"So they probably wouldn't want you to die, right?"

He gave her a dark look. "No, probably not."

"I'm sure, if they knew the whole story, they would *want* you to borrow this car."

"*Borrow* implies we're bringing it back."

"Which of course we will. Unless we're dead. Do you think anything but death could keep Kevin from retrieving his favorite ride?"

Daniel was abruptly much more serious. He folded his arms across his chest and turned to face the car rather than her. "Don't joke about that."

Alex was a little confused by his mood shift. "I'm not actually joking," she clarified. "I was trying to make you feel better about taking the car. We'll bring it back if we can, I promise."

"Just . . . don't talk about dying. Not like that. So . . . casually."

"Oh. Sorry. It's just, you know, laugh about it or cry about it, that's the only choice. I'd rather laugh while I can."

He looked down at her from the corner of his eye, his posture still rigid for a moment. Then suddenly he softened, freeing one hand to place it on the side of her face.

"Maybe we don't do what Kevin wants. Maybe we just stay here."

She put her hand over his. "We would if we could. They'd find us eventually."

He nodded, almost to himself.

"Okay, then. Shall we start loading?"

"Sure; let me call Kevin first."

Daniel started shifting bags from the Humvee to the Toyota while Alex enthused about the car to Kevin. Kevin wasn't much more excited than Daniel, but he got it immediately.

"That's great, kid. Now hurry up. The clock is ticking."

"We don't want to get to Atlanta before nine, so we don't need to leave here till, what, two a.m.?"

"All right. So I'll expect you here around five p.m."

"Counting down the seconds," she gushed facetiously. The car—or the afternoon with Daniel—had put her in an ebullient mood.

"I'm glad you'll be driving all night," Kevin said. "I think I like you better sleep-deprived." With that, he hung up on her again.

"I should probably walk Einstein," Alex mused. "Redo Lola's bandages. Pack up the food. Then we should try to force ourselves to get a nap. We're flipping our sleeping routine again."

"I suppose I'm not allowed to walk the dog," Daniel said.

"Sorry, America's Most Wanted. My sad little face is better than yours right now, beard or no beard."

"It's dark out—are you sure it's safe for you to go alone?"

"I won't be alone. I'll have a supernaturally intelligent attack dog and a SIG Sauer P220."

He almost smiled. "Tough luck for the hungry gators."

She hid her frown. Alligators. She hadn't been thinking about things like *that*. Well, she'd stay away from the water. And hopefully Kevin had trained Einstein for more than just human attackers.

The walk wasn't long, just enough for Einstein to stretch his legs a little. She couldn't stop thinking about giant reptiles. The road was black, but she didn't want to use a flashlight. She saw no headlights or house lights, heard nothing but swampy noises. It was still hot enough to have the perspiration rolling down her temples, but she was glad she'd brought the hoodie—the mosquitoes were definitely active.

When she returned, the Toyota was in front of the house and the Humvee invisible inside the garage. Daniel had taken care of everything but Lola's dressings. Alex did that, trying to make her work look professional. Hopefully the boarding place would believe a vet had tended her. She stroked Lola's ears sadly. It would be better for Lola to be somewhere people could take care of her, but Alex would miss her. She wondered what would happen to the dog if they weren't able to come back for her. Lola was beautiful. Someone would want her. Alex remembered imagining taking Lola home with her in some safe, unlikely future. If only.

Alex set the alarm clock by the bed for 1:45, but it was obvious that Daniel wasn't interested in stocking up on sleep.

"We're going to regret this around eight a.m.," she promised him as his lips trailed down her sternum.

"I won't ever regret this," he insisted.

He was probably right. Given the abbreviated timeline they were working with, it didn't make sense to waste even a second she got to have with him. Happiness with a deadline, just like she'd thought before. Only the happiness was greater now. And the deadline was crueler.

CHAPTER 23

Alex did manage to get a little bit of sleep, maybe thirty minutes by the time the alarm sounded. Just enough that she was completely dragging as they set off. Daniel was more alert, so he took the first shift and she reclined the passenger seat as far back as it would go. The seats were much more comfortable, the suspension smoother, and it was easier to doze. The dogs seemed happy in the back, as if they appreciated the new ride, too.

She was herself again by the time they got to the dog-boarding facility north of Atlanta. It was after nine thirty; they were running a little behind, thanks to some construction delays on I-65.

Daniel stayed with the car as she carried Lola into the front office. It was a casual place, homey, with lots of fenced acres lining the road in. The dogs that ran alongside the car as they passed looked happy and healthy. Of course, Lola wouldn't be running anywhere for a while.

The man behind the desk was all sympathy as Alex came in. He obviously had linked her to the reservation before she introduced herself as Ms. Wells. She followed patiently as he showed her the spacious kennel Lola would occupy and explained the visiting vet's schedule. She thanked him and paid him for a month in advance, then gave Lola one last hug. As Kevin had promised, the man never commented on Lola's injury in a specific way, and he didn't mention

Alex's face. Twenty minutes later, she and Daniel were back on the road. Alex was glad it was her turn to drive. She needed something to concentrate on so she wouldn't think about leaving Lola behind.

She thought Daniel would crash, but he was still bright-eyed and in a talkative mood. Or maybe he could see how she was trying to fight off the sadness and wanted to help. Knowing him, that was probably it.

"You know almost everything about me from that stupid file," he complained. "But there's so much I don't know about you."

"I've actually told you most of it. When my life wasn't bizarre, it was pretty boring."

"Tell me something embarrassing about you in high school."

"Everything about me was embarrassing in high school. I was a huge nerd."

"Sounds sexy."

"Oh, really? My mother cut my hair at home and I had the most outrageous bangs the nineties had ever seen."

"Please tell me there's a picture."

"You wish. When my mother died, I burned all the incriminating stuff."

"Who was your first boyfriend?"

Alex laughed. "Roger Markowitz. He took me to senior prom. I had the most totally awesome puffy sleeves on my dress. Electric blue, naturally. Roger tried to slip me the tongue in the limo on the way to the ballroom, but he was so nervous that he threw up on me. I spent the whole dance in the ladies' room trying to clean up. I broke up with him that night. One might describe it as an epic romance."

"What a tearjerker!"

"I know. Romeo and Juliet had nothing on us."

Daniel laughed. "Who was your first serious relationship?"

"Serious? Wow. Hmm, I don't know if anyone would qualify besides Bradley. First year of med school at Columbia."

"You went to Columbia med?" he asked.

"I was a very brainy nerd."

"I'm impressed. Back to Bradley."

"Do you want to hear something really and truly embarrassing?"

"Very much."

"The reason I was first attracted to him..." She paused. "Maybe I shouldn't admit this."

"It's too late to turn back. You have to tell me now."

She took a deep breath. "Okay, fine. He looked like Egon. You know, from *Ghostbusters*? Just exactly like that, bouffant hair, round glasses, everything."

Daniel worked to keep a straight face. "Irresistible."

"You have no idea. *So* hot."

"How long were you together?"

"Through that first summer. Then I won a scholarship in my second year. We both applied, and he thought he was a shoo-in. He didn't take it well when I, as he put it, *took it from him.* He went in and demanded to see our scores. Something I noticed multiple times throughout my wild and crazy romantic period: lots of guys don't like girls to be smarter than they are."

"That must have really limited your dating pool."

"Right down to zero."

"Well, rest assured, I've never had a problem with a woman who is smarter than me. I wouldn't want to limit *my* pool by that much. I think that kind of childishness usually goes away when men grow up."

"I'll have to take your word for it. I never dated anyone outside of school. I didn't get to explore the adult stage of the human male. Well, till now."

"Never?" he asked, shocked.

"I was recruited while I was still in school. I told you what it was like after that."

"But... you must have met people outside of work. You got vacation time, didn't you?"

She smiled. "Not very often. And it was hard for me to talk to people outside of the lab. Everything was classified. *I* was classified. I couldn't be myself in any way or talk about any part of my real life with a person on the outside. It was too hard being some imaginary character. I preferred isolation. It embarrassed me to try to play a role. Ironic, isn't it? Now I have a new name every other week."

He put his hand on her knee. "I'm sorry. It sounds horrible."

"Yeah. It frequently was. That's why I'm so backward when it comes to interpersonal relations. But on the plus side, I got to do some really cutting-edge work with monoclonal antibodies — I'm talking about sci-fi stuff here, the kind of thing people don't believe exists. And I had essentially no limits on my practical research. I got everything I wanted in the lab. My budget was amazing. I'm responsible for a larger chunk of the national debt than you know."

He laughed.

"So was your ex-wife smarter than you are?" she asked.

He hesitated for a moment. "It doesn't bother you to talk about her?"

"Why would it? You didn't get jealous over the eternal flame I will always carry for Roger Markowitz."

"Good point. Well, Lainey was very bright in her own way. Not book-smart, but clever, shrewd. When we met, she was so...vivid. She wasn't like other women I'd dated, easygoing girls who were content with easygoing me. Lainey always wanted more — from every aspect of life. She was a little...contrary. In the beginning, I thought she just had very firm opinions and wasn't afraid to disagree. I loved that about her. But then, over time...well, she wasn't really opinionated, she just loved the drama. She would argue if you told her the sun rises in the east. It was always exciting, at least."

"Ah, so you're an adrenaline junkie. This all starts to make sense now."

"What makes sense?"

"Your attraction to me."

He stared at her, blinking owlishly the way he did when he was surprised.

"Admit it," she teased. "You're just in this for the thrill of the near-death experiences."

"Hmm, I hadn't considered that."

"Maybe we should forget this gig in DC after all. If I eliminate my hunters and life gets all safe and boring, you'll be out the door, won't you?" She sighed theatrically.

She couldn't tell if he was serious or playing along when he answered, "I was never fond of this plan to begin with. Maybe it *is* smarter to run."

"On the other hand, if I do a bad job in DC, it's going to get a lot more dangerous. You'll love that."

He gave her a bleak stare.

"Was that over the line?" she asked.

"A little too close to home."

"Sorry."

He sighed. "Your theory is incorrect, though, I'm afraid. See, I got over my love of drama early on. It was still exciting, but so is drowning in quicksand, I'd imagine. Exciting is not the same thing as enjoyable."

"But you didn't leave."

Daniel stared at his hand—curled tensely around her thigh now—as he answered. "No. I thought . . . well, this makes me sound like a first-class sucker. I thought I could fix her. She had a lot of issues from her past, and I let those issues be the excuse when she did things to hurt me. I never blamed her; I always blamed her history. Cliff—that's the man she left me for; what a fantastic name to be left for, don't you think?—Cliff wasn't her first fling. I found out about the others later." He glanced up at her suddenly. "Was that all in the file?"

"No."

He stared out the windshield. "I knew I should give up. I knew I wasn't holding on to anything real. The Lainey I loved was just a construct in my head. But I was stubborn. Stupidly so. Sometimes you cling to a mistake simply because it took so long to make."

"It sounds miserable."

He looked over and smiled at her weakly. "Yes, it was. But the hardest part was just admitting none of it had ever been real. It's humiliating, you know, to be duped. So my pride was hurt worse than anything else."

"I'm sorry."

"And I'm sorry, too. My stories are so much less entertaining than yours. Tell me about another boyfriend."

"I have a question first."

He stiffened a little bit. "Go ahead."

"That story you told the hooker, Kate, what was that about?"

"Huh?" His eyebrows pulled together in confusion.

"The one who was supposed to plant your tracker. Kevin said you told her your divorce wasn't final. But he also said this conversation happened two years after you split. You didn't contest the divorce, it went through in months. So why did you say that?"

Daniel laughed. "Thank you, seriously, from the very bottom of my heart, for not voicing that question in front of Kevin."

"You're welcome."

"Yes, the divorce was ancient history by then. But this girl... girls like *that* did not wander into the dive bar where I used to hang out. And if one happened to, I would not have been the guy she approached."

"What was she like?"

"If memory serves, she was stunning. And predatory. And oddly... frightening. I never believed for an instant that she was really attracted to me. I could sense there was an agenda, and I didn't want to fall for it. I was a little sensitive, at that point, to the idea of being duped again. But of course I didn't want to be rude, so I went with the politest refusal I could think of."

Alex chuckled. "You're right. Never, ever tell Kevin that you were afraid of the stunning hooker."

"Can you imagine?" He laughed with her. "Your turn. Another boyfriend."

"I'm running out...Let's see, I dated a guy named Felix for a couple of weeks in undergrad."

"And what extinguished the flames of your passion?"

"You have to understand, the only place I ever met boys was in a lab."

"Go on."

"Well, Felix worked with animals. Rats, mostly. He kept a lot of them in his apartment. There was a...smell problem."

Daniel threw his head back and howled with laughter. The sound of it was infectious. She couldn't help chortling along with him. It was not as out of control as that first afternoon in Kevin's secret lair, but it was close. All the stress seemed to drain out of her body, and she felt more relaxed than she would have thought possible in light of where she was headed.

Eventually, Daniel fell asleep, midsentence, as he described his fifth-grade crush. He'd been fighting his droopy eyelids for a while, and she suspected again that he'd been trying to keep her mind off the negatives.

It was relaxing to have him sleeping peacefully next to her. Einstein was snoring on the backseat, a nice counterpoint to the even sound of Daniel's breathing. She knew she should be thinking of a variety of plans, ways to get to Carston without exposing herself too greatly, but she just wanted to enjoy the moment. Peace was going to be a limited commodity in her near future. If this was the last moment that she got to be entirely content, then she wanted to experience it fully.

She was in a rare state of calm when she woke Daniel a few hours later, as they were entering the outskirts of DC. The last time she'd pulled into this city, she'd been furious and terrified. She probably had even more reason to feel that way today, but she was still enjoying the time she had left alone with Daniel, and she wasn't going to let that go before she had to.

Daniel read the directions to her as she got closer to their target. As she'd originally thought, this was a nice neighborhood, and it was only getting nicer. Wasn't that like Kevin, to hide somewhere so incongruous? She circled the building with the matching address twice, doubting whether this could be the place.

"I'd better call him."

Daniel handed her the phone. She hit Redial, and it rang once.

"You're late," Kevin answered. "What's wrong now?"

"Traffic. Nothing. I *think* we're outside, but . . . this place doesn't look right."

"Why?"

"We're hiding out in a fancy art deco high-rise?"

"Yeah. A friend of mine is letting us crash. There's parking under the building. Go to the fourth level down, I'll meet you." He disconnected.

She handed the phone back to Daniel. "Just once, I want to hang up on him first."

"You did the very first time he called, remember? Fairly spectacularly."

"Oh, right. That does make me feel better."

All the tension came back as they rounded the corner into the parking garage, and the daylight disappeared. She drove in a claustrophobic downward spiral until she reached the right level, and then saw Kevin standing impatiently beside an empty space marked RESIDENTS ONLY. He waved her into it.

She braced herself as she opened the door, expecting a few snide comments about her face or disparaging observations about Daniel's screwups, but Kevin said only, "Don't mind the cameras, I took them offline this morning," and then opened the back of the SUV to let Einstein out.

There was a real reunion with Einstein, who threw Kevin to the ground and attempted to lick the skin off his face. Trying to pretend that she wasn't the slightest bit jealous of Einstein's affection for his man, Alex ignored them both until she and Daniel were loaded up with as much as they could carry.

"Um, which way?" she asked.

Kevin got up with a sigh. "Follow me."

To his credit, he did grab the remaining duffel bags as they went to the elevator.

"Do I need a hat?" Alex asked. "Is there a lobby? I'm not exactly ready for my close-up."

"No worries, Ollie, this goes straight to the apartment. By the way, bro, nice beard. It's a good look on you. In that you don't look like you as much anymore."

"Um, thanks?"

"About this friend..." Alex began.

Kevin sighed again. "They can't all be Arnies. Sorry, shorty, this might get rough."

"You don't trust him?"

The elevator opened into a plush hallway... or was it an anteroom? There was only one door in the space.

"I've paid her through next week, so I trust her about that far."

The hair on the back of Alex's neck stood up. Daniel had gotten her more used to human interaction, but she knew she still had some pretty severe people issues. As they walked the length of the short hall, she struggled with the duffel in her right hand, trying to free some fingers so she could pull a syringe from her belt. Just as she caught hold of the one she wanted, Daniel touched her wrist. She glanced up, and he was giving her a look that seemed to imply she was overreacting. Frowning, she slid the syringe back into place. It wouldn't take long to draw it if the need arose anyway.

Kevin had a key to the single door. He took a deep breath as he pushed it open.

At first Alex wasn't sure they hadn't stumbled into the lobby after all, because she'd never been inside an apartment with a wide marble staircase up to another story. The place was lavish, sleek and modern, and lined with floor-to-ceiling windows that immediately had her feeling exposed. Through the glass, the sun was just beginning to droop toward the DC skyline. There didn't *seem* to be any other apartments close enough to look into this one, but a telescope would make it possible. Or a rifle sight.

"No," a hard—but somehow still velvety—voice announced from behind them.

Alex whirled. The apartment stretched back the other way, too, wrapping around the front door and the hallway beyond. On one side was a huge white kitchen; on the other a dining room with seating for ten, with more window-walls framing each. Leaning against the marble kitchen island was the most exquisite human being Alex had ever seen in real life.

The woman looked exactly like the facetious description Alex had conjured up to describe Kevin's improbable mental image of the Oleander. She had honey-blond hair, thick and long, that stood out from her head in full waves like a Disney cartoon's. Sapphire-blue doe eyes, full red lips turned up at the corners, and a straight, narrow nose, all set with flawless symmetry in an oval face with prominent cheekbones. Swan neck over elegant collarbones. Of course, the generous hourglass figure with a tiny waist and legs that seemed longer than Alex's entire body. The woman was wearing only a short, black kimono and an irritated expression.

"It's temporary," Kevin said in a conciliatory voice. "Obviously, I'll pay you the same for each of them. Three times what we originally agreed on."

The surreally perfect woman raised one eyebrow and looked pointedly at Einstein. His tail was wagging furiously. He stared up at the blonde with the proverbial puppy-dog eyes.

"Four times," Kevin promised. He dropped the bags he was carrying. "You *like* dogs."

"Kate?" Daniel asked suddenly, surprised recognition saturating his tone.

The woman's face dimpled into a toothpaste-commercial-quality smile.

"Hi, Danny," she purred. "I almost didn't know you with all that scruff. Well, that *does* make me feel better. You left a nasty welt on my ego, but at least you didn't forget me."

"It's, er, nice to see you again," Daniel stammered, flummoxed by her greeting.

The blonde's eyes cut to Kevin. "Okay, *he* can stay."

"It's just a few nights," Kevin said. "I need the little one, too."

"You know I don't like women in my space," she said in a flat voice, flicking her eyes to Alex, then back to Kevin.

"Oh, that's okay, Ollie's not a *real* girl," Kevin assured her.

Daniel dropped his bags and took half a step forward before Alex hooked the back of his shirt with her one free finger.

"Not now," she muttered.

Kate — or whatever her real name was — shrugged gracefully away from the island and glided toward them. She looked down her nose at Alex; easy to do, as she was a good six inches taller.

"So what happened to your face? Your boyfriend tune you up?"

Daniel stiffened. Alex wasn't sure what this was — maybe some kind of territorial thing? It was only a guess; Alex didn't have a lot of experience with other women. In the distant past, she'd suffered through a couple of immature roommates, liked a few other lady science geeks, and made small talk with the rare female underling who didn't flee her presence. Mostly she'd worked with men, and she didn't know all the rules for double-X-chromosome interactions. At a loss, she went with the truth, though she probably should have waited to see what Kevin had told the woman.

"Um, no, it was a Mafia assassin." Alex worked her jaw, feeling the bandage pull against her skin. "Oh, and the older stuff was just Kevin trying to kill me."

"If I'd actually been trying to kill you, you'd be dead," Kevin grumbled.

Alex rolled her eyes.

"What, you want to go another round?" Kevin demanded. "Anytime, sweetheart."

"The next time I put you down," Alex promised, "it will be permanently."

Kevin laughed—not derisively, like she expected, but with genuine delight. "See what I mean, Val?"

The woman looked like she was trying not to smile. "Okay, you've piqued my interest. But I have only the one extra room."

"Ollie's good at roughing it."

"Whatever," the woman said. Apparently it was an agreement. "Get all that mess out of my living room."

She skimmed close by Daniel as she passed them. Without a backward glance, she headed upstairs. The kimono was very short, and both brothers watched her climb with partially open mouths.

"You turned *her* down?" Alex muttered under her breath.

Kevin heard her and laughed again. "Let's move this stuff before she kicks us all out."

• • •

THE EXTRA BEDROOM was bigger than Alex's entire DC apartment had been. And it wasn't as if she'd been living in a dive; her place was what real estate agents described as a luxury apartment. This place, though, was several degrees beyond mere luxury. Kevin had seemed on the level when he said the woman was a hooker, but Alex hadn't had any idea that profession could pay so well.

Kevin stacked the duffels against one wall.

"Ollie, you've still got that cot, right? There's a huge walk-in closet off the bathroom. Check it out and see if it will work for you. You *could* set up on one of those couches out there, but it might be best to keep you out of Val's line of sight as much as possible."

"Of course Alex will sleep in the bed," Daniel said.

Kevin's eyebrows pulled together skeptically. "Really? You're going to get all chivalrous about *Ollie?*"

"It's like you never even met our mother."

"Relax," Alex said as Kevin bridled. "We'll work it out."

"Fine," Kevin said.

"Should I have been more careful with my words out there?" Alex asked Kevin. "You said she's not trustworthy."

Kevin shook his head. "No, you're fine. Val might kick us all onto the street when she's tired of us, but she won't sell us out. I've bought her time and her discretion. What happens with Val stays with Val. She has a reputation to protect."

"Okay," Alex agreed, though she wasn't sure she entirely understood Val's policies.

He moved to the door, then paused with his hand on the knob. "There's plenty of food in the fridge if you're hungry, or we can order something in."

"Thanks," Alex said. "I'll sort my stuff out first."

"Yes," Daniel said. "Let us get situated."

Kevin hesitated one more second, then stepped back into the room. "Uh, Danny, I just wanted to say . . . it's good to see you. I'm glad you're safe."

Like before, as he was leaving the ranch, Kevin looked like he wouldn't be opposed to a hug. Daniel stood awkwardly, his body language full of ambivalence.

"Yes, well, thanks to Alex," Daniel said. "And I'm glad you're not dead like she thought you were."

Kevin barked a laugh. "Yeah, me, too. And thanks again, poison woman. I owe you one."

He exited on another laugh, leaving the door cracked behind him.

Daniel gave Alex a long stare, then went to the door and quietly shut it all the way. He turned back to her, and there was clearly an argument about to begin. She shook her head and motioned him to follow her farther into the guest suite.

For a second, the bathroom made her forget why she'd come this way. A swimming pool–size tub was set into the floor, surrounded by marble and a faintly blue tile wall that shimmered like a pale sea. A showerhead the diameter of a truck tire was suspended from the ceiling over it.

"What *is* this place?" Alex gasped.

Daniel shut the door behind them. "Kate — or rather Val — is apparently quite successful."

"Do you think she's really a prostitute, or was that just Kevin trying to make the story better?"

"I didn't come in here to talk about Val."

She turned to face him, her lips twisting sideways into a pucker. "Alex, I don't like lying to him."

"Who's lied?"

"Acting, then. Pretending that we're nothing to each other."

She huffed a sigh. "I'm just not ready to deal with the inevitable fallout. I have enough stress."

"We're going to have to tell him eventually. Why not get it over with?"

He saw her expression change as she weighed the options.

"You still don't believe we have an *eventually,* do you?" he accused.

"Well...there *is* a good possibility either he or I will be dead within the next week, so why rock the boat?"

Daniel abruptly pulled her into a rough hug that was somehow more reproachful than comforting.

"Don't say that. I can't stand to hear you talk that way."

"Sorry," she said into his shirt.

"We can run away. Tonight. We'll hide. You know how."

"Can we at least wait till we've slept and eaten?" she asked plaintively.

He laughed unwillingly at her tone. "I suppose I could allow that much."

She relaxed into him for a moment, wishing again that running were the right option. It sounded so much easier, restful almost.

"Let's just walk out there hand in hand," Daniel suggested, "and then make out on the sofa for a bit."

"First, eating and sleeping. I am not dealing with the aftermath of some grand reveal until I'm sure I've considered all the possible forms the backlash might take and whether I need to be armed — or, rather, *how* armed I need to be. I can't even think straight right now."

"All right," he said. "I'll give you tonight, because I know how exhausted you are. But we're revisiting this discussion in the morning, and I intend to be quite inflexible."

"Will Kevin be in here too?" she wondered. "The woman said there was only one extra room. That won't make discussing anything very easy."

"I doubt it." She could hear the eye roll in his voice and she pulled away to look at his face. He didn't let her go, but he dropped his arms to rest more casually around her waist.

"Oh, do you think she meant this was the only *empty* extra room?"

"No, I think he's staying with her."

She wrinkled her nose. "Really? She didn't seem to like him very much."

"The women in his life never do."

She was still unconvinced. "But . . . she could do so much better."

Daniel laughed. "I won't argue with that."

367

CHAPTER 24

Val's huge double fridge was much better stocked than Arnie's. In fact, it was much better stocked than the average restaurant's. It looked like she was planning to feed a dozen more guests than those she already had in residence—though she apparently had not been apprised of Alex's and Daniel's existence until moments before they arrived.

The incongruity bothered Alex a little, but not enough to deter her from the bowl of grapes. She felt like she hadn't eaten anything fresh in weeks, though it really hadn't been so very long. The ranch seemed months ago. She could barely wrap her head around how short the time actually was.

Alex sat on one of the pure white, ultramodern bar stools. It wasn't terribly comfortable.

Daniel was humming with pleasure as he examined the accoutrements. "Now, this is a kitchen," he murmured. He started sorting through the lower drawers, evaluating the pots and pans available.

"Making ourselves right at home, are we?"

Daniel jerked upright. Alex paused with a grape halfway to her mouth.

Val came into the room laughing, still in the brief kimono. "Relax. All this stuff is here for you. I don't really use this room."

"Um, thank you," Daniel said.

She shrugged. "Kevin paid for it. So, you like to cook?"

"I dabble."

"He's being modest," Alex told her. "He's a five-star chef."

Val smiled warmly at Daniel as she stretched her whole torso across the island toward him so her chin nearly touched the marble. "Well, that's nice. I've never had a live-in chef before. It sounds...fun."

Alex wondered how Val was able to load so many different implications into one common word.

"Er, I suppose so," Daniel said, flushing a little. "Where is Kevin?"

"Walking the dog."

Val turned her face toward Alex, and Alex braced for more aggression.

"I asked Kevin about you. Kevin says you tortured *him*." Val jerked her head toward Daniel.

"Ah, well, technically, that's correct. It was a case of mistaken identity, though."

Val's eyes glowed with interest. "What did you do? Did you burn him?"

"What? No, no... Um, I used injectable chemical treatments. I find them more effective, and they don't leave scars."

"Hmm." Val rolled her body sideways along the marble so she was turned to Daniel again, then pillowed her head against her arm. The kimono was partially dislodged by this maneuver, and Alex imagined his view was quite interesting. He stood awkwardly, one hand on the refrigerator door.

"Was it really painful?" Val demanded.

"Beyond anything I'd ever imagined," Daniel admitted.

Val seemed fascinated. "Did you scream? Did you beg? Did you *writhe?*"

Daniel couldn't help but smile at her enthusiasm. "All of the above, I believe. Oh, and I cried like a baby as well." Still smiling, he seemed suddenly comfortable; he turned back to the fridge and started rummaging.

Val sighed. "I really wish I could have seen that."

"You're into torture?" Alex asked, hiding her concern. Of course Kevin would move them in with a true sadist.

"Not torture per se, but it's so intoxicating, isn't it? That kind of power?"

"I guess I've never looked at it quite that way . . ."

Val cocked her head, looking at Alex with undisguised interest. "Isn't everything about power?"

Alex thought about it for a moment. "Not in my experience. Back when that was my job, honestly — it sounds naive now, even to me — I was really just trying to save people. There was always a lot hanging in the balance. It was stressful."

Val considered that, pursing her lips. "That does sound naive."

Alex shrugged.

"It never gave you a rush? Being in control?" Val's wide lapis eyes bored into her.

Alex wondered if people felt this way in a psychiatrist's office — this compulsion to speak. Or maybe it was more like being shackled to Alex's own table. "I mean . . . maybe. I'm not a very dangerous person on the surface. I guess there were times that I appreciated the . . . respect."

Val nodded. "Of course you did. Tell me, have you ever tortured a woman?"

"Twice . . . well, once and a half."

"Explain."

Daniel's head was leaning back as he adjusted the flame under the stovetop grill; he was paying close attention. Alex hated talking about this in front of him.

"I didn't actually have to do anything to the first girl. She was confessing before she was even strapped to the table. She didn't belong in my lab anyway — any normal interrogation would have gotten the same results. Poor kid."

"What was she confessing to?"

"A terrorist cell was trying to coerce some suicide bombers in New York. They'd kidnap someone's family back in Iran—in this case, her parents—and kill the hostages if the subject wouldn't do as directed. The NSA had it under control before any of the bombs were detonated, but they lost several of the hostages." She sighed. "It's always messy with terrorists."

"What about the second?"

"*That* was an entirely different situation. Arms dealer."

"Was she tough to break?"

"One of the toughest in my career."

Val smiled as if the answer greatly pleased her. "I've always thought that women can handle a lot more pain than the so-called stronger sex. Men are all just oversize children, really." Then she sighed. "I've made men beg, and I've made them writhe, and maybe there have been some tears here and there, but no one's ever *cried like a baby*." Her full lower lip pushed out into a pout.

"I'm positive they would if you asked them to," Alex encouraged.

Val smiled her glittery smile. "You're probably right."

Daniel was chopping something now. Alex decided she should slow down on the grapes. Dinner was sure to be worth the wait. Val rolled to the side again to watch him, and Alex felt a sudden urge to distract her.

"This is a beautiful place."

"Yes, it's nice, isn't it? A friend gave it to me."

"Oh, does he stay here often?" How many people were going to know about them? She'd already been stupidly and bizarrely honest with this strange woman. It would surely come back to bite her.

"No, no, Zhang and I broke up *ages* ago. He was too stuffy."

"And he let you keep the place?"

Val stared at Alex, disbelieving. "*Let* me? What kind of a gift is it if the deed's not in your name?"

"That's a good point," Alex agreed quickly.

"What was that you were saying earlier, about putting Kevin down?"

"Oh, can I tell the story, please?" Daniel butted in. "It's my favorite."

Daniel stretched the story out, milking it for Val's laughs and coos. He made Alex sound more in control than she had been and fictionalized the parts he wasn't awake for. It was a better story his way, she had to admit. Val's expression as she assessed Alex now was one hundred eighty degrees from what it had been at their first meeting.

Then the food was ready, and Alex stopped caring about much else. It had been a while since she'd had red meat, and her inner carnivore took over. When she came out of the frenzy, she saw that Val was watching her again, engrossed.

Alex glanced down — Daniel had given Val a plate, too, but she'd eaten only a few slivers off the side of her steak.

"Do you always eat so much?" Val asked.

"When it's available, I guess. When Daniel is cooking, definitely."

Val's eyes narrowed. "I'll bet you never gain an ounce, do you?"

"I don't know. I probably must sometimes, right?"

"Do you even own a scale?" she demanded.

"I've got one that weighs milligrams," Alex answered, confused.

Val blew out a puff of breath that ruffled the waves of hair over her forehead. "People with naturally high metabolisms piss me off."

"Seriously?" Alex said, looking her up and down. "You're going to complain to *me* about our relative genetic heritages?"

Val stared at her for a few seconds, then smiled and shook her head. "Well, I suppose a girl can't have everything."

"And you're just the exception that proves the rule?"

"I think I like you, Ollie."

"Thanks, Val. It's actually Alex, though."

"Whatever. You know, you've got a lot of untapped potential. With decent hair, some makeup, and a midsize boob job, you could do all right."

"Er, I do fine as is, thanks. I have lower expectations out of life. It makes things easier."

"Seriously, you cut your own hair, don't you?"

"I don't have another option."

"Trust me, there's always another option to *this*." She stretched across the counter and tried to touch the hair hanging in Alex's eyes, but Alex flinched out of her way. It was true that it was time for another trim.

Val turned to Daniel, who was trying to be unobtrusive, leaning against the counter directly behind Val as he finished his food, almost like he was hiding from her. Well, Alex could understand that. And she completely understood why Daniel had found Val frightening on their first meeting.

"Back me up, Danny. Don't you think Ollie could be pretty if she tried?"

Daniel did the blinking thing he always did when taken by surprise. "But Alex is pretty now."

"What a gentleman. It's like you're Bizarro Kevin."

"I'll take that as a compliment."

"It *is* a compliment. Maybe the best I've ever given," Val agreed.

"How long have you known him?" Daniel wondered.

"Too long. I don't know why I keep opening the door when he comes begging. I guess it's that power thing." She shrugged, and one shoulder of her silk robe slid down her arm. She didn't fix it. "I like watching someone so strong have to do what I say."

A key jangled in the front door. Alex slipped from the stool to her feet, muscles tensing automatically. Val watched as Daniel looked to Alex, tensing, too, ready to follow her lead.

"You two are funny," she murmured.

Einstein ran panting into the kitchen, and Alex relaxed.

Val eyed the dog, his tongue lolling out and his eyes eager. "Does it want something?"

"He's probably thirsty," Alex told her.

"Oh." She glanced around the kitchen, then grabbed a decorative crystal bowl from the center of the island and filled it in the sink. Einstein licked her hand gratefully and then started lapping up the water.

"Smells good," Kevin commented as he came around the corner.

"You can finish mine," Val said without looking at him. "I'm done." Experimentally, she stroked one of Einstein's ears.

Kevin leaned comfortably against the island, looking very at home as he started cutting into Val's food. "Everyone getting along?"

"You were right," Val answered.

Kevin grinned triumphantly. "I told you she wouldn't bore you."

Val straightened up and smiled back. "Anyone who's chained you to the floor is bound to get along with me."

Kevin's grin disappeared. "It was a draw."

Val threw back her chin and laughed, her long neck looking even more swanlike than before.

Daniel turned the sink on and rummaged for dish soap. Alex joined him automatically, comforted by even just the opening chords of their usual routine. Once again she was in an unfamiliar place, well out of her league, unsure and unsafe, but with Daniel there, she could handle it. He was like a gas mask — a touchstone of refuge. She smiled to herself, thinking how little he would care for that comparison. Well, she wasn't the romantic one.

"Oh, don't bother with that, sweetie," Val told Daniel. "The housekeeper comes every morning."

Alex shot Kevin a loaded glance, which Val caught. "I'll leave a note on the counter, and he'll stay out of the bedrooms," Val assured her. "I know this is all very cloak-and-dagger. Don't worry, you won't be exposed on my account."

"I don't mind," Daniel said. "Dishes relax me."

"What *is* this brother of yours?" Val asked Kevin. "Can I keep him?"

Alex smiled when Daniel's eyes widened in panic, but he kept his face down over the sink so Val didn't see. He handed Alex a clean pair of tongs and she dried them with a dish towel that felt like silk and was probably meant to be ornamental. She had a feeling Val didn't care about things like that.

"He's not your type," Kevin answered.

"I have many types, though, don't I?"

"Fair enough, but I don't think he'll hold your interest long."

She sighed. "They so rarely do."

"So, um, back to this housekeeper — what time will he arrive, leave, et cetera?" Alex asked.

Val laughed. "You take things very seriously."

"People try to kill me a lot."

"That must get irritating," she said casually. "When I'm in residence, Raoul comes early and leaves quickly. He won't even wake you. He's good."

"I'll just lock the door, then."

"If you like."

"We're not sleeping in tomorrow, Ollie," Kevin interjected. "There's a lot to get set before we act, and I don't want to waste more time."

"Give her the one morning off," Daniel insisted. "She's been driving all night for a week, sleeping in the back of cars. She needs rest."

Kevin made a disgusted face. "She's not a child, Danny. The big kids have work to do."

"It's not a problem," Alex said quickly. She glanced at the clock on the oven; it was only seven. "I'm crashing now anyway, so I'm sure I'll be up long before Raoul arrives."

"I'll walk you through my inventory, then you can tell me what else you need. I've got the video footage of your subject, which I'm sure you'll want to review, and then—"

"Tomorrow, Kevin," Alex interrupted. "Now, sleep."

Kevin inhaled noisily through his nose and rolled his eyes to the ceiling.

Alex almost reached for Daniel's hand as she left the kitchen. She had to curl her fingers into a fist and hope Kevin hadn't noticed. It felt unnatural, and she knew Daniel felt it, too. He followed close behind her, almost as if he were thinking about doing something to instigate the conversation—or possible altercation—that she was trying to avoid. *Not now,* she tried to communicate to him telepathically without turning. She walked faster, but it was a wasted effort. Daniel's legs were too long for her to build any kind of lead.

She felt much better when she heard him close the door behind him and click the lock into place.

"Thanks," she said, turning to wrap her arms around his waist.

"Only because we're exhausted," he reminded her. "I will be much more tenacious tomorrow."

She was really dragging, so she went through only the most important parts of the routine. She didn't want to bother with rebandaging her face, so she decided to let her skin breathe for the night. The wound was still bright red and puckered, and the stitches in her ear—though she'd used a flesh-toned suture thread—were hard to miss. It looked like the two halves of her lobe would rejoin, though. She'd have a nasty scar, but she didn't want to think about that now.

She thought about setting up the cot in the closet for show but decided to wait till morning. It wasn't like Kevin was going to do a room inspection. She also considered stringing a gas-canister line around the door. She didn't think she had the energy, and anyway, an intruder would surely check the master first, if he got past Einstein. She settled for putting her SIG and belt on the bedside table.

Daniel was in the bed before her, but he was still awake.

"Should I leave my rifle out, do you think?" he asked.

"It's a big room, but probably a little tight for the rifle. I can go grab the shotgun."

He gave her an exasperated look. "I was joking."

"Oh. Right."

He held his arms open for her. She switched off the lamp and climbed into her now usual place. The bed was absurd—some kind of soft, supportive cloud that was probably made from spun gold or unicorn mane.

"Good night, Alex," he whispered into her hair, and then she was asleep.

· · ·

SHE WOKE WHILE it was still dark outside; the faint light glowing from around the edges of the shades was the unnatural yellow-green of city lights. She couldn't see a clock, but she'd guess it was around four. A solid night's rest and then some. She was glad; today would be long. For years now, all she'd been doing was running and surviving. Now she had to shift into a more proactive mode and she dreaded it. There had been her one uncharacteristic adventure in Texas, but she blamed that on the adrenaline of the moment and the unfamiliar responsibility of having a liability. It wasn't something she would ever have *planned* to do.

So when Daniel, woken by her movements, started to kiss her throat, she didn't mind procrastinating for a bit.

She wondered what it would be like to be a normal person. To be able to expect that mornings like this—waking up with someone you'd chosen—would happen over and over again. To go through the day certain that you'd lie back down at the end of it in the same bed, with that same person next to you. She doubted many people appreciated that certainty when they had it. It would be too much a part of everyday life to them, taken for granted, not something they would think of feeling grateful for.

Well, she couldn't count on another morning like this, but she could be grateful for it now.

She yanked on his T-shirt and he pulled his hands out of her hair long enough to remove it. Alex tugged her own shirt out of the way, greedy for the feeling of his skin next to hers. His kisses, which had begun so tenderly, started to veer more toward the unrestrained, though she could almost hear him reminding himself to be careful with her. She didn't want any of that. She kissed him back in a way designed to make him forget any other consideration.

There was no sound, no warning. She didn't hear the lock turn or the door open. And then, suddenly, the metallic click of a gun safety sliding off, just inches from her head. She froze and felt Daniel do the same. She wasn't sure if he'd recognized the quiet click, as she had, or was just responding to her.

From the sound, she knew the intruder was closer to the gun on the nightstand than she was. She cursed herself for neglecting basic security and worked to think of any move left to her. Maybe if she tried to spin and kick the gun away, it would give Daniel time to get around him.

And then the intruder spoke.

"Step away from the civilian, you poisonous little *snake*."

She blew out the huge gasp of air she'd been holding in. "Hoo! Huh! Okay. Ah! Let's put the gun down now, psychopath."

"Not until you get off my brother."

"This is so far beyond crossing the line, I don't even know what to call it," Daniel said in a harsh tone. "Did you *pick the lock?*"

"Danny, listen to me, she's drugged you again. That's what's happening here."

"As if I would waste my limited supply on recreation," she muttered. She rolled, tugging the sheet up to cover herself, and reached for the lamp. She felt the cool barrel of the gun press into her forehead.

"You're ridiculous," she told him as she switched the light on.

Kevin stepped back, blinking in the light. He still had his long, silenced pistol aimed at her face.

The bed rocked as Daniel vaulted agilely over her body and placed himself between her and Kevin. "What are you *doing?* Don't point that at her!"

"Danny, I don't know what she has you on, but we'll get it out of your system, I promise. Come with me."

"If you know what is good for you, you will turn around and walk away *now.*"

"I'm saving you here."

"Thanks, but no thanks. I was quite happy with what I was doing before you so rudely interrupted, and I'd like to return to it. Shut the door behind you."

"What's happened?" Alex asked, yanking her T-shirt on. There was no time for this squabbling. Kevin was wearing only a pair of pajama pants, so whatever the catalyst was, he hadn't had time to prepare himself. It wasn't like Kevin to let something—even something this offensive to him—distract him when there was trouble. She leaned around Daniel to grab her belt and then wrapped it around her waist as she spoke. "Do we need to move?" She reached for the SIG next and shoved it into the back of her belt.

Kevin's gun lowered slowly, and he started to look less confident as he was confronted with her practicality.

"I didn't believe her, so I came to check," he admitted, suddenly sheepish. "I wasn't planning on Danny ever knowing I was here."

"Her?" Daniel asked.

"Val...she said you two were together. She was so sure of herself. I said there was no way in *hell.*" His voice was outraged again by the end.

Daniel exhaled, irritated. "Well, I hope you made some kind of bet. With a very humiliating consequence for losing."

"This is punishment enough," Kevin grumbled.

"In all seriousness," Daniel said, "get out, Kevin."

"I can't believe this, Danny. What are you thinking? After what she did to you?"

Daniel was still between Alex and Kevin, so she couldn't see his face, but she could suddenly hear a smile in his voice. "You're supposed to be so tough, so dangerous. And yet you're saying you'd let a little pain come between you and the woman you wanted? Really?"

Kevin rocked a step back and took a few seconds to respond. "But why? Why do you want *her*?" The anger had vanished; when he looked at Alex, there was only bewilderment.

"I'll explain it to you when you've grown up. Now, for the last time, get out, or"—and he reached one long arm around Alex's body and pulled the gun from her back—"I'll shoot you."

He pointed the gun at Kevin's torso.

"Um, the safety is off on that," Alex murmured.

"Counting on it," Daniel replied.

Kevin stared at them—Daniel holding the gun steady, Alex watching from behind his arm—and then his shoulders squared.

He pointed at Alex with his free hand. "You. Just…stop…" He waved his hand in a big, inclusive gesture, taking in the two of them and the bed. "All of this. We leave in fifteen. Be ready."

His hand shifted to Danny. "I…" He blew out a deep breath, shook his head, and then turned and walked out the door. He didn't bother closing it. "Damn it, Val!" he shouted as he headed through the dark hall, as if all of this were somehow her fault. Einstein barked from upstairs.

Alex sighed and stretched. "Well, that went about exactly as I thought it would. No shots fired—this was the best-case scenario, I guess."

"Where are you going?" Daniel asked.

"To shower. You heard the man. Fifteen minutes."

"It's the middle of the night!"

"All the better to hide my face. You're not tired, are you? I think we've been asleep for nine hours, at least."

Daniel scowled. "No, I am not in the least bit tired."

"Well, then..." She started toward the bathroom door.

"Wait."

Daniel jumped up, ruffling his hair as he walked to the bedroom door. He shut it and then locked it again.

"What's the point of that, really?" Alex asked.

Daniel shrugged. "Touché."

He walked to her and wrapped his hands around her upper arms, holding her securely. "I wasn't ready to get out of bed."

"Kevin's not going to knock," she reminded him. "He probably won't even give me the full fifteen."

"I don't like letting him call the shots. Not only was I not ready to get out of bed, I was not ready for you to get out of bed, either."

He bent his head down to kiss her, his hands running slowly up her shoulders till they were cradling her face. She knew that under normal circumstances, it would have taken very little convincing on his part to get her to agree. But these were not normal circumstances, and the idea that Kevin might walk into the room at any moment—probably with gun in hand again—tempered her response.

She pulled back. "What about a compromise?"

The look he gave her was less than thrilled. "I categorically refuse to compromise in any way for Kevin's sake."

"Can I please at least make my case before you dismiss it?"

He kept his expression stern, but she could tell he wanted to smile. "Do what you have to do, but I will not be swayed."

"We have limited time, and we both need to clean up. That shower–slash–lap pool in there will easily fit two—well, actually it could fit twelve—and I was thinking we could multitask."

The hard-line expression disappeared. "I immediately withdraw my opposition and offer my full cooperation."

"I thought you might see it that way."

CHAPTER 25

Because there's no reason for you to go," Kevin objected.

Kevin stood in front of the elevator doors, blocking the call button, arms crossed over his chest.

"Why not?" Daniel demanded.

"You're not going to be a part of the offensive, Danny, so you don't need to be a part of the preparation."

Daniel's lips mashed together into a scowl.

"It doesn't hurt anything for him—" Alex began mildly.

"Except someone could see his face," Kevin growled.

"You mean *your* face?" she countered.

"*I'm* smart enough to keep my head down."

Daniel rolled his eyes. "I'll ride in the trunk if you want."

Kevin evaluated the two of them for a long second. "Are you going to let me focus?"

"What do you mean?" Alex asked.

Kevin closed his eyes; he seemed to be calming himself. He inhaled through his nose, then looked at Daniel.

"Here are my requirements for you to join us on this very boring, standard recon exercise: No one will speak of what happened this morning. I will not be forced to remember the nauseating things I witnessed. There will be no discussion that might allude to said nauseating things. This is business, and you will conduct yourself appropriately. Agreed?"

Daniel's neck started to flush. She was sure he was going to mention the fact that if Kevin hadn't broken in to a locked room in the middle of the night, he wouldn't have seen anything. Before Daniel could object, Alex said, "Agreed. Appropriate businesslike behavior."

Kevin glanced back and forth between them, measuring again. After a second, he turned and hit the call button.

Daniel gave her a *Really?* look. Alex shrugged.

"None of that!" Kevin commanded, though he still had his back to them.

"What?" Daniel complained.

"I can *feel* you two silently communicating. Stop it."

• • •

IT WAS A quiet drive in the average-looking black sedan. She didn't know if it was Val's car or something Kevin had acquired. It didn't seem like Val's style, but maybe she liked to be incognito sometimes. Alex appreciated the heavily tinted windows. She felt less exposed as she sat with her ball cap pulled low over her face and stared out at the still mostly sleeping city. They were early enough to beat the morning rush.

Kevin drove through a seedier section of town—more the kind of neighborhood she would have expected his hiding place to exist in. He pulled in at a storage facility that seemed to be mostly enormous cargo containers. There was no guard posted, just a keypad and a heavy metal gate with razor-wire coils on top. Kevin drove them to a spot near the back of the fenced lot and parked behind a dingy orange container.

The lot appeared to be empty, but Alex kept her face down and her walk unfeminine as they moved to the wide double doors that made up the front wall of the container. Kevin plugged a complicated sequence of numbers into the heavy-duty rectangular lock, then pulled it out of the way. He opened one door just a few feet and waved them inside.

It was black when Kevin pulled the door shut behind himself. Then there was a low click, and rope lights lining the ceiling and the floor glowed to life.

"Exactly how many Batcaves do you *have?*" Alex demanded.

"Just a few, here and there, where I might need them," Kevin said. "This one's mobile, so that helps."

The inside of Kevin's cargo container was tightly packed but compulsively organized. Like the barn in Texas, there was a place for everything.

Racks of clothing—costumes, really—were wedged against the wall by the double doors. She was sure that was on purpose—if someone got a glimpse inside while the doors were open, all he would see was clothes. A casual observer wouldn't think anything of it. A more careful observer might think it was odd that uniforms for every branch of the military were hanging together, along with mechanic's coveralls and several utility companies' official garb, not to mention the raggedy components of a homeless man's outfit hanging a few feet down from a row of dark suits that ranged from off-the-rack to high-end designer. A person could blend into a lot of situations with these clothes.

The props were in bins over the clothes racks—briefcases and clipboards, toolboxes and suitcases. The shoes were in clear plastic boxes underneath.

Beyond the costumes, deep floor-to-ceiling metal cabinets were installed. Kevin guided her through each; she took note of the things she might need. As in the barn, there was a space for guns, for ammo, for armor, for explosives, for knives. There were other things that hadn't been in Texas, or if they were, they'd been better hidden than the rest. He had a cabinet full of various tech items—tiny cameras and bugs, tracking devices, night-vision goggles, binoculars and scopes, electromagnetic-pulse generators of various sizes, a few laptop computers, and dozens of gadgets she didn't recognize. He identified the code breakers, the frequency readers, the frequency jammers, the system hackers, the mini-drones...She lost track after a while. It was unlikely that she would want to use anything she wasn't familiar with.

The next cabinet was chemical compounds.

"Yes," she hissed, digging past the front row to see what was behind. "*This* I can use."

"Thought you'd appreciate that."

"Do you mind?" she asked, holding up a sealed cylinder of a catalytic she knew she was almost out of.

"Take whatever you want. I don't think I've ever used any of that stuff."

She crouched down to the lower shelf and loaded several more jars and packages into her backpack. *Ah,* this one she needed. "Then why do you have it?"

Kevin shrugged. "I had access. Never look a gift horse—"

"Ha!" She stared up at him triumphantly.

"What?"

"You told me that was a stupid saying."

Kevin raised his eyes to the ceiling. "Sometimes it's really hard not to kick you."

"I know precisely how you feel."

Daniel moved to stand between her and Kevin. She shook her head at him. It was just banter. With the brief lecture on appropriate behavior out of the way, Kevin had shifted back to his normal self—something in between a serial killer and the world's most obnoxious big brother. Alex was getting used to it; she didn't mind him as much anymore.

Grumbling about *silent communication,* Kevin stalked back to the ammo cabinet and started filling a large black bag with reserves.

"First aid?" she asked.

"In the knife locker, top shelf."

There were several zippered black bags over the knives, some of them about the size of a backpack, others smaller, like shaving kits.

She couldn't reach any of them, so Daniel pulled them down and she combed through them on the floor.

The first smaller bag she opened had no medical supplies — instead, there were little packets of documents neatly rubber-banded together for easy sorting. She quickly pulled out a Canadian passport and glanced at the ID page. As she'd expected, there was a photo of Kevin with a different name — Terry Williams. She glanced up. Kevin had his back to her. She grabbed two of the packets and stuffed them into the bottom of her backpack, then zipped the bag closed.

These particular items wouldn't be of any help to her, but she had to be prepared for other outcomes. She peeked at Daniel; he wasn't paying attention to her, either. He was looking at the array of knives with a disbelieving expression. It made her wonder how long he could survive on his own with what he'd learned so far.

Alex pulled open one of the bigger bags but wasn't thrilled with what she found inside. It was a fairly basic kit, with nothing that she didn't already have. She checked the next bag, then the last. Nothing that wasn't in the first.

"What's missing?" Kevin asked.

She jumped slightly; she hadn't heard him approach. He must have read her disappointed expression.

"I'd like access to some decent trauma supplies, just in case..."

"Okay. Grab up whatever else you want here, and then we'll go get some."

"Just that easy?" she asked skeptically.

"Sure."

She raised one eyebrow. "We're going to walk into a medical facility and ask to purchase some surplus?"

"No!" He made a face implying the stupidity of her suggestion. "Haven't you ever heard the phrase *It fell off a truck*? You got some of that knockout stuff on you now?"

"Yes."

"Then hurry, so we can get out there before all the trucks have finished their deliveries."

● ● ●

ALEX'S BACKPACK WAS now stocked with ammo for her various appropriated guns — the SIG Sauer, the Glock she hadn't abandoned, the shotgun, Daniel's rifle — and her own PPK. She'd taken two extra handguns from the stash, because you never knew, and ammo for those as well. From the tech case she'd grabbed two sets of goggles, some trackers, and two EMP generators of different sizes. She wasn't sure what she would use any of them for, but she might not have time to get back here if there was an emergency. While she shopped through his gear, Kevin reset the lock so that the usual birth-date code would let her back in.

Or Daniel, if things really went south.

"So, what are my options for chemically incapacitating another human being?" Kevin asked when they were back on the road. Alex drove this time.

"Let's see... do you want airborne or contact?"

Kevin gave her a sidelong look. "Which do you recommend?"

"Depends on your approach. Will the target be in an enclosed space?"

"How would I know? I'll be improvising."

She huffed out a breath. "Fine. Take both. Daniel, can you grab the perfume bottle in the outside pocket of my backpack? It's in a Ziploc bag."

"Found it," Daniel said after a minute. "Here." He passed it up to Kevin. Kevin turned it over in his hands.

"Looks empty."

"Mm-hm," Alex agreed. "Pressurized gas. Now," she said, stretching her left arm across her body and holding her hand toward him. "Take the silver one."

He pulled the ring off her third finger, and then his eyebrows mashed down in surprise when the tiny clear tube and attached rubber squeeze pouch came out one after the other, like a couple of handkerchiefs from the sleeve of a mediocre magician. His expression turned skeptical.

"What's this supposed to do?"

"See the little hatch on the inside? Swing it open. Be careful."

Kevin examined the tiny hollow barb, then looked at the little round rubber bag. It was quiet enough to hear the faint sound of liquid sloshing inside.

"Hold the pouch in your palm," she directed, pantomiming as she explained. "Put your hand down hard on your target." She gestured to Daniel, who obligingly held out his arm. She grabbed his wrist—not violently, just forcefully. "The subject will feel the prick and try to pull away automatically. Hold on. If you're doing it right, the liquid in the pouch will be expelled through the barb." She released Daniel when she finished.

"And then what happens?" Kevin asked.

"Your target takes a nap—for an hour, maybe two, depending on his or her size."

"This thing is tiny," he complained, holding the ring between his thumb and forefinger and staring through the hole.

"Sorry. I'll try to have bigger hands for you next time. Put it on your pinkie."

"Who wears a pinkie ring?"

She smiled. "I think it will suit perfectly."

Daniel chuckled.

Kevin shoved the ring onto his littlest finger, but it made it only over his first knuckle. The pouch barely reached his palm. He'd need more tubing if he ever wanted to hide it in his sleeve. He frowned at the apparatus for a moment, then suddenly grinned. "Neat."

Daniel leaned forward and gestured to the rings Alex still wore. "What do those other two do?"

She lifted her right hand, wiggling her ring finger with the gold band. "Kills you easy." She held up the middle finger of her left hand with the rose-gold band. "Kills you hard."

"Oh, hey!" Kevin said in sudden realization. "Is that what that girlie slap back in West Virginia was about?"

"Yes."

"*Damn.* You're one dangerous little spider, Ollie."

She nodded in agreement. "If I were taller or you were shorter, we wouldn't be having this conversation."

"Well, I guess that was your lucky day."

She rolled her eyes.

"Which one did you try to hit me with?"

She held up the middle finger on her left hand again.

"Harsh," Kevin commented. "Why don't those rings have all the extra stuff?" He waved his hand so that the tube and pouch swung beneath his hand.

"Be careful," she warned. "That could detach."

Kevin caught the little bag and cradled it in his palm. "Right."

"My other rings are coated with venom. A little goes a long way. Just one drop of cone snail venom is enough to kill twenty men your size."

"Let me guess, you keep cone snails and black widow spiders as pets back home?"

"No time for pets, and really, black widow venom is on the very weak end of the damage scale. No, I used to have access to a lot of things. I studied cone snail venom briefly because of the way it targets particular classes of receptors. I was never one to waste an opportunity. I kept what I could and I'm careful with my supplies now."

Kevin looked down at the ring he wore again, considering. It kept him quiet, which Alex appreciated.

She chose Howard University Hospital, because it was a level-one trauma center and she knew her way around the facility—unless a lot had changed in the past ten years.

She did a slow loop around the buildings, scanning for camera placement and police presence. It was not even seven a.m., but there were plenty of people coming and going.

"How about that one?" Kevin asked, pointing.

"No, that will mostly be linens and paper goods," she muttered.

"Take a break before you do another lap; we don't want to be noticed."

"I know how this works," she lied.

She drove a few streets west and stopped at a small green space. A handful of joggers were doing their rounds, but it was otherwise fairly empty. They waited in silence for ten minutes, then she pulled out and drove a wider circle, staying two blocks out from the roads around the hospital. Eventually she spotted something promising — a white truck labeled HALBERT & SOWERBY SUPPLIERS. She was familiar with the company and was pretty sure they would have usable goods on board.

She tailed the truck into a loading area behind the main building of the hospital. Kevin was ready, fingers already wrapped around the door handle.

"Just drop me behind them, then wait a block up," he told her.

Nodding, she slowed to a brief pause just behind the truck, too close for Kevin to be seen in the mirrors. Once he was out, she reversed a couple of feet and then drove away at the exact posted speed. She glanced into the truck from under her hat as she passed; there was only a driver, no passengers. Still, there were plenty of people in scrubs and maintenance uniforms on the sidewalk. She hoped Kevin could be unobtrusive about this.

She braked at the stop sign on the corner, wondering how she was supposed to wait here when there was no parking. Before she could decide, she saw the white truck coming up behind her, one car back. She drove ahead slowly, goading the car between them to pass, then letting Kevin pass, too. She could see the driver — a very young-looking black man — leaning against the passenger-side window with his eyes closed.

"Well, there aren't any cops following him... yet," she muttered as she began following.

"Will it hurt the guy?" Daniel asked. "What Kevin stuck him with?"

"Not really. He'll have an awful hangover when he wakes up, but nothing permanent."

Kevin drove for about twenty minutes, first putting some distance between them and the hospital, then seeking the right place for the transfer of goods. He decided on a quiet industrial park, pulling to the back where there were several empty loading spaces near closed, roll-down access doors. He backed into one and she parked next to him, on the lee side, where she would be invisible to anyone entering the lot.

She yanked on a pair of latex gloves, handed another to Daniel, and shoved a pair into her pocket.

Kevin already had the back door of the truck open. She handed him the extra gloves, then boosted herself up onto the floor of the cargo hold. Everything inside was secured in opaque white plastic bins, stacked high and anchored to the walls with red nylon cords.

"Help me get these open," she instructed. Kevin started pulling the bins down and removing the lids. Daniel climbed in and followed his lead. Alex went behind them, sorting through her options.

Her main worry was being shot. It seemed the most likely fallout from an offensive action. Of course, she couldn't rule out being knifed or beaten with a blunt object. Still, she was very happy when she found a bin with blowout kits; each had tourniquets, gauze impregnated with QuikClot, and a variety of chest seals. She started a pile, adding different kinds of closure strips and gauze packs, dressings and compression bandages, chemical heating and cooling packs, resuscitation kits, a few bag-valve masks, alcohol and iodine wipes, splints and collars, burn dressings, IV catheters and tubing, saline bags, and handfuls of sealed syringes.

"You planning to start your own field hospital?" Kevin asked.

"You never know what you might need," she countered, then added in her mind, *You might be the one who needs this stuff, idiot.*

"Here," Daniel offered, turning one of the half-depleted bins upside down and dumping what was left into another. He took the now-empty bin and started organizing her pile inside.

"Thanks. I think I've got everything I want."

Kevin secured the bins to the wall, then wiped down the door. She followed him again until he found a place to leave the truck and driver, behind a small strip mall. He quickly cleaned his fingerprints from the cab, and they were on their way.

When they got back to the apartment, Raoul the housekeeper had been and gone, and Val was lying across a low sofa watching a big-screen TV that Alex could have sworn was not there yesterday. It was playing a black-and-white movie.

Today Val wore a pale blue jumpsuit with short shorts and a plunging neckline. Einstein lay on the sofa beside her with his muzzle on her arm. She was petting him rhythmically, and he didn't get up to greet them as they came through the door. He only pounded his tail against the sofa when he saw Kevin.

"So, how did all the spying go?" she asked lazily.

"Just boring groundwork," Kevin said.

"Ugh, then don't tell me about it. And don't leave any of that new stuff in here, either. I don't want the clutter."

"Yes, ma'am," Kevin agreed docilely, and he headed back to Alex and Daniel's room to add to the storage pile.

"I'll get you hooked up on my computer, Ollie," he said as he stacked. "You can watch the playback from the cameras I've got on Carston. And you can listen—there's a bug in the car and a directional mike on the office. The car has a tracker, too, so you can follow his movements for the past several days."

Alex exhaled, already exhausted by the mound of intel to assess. "Thanks."

"I'm starved," Daniel said. "Anyone else for breakfast?"

"Yes, please," Alex said at the same time that Kevin answered, "Hell, yeah."

Daniel smiled and turned for the door.

Alex watched him walk away, then realized that Kevin was watching her watch Daniel.

"What?"

Kevin pursed his lips, as if he were looking for the right way to express himself. He automatically glanced at the bed—still rumpled; Raoul had not been allowed in here—and shuddered.

Alex turned her back on him and went to retrieve her own computer. She'd want to move the important files onto it.

"Ollie…"

She didn't look up from what she was doing. "What?"

"Can I…"

She held her computer to her chest and turned to face him, waiting for him to finish. Unconsciously, she squared her shoulders.

He hesitated again, then asked, "Can I ask you some questions without getting any specific or graphic answers?"

"Like what?"

"This thing with Danny…I don't want him to get hurt."

"That's not a question."

He glared, then took a deep breath, forcing himself to relax. "When we finish up here, where do you go?"

It was her turn to hesitate. "It…well, it kind of feels like a jinx to assume that I'm going to survive. I honestly haven't thought about what's next."

"C'mon, this isn't that hard," he said disparagingly.

"It's not what I do. You handle it your way, I'll handle it mine."

"You want me to take care of Carston, too?"

"No," she growled, though if his tone hadn't been so condescending, she would have been tempted. "I'll take care of my own problems."

He paused, then asked, "So . . . what? Do you think you're just going to tag along with us after?"

"That wouldn't be my first choice, no. Going with the theory that I'm still alive then, of course."

"You're a real pessimist."

"It's part of the way I plan. Expect the worst."

"Whatever. Back to my point — if you go your own way, what about Danny? Is it just *Good-bye, thanks for the laughs?*"

She looked away, toward the door. "I don't know. That depends on what he wants. I can't speak for him."

Kevin was silent long enough that she finally had to look back. His face was uncharacteristically vulnerable. Like always, when his features were allowed to relax, he looked a lot more like Daniel.

"You think he'd choose to follow you?" Kevin asked very quietly. "I mean, he just met you. He barely knows you. But . . . I guess he probably feels like he barely knows me, too, at this point."

"I don't know what he'll want," she said. "I would never ask him to make that choice."

Kevin focused on the air a few inches above her head. "I really wanted the chance to make things up to him. To set him up in a life he could live with. I was hoping, after a while, we could be brothers again."

She had an odd urge to walk across the space between them and put her hand on his shoulder. Probably just because he was still looking like Daniel.

"I won't get in the way of that," she promised. She meant it. Whatever was best for Daniel, that was the main thing.

Kevin stared at her for a minute, his face hardening and turning back to normal. He blew out a huge sigh. "Well, damn it, Ollie, I wish I'd just left that Tacoma thing alone. Millions of lives saved — really, what does that add up to in the face of my brother sleeping with Lucrezia Borgia?"

Alex froze. "What did you say?"

He grinned. "Surprised that I know the appropriate historical analogy? I did pretty well in school, actually. I've got just as many brain cells as my brother."

"No, about Tacoma. What do you mean?"

His grin shifted to confusion. "You know all about that—they gave you the file. You interrogated Danny—"

She leaned toward him, unconsciously clutching her computer more tightly against her ribs. "This is about the job you did with de la Fuentes? Does the *T* in TCX-1 stand for *Tacoma?*"

"I've never heard of TCX-1. The de la Fuentes job was about the Tacoma virus."

"The Tacoma Plague?"

"I never heard it called that. What's going on, Ollie?"

Alex yanked open her computer as she climbed onto the foot of the bed. She pulled up the most recent file she'd worked on—her coded case notes. She scrolled through the list of numbers and initials, feeling the bed shift as Kevin put one knee on it, leaning to read over her shoulder.

It felt like a long time since she'd written these notes. So much had happened, and the thoughts she'd attached to these brief lines were faded.

There it was—terrorist event number three, *TP,* the Tacoma Plague. The letters danced in front of her eyes, only some of them resolving into words in her memory. *J, I P,* that was the town in India, on the Pakistani border. She couldn't remember what the name of the terrorist cell was, only that they originated out of Fateh Jang. She looked at the initials for the connected names: *DH*—that was the scientist, Haugen; *OM* was Mirwani, the terrorist, and then *P* . . . The other American she couldn't remember. She pressed her fist to her forehead, trying to force her recall.

"Ollie?" Kevin said again.

"I worked this case—years ago, when the formula was first stolen from the U.S. Long before de la Fuentes got hold of it."

"Stolen from the U.S.? De la Fuentes got it out of Egypt."

"No, it was developed in a lab just outside Tacoma. It was supposed to be theoretical, just research. Haugen...Dominic Haugen, that was the scientist." The story came back to her as she concentrated. "He was on our side, but with the theft, the situation became too sensitive for him to continue where he was. The NSA buried him in a lab somewhere under their control. We had the terrorist cell's second in command. He gave up the location of the lab in Jammu that was successfully creating the virus from the stolen blueprints. Black ops razed the lab. They thought they had the biological-weapon aspect locked up, but there were members of the cell who slipped through. As far as I know, the department was still working with the CIA on hunting them down a couple of years later...when Barnaby was killed."

She looked up at him, the wheels in her head spinning so fast that she felt physically dizzy.

"When the CIA called you in, when they burned you—you said there were issues you were trying to track down. What were they?"

He blinked fast, reminding her of Daniel again. "The packaging on the vaccinations—the outside was in Arabic, but the inside packaging, the original labels—everything was in English. And the name, too: Tacoma. It didn't make sense. If de la Fuentes had wanted them translated, he would have had it changed from Arabic to Spanish. I wanted to trace the virus back. I was sure it hadn't originated in Egypt. I figured there had to be an American or a Brit working with the developers somewhere. I wanted to find the guy. You're saying this thing started in *Washington State?*"

"It's got to be the same thing. The timing's right. We get some info about this virus, suddenly they start watching me and Barnaby. Two years later—around the time de la Fuentes got his hands on it, right?—they murder Barnaby. That has to be the catalyst. That's why they killed him and tried to kill me. Because the virus was out there again, and if the public found out, we knew something that could connect it back..."

Barnaby had never told her what had triggered his paranoia, why he'd decided they needed to be ready to flee. She looked at the letters on her screen. *DH,* Dominic Haugen. It was unlikely that the bad guys would leave Haugen alive if they'd felt the need to erase her and Barnaby. Had Haugen been the first to die? Probably in some totally normal, expected way. Car accident. Heart attack. There were so many methods to make it look innocent. Had Barnaby seen some notice of Haugen's death? Had that been the tip-off?

She wanted to do a quick search online, but if she was right about this, then Haugen's name was sure to be flagged. Anyone inquiring into his death—no matter how anonymous the method—would be noticed.

Who was the *P?* She couldn't even be positive she had that letter right. It had been a fleeting mention. Something short, she thought, something snappy...

"Ollie, the packaging...it looked...professional? Is that the right word? It wasn't something put together in a makeshift lab somewhere in the Middle East."

They stared at each other for a moment.

"I always thought it was a stretch," she murmured. "That someone could actually fabricate the virus from nothing more than Haugen's theoretical design. It seemed the equivalent of winning the terrorist lottery."

"You think they stole more than notes?"

"Haugen must have done it—actually created the thing. If there was a supply that large, if the vaccine was packaged up so neatly... they must have been producing it. So working on weaponized viruses wasn't just Haugen's weekend hobby. It was a military project. There were hints of that...something about a lieutenant general's involvement. No one wanted to follow up on the American side of things. They kept us focused on the cell. Usually they let us ask the questions that naturally followed...but I remember, this was different. Carston fed me the questions he wanted."

"So we got burned on the same case," Kevin said darkly.

"I don't believe in that big a coincidence."

"Neither do I."

"Who are they protecting?" Alex wondered. "Whoever it is, he's got to be calling the shots. Which means he knows about both of us."

"Which means we've got to get to him, too."

They stared at each other again.

"Alex? Kev? Guys? Is this place soundproofed?"

Alex looked up slowly, her eyes not totally focusing on Daniel walking through the doorway.

"Is something wrong?" Daniel asked in a quieter tone as he took in the tableau. He hurried to the bed and put one hand on Alex's shoulder.

"Just putting a few things together," Kevin said grimly.

Daniel looked to Alex.

"We need to add another name to our list," she told him.

"Who?"

"That's the problem," Kevin said.

"Let me think," Alex said. "If I didn't know the answer to that question, they wouldn't be trying to kill me." She glanced up at Kevin. "I know this is incredibly nonspecific, but did you ever hear a name beginning with a *P* involved with this on your end?"

"A *P?* I'll have to think about it, but not offhand. I'll go through Deavers's calls again, see if I can turn anything up."

"I'll work on it while I go through the Carston stuff."

Kevin nodded, then looked at Daniel. "I hope you came in here because there's some food ready. Got to feed Ollie's big brain so she can figure this out."

• • •

THEY SET THEIR computers up on the big kitchen island and started into it while they ate. Val and Einstein hadn't moved, but they were watching the shopping channel now. Daniel pulled a stool up beside Alex and looked on as she scanned through the video of the front of Carston's very respectable-looking town house. She fast-forwarded through the downtime when no one was in residence, simultaneously listening to Carston's phone calls on her earbuds. Carston was careful—his work conversations were vague, never naming any person or project specifically, and since the office calls were recorded on an exterior microphone, she could only hear his side. He used so many pronouns it was impossible to follow. She could tell only that there were a few *he*s and *him*s that were getting on Carston's nerves in a bad way and that at least one project was not going well. He sounded stressed. That could have been because of what happened in Texas and the e-mail to Deavers. Did Carston feel in danger? Did he think Kevin knew about him? He would have to play it safe, just in case. Carston didn't get to where he was now by not being paranoid enough.

His house had an alarm system, ornamental bars on the first-floor windows, and exterior cameras. Some of the footage Kevin gave her appeared to be from those cameras—he must have hacked into the system. The street wasn't ideal—lots of close neighbors, lots of activity on the street both morning and night. A plethora of witnesses.

"You have to break into *that?*" Daniel muttered as she pulled up yet another camera angle of the barred windows.

"Hopefully not."

Alex pointed to the small woman who was walking up the front stairs. She had several paper grocery bags weighing her down as she stuck her key in the door and unlocked the dead bolt. From this angle, Alex could see as she paused in the doorway and punched in the code for the alarm. Her hand covered the keypad; there was no way to read the sequence.

"Housekeeper?" Daniel asked.

"Looks like. And she does his shopping."

"Is that good?"

"It might be. If I could get a new face so I would be able to follow her around a bit."

"What about me?" Daniel asked. "I haven't been on the news in a while."

"Daniel, we haven't watched the news in a while," she pointed out.

"Oh. You think they're doing the bad-guy story now?"

"It's possible. We should check it out."

"You want the news?" Val called from the sofa in the adjacent room.

"Um, not if you're using the TV now," Daniel said politely.

"There's another one in the cabinet to the left of the fridge, two over," she told them.

Daniel walked to the indicated cupboard and pulled the door open to reveal a television screen recessed into the space. The door rolled back into a side pocket.

"Sweet," Kevin muttered, glancing up from his own computer for half a second.

Alex went back to her research while Daniel flipped through channels until he found a twenty-four-hour news network. He set the volume low, then came back to sit with her.

Alex didn't hear Val get up, but suddenly the blonde was leaning over her shoulder.

"That looks really dull," she commented.

"Well, adding my mortality into the equation spices it up a bit," Alex told her.

"Did you say you needed a new face?"

"Um, yes. See, the bruises and bandages make me too memorable."

"And being memorable isn't a good thing in your case?"

"No."

"I could do that."

"Huh?" Alex asked.

"Give you a new face."

Alex turned to give Val her full attention. "What do you mean?"

CHAPTER 26

"T his would be easier if you'd stop trying to do two things at once," Val complained.

"Sorry. I'm sort of on a deadline."

"Just hold your head still."

Alex did the best she could. She had Kevin's laptop on her knees with her earbuds plugged into it. While Carston was in his car, she could hear both sides of the conversation. Unfortunately, it seemed Carston usually chose to use his driving time to connect with his only daughter, Erin. They spoke almost nonstop about the granddaughter—the one whose picture was in Alex's locket—and after the first forty-minute discussion about which prekindergarten program was most likely to result in an Ivy League happy ending, Alex had started fast-forwarding as soon as she heard the daughter's voice or, if Carston was in the office, the special tone he used only to speak to Erin. They talked a lot more than Alex would have expected. She stretched her fingers down and touched the Play button. Erin was still blathering on, something about taking Livvy to the zoo. Alex hadn't missed anything. She hit fast-forward again.

"I want you to know this is an imperfect job, and it's your fault."

"Any imperfections are on me, agreed," Alex said.

Val had turned Alex away from the wall of mirrors in the bathroom so she couldn't see what was being done. She knew only that it felt like a coat of heavy, oil-based paint had been applied to her skin. Something pulled across the slash on her jaw, tight and constricting.

She'd thought the guest bathroom was opulent, but this palace was insane. Two families of five could live comfortably in just this room.

She focused her attention back on her computer screen. The housekeeper was arriving again at Carston's. It looked like she brought groceries in about every other day. Alex noted the things she could see in the tops of the bags—a quart of organic skim milk, a box of bran cereal, OJ, coffee beans. She had the housekeeper's license plate, and Kevin had gotten an address. After dark, Alex could run out and put a tracker on the woman's car so she could follow her to the store.

She checked the audio again, and Erin was saying her good-byes. Alex didn't know how Carston was able to devote so much time to listening to his daughter talk. It was a good thing he had only one child. Probably he multitasked, just like Alex was doing.

On his work calls, there had been no names mentioned at all, let alone one that started with a *P*. She felt as though if she could just push this worry to the back of her mind, her subconscious would figure it out for her. Unfortunately, she couldn't stop obsessing about it, so of course she wasn't making any progress.

"Okay, the final touch," Val said, wrestling a wig onto Alex's head.

"Ouch."

"Beauty is pain. You can look now."

Alex stood stiffly—she'd been immobile for too long—and revolved to face the mirrors.

It gave her a start. She didn't recognize herself right away as the short woman standing next to Val.

"How..." Her fingers went automatically to the place where her scabbed wound should be.

Val slapped her hand away. "Don't touch anything, you'll smear it."

"Where did it all go?"

The face of the woman in the mirror was unmarred and perfect. Her skin looked like it belonged to a dewy fourteen-year-old. Her eyes were huge, enhanced without looking overdone. Her lips were fuller, her cheekbones more pronounced. She had shoulder-length, medium brown hair with reddish highlights. It fell in flattering layers around those suddenly high cheekbones.

"Voilà, your new face," Val said. "That was fun. Next time, I'm trying you as a blonde. You have a good skin tone—it will look natural with a lot of shades."

"This is amazing. I can't believe it. Where did you learn how to do this?"

"I play a lot of different roles." Val shrugged. "But it's fun having a model. I always wanted one of those big Barbie styling heads when I was a kid." She reached out and patted the top of Alex's wig. "Or a little sister. But the plastic head was my preference."

"I'm probably ten years older than you," Alex protested.

"What a nice compliment. But whatever my age might actually be, you're still not older when it comes to the things that count."

"If you say so." Alex wasn't about to argue; Val had just handed her an unexpected get-out-of-jail-free card. "My own mother wouldn't know me."

"I can go sexier," Val promised. "But you wanted inconspicuous..."

"This is probably the sexiest I've looked in my whole life. I'd be scared to see what *sexier* looks like."

"I bet Danny would like it," Val purred.

"By the way...where did I screw that up? What tipped you off there?"

Val smiled. "Please. When two people are that into each other, it *radiates* off them. You didn't do anything."

Alex sighed. "Thanks for passing your observations on to Kevin."

"You're being sarcastic, but you *should* thank me. Aren't things easier now, without the secrecy?"

"I guess so . . . but he nearly shot me in the head, so there's that."

"Little ventured, little gained."

Alex approached the mirror wall and leaned in close to examine the disguise. There was some kind of prosthetic skin covering the wound on her jaw. She moved her mouth carefully, watching for expressions that might pull too far, make the fraud obvious. She could see a slight ripple when she smiled, but the layers of the wig mostly obscured that part of her face anyway. She wouldn't have to worry about someone noticing something wrong with her, even close up. Sure, people would be able to tell she was wearing makeup, but most normal women did. Hardly something that would draw attention.

She could accelerate her plans now. She didn't need to wait for dark. She grinned, then smoothed the expression to ease the tension in her fake skin. The new freedom was a heady thing.

Alex skipped quickly down the stairs, computer tucked under her arm. She already had a pretty workable plan—low risk, minimal exposure—so she was listening to the calls only in the vain hope that Carston would screw up and say something meaningful. It was unlikely, but she'd finish it out. Later. Right now she could get started on the specific preparation.

"Huh," Kevin grunted. Alex saw him look past her to where Val followed. "Hey, Val, how many virgins did you have to sacrifice to make her look like that?"

"I don't need any satanic help to do what I do," Val responded. "And virgins aren't useful for anything."

Daniel got up from the couch where he was watching the news— taking it seriously as his assignment—and came around the stairs to see what Kevin and Val were talking about.

Alex hesitated on the bottom stair, feeling oddly vulnerable. She wasn't used to caring if she looked pretty or not.

Daniel did a small double take, then his face relaxed into a smile.

"I'd gotten so used to seeing you with the bruises, I'd almost forgotten what you looked like without them," he said, and then his grin got wider. "It's nice to see you again."

Alex knew she hadn't looked like *this* on the train, but she let it go.

"I'm headed out to place the tracker," Alex told them. "Shouldn't take me long."

"Do you want me to come?" Daniel asked.

"Better to keep your face hidden in the daytime," she told him. He didn't look happy about it, but his expression was resigned. She imagined how she would feel if he ran out to do some surveillance, and she could understand his reluctance.

"It won't be anything," she promised.

"Take the sedan," Kevin said, gesturing to a set of keys on the counter.

"Wilco," Alex said, imitating his soldier tone. He didn't seem to notice.

Carston's housekeeper would probably be home by now, unless she had errands to run. She only worked mornings there. Of course, she could have other clients, but Alex imagined that Carston would pay well so he wouldn't have to share—he would want her free if he needed something. Alex drove the black sedan across town, not all that far, really, from Daniel's empty apartment. She was glad he was safely tucked away at Val's. She was sure they'd have some kind of surveillance on his place, just hoping he'd be stupid enough to come back for his toothbrush or favorite T-shirt.

The housekeeper's neighborhood had street parking only. She found the decade-old white minivan a block over from the apartments where the woman lived. There was plenty of traffic, both cars and pedestrians. She found a spot near the minimart on the corner and set off for a walk.

The early-summer heat had her sweating almost immediately. Unlike Kevin, she didn't have a myriad of costumes to choose from, so she was in her blazer again today, and it felt twice as thick as usual. Oh, well, she needed the pockets. Hopefully the makeup wouldn't sweat off.

There were enough people around her that she felt invisible, just one of the herd. The numbers dwindled as she crossed over to the next block, but she still didn't stand out.

She pulled her phone out of her pocket and hit Redial.

Kevin answered on the first ring. "What's the problem, Oleander?"

"Just calling to say hi," she told him.

"Ah. Blending?"

"Of course."

"Talk to Danny. I don't have time to blend with you."

"I'd prefer it anyway," she said, but he was already gone.

She heard a thud as the phone hit something, and then Daniel said, "Ouch."

Alex took a deep, calming breath. Kevin always made her want to stab things.

"Alex, are you all right?"

"Absolutely."

Kevin shouted something in the background.

"Kevin says you're trying to look natural," Daniel said.

"That's part of it," she agreed.

She was only two cars from the minivan now. There was a man ahead of her but walking in the same direction so his back was to her. She couldn't hear anyone close behind her, but there could be someone who had her in his sight line. She didn't turn to look.

"So I guess we should talk about something normal people talk about," Daniel was saying.

"Right."

"Um, what would you like for dinner? Do you want to stay in again?"

Alex smiled. "Staying in sounds great. I'll eat anything you feel like cooking."

"You make things too easy for me."

"There are enough difficulties in the world without adding my own." She flipped a few locks of the wig out of her eyes, her fingers knocking into the phone. It skittered across the sidewalk and teetered on the edge of the curb. "Hold on," she called toward it. "I dropped the phone."

She knelt and swiped the phone up, holding on to the edge of the minivan's wheel well for support. She jumped back to her feet, brushing at the knees of her leggings.

"Sorry about that," she said.

"Did you just plant the tracking device?"

She started walking again, heading for the end of the block, where she could begin circling back to the car. "Yes."

"Very smooth."

"I told you it was nothing. I'll see you soon."

"Drive safe. I love you."

Kevin shouted something in the background, and there was another thud close beside the phone.

"Are you *kidding?*" Daniel shouted back. "A knife?"

Alex ended the call and picked up the pace a little. She couldn't leave them alone for twenty minutes.

Things had returned to normal — or her new version of it — by the time she got back to the apartment. Daniel was still studiously watching the news. Val had just brought Einstein back from a walk and was filling the lovely crystal bowl with water for him. Kevin was watching the feed from his cameras and sharpening a machete. Home sweet home.

"Anything?" she asked Daniel.

"Nothing about me. Apparently the vice president is bowing out before the election after all. I guess those recent scandal rumors aren't entirely unfounded. So of course, everyone is speculating about who President Howland will select for his running mate."

"Fascinating," Alex murmured in a tone that implied the

opposite. She dumped her bag onto one of the white bar stools, sat on the next one over, and opened her computer. All seemed quiet at Casa Carston, so she started scrubbing backward to see if she'd missed anything while she was out. So far she hadn't discovered any regular visitors besides the housekeeper and the security service that drove by once daily in the afternoon.

Daniel flipped to a different news network, where another version of the same story was running. "You don't care who the president runs with?" he asked. "Howland's pretty popular. Whoever he chooses will probably be the vice president, and possibly the president four years from now."

"Ventriloquist dummies," Kevin grumbled, setting down the machete and starting to work on a long boning knife.

Alex nodded in agreement as she slowed the feed to watch two teenagers amble past Carston's house and up the block.

"What do you mean?" Daniel asked.

"I don't worry about the puppet," Kevin said. "I worry about the guy pulling the strings."

"That's a pretty cynical attitude about the democratic nation you used to work for."

Kevin shrugged. "Yup."

"Alex, Republican or Democrat?" Daniel asked.

"Pessimist."

She reached for the other computer, the one with the bugged calls on it, and plugged in her headphones.

"So nobody cares that the front-runner is some ultra-right senator from Washington State who used to work for the Defense Intelligence Agency?"

The first call Alex had missed was from the daughter again — she could tell from Carston's warm, fatherly voice. She started fast-forwarding.

"Makes sense," Val was saying, pulling a rubber band out of her hair. She was wearing sweaty workout clothes and looked like she should be on a *Maxim* cover anyway. "Howland is soft. Get someone with a conservative edge, pull some voters off the fence. Plus, the new guy is one part grandpa, one part silver fox, with a catchy two-syllable name. Howland could do worse." She shook her golden hair out, and it fell into perfect waves down her back.

"It's sad, but you're probably right. Just a beauty pageant."

"Everything is, honey," Val told him.

Alex stopped to check the recording, but Carston was still just listening and muttering kindly *mm-hmm*s. She sped it up again.

"I suppose I should get used to it, since I imagine I don't get to vote anymore." Daniel frowned. "Vice President Pace. Do you think he was born with that name, or did he alter it to make it voter-friendly? Wade Pace. Is that something you would name a kid?"

"I wouldn't name a kid anything," Val said. "Because I would never be dumb enough to bring one home."

Alex's fingers reached down automatically to stop the recording.

"What was that?" she asked.

"Just explaining that I'm not the mom type," Val said.

"No, Daniel, what was that name?"

"Senator Pace? Wade Pace?"

"That name...it sounds familiar."

"I think everyone knows his name," Daniel said. "He's been positioning himself for this kind of promotion, not exactly low profile."

"I don't follow politics," Alex said. She stared at the TV now, but it just showed some news anchor. "How much do you know about this guy?"

"Just the stuff they're running on the news," Daniel answered. "Sterling service record, all the normal clichés."

"He was military?"

"Yes, some kind of general, I think."

"A lieutenant general?"

"Maybe."

Kevin was paying attention now. "Wade Pace. Pace with a *P*. That our guy?"

Alex stared into space, unconsciously rocking slightly back and forth on her stool. "He's from Washington State...he worked defense intelligence..." She looked up at Kevin. "Let's say the DIA is theoretically exploring some biological-weapons options. This guy's already got some political aspirations, so of course he makes sure the money gets spent in his hometown. They would have had plenty of innocuous goals on the surface—all the outsiders would see was the economic boost. Probably helped get him his seat in the Senate. Great. But then, years later, the fabricated virus is stolen. Obviously, no one can know that he ever had a hand in its creation. No one can know it exists. We track down the bad guys, and they give up too much information. Wade Pace has big dreams. Anyone who heard his name in connection with this virus—"

"Has to be preemptively silenced," Kevin finished. "And who knows exactly what the too-thorough CIA agent might have seen? Better shut him up, too."

"Can't take any chances," Alex whispered. "Not when you're reaching this high."

It was silent for thirty seconds.

"Wow," Val said, so loudly it made Alex jump. "Are you guys going to assassinate the vice president?" She sounded utterly thrilled by the idea.

"He's not the vice president yet," Kevin said. "He's nothing, officially. That means no Secret Service."

Daniel's mouth was hanging open.

Higher stakes again, but not by so very much. In the end, no matter what else he represented, Wade Pace was just one beating heart.

Kevin locked eyes with Alex. "So he put a hit out on me, my

brother, you, your friend... so he could try to be president. Oh, I'm going to *enjoy* this one."

She opened her mouth but then quickly snapped it shut again. It would be a lot easier and safer — for her — to let Kevin do as much of the wet work as possible.

But there was her anonymity — Daniel's, too, so she might as well lump in Kevin's matching face — which had to be protected above all else if this plan was going to work. Kevin might be better at killing people than she was, but she was pretty sure that she was better at doing it with minimal ripples. *If you want something done right...*

"As much as I hate to deprive you of any fun, I think you might want to let me take this one." She shivered slightly. This was probably a big mistake. Was she turning into the adrenaline junkie she'd accused Daniel of being? She didn't *think* so. She felt nothing but dread at the idea of adding another job to her list. "Quiet is the goal, right? It won't get too much attention if our wannabe president dies of a heart attack or a stroke — not the same coverage as if he were found shot in some kind of home invasion."

"I can be quiet," Kevin insisted. His eyebrows were pulling down into a scowl.

"Natural-causes quiet?"

"Close enough."

"*Close enough* puts our other targets on high alert."

"They're already on high alert."

"So how do you see this happening?"

"I'll improvise when I get there."

"Sound plan."

"You know how many people die in household accidents every day in this country?"

"No. But I'm positive that more white men in their early sixties die from health-related problems than from any other reason."

"Okay, great, a heart attack would be the *quietest* way for Pace to die, agreed. How are you going to get in, shorty? Knock on the door and ask to borrow a cup of sugar? Be sure to wear your frilly apron—really sell it."

"I can adapt the Carston plan. I'll just need a few more days of research on Pace—"

Kevin's hand slapped loudly against the counter. "We don't have that kind of time. We've delayed too long as it is. You know Deavers and Carston aren't wasting the prep time we've already given them."

"Rushing just leaves openings they can take advantage of. Proper preparation—"

"You are *so annoying!*"

She hadn't realized how close together she and Kevin had gotten—pretty much spitting in each other's face from about six inches away—until Daniel's hand suddenly shot in between them.

"Can I interrupt to suggest the obvious?" he asked.

Kevin smacked his hand away. "Stay out of it, Danny."

Alex took a deep, calming breath. "What's obvious?" she asked Daniel.

"Alex, you have the best plan for how to ... um, assassinate the senator." He shook his head quickly. "I can't believe this is real."

"It's real," Kevin said harshly. "And I wouldn't call a plan with no entry point the best plan."

"Let me finish. Alex has the best ... methodology. Kevin, you have the best chance of getting in undetected."

"Yeah, I do," Kevin said belligerently.

"Oh," Alex said, feeling suddenly disgruntled for some reason. Probably just bruised pride and the irritation of having to cooperate with someone so obnoxious. "You're right," she admitted to Daniel. "Again."

He smiled.

"What?" Kevin demanded. "And stop with the goo-goo eyes, you'll make me vomit."

"Obviously"—Alex drew the word out into almost five syllables—"we have to do this together. You go in with my premixed solution in hand. Actually..." Her brain started turning over options. "More than one solution, I think. We'll have to stay in contact so I can guide you to the best application—"

Kevin gave her a withering look. "*You're* in command, and I'm just following orders on the ground?"

Alex stared him down. "Tell me your better plan."

Kevin rolled his eyes, but then refocused. "Fine. It makes sense. Whatever."

Alex felt better already. She could perform her part without any risk. And though she didn't love to admit it, she knew Kevin could do his.

Kevin snorted like he could hear her thoughts, then said, "Can I ask one favor?"

"What do you want?"

"When you're mixing your little beakers of poison, could you make this one hurt? Hurt *bad?*"

Alex smiled in spite of her fear. "*That* I can manage."

He pursed his lips for a minute. "This is weird, Ollie. I... well, I almost like you right now."

"The feeling will pass."

"You're right—it's fading already." He sighed. "How long will you need with your chemistry set?"

Alex calculated quickly. "Give me three hours."

"I'll research my new target, then."

Kevin grabbed his machete and other knives and headed upstairs, whistling.

Alex stood and stretched. Even with the new pressure and attached dread, it felt good to have the answer. The missing name had been an irritant, like an itch on the inside of her skull. Now she could concentrate on her next move.

• • •

"ALL RIGHT, I'M in the master bath."

Kevin's voice was muted, for Kevin, but still louder than Alex felt was safe. If she'd mentioned her concern, he would only have reminded her that he was the expert now, but still. He was just so cocky.

Alex wondered if he'd brought Einstein into the house with him. Probably, she thought, but of course the dog made no sound.

"Make sure you've got his side of things. I don't want to kill the wife." Alex couldn't bring herself to speak above a whisper despite his apparent comfort.

"What?"

"Make sure you find *his* stuff," she murmured a little louder. "Nothing unisex, like toothpaste."

"I'm pretty sure the right-hand side medicine cabinet belongs to our guy. Refill safety razor blades, Excedrin, SPF forty-five sunblock, Centrum Silver, some makeup, but it's all flesh tones . . ."

"Be positive."

"I am. Lots of lipsticks and perfumes on the left side."

"Some things they might share . . . check the drawers under the medicine cabinet."

Alex pictured the pretty blond woman she'd seen standing beside Wade Pace in the official photos. Carolyn Josephine Merritt-Pace. She was only ten years the senator's junior, but she looked a full quarter of a century younger. Whatever surgeries she had undergone, she'd been circumspect enough to keep things minimal; she'd retained her warm, beaming smile that crinkled the corners of her eyes and had every appearance of being genuine. She'd inherited a fortune from her aristocratic southern family, much of which she used to fund her various causes—literacy, feeding hungry children, saving music programs in inner-city schools, building shelters for the homeless. Never anything controversial. She had been a stay-at-home mother for their two daughters, both of whom had graduated from Magnolia League schools and were now married to respectable men—a pediatrician and a college professor.

From everything Alex had learned in her hurried research about the senator's wife, Mrs. Merritt-Pace seemed a pleasant enough woman. Certainly not deserving of the painful death her husband was about to suffer. *Hopefully* about to suffer, Alex amended. There was still so much that was left to luck.

"I've got three boxes of bar soap, a pack of extra toothbrushes, ChapStick in two flavors, cherry and strawberry...pomade, cotton pads, Q-tips...Next drawer down—oh, now here we go. Hemorrhoid cream. That's fitting. Suppositories, too. Whatcha think, Ollie?"

"That might work. I'd love to use something topical rather than going the oral route, just to separate this as much as possible from Carston. But he might not use either the cream or the suppositories regularly."

"A good point. Though it would be so great to literally shove this poison up—oh, hey, is our guy a smoker?"

"Um...hold on one second."

Alex typed the phrase *Does Wade Pace smoke?* into her open browser window. She was immediately flooded with articles and pictures. She clicked on the images—poor-quality photographs taken from behind or at a great distance. Wade Pace—younger than he was now, still some dark in his hair, usually in a military uniform— was never at the center of the photo, but it was easy enough to pick him out, cigarette in hand. And then the more recent photos where he *was* centered; these were after he'd morphed into the "silver fox" Val had called him, and he never held a cigarette. But several photographers had focused in on the nicotine patch just slightly visible through the sleeve of his white button-down. Another on vacation, in a garish Hawaiian shirt, the bottom corner of the tan patch showing just below the sleeve. The vacation picture was from April. Not that long ago.

"Looks like he used to be," Alex said. "Tell me you found the patches."

"NicoDerm CQ. One half-used box, with three unopened packages behind it. I'll check the trash."

Alex waited eagerly through the short silence.

"Affirmative. Used patches in the trash under his sink. I'd say this bin gets emptied regularly. So he's still actively using them."

"This couldn't be more perfect," Alex said through her teeth. "Use the syringe marked with the number three."

"Got it."

She could hear the quiet pull of a zipper.

"Don't let the liquid come in contact with your skin. Come at it from the seam—don't leave an obvious pinhole."

"I'm not an idiot. How much?"

"Depress the syringe halfway."

"It's pretty small, are you sure—you know what, never mind. How soon will it dry?"

"A few hours. Put it—"

"Underneath the top patch, right?" Kevin interrupted. "Second down."

"Yes, that will work."

Alex heard Kevin's low chuckle.

"Mission accomplished. Wade Pace is one very deserving dead man walking. Moving on to target number two."

"Will you check in when you're in position?"

"Negative. Should be less than twenty-four. I'll see you back at the apartment."

"Fine."

"Get on your guy, Ollie."

Her voice was a little higher-pitched when she answered. "Yeah. I'll have that, um, done before you're back."

He tuned in to her nervousness, and his tone became gruff, commanding. "You'd better. If I cause ripples, your plan might not work."

"Right."

He disconnected before she could. Again.

Alex took a deep breath and set the phone and the computer down on the bed next to her.

Daniel was cross-legged on the floor at her feet, one hand curled loosely around her calf. His eyes hadn't left her face throughout the phone call.

"Did you get all that?" she asked.

Daniel nodded. "I can't believe he didn't wake anyone. Tell me my voice isn't so piercing."

She grinned. "It's not."

He leaned forward to put his chin on her knee. She felt his hand tighten around her leg.

"And now it's your turn." He said the words in barely more than a whisper, but the volume didn't disguise his intensity.

"Not quite yet." She glanced automatically at the digital clock she'd set up as part of her temporary lab. The display read 4:15. "I've got a few hours till showtime."

She felt the shift against her skin as his jaw tightened.

"I'm not doing anything dangerous," she reminded him. "I won't be breaking into anyone's fortress. It's not so different from placing the tracker."

"I know. I keep telling myself that."

Alex stood, stretching, and Daniel leaned back to give her room. She nodded to the corner where her lab equipment was spread out inefficiently across a variety of end tables. She'd taken advantage of the setup to create a healthy supply of *Survive* after she was done with the recipes for Pace.

"I suppose I should clean this up before it upsets Val."

Daniel got to his feet. "Can I help?"

"Sure. Just don't touch anything without gloves."

It didn't take long; she'd had so much practice setting her lab up and taking it down, sometimes with an urgent deadline. Daniel was quick to grasp the order of things, and soon he had the proper case ready before she had the equipment totally dismantled. As she carefully wrapped up the last round-bottomed flask, she glanced at the clock again. She still had hours before Val would need to start on her makeup.

"You look exhausted," Daniel commented.

"We got an early start. Val will fix me up so I'm presentable."

"A nap might not hurt, either."

Alex was fairly sure that she wouldn't be able to fall asleep. She was working to seem composed so that Daniel wouldn't worry, but in truth she could feel the seeds of panic beginning to take root in her stomach lining. Not that she'd lied to him about anything she would be doing, but she wasn't anywhere close to relaxed about the next phase. The actual action part. The truth was, she'd fallen back into her usual mind-set, gotten very comfortable with preparation. Now that it was time for her to implement the plan, her nervous system was in overdrive. Still, even just resting would probably be smart.

"Good idea."

• • •

AS ALEX WATCHED Carston's housekeeper walk through the automatic doors into the huge supermarket, she took a few slow, deep breaths, trying to center herself. She examined her face in the visor mirror and was reassured by the illusion Val had created. Alex was sandy blond today, quite believably so. Her makeup appeared understated, despite all the coverage. Alex was happy to see that her nose was settling into its new shape, probably permanently. Every little bit helped.

A few other shoppers parked and entered, and Alex knew it was time to move. One more deep breath. This wasn't that hard. Just a normal shopping trip for now.

Inside, the market was busy. It was a diverse group of patrons, and Alex was sure she wouldn't stick out. She was suddenly reminded of Daniel's catastrophic shopping spree in Childress, and she was surprised to find herself smiling. She blamed her reaction on nerves.

Despite the traffic, it wasn't hard to find the woman she was looking for. The housekeeper was wearing a bright yellow cotton wrap dress, and the color stood out. Rather than follow her through the store, Alex worked the opposite pattern and crossed paths with her every other aisle. It put Alex in the woman's sight line more often but seemed more natural, less creepy. The woman — who appeared to be about fifty from close up, in good shape and fairly attractive — paid Alex no attention. Meanwhile Alex filled her cart with random items that seemed innocuous — milk, bread, toothpaste — and then added the few items that mattered.

Carston liked these small bottles of organic orange juice. They must expire quickly, because the housekeeper bought a few every trip but never stocked up. Alex grabbed three — the same number as in the housekeeper's cart — and put them in the front child seat of her own.

She wheeled over to an empty aisle — no one was looking for birthday cards or office supplies this morning — and then uncapped the small syringe in her pocket. It was a very slender needle, and it left almost no mark behind when she pushed it through the plastic of the orange juice bottle, just under the screw-off cap. She kept her body turned toward the cards, as if she were looking for the perfect sentimental phrase. When she was done, she grabbed a glittery congratulations card in hot pink and put it in the cart. Maybe she'd give it to Kevin when he finished his mission. It was the kind of glitter that would stick to someone for days.

She and Barnaby had called this drug simply *Heart Attack*, because that's what it caused. Sometimes after the interrogation was over, the department needed to dispose of a subject in a way that looked natural. After about three hours, *Heart Attack* broke down into a metabolite that was nearly impossible to trace. A man of Carston's age, in his physical condition, and factoring in the high-stress job—well, Alex greatly doubted that anyone would look too carefully at the cause of death, at least in the very beginning. Sure, if he were twenty-five and ran marathons, it might look more suspicious.

Alex moved to the bakery next, because it was near the cashiers and had an unobstructed view of the shoppers waiting to pay. It took about ten minutes as she pretended to dither between a baguette or ciabatta rolls, but then the housekeeper appeared from aisle 19 and got into the checkout line. Alex threw the baguette in her cart and joined the next line over.

This was the tricky part. She'd have to stay pretty close to the woman as they left the store. Alex's inconspicuous black sedan was parked right next to the minivan. As the woman was loading her groceries, Alex was going to trip with her arms full of bags and fall into the minivan's bumper. It shouldn't be too hard to leave her juice in the back of the car. Hopefully snagging the woman's juice bottles would be possible, but if not, she assumed the housekeeper would load them all into the fridge, even if she didn't have the right number.

Alex eyed the conveyor belt next to hers, double-checking that the juice was there. She spotted what she was looking for and glanced quickly away.

As her own purchases slid across the scanner, her brows furrowed. Something was off. Something wasn't matching the mental picture. She glanced back at the other conveyor belt, trying to pin it down.

The bagger was packing a box of Lucky Charms. The housekeeper had never bought that kind of cereal for Carston, as far as Alex had been able to see. Carston was a creature of habit, and he ate the same fiber-heavy cereal every morning. Sugary marshmallows with plastic prizes were not his MO.

Another quick peek, head down. The usual coffee beans, the low-fat creamer, the quart of skim milk, but there was also a half a gallon of whole milk and a box of Nilla Wafers.

"Paper or plastic, miss? Miss?"

Alex quickly refocused, pulled her wallet open, and grabbed three twenties. "Paper, please," she said. The housekeeper always got paper.

Her mind was turning over and over as she waited for her change.

Maybe the housekeeper got groceries for herself while she was shopping for Carston. But if she got her own milk, she'd have to carry it inside and put it in Carston's fridge until she was done for the day, so it wouldn't spoil in the heat. And she'd never done that in the past.

Was Carston expecting guests?

Alex's heart pounded uncomfortably as she followed the woman through the automatic front doors, her two bags both gripped in her left hand.

She needed Carston to be the one who enjoyed that bottle of OJ. But what if a friend grabbed it instead? A friend who *was* twenty-five and a marathoner? It would be obvious what she had attempted. Carston would change his habits, beef up his security. And he would know it was Alex, without a doubt. That she was alive, and nearby.

The hunt would begin again, closer than ever.

Should she go with the odds? The juice was Carston's thing. Probably he wouldn't offer it to someone else. But what if?

As her mind raced through the possibilities, a small piece of meaningless information—or so she'd categorized it—popped into her head and suggested a new prospect.

The zoo. The daughter had kept going on and on about the zoo. And all the calls, every day, some of them hours long. What if Erin Carston-Boyd wasn't always in such close touch with her father? What if Alex, in her hurry to get to the important calls, had fast-forwarded through vital information—like a pending visit from his daughter and granddaughter? The DC zoo was famous. Exactly the kind of place you'd take your out-of-town granddaughter. Just like Lucky Charms was exactly the kind of cereal an indulgent grandpa would have on hand for her breakfast.

Alex sighed, quietly but deeply.

She couldn't risk poisoning the child.

Now what? The coffee beans? But Erin would drink coffee, too. Maybe another kind of toxin, something that looked like salmonella?

She couldn't wait until the family went back where they belonged. Deavers and Pace would be dead by then — if they weren't already — and Carston would be on high alert. This was her one chance to stay ahead of the panicked reaction. There would be six bottles of juice, only one poisoned... odds were Carston would drink it... it was unlikely the child would be hurt...

Ugh, she groaned mentally, and slowed her pace. She knew she wasn't going to do it. And she couldn't go back to his favorite sidewalk café and add an extra ingredient to his chicken parm; he'd surely given up that habit once she'd contacted him there. She'd be stuck with something really obvious and dangerous now, like borrowing Daniel's rifle and shooting Carston through his kitchen window. Her chances of getting caught — and killed — would be much, much higher than she'd planned.

Kevin was going to be disgusted with her. Only one person on her list, and she'd already blown it. She couldn't resent that reaction; she was disgusted with herself, too.

As though he could read her mind, just then Kevin called. She felt the vibration in her pocket, then pulled the phone out and read the number. She hit Answer and put it to her ear, but didn't say anything. She was still too close to the housekeeper, and she didn't want the woman to hear her voice and turn, getting another, closer look at the blond woman shadowing her. Perhaps the housekeeper was still the way in. Alex couldn't afford to be noticed.

Alex waited for Kevin to start in on her, irrationally sure he had somehow sensed that she was failing; *Way to drop the ball, Oleander,* in the half shout that was his normal volume.

Kevin said nothing. She pulled the phone back to look at the screen. Had they been disconnected? Had he dialed her by accident?

The call was live. The seconds counted upward in the bottom corner of the screen.

Alex almost said, *Kevin?*

Four years of paranoia stopped her tongue.

She pressed the phone to her ear and listened intently. There was no ambient sound of a car or movement. No wind. No animal sounds, no human sounds.

Goose bumps erupted on the backs of her arms, raised the hair on her neck. She'd walked past her car, and now she had to keep going. Her eyes darted around while she kept her head still; she focused on a dumpster in the back corner of the lot. Her pace quickened. She was too close to the center of her enemy's power. If they were tracing this call, it would not take them long to get here. She wanted to run, wanted it badly, but she kept herself to a quick, purposeful walk.

Still no sound from the other end of the line. The cold, heavy hollow in the pit of her stomach grew larger.

Kevin wasn't going to suddenly start speaking to her, she knew that. Still, she hesitated for one more second. Once she did what she knew she had to do now, it was over. Her only connection to Kevin was severed.

She hung up. The numbers at the bottom of the screen told her the call had lasted for only seventeen seconds. It felt like much more time had passed.

She walked around the side of the dumpster, where she wasn't visible from the parking lot. She couldn't see anyone, which hopefully meant no one could see her.

She set the groceries on the ground.

In the lining of her purse, she had a small lock-picking kit. She'd never had to use it for its real purpose, but it came in handy now and then when she worked with some of her smaller reflux rings and adapters. She pulled the thinnest probe, then used it to pop the SIM card tray out from her phone. Both card and tray went into her bag.

Using the hem of her T-shirt, she carefully wiped the phone down, handling it only through the fabric. The tether of the shirt's length made it hard to get the phone through the side hatch on the dumpster; it was too high up. She had to toss the phone when she couldn't reach far enough, but she got it through in one try.

Alex grabbed the paper bags, spun back around, and walked quickly to her car. The minivan was just exiting the lot. She couldn't tell if the housekeeper had noticed her side trip. She took the longest strides she was capable of as she hurried back.

The phone was gone, but she could almost see the seconds still ticking away in the corner of the screen. There were two possibilities now, and one of those possibilities gave her a very tight deadline indeed.

CHAPTER 27

"Alex, he just pocket-dialed you," Daniel argued.

"Danny's right," Val agreed. "You're overreacting. It's nothing."

Alex shook her head, feeling the pull in her jaw as her teeth clenched. "We need to move," she said flatly.

"Because the bad guys might be torturing Kevin for information as we speak," Val recapped. She used the patient, humoring voice people used with very young children and the elderly.

Alex's answer was cold and hard. "It won't be a joke if they come for you, Val. I can promise you that."

"Look, Alex, your own plan had just failed," Val reminded her. "You were already upset. Kevin called you and didn't say anything. That is all that happened. I think it's a little bit of a leap to assume it was more than an accident."

"It's what they do," Alex said in a slow, even voice. Even before Barnaby had gotten her the appropriate classified reading material, she'd seen some of this in action. "The subject has a phone with one number on it. You call that number and see what kind of information you can get from it. You track the signal you've just created. You find the person on the other end."

"Well, there's nothing to find, though, right?" Daniel asked encouragingly. "You tossed the phone. It can't lead them to anything more than a parking lot that's not connected to us."

"The phone is a dead end," she agreed. "But if they have Kevin…"

Doubt rippled across Daniel's face. Val still wore a patronizing expression.

"Do you think they would have killed him?" Daniel asked in a voice that was almost a whisper.

"That's the best-case scenario," she said bluntly. She didn't know how to sugarcoat it or say it in a gentler way. "If he's dead, they can't hurt him anymore. And we're safe. If he's alive…" She took a deep breath and refocused. "Like I said, we need to move."

Val was unconvinced. "You really think he'd sell Danny out?"

"Look, Val, I would never question your understanding on anything remotely feminine. That's your world. This is mine. I am not exaggerating when I say that everyone breaks. It doesn't matter how strong Kevin is or how much he loves his brother. It may take a while, but he *will* tell them where we are. And for his sake, I hope it doesn't take that long."

It would, though, and she knew it. Rocky as her relationship with Kevin had always been, she had learned to trust him, to *know* him. He would buy her the time she needed to get Daniel and Val somewhere safe. Partly because he did love his brother, and partly because of his pride. He'd never give Deavers what he wanted easily. Kevin would make them work for every word they pried out of him.

She was glad it wasn't her job to break Kevin. She was sure he would be the hardest case she'd ever faced. If anyone could do it — actually take his secrets to the grave with him — that person might be Kevin Beach. Maybe he would have broken her perfect record.

For a second, she could see it vividly — Kevin restrained on the state-of-the-art table in the old lab, herself standing over him. How would she have worked the case? If things had panned out just slightly differently — if her Pakistani subject had never murmured the name Wade Pace — the scenario she pictured could have been her reality.

She shook the image away and looked up at Daniel and Val. Alex could see that her tension—her intensity and dark certainty—were finally getting to Daniel, at least.

"If they did get Kevin...what do you think would happen to Einstein?" Val asked, still skeptical, but her lapis eyes were abnormally vulnerable.

Alex winced. Why had she learned to care so much about an animal on top of everything else? What a stupid thing to do.

"We don't have time to figure everything out right now," she said. "Do you have a place to go, Val? A place Kevin wouldn't know about?"

"I've got a million places." Val's face hardened. Her perfect features suddenly looked like they belonged to a beautiful doll, cold and empty. "You?"

"Our options are a little more limited, but I'll figure something out. Pack up the things you want to save—it won't be safe to come back here. Can I keep the wig?"

Val nodded.

"Thanks. Do you have another car besides the one we've been using?" Kevin had taken the McKinleys' SUV when he and Einstein had set off just after midnight.

"I've got a couple here. That one isn't mine. Kevin was driving it when he got here."

Val pivoted slowly, gracefully, and then sauntered to the stairs. Alex couldn't tell if she was going to pack or headed up to catch a nap. Val didn't believe her.

Alex's mind was racing in a hundred different directions. They'd have to get a new car quickly and dump the one Kevin knew about. There were so many details she had to think through, and she had to do it fast.

Alex turned and hurried back to the guest room. She had to pack, too.

And think. She hadn't planned for this. She should have.

Daniel followed her down the hallway. "Tell me what I need to do," he said as they walked through the door.

"Can you get everything back into the duffel bags? I...I need to think for a few minutes. We can't afford any mistakes today. Just let me concentrate, okay?"

"Of course."

Alex lay down on the bed, then crossed both arms over her face. Daniel worked quietly in the corner; the noise wasn't distracting. She tried to think through all the moves they had available to them, everything Kevin didn't know.

There wasn't much. She couldn't even go back for Lola—Kevin had picked the boarding facility.

She took another centering breath and put that thought away. There was no time for sadness now.

It would be small motels for a while. Cash only. Luckily she had plenty of Kevin's drug money. They'd be able to keep their heads down.

Of course, Carston would expect that. Her face and Daniel's would end up on a police flyer e-mailed to all the potential stops for a thousand miles. Since they'd already rolled the Daniel story, maybe they'd cast her as his captive. It would be hard to sell the other version, given Alex's and Daniel's relative sizes.

They could camp out of whatever car they found, as they'd done before. The scrutiny would be intense. Once Carston's people located Kevin's vehicle, they'd trace every used car sold, every want ad, every stolen car for a hundred miles in any direction. Any description that fit the scenario would go onto a list, and if a cop reported that vehicle, Carston's people wouldn't be far behind.

Maybe it was time to go back to Chicago. Maybe Joey Giancardi wouldn't kill her immediately. Maybe he'd be willing to trade some kind of indentured servitude for two sets of facial reconstruction. Or maybe he'd get one whiff of her desperation and know there was good money to be made in selling her back to the people who wanted her.

She had identities that Kevin knew nothing about, but Daniel didn't. The documents she'd grabbed from Kevin's mobile Batcave wouldn't be safe.

Unless Daniel acted fast enough.

She uncovered her face and sat up.

"Do you think you've grasped the basic principles of hide-and-seek?"

Daniel turned with two clear bags of ammo in his hands. "Maybe the *very* most basic of the basics."

Alex nodded. "You're smart, though. You speak Spanish pretty well, right?"

"I can get by. You want to go to Mexico?"

"I wish I could. Mexico probably isn't totally safe for your face since you've been there so many times, but there are a lot of good hiding places in South America. It's cheap, too, so you won't run out of money for a while. You won't blend in, but there are lots of expats..."

Daniel hesitated for a second, then carefully placed the ammo in one of the duffels. He came to stand next to her.

"Alex, you're using a lot of second-person pronouns there. Are you...talking about us splitting up right now?"

"You'll be safer outside the country, Daniel. If you laid low in a quiet little place somewhere in Uruguay, they might never find—"

"Then why can't we go together? Is it because they'll be looking for a couple...if...if Kevin talks?"

She hunched her shoulders; it was half a shrug, half a defensive motion. "It's because I don't have a passport."

"You don't think they'll be waiting for Daniel Beach to try to board a plane?"

"You won't be Daniel Beach. I've got a couple of Kevin's ID sets. It will be a long while till they get around to asking him about false identities, if they ever do. You'll have plenty of time to catch a flight to Chile tonight."

His expression was suddenly hard, almost angry. He looked like Kevin, and she was surprised at how sad that made her.

"So I just save myself, then? Leave you behind?"

Another almost-shrug. "Like you said, they'll be looking for a couple. I'll slip through the holes in the net."

"They'll be looking for *you,* Alex. I won't—"

"Okay, okay," she interrupted. "Let me think some more. I'll come up with something."

Daniel locked eyes with her for a long second. Slowly, his expression softened until he looked like himself again. Finally, his shoulders slumped and his eyes closed.

"I'm sorry," she whispered. "I'm sorry this didn't work. I'm sorry that Kevin..."

"I keep hoping he'll walk through the door," Daniel admitted, opening his eyes and staring down. "But I can feel it in my gut— that's not going to happen."

"I know. I wish I were wrong."

His eyes flashed up to hers. "If our positions were reversed, he'd do something. He'd find a way. But there's nothing *I* can do. I'm not Kevin."

"Kevin would be in the same position we are. He wouldn't know where they were keeping you. If he did, he'd still be impossibly outgunned. There wouldn't be anything he could do."

Daniel shook his head and sank down onto the bed. "Somehow, none of that would have stopped him."

Alex sighed. Daniel was probably right. Kevin would have some secret informant, or another camera angle, or a way to hack into Deavers's system. He wouldn't give up and run. But Alex wasn't Kevin, either. She couldn't even poison Carston while he was still oblivious. He wasn't anymore, she was sure of that.

"Let me think," she repeated. "I'll try to figure a way out."

Daniel nodded. "But together, Alex. We leave together. We stay together."

"Even if that puts both of us at risk?"

"Even then."

Alex threw herself back onto the bed, hiding her face again with her arms.

If there had been some perfect escape for them, she would have tried it earlier. The whole reason she was here in the first place was that the escape option had failed. Now the attack option had failed. It didn't leave her feeling very optimistic.

It was funny how you didn't realize how much you had to lose until it was gone. Yes, she knew she was in deep with Daniel; she'd embraced that disadvantage. But who would have thought she would miss Kevin? How had he become her friend? Not even a friend, because you chose your friends. More like family — the brother you tried to avoid at family gatherings. She'd never had anything like that, but this must be what it felt like, the pain of losing something you'd never wanted but had come to count on anyway. Kevin's arrogant self-assurance had made her feel almost safe in a way she hadn't for years. His team was the winning team. His invulnerability was the safety net.

Or used to be.

And the dog. She couldn't even think about the dog or she'd be incapacitated. She wouldn't be able to make her brain work toward any kind of solution.

Again, the image of Kevin on her table flashed across the black insides of her eyelids. If only she could know that he was already dead, that would be something. If she could believe he wasn't in agony right now. Surely he was smart enough to have had a way out. Or was he so certain of himself that failure was never part of the plan?

She thought she knew enough about Deavers from his moves up to this point to be sure he wouldn't waste an opportunity if there were any way to find an edge in it.

She honestly wished the situation were reversed. If she'd been the one caught, she would have been able to take a quick, painless exit, leaving Deavers and Carston no information about the others. Whatever Kevin had done wrong, however he had failed, he was still the one best qualified to keep Daniel alive. And Val, too, for that matter. Val would have the easiest escape in the short term, but neither Carston nor Deavers seemed like the type to give up on a witness.

If Kevin were the one in Alex's place, trying to come up with a plan, what would he do?

Alex didn't know. He had resources she knew nothing about, resources she couldn't duplicate. But even then, running would have to be his only option. He might come back to try again later, but it wasn't like he could keep going after the potential vice president's kill team today. Now was the time to disappear and regroup.

Or, in her case, disappear and try to stay gone.

That obnoxious image of Kevin on the table wouldn't leave her head. The problem with being a professional interrogator was that she knew, in intimate detail, all the options for what they could be doing to him now. It was impossible not to mark the passing minutes, imagine how the questioning was progressing.

Daniel was quiet. The packing hadn't taken him long; they hadn't spread out here, gotten comfortable. They'd known from the beginning that they might have to leave at any moment, whether because of another disaster or simply wearing out their welcome with Val.

She could guess what he was feeling. He wouldn't want to believe things had gone so wrong. He wouldn't want to believe Kevin could be dead or that death was the best outcome for Kevin now. He would remember how Kevin had come through the roof in the middle of the night to save him and feel guilty that he couldn't do the same. More than guilty—helpless, weak, furious, culpable, cowardly...All the things she was already starting to feel.

But there was nothing she could *do* about Kevin. If she and Kevin switched places, there would be nothing Kevin could do, either. He wouldn't know where they were keeping her. The bad guys wouldn't choose a location that either Alex or Kevin would know about. They had thousands of options open to them. And if there *were* some way to know where their hideout was, they certainly wouldn't be careless about the security there. Kevin would be just as helpless as she was.

She shouldn't waste time thinking about the impossible. She needed to focus.

She had to operate under the assumption that Kevin was still alive, and the bad guys would soon know both she and Daniel were also alive, and nearby. They would know Val's name and address. They would know the make, model, color, and probably plate number of the only two cars they currently had access to. It was time to distance themselves from as many of those facts as possible.

Alex sat up slowly. "We'd better load the car and get moving."

Daniel was leaning against the wall beside the stack of bags with his arms crossed over his chest. Red rimmed his eyes. He nodded.

Val was nowhere to be seen as they ventured out into the great room, both weighed down with bags. The space seemed colder, bigger without the dog in it. Alex walked quickly to the front door.

They didn't speak in the elevator or as they walked to the car. Alex dropped her bags by the trunk and fished the keys out of her pocket.

A hushed scraping sound broke the short silence. It sounded like it was coming from close beside or maybe underneath the car.

I'm an idiot, Alex thought to herself as she dropped into a crouch next to the bag that she desperately hoped contained the guns but most likely held medical supplies. She knew how precarious their situation was, yet she'd walked into the parking garage unarmed.

She'd relied on Kevin to hold out longer. Stupid.

Daniel had the heavier bags. She could tell as soon as her hand rested on the bag in front of her that it contained first-aid gear — first aid she wouldn't have a use for now. At least she had her rings and belt. So she'd have to be close. No resisting at first. That was, if they didn't just shoot her immediately.

Not even a full second passed as she made these calculations. The first noise was quickly followed by another, a low whine that definitely came from under the car. The sound took her back to a different panicked moment, by a dark porch in Texas. It wasn't a human sound.

Alex crouched lower, leaned her head down so it was almost touching the asphalt floor of the garage. The dark shadow beneath the sedan pulled itself closer.

"Einstein?" She gasped.

"Einstein?" Daniel echoed behind her.

Alex crawled around to the side of the car to where Einstein was closest. "Einstein, are you okay? Come here, boy."

The dog crept toward her until he was free of the car. She ran her hands along his back and legs.

"Are you hurt?" she crooned. "It's okay. I'll take care of it."

His fur was matted and wet in a few places, but when she pulled her hands away to check, they weren't red—just dirty. His paws were cut up a bit and he panted like he was dehydrated or exhausted or both.

"Is he all right?" Daniel asked, close beside her.

"I think so. It looks like he's had a rough night, though."

"C'mere, boy," Daniel said, reaching for him. Einstein got to his feet, and then Daniel scooped him up. Einstein licked his face over and over again.

"Get him upstairs. I'll load this stuff in the car and follow."

"Okay." Daniel hesitated, then gulped a ragged breath. "It's all true."

"Yes." She popped the trunk without looking up.

She heard him turn and walk away. The sound of Einstein's panting faded.

It didn't take her long to get things squared for their departure. The garage stayed quiet and empty of people, as usual. Maybe this was Val's private floor of the parking garage. Maybe all these cars belonged to her. Alex wouldn't be completely shocked if that was the case.

Shouldn't Alex feel better that the dog was okay? Part of her must have been hoping that she was wrong, that she'd overreacted. That it was just a mistake.

When she walked back into the living room, Val was on the floor with the dog. Einstein was curled in her lap with his head on her shoulder, and Daniel knelt beside them.

Val looked up at her, still wearing the hard-doll face. "Now is when you get to say *I told you so*."

"Do you need help getting out of here?" Alex asked.

"I've had to disappear before. It's been a while, but that's not something you forget."

Alex nodded. "I'm sorry, Val."

"Me, too," Val responded. "Do you think...are you going to take the dog?"

Alex blinked in surprise. "Yes."

"Oh." Val pressed her face into Einstein's fur. "Gimme a minute." Her voice came out muffled.

"Sure," Alex said. They had a few hours. This location was the last thing Kevin would give up. He'd sent the dog back to warn them. He was fighting for them.

Besides, she still had one unlikely avenue of information, and she should probably check that out while she had access to a high-speed Internet connection. She went to the computer on the island.

Carston had been pretty tight-lipped up till now, but maybe he'd finally give something away. At the least, she should be able to construe the approximate time Kevin had been taken. Surely there would be a call to mark that. Maybe some travel. Carston was the expert on this front, not Deavers.

The tracker was an easy check. Carston's vehicle was at his office, as usual for a workday. He might have taken another car, though. She checked the sound feed—Carston was in the office. She scrolled back to listen to his conversations.

Here was something telling. Carston had been in the office for a while—usually he got in at six, but there was activity beginning around three thirty a.m. She wanted to kick herself for not checking backward on the recording before heading out this morning.

His first call was short. Just "I'm here" and "What's the status?" It wasn't hard to draw conclusions from that. Someone had woken Carston up with the news and he'd headed to the office. With zero traffic, it would only have taken him ten minutes to make the drive. Factor in throwing some clothes on, brushing teeth, et cetera, and the call could have come in anywhere from two thirty to three fifteen.

She looked at the clock on her computer, calculating how long they'd had Kevin. They would have had to subdue him in the begin-ning, then wait for him to be fully cognizant if they'd knocked him out. Then they'd have to decide on a course of action and bring in a specialist...

Was that Carston's second call? At three forty-five, Carston had dialed out.

"What's the play?...I don't like it...Fine, fine, if that's the best option...What?...You know how I feel about it...Like you say, it's *your* problem...I want updates."

He never said much, and the words had probably a thousand possible interpretations, but she couldn't help applying her own.

No, Kevin wasn't dead.

There was a long stretch of silence. Typing, pacing, breathing; that was all. No calls. It didn't sound like he left the room once. She could almost hear Carston's anxiety and it made her more anxious than she already was. Where were his updates? Was he getting them in e-mails?

Maybe they were lucky. Maybe the specialist had to be brought in from a distance. Maybe Kevin was just being held, anticipating. That was one face of the game, and she'd played the card before—let the subject wait, visualize, panic. Let him lose the fight in his own head before it began.

Not likely, in this case. They knew Daniel was alive. They'd sus-pect he had other help here in the city. They would not want to give Kevin's confederates time to escape.

The clock was ticking for Carston and Deavers, too. They'd made the call. They'd heard her pick up, then disconnect. She hadn't called back to see if it was an accidental dial. The phone was ditched. They would guess the partner was already running.

Like she *should* be.

Alex came out of her intense reverie, realizing for the first time that Daniel was perched on the stool beside her, watching the reac-tions play across her face. Val was leaning against the counter by the sink, Einstein at her feet, also watching.

"Just a little longer," she told them, scrubbing through the long silence in Carston's office. She didn't want to miss anything, but she couldn't afford to listen through the empty spaces in real time.

She paused when his voice began, and then carefully backed up. He'd dialed out again. The tone of his voice was one hundred eighty degrees from what it had been. It was such a shift it jarred her. She wondered if she'd somehow messed up the program and pulled up an earlier recording.

It was his kindly-grandpa voice.

"I didn't wake you, did I? How did you sleep? Yes, sorry, I have a small emergency on my plate. I had to come into the office...No, don't cancel the plans. Take Livvy to the zoo. It's going to get hotter tomorrow...You know I don't have a choice in these things, Erin. I am sorry I can't be there today, but there's nothing I can do about it...Livvy will have a great time without me. She can tell me all about it tonight at dinner. Take lots of pictures...I can't make any promises, but I hope to be free by dinnertime...That's not fair... Yes, I remember that I told you this would be a light week, but you know how the job works, honey. No guarantees."

A big sigh.

"I love you. Give Livvy a kiss for me. I'll let you know when I'm free."

She had chills when he hung up. Carston thought it would be over by *dinnertime?* Or was he just placating his daughter?

More silence, more typing. He must be getting the updates electronically. Kevin was in the thick of it, Alex was sure. Was he talking yet? She didn't have a clue.

There was nothing more until she caught up to the present time. She checked the tracker. Carston wasn't going anywhere. Deavers must be handling *his* problem.

Still listening through her earbuds, Alex leaned her forehead against her arms. Carston was typing again.

She pictured him at his desk, poker face in place as he sent out directions or questions. Would he be flushed with anxiety? Would tension sweat drip off his pale, bald head? No, she was sure he would be cool and precise, no more worked up than if he were typing out a request for paper supplies.

He'd know the right things to ask, even if Deavers didn't. He could manage the whole operation from his ergonomically correct desk chair. He'd see Kevin tortured to death, then run out for his dinner reservations without a second thought.

The sudden anger that flared up almost choked her.

What was happening now had nothing to do with national security or saving lives. Carston was running a private vendetta for a man who was quite possibly the kind of person who actually belonged on an interrogation table. Carston had crossed the line from arguably necessary black ops to purely criminal acts a long time ago, and it didn't seem to have affected him at all. Maybe it had always been this way. Maybe everything she'd done for him, every inhuman action she'd performed in the name of public safety, had been a scam.

Did he think he was so untouchable? That these hidden choices would never touch his public life? Did he think he was exempt? Did he not realize that he had liabilities, too?

There were worse things than being poisoned.

Alex's breath caught. Unexpectedly, a new avenue, something she'd never considered before, opened up inside her mind. It was a reach, and she knew it. There were a thousand things that would probably go wrong, a million ways to screw it up. It would be almost impossible, even with a year to plan every detail.

She felt Daniel's hand on her back. Through her earbuds, she heard him ask, "Alex?" in a worried tone.

She looked up slowly. She stared at Daniel, assessing. She examined Val the same way.

"Give me ten more minutes," she said, then she put her head down on her arms and concentrated once more.

CHAPTER 28

Alex spoke quickly as she laid out her plan, emphasizing the details she was sure of a little more than necessary. She tried to make it sound well thought out, like she was confident about it. Daniel seemed to be buying her version, listening intently, nodding at certain intervals, but Alex couldn't read Val at all. Her eyes were focused toward Alex, but almost like she was looking through Alex's face to the back of her head. Her expression was politely distant.

Alex talked through the conclusion, which wasn't nearly as fail-safe as she would have liked it to be, and she could tell she wasn't selling the outcome as well as she had the preliminaries. She looked down at Einstein's face resting on her leg instead of at the human faces, petting him more frequently as her discomfort grew. Trying to wrap it up on a positive note, she went on a little longer than she should have. She was still midsentence when Val interrupted.

"No," Val said.

"No?" Alex repeated. She said the word like a question, but she was already resigned.

"No. I won't do that. You're going to get killed. It's nice that you want to go back for Kevin, but be realistic, Alex. This isn't going to work."

"It might. They won't be expecting this. They won't be ready."

"It doesn't matter if they're ready or not. There will be more than enough of them to make up for it. So you get off a lucky shot and take one down. The guy next to him will get you."

"We don't even know how many people will be there."

"Exactly," Val said in a flat voice.

"Val, they won't pay attention to you. You'd just be an anonymous aide. These people see hundreds of assistants every day. You'll be invisible to them."

"I have never been invisible in my life."

"You know what I mean."

Val looked at her with a perfectly smooth face. "No."

Alex took a deep breath. She knew it wasn't fair to involve Val. She would have to make do.

"Okay," she said, wishing her voice sounded stronger. "I'll do it by myself, then."

"Alex, you can't," Daniel insisted.

She smiled weakly at him. "I can. I don't know how well I'll do, but I have to try, right?"

Daniel looked at her, torn. She could see that he wanted to argue. He wanted to say no, she didn't have to try, but that would mean walking away, leaving Kevin to die in agony. His was an untenable position. Now that there was any hope at all, how could he turn his back on it?

"Together, we'll be able to get the first part done," she told him. "It won't take more than the two of us."

"But the second you're separated from Carston, he'll double-cross you."

Alex shrugged. "I'll just have to sell my threat. If he thinks betraying me means the hostage dies, maybe he'll play it clean."

"You won't know how he's playing it. You won't be prepared."

"Val doesn't want to risk her life. Can you argue with her?"

Val watched Daniel with half-lidded eyes as he hesitated.

"No," he said. "But I can do her part. We'll trade. Val, you could do mine, right?"

Alex squeezed her eyes shut and then slowly opened them again. "Daniel, you know that won't work. Even if you weren't Kevin's twin brother, these are the people who put your face on the news."

"Val can fix me up, can't you, Val? Make me look different enough?"

Val's expression shifted abruptly, became more engaged. She examined his face closely.

"Actually...I think I could." She turned to Alex. "It's not like anyone is going to be looking for him there. Trust me, a lot more people would look at me—even as a nameless assistant. I think I can make him different enough for them not to give him a second glance."

"I'm not doubting your abilities, Val...but they're *twins*."

"Let me try?" she asked, an unfamiliar pleading tone coming into her voice. "I do want to help Kevin." When she said his name, Einstein looked up. "I just won't die to do it. Let me do something."

Einstein put his head on Alex's leg again.

"I guess I could let you try. But it's a waste of time and we don't have enough of that as is."

"It won't take me that long."

"And you'd be willing to do Daniel's part of the plan?"

"Sure, that's easy. No one will be shooting at me."

Alex winced.

What was she contemplating here? People would be shooting at Alex for certain, she'd already come to terms with that. But if Val could disguise Daniel enough, which Alex couldn't even *imagine,* then they might be shooting at Daniel, too. She reminded herself of all the reasons they had to go after Kevin. He had too much vital information. If he told the bad guys everything he knew about Alex and Daniel, the cars they were in, the places they had to go to ground, the way Alex operated, it wouldn't be that hard for the Agency to track them down. Val, too. Most likely, they'd all die anyway.

Die like cowards, running.

But the reasons were moot. If there was a way to save Kevin from what was happening to him, she had to do it. There was a bond there now that she hadn't even realized was forming. He was her friend. Her second liability. They were hurting him, even as she sat here considering. She had to stop it.

"Get to work, Val. This first part will take me two hours, if I'm lucky. When I get done, we'll reevaluate."

• • •

THOUGH SHE'D LIVED in DC for almost a decade, Alex had never visited the National Zoo. She'd always thought of it as something for children, but there seemed to be plenty of adults attending today unencumbered by offspring.

There were still many, many children—it seemed like thousands of them yapping in high-pitched voices and flailing around their parents' feet. All appeared to be under the age of five, so she guessed school wasn't done for the year yet, though it must be close.

She tried to think how long it had been since she'd first met with Carston, but she couldn't tally up the days in a way that made sense. Daniel had had around three weeks left of school then. More time had passed than that...hadn't it? Maybe Daniel's school finished earlier than average.

Alex's first stop was the rental line at Guest Services. It wasn't long. Most of the visitors would have arrived earlier, in the cool of the morning. Lunchtime was approaching, with the sun beating down almost directly overhead. Some people would leave then, avoid the high prices of the food inside the park. Head home for naptime.

She had quite a bit of information about Erin and Olivia, all gleaned from Erin's Facebook page. It was the same place that, months ago, she'd found the picture of Olivia that hung around her neck now.

Alex knew Olivia was three and a half. Still small enough that she would fit in a stroller. Alex knew what Erin looked like from nearly every angle and had a good idea of the kinds of clothes she wore. She knew Erin was a late riser and probably wouldn't have gotten to the zoo right as it opened. She knew Olivia was most excited about seeing the pandas.

Alex paid nine dollars cash for a single stroller, then put her backpack in it and headed into the park. She craned her neck around, searching. It made sense that she would be looking for someone—maybe her sister and nephews, or her husband and their child. There were lots of other patrons looking for their parties. She didn't stand out.

Erin and Livvy would be past the pandas by now, probably thinking about lunch. She analyzed the map she'd gotten with the stroller. She'd try across from the apes first, then near the reptiles.

She walked fast, ignoring the turnoffs and viewing areas.

Erin had the fair skin of a redhead, like her father. She'd posted pictures of herself sunburned and moaned about freckles. Erin would be in a hat and probably light long sleeves. Her hair was bright and hung halfway down her back. It would catch the eye.

Alex scanned the crowds as she moved quickly through them, looking for a woman with a child, ruling out those with friends and spouses and multiple children. For a while, she followed a woman with her hair rolled up under a wide-brimmed straw hat pushing a single stroller, but then the child climbed out to walk with her—it was a boy.

A quick loop around the big cats, and then down toward the petting zoo. All the while, she was conscious of how she looked— map in hand, vigilantly searching for her companions. She wore a straw hat of her own over the dark blond wig and wide-framed sun-glasses. She had on a plain T-shirt, boyfriend jeans, and the sport-shoe/ballet-flat hybrids that would let her run if she had to. Nothing about her would be particularly memorable.

Several shades of red hair had grabbed her attention throughout the course of her search, but many of them had been clearly unnatural. Others had been on women too old to be Erin, or too young, or holding extra children. Now she spotted one headed along the trail toward the Amazon exhibit—a long braid of golden-red hair swinging from beneath a white bucket hat. The woman was pushing a single stroller; it looked exactly like Alex's, tan molded plastic with a dark green shade. She wore a sleeveless tank, and her arms were thick with freckles. Alex walked quickly after her.

The woman wasn't moving fast; it didn't take long for Alex to pass her. Alex kept her head down and glanced into the stroller as she walked alongside it.

The little girl looked right. Her face was turned away, but the fluffy blond hair seemed the same. Her size fit the profile.

Alex kept walking and beat the mother and daughter to the exhibit. She parked her stroller in the designated space beside the bathrooms, inconspicuously wiping the handle with the hem of her shirt before she removed her backpack and shrugged into it. Now that she was fairly certain the woman was Erin and that Erin had her own stroller, she didn't need this one.

She located the woman and child dawdling along the trail. A larger group had caught up to them and flowed around them from both sides. Alex could see the woman's face clearly now—it was definitely Carston's daughter. Erin had paused to offer Olivia a sippy cup.

The path was getting more crowded. It was hot, and the wig was making her head itch and sweat. The straw hat wasn't helping.

Alex focused on an empty bench about ten feet ahead of the duo. There was another large crowd behind the first. If she timed it right, she could intercept Erin at the bench while the second crowd was passing.

Alex moved purposefully back the way she'd just come, watching through her dark glasses to see if anyone was paying attention to her. The first group—a loud extended family, it looked like, with several toddlers, multiple parents, and one older woman in a wheelchair—enveloped her for a moment. She dodged through them and then slowed a bit.

The second crowd was all adults—foreign tourists on a day trip, she guessed, many of them wearing fanny packs—and they reached Erin as she was almost to the bench. Alex moved against the flow until she was just ahead of her quarry. As Erin passed a foot away from the bench, Alex turned, twisting around an older man, and pretended to stumble. She reached out and grabbed Erin's hand on the stroller handle. Her palm mashed the pouch of clear fluid and forced it empty with one strong squeeze.

"Hey!" Erin said, turning.

Alex ducked back, twisting partially behind the closest guest. Erin came face to face with the bald septuagenarian.

"Excuse me," he said hesitantly to both of them, not sure how he'd become entangled. He pulled free of Alex and stepped around Erin and the stroller.

Alex watched as Erin blinked once, then again. Her eyelids seemed to get stuck on the second blink. Alex jumped forward and grabbed Erin around the waist as she started to crumple, then jerked her toward the bench so that they fell heavily onto it together. Alex jammed her elbow against the wooden back; it would leave a bruise, but one she could easily cover. Erin was taller and weighed more than Alex, so Alex wasn't able to keep them from slumping awkwardly. Alex loosed a slightly manic laugh—hopefully anyone watching would think they were playing around.

The little girl was singing to herself inside the stroller. She hadn't seemed to notice that she'd stopped moving. Alex extricated herself from the mother and pulled the stroller closer, angling it so that Olivia was facing away from Erin.

Erin lolled on the bench, her head falling onto her right shoulder and her mouth hanging open.

A third conglomeration of visitors moved past them. No one stopped. Alex was operating quickly, so she couldn't keep close tabs on any reaction, but no one had raised an alarm yet.

She pulled the bucket hat lower over Erin's face, shading her lifeless expression. Out of the side pocket of her backpack, Alex drew the little perfume bottle. She reached around the edge of the stroller's shade and pressed the nozzle down for two seconds. The singing ceased, and then Alex felt the light thud through the plastic frame of the stroller as the child fell back against the seat.

Moving as casually as she could, Alex patted Erin's shoulder, then stood up and stretched.

"I'll get her some lunch, you go ahead and rest," Alex said, smoothing the wig under her hat in case her tumble had disarranged it. She glanced around, eyes hidden behind her glasses. No one seemed to be focused on the little tableau she'd created. She grasped the stroller's handle and started moving back toward the parking lot. At first she kept the pace easy. She looked toward the animal cages like the others were doing. As she got farther from the bench, she began moving faster. A mother with an afternoon appointment.

Outside the bathroom at the visitors' center, she parked the stroller and pulled Olivia into her arms. The child had to weigh over thirty pounds and felt heavier because her body was slack. Alex tried to arrange the unconscious child into the same position she'd seen other parents use — straddling one hip, legs on either side, head cradled on the shoulder. It didn't feel like she'd gotten it right, but she had to move anyway. She gritted her teeth and walked as quickly as she could through the gate. She wished she'd been able to park closer, but eventually, with sweat soaking her T-shirt, she reached the car.

Alex hadn't had time to get a car seat. She glanced around surreptitiously to see if anyone was watching, but the area of the parking lot she was in was mostly full, and the people arriving now were far away. The early quitters had already left; she was alone.

She laid the child on the backseat and wrapped a seat belt around her waist. Then she covered Olivia with a blanket to conceal her.

Alex straightened up and checked for witnesses again. No one was nearby; no one was watching her. She pulled a syringe from the inside pocket of her pack and leaned in to administer the drug to the sleeping child. She'd calculated the dose for someone weighting thirty to forty pounds. It should keep Olivia under for about two hours.

Alex turned the car on and cranked up the air-conditioning. She started breathing again for what felt like the first time since she'd entered the zoo.

Phase one was successful. Erin would wake up in forty-five minutes, more or less. Alex was sure that paramedics would be attending to her by then. When she woke, she'd sound the alarm about her missing daughter. The zoo would be searched first, then the police would be brought in. Alex had to be in position when Erin realized her daughter had been taken, that she'd not merely wandered off while her mother was having some sort of seizure. Alex was 85 percent sure which call Erin would make first.

She really hoped that Val would be done working her magic by the time she arrived at the new hiding place so Alex would know exactly which plan was moving forward—not because she'd made up her mind as to which outcome she wanted most. Going in alone...that was suicide. But taking Daniel...was that murder-suicide?

Maybe Val's confidence in herself was misplaced. Maybe Daniel would just look like himself in a wig.

Alex could do it alone. She'd just make it very clear what would happen to Olivia if she, Alex, didn't live through the night. That would keep Carston in line, wouldn't it?

She didn't want to think about the things Carston could set in motion. The traps he could lay so that once he had Olivia back, Alex would be his.

Alex called Val as she approached the new building, and when she pulled into the underground garage, Val was waiting by a set of elevators with a wheeled cart—it looked like something a hotel visitor would receive room service on. The garage was otherwise empty of other people. Alex couldn't spot any cameras, but she kept her body between the open back car door and the best view inside. Neither Val nor Alex spoke. Alex shifted the sleeping child to the bottom shelf of the cart, then rearranged the blanket around her so her shape was obscured.

This elevator was more normal than the one that led to Val's penthouse—just a silver box, as in most of the buildings where Alex had lived. It made her nervous that the box would suddenly slow and the doors would open, exposing them. Val must have felt similarly. She kept her hand on the button for the sixteenth floor, as if holding it down would guarantee them express service.

While the elevator climbed, Alex noticed Val's expression for the first time. It was . . . a little too stimulated. Alex hoped Val wasn't heading into some kind of power-mad version of a sugar rush.

The elevator doors opened to an empty hallway. It was a nice building, with fancy moldings and marble floors, but it looked pedestrian after Val's other place.

Val pushed the cart down the little hall, motioning for Alex to go ahead.

"Number sixteen-oh-nine, on the end. It's not locked," she said, and the eager tone of her voice made Alex wary again. Though maybe if Val got hyped up enough, she'd change her mind and come with Alex for the main event.

Alex walked into the apartment in a hurry—there was a lot to set up and she needed to be fast. She barely took in the routine living room–kitchen spread, the fabric-shrouded windows, or the beige color scheme. She noted an open door on the far wall, revealing a brightly lit room with a queen bed, and headed for it. She could see some of her duffel bags leaning against the flowered bedspread.

She was halfway to the door before she really absorbed the whole space, and then her eyes focused on the man standing in the dimly lit kitchen.

Even though she'd been expecting *something,* it didn't stop her from spooking. She jumped a step back, her thumbs automatically going to the little hatches of her poisoned rings.

"Well?" he asked.

The tall man in the cheap black suit waited, fighting a smile.

"Told ya," Val said from behind her, and Alex could hear the smug grin on her face without looking.

The man looked Nordic with his fair skin and pale, white-blond hair. His blond beard was neatly trimmed and reminded her of a college professor's. His eyebrows were so pale against his forehead they were nearly invisible, completely changing the look of his eyes and his forehead. The hair around the edges of his head was straight, short, and neatly combed. The top of his head was pale, shiny, and totally bald. It changed the perceived shape of his head and made him look ten years older. He wore thin silver glasses, and his cheeks were unexpectedly round. His most striking features were his bright, icy-blue eyes, framed by nearly white lashes.

"You look like a Bond villain," Alex blurted out.

"Is that good?" Daniel asked, his voice not quite right — it was clipped, somehow, a little slurred.

Alex felt her heart sink as she more closely examined the transformation. If she hadn't been looking specifically for a disguised version of Daniel, she would have walked right past this man on the street. Even if she had been looking for Daniel, only his height would have made this man a suspect. As the despair settled sickeningly into her stomach, Alex knew she'd really been counting on Val's failing.

"Val did a good job," Alex said, and then she started moving again. "Let's get Olivia set up."

Einstein was sniffing around the blanket-covered child. He whimpered quietly, ill at ease.

"Is it good *enough?*" Daniel persisted while pulling the child out from under the cart and cradling her against his chest.

"Let me think about it while I do this," Alex hedged.

Daniel laid Olivia on the flowered coverlet, smoothing the sweaty fluffs of hair back from her forehead. It took Alex only a few seconds to get the IV bags hanging. One clear, one white and opaque, and then a very small bag with a dark green fluid inside. She quickly placed the IV catheter using the smallest needle she had and then started the fluids.

"Back out of the way," she told Daniel.

Alex pulled up the camera on a phone Val had given her—left behind by a *friend*, Val said—and snapped a few pictures of Olivia sleeping. She flipped through them and found one that she decided would do.

"This is my least favorite part of the plan," Daniel muttered.

She glanced up and saw his pained expression. It looked strange on his new face.

"Let's hope Carston feels similarly."

His frown deepened. Alex took his hand and pulled him from the room. The way he was holding his mouth made the round shape of his cheeks more prominent.

"What did she do to your face?" Alex asked.

Daniel stuck two fingers in his mouth and pulled out a little piece of plastic. "These make it a little hard to talk." With a sigh, he replaced the plastic, and his cheek rounded out again.

Val waited for them in the big living room, eyes still lit up with her success.

"That baby's not going to wake up, right?" she asked.

"Right."

"Good. I wouldn't know what to do with a kid. Now, what do you think? Totally altered, yes?"

Alex looked at Daniel again, and her shoulders slumped. He was thicker around the middle, too; she hadn't noticed that before. It all looked so real.

"You don't think it's good enough, do you?" Daniel asked.

"It's good enough," Val answered for her. "And she knows it. That's why she looks so glum. She'd much rather risk my life than yours."

Daniel looked at Alex, waiting for her answer.

"Val's right. Except for the part about risking her life. I don't want to risk anyone's."

Val snorted.

Daniel grabbed Alex's hand and pulled her against his chest. "It's going to be fine," he murmured. "We can do this together. Your plans always work. I will follow your instructions to the letter, and we'll make it through. I promise."

Alex squeezed her eyes tight, trying to force the tears back into their ducts.

"I don't know, Daniel. What am I doing?"

He kissed the top of her head.

"Cut it out," Val interrupted. "You two are making me jealous, and that's never a safe thing to do."

Alex opened her eyes and pulled away, brushing at Daniel's suit to make sure she hadn't left any makeup on it.

"I see you had time to get the things I needed from the Batcave. This toolbox is perfect."

"More than perfect—check the fifth drawer down. I packed the rest how you asked," Daniel told her. "Do you want to go through it before I put it in the car?"

"That's a good idea."

The silver toolbox—one of the props from Kevin's stash, she assumed—had wheels and a pull-up handle, like a suitcase, but unlike a suitcase, many locking drawers that pulled forward out of its face. She went swiftly through the top drawers, identifying the location of the different drugs by the color rings on the syringes. The syringes were stacked in the rubber trays she usually stored them in. The next drawer down had a variety of scalpels and razor blades. She wouldn't need so many; the point was to make the

drawer look full. Saline bags and tubing were next, along with needles and catheters in different sizes. The next compartment was
deeper. It held her pressurized canisters and several random chemicals from Kevin's stores.

The second-to-last drawer was key. It held another tray of
syringes—these empty—and seemed shallower than the last. She
traced the edges of the bottom of the drawer—of course Kevin
would have something like this. She could fit her fingernails around
and lift up the false bottom. She peeked at what was underneath.

"Let's hope Carston's up for some Oscar-level acting," she murmured to herself.

She went through the final, deepest drawer, where Daniel had
stowed her more ostentatious props—the blowtorch, the wire snips,
the pliers, along with several arbitrary tools Daniel had added from
the items available in Kevin's hoard.

There was one more useful thing she needed—just a tiny config-
uration of wires that she'd picked up the first time they'd visited the
local Batcave. She pulled it from her backpack now and hid it in the
third tray of the first drawer, under a syringe. She would want easy
access to that one.

Alex straightened. "Perfect. Thank you."

"You," Val said, pointing to Daniel. "Get to the rendezvous
point. You," she continued, moving her index finger toward Alex's
face. "Let's fix you up and get going. The clock is ticking." She
motioned to a set of double doors across the room.

"I'll be there in thirty seconds," Alex promised.

Val rolled her eyes. "Fine, have your little good-bye scene." She
turned and walked through the doors.

"Alex—" Daniel began.

"Wait."

She took his hand again and led him out the front door, pulling
the toolbox with her free hand. He had the big first-aid bag slung
over his shoulder. Einstein tried to follow and then whined when
she shut the door on him.

They walked down the quiet hall to the elevator. Alex pressed the button. When the doors slid apart, Daniel walked in and she followed, putting one foot across the breach to hold it open. She dropped the toolbox's handle and reached up to hold Daniel's face between her hands.

"Listen to me," she said quietly. "In the glove compartment of the sedan there's a manila envelope. There are two sets of IDs — passports, driver's licenses, and a bunch of cash."

"I don't look that much like Kevin now."

"I know, but people age, lose hair. You can toss the glasses, shave, dye your hair back to brown. And if things go badly, you'll need to do all of that. Then get to the nearest airport. Get on any plane that's leaving North America, okay?"

"I won't leave you behind."

"When I say *go badly,* I mean that I won't be around for you to wait for."

He stared at her with that odd new version of his troubled face.

"Okay?" she repeated insistently.

He hesitated, then nodded.

"Good," she said, trying to sound like that discussion was closed. She wasn't feeling the conviction behind his nod, but there wasn't time to argue about it.

"You stay quiet tonight," she instructed. "Don't speak to anyone unless you have to. Think like an underling. You're just there to drive the car and carry the bags, okay? This is just a paycheck. None of what's happening means anything to you. No matter *what* you see, it doesn't affect you. You have no emotional response. You got that?"

He nodded seriously. "Yes."

"If things get dicey, it will make sense for you to run. This isn't your problem."

"Right," he agreed, but his answer was less decided this time.

"Here." She yanked the gold ring from her finger. It was the bigger of the two. She removed his arms from around her and tried it on all his fingers. As with Kevin, it fit only on his pinkie. At least she was able to get it all the way down over his knuckles. Hopefully it wouldn't look too out of character.

"Be *extremely* careful with this," she told him. "Slide this little hatch out of the way if you need to use it. Whatever you do, don't touch the barb. If you're not in the act of using it, keep it closed. But if you're trying to get out, and someone's in your way, all you have to do is put that barb in contact with his skin."

"I got it."

Alex looked into the startling blue eyes, searching for Daniel behind the strangeness of his oddly simple disguise. She was out of instructions, and the feelings she wanted to share with him didn't seem to have corresponding words.

"I . . . I don't know how to go back to my old life," she said, trying to explain. "I don't know how to do that anymore, without you. Having you as my liability is the best thing that ever happened to me."

He smiled just a little bit, though it didn't reach his eyes. "I love you, too," he whispered.

She tried to smile back.

Daniel put his hands on her shoulders and kissed her for one lingering second. Then he smiled at her again, unfamiliar and familiar at the same time. She took a step away from him.

"I told you I'd be there when you needed backup," he said.

The elevator doors closed.

CHAPTER 29

There was no wig involved this time, just a quick trim that left her real hair looking like it had an actual style. A pixie cut; that's what people called it, she thought. The color was medium blond now, and it lightened up her complexion. It was also flattering to her face shape the way her real hair hadn't been since...she couldn't remember the last time her hair had been attractive.

"Seriously," Alex said. "Did you go to cosmetology school?"

Val applied mascara with a hand as steady as a surgeon's. "No. I never liked school that much. It always seemed a little bit like prison to me—I wasn't going to sign up for extra. I just liked playing with my appearance, having a face for every mood. I practice a lot."

"I think you've got a real aptitude. If being the most beautiful woman on the planet ever gets dull, you could open a salon."

Val flashed her brilliant teeth. "I never thought I would want an actual woman friend. It's more fun than I imagined."

"Ditto. Just curious, and you don't have to answer, but is Val for Valerie?"

"Valentine. Or Valentina. It changes, depending on mood and circumstance."

"Ah," Alex said. "That fits better."

"It's very *me*," Val told her. "It's not the name I was born with, of course."

"Whose is?" Alex murmured.

Val nodded. "It's only logical. My parents didn't even *know* me when they picked a name out. Of course it didn't fit."

"I never really thought of it that way, but it does make sense. My mother picked a name for a much more . . . feminine kind of girl."

"My parents evidently assumed I would be very boring. I cleared that misconception up pretty quickly."

Alex chuckled once. As was so often true lately, the laugh carried with it the barely disguised sound of panic. It was nice to talk like she imagined normal people did, to try to forget that this might be the last friendly, mundane conversation she would ever have, but she couldn't keep her thoughts focused on pleasantries.

Val patted her head. "It's going to be okay."

"You don't have to pretend to have faith in the plan. That's only for us suckers who are putting ourselves into the line of fire."

"It's not a bad plan," Val assured her. "I'm just not a risk taker. I never have been." She shrugged. "If I were brave, I would do it."

"It wasn't fair for me to ask you."

"No, it was. I do . . . care about Kevin. Part of me just can't believe that what you say is happening to him is actually happening. He's always seemed so invulnerable. That's what pulls me to him. Like I said, I'm not brave, so I'm fascinated with people who are. The other part of me . . ."

Val leaned back for a moment, the little brush with lip gloss on it trembling suddenly. Her face was still perfect, but suddenly it was the doll's face again. Exquisite, but empty.

"Val, are you okay?"

Val blinked and her face came back to life. "Yes."

"You'll leave here, after your part, right?"

"Absolutely. I have lots of friends who can protect me. Maybe I'll go visit Zhang. I'm sure he's still stuffy, but he has an amazing place in Beijing."

"Beijing sounds lovely," Alex half sighed. If she lived through tonight, she'd do whatever she had to in order to get her hands on a passport. She'd blow the rest of her savings — all of Kevin's drug money. To be out of the easy reach of the American government sounded like a practical version of heaven.

"If . . ." *Though when was probably more appropriate,* Alex thought to herself. "If you don't hear from any of us by sunrise, go see Zhang. If I can, I'll call you from a pay phone."

Val smiled a little. "You have my number." Her lips pursed. "You know, there's a guy . . . I might be able to get my hands on a service-dog vest."

Alex stared at her for a moment, then felt her face start to crumple. With the new plan, the suicidal plan, there was really no way for Alex to keep Einstein safe.

"That's a brilliant idea. That makes me feel better." Her positive words didn't match her expression.

Val reached out with one bare foot and stroked it along Einstein's back. His tail thumped once against the marble floor, but without much enthusiasm.

"Okay," Val said in a brighter voice. "You're done. I'll throw on my things, and we're off."

While Val disappeared into the closet, Alex checked out her face. Val had done another excellent job. Alex looked pretty, but not flashy. The hair was obviously hers, which was important; she would definitely be scrutinized tonight, and a wig would be the most obvious tell. She looked more or less credible for the role she'd chosen. Of course, she'd feel more comfortable with no makeup at all — in her experience, that was the way people in this specific role presented themselves, without fuss or vanity. But that was just baggage from her past.

She knelt down on the floor beside Einstein. He looked up at her with eyes that were unmistakably pleading. She stroked his muzzle, then rubbed his ears.

"I'll do everything I can," she promised. "I won't come back without him. If I screw this up, Val will take care of you. It will be okay."

Einstein's eyes didn't change. They accepted no excuses or consolation prizes. They just begged.

"I'll *try*," she vowed. She laid her forehead against his ear for just a moment. Then, with a sigh, she got to her feet. Einstein put his head on his paws and huffed out his own sigh.

"Val?" Alex called.

"Two seconds," Val called back. Her voice sounded far away, like she was at the other end of a football field. This bathroom was nice — like the bathroom in a fancy hotel suite — but not insane like Val's other place. Maybe the excess here was saved for the closet.

She heard Val shut the closet door and glanced up; she felt a brief jolt of shock at the change, then nodded.

"That looks about right," she approved.

"Thanks," Val replied. "Some parts of being a spy I could handle."

The outfit Val was wearing was not inconspicuous. She had on a long flowy dress kind of thing that covered her from chin to wrist to floor, similar to a sari, but with more coverage; it had scarf-like pieces that cascaded around her, obscuring the shape of her body. It looked like something straight off an avant-garde runway, and probably was. It was memorable. But from behind, all you could see about her body was that she was tall. She wore a thick, dark wig with corkscrew curls that jutted out wildly in every direction. It, too, called attention at the same time that it obscured the shape of her head and covered parts of her face. With the wide-framed black sunglasses she held in her hand, she would be well hidden.

"Shall we?" Val asked.

Alex took a deep breath and nodded.

. . .

ALEX PARKED VAL'S tacky green Jaguar at a meter on the hill overlooking a large, dingy-gray concrete office block. Val had insisted on the green car — a gift from another admirer, naturally. It was the one, she said, that she wouldn't miss if she had to submerge it in a lake.

From this angle, Alex could see the entrance to the underground parking garage. It was kind of sad, actually, that Carston had never moved to a better office. Maybe he liked the depressing surroundings. Maybe it seemed appropriate to the job and he liked things to conform. Making things easier for Alex had probably not been on his agenda, but it was nice it had worked out this way.

She and Val sat in the Jag for more than an hour, Val getting out to feed the meter once. They didn't talk; Alex's mind was miles away, working overtime to think through the flaws in her plan and try to fix them insofar as that was possible. There was so much that had to be left up to chance; she hated chance.

Alex imagined Val's mind was in Beijing. It was a good place to run to. Val might even be safe there. Alex wished she and Daniel were getting on a plane to Beijing right now.

Daniel probably wasn't enjoying the wait any more than she was. He'd be at the park now, nothing to fill his time until Alex arrived, no way to know what was happening. At least she had Val to sit with, even if neither of them was very good company at the moment.

Finally there was movement below, and she sat up straighter. The white-and-red-striped arm at the mouth of the garage was rising to let someone out. The last two alarms had both been delivery trucks, but this time a dark sedan was pulling out of the garage. Alex started the engine and rolled out onto the street. Someone honked behind her, but she didn't spare him a glance. She didn't take her eyes off the car. From this distance, it appeared to match Carston's black BMW. It was only just after four o'clock now, not quite time for government employees to be heading out.

Here was the first big chance. Once Erin Carston-Boyd was sure her daughter was missing, she would have called her father in a panic. Right? She knew he had some kind of important government job. She would consider him powerful and capable. She wouldn't rely on just the police with her daughter kidnapped. Should it have taken this long? When Alex had last been able to check, no call had come and Carston was still in his office. Managing Kevin's interrogation, no doubt.

She thought he would head to his daughter's side. It seemed the only response. But what if Carston had other options? What if he sent a special ops team instead? Was he that cold? If he had to be... probably yes.

But surely Deavers could manage the interrogation by himself for a few hours. Right?

Alex's driving was much more offensive than defensive as she weaved her way forward, refusing to stop for even the pinkest of yellow lights. She knew the two best routes from Carston's office to the zoo, where she assumed Erin's call had come from. Would the terrified mother leave the last place she'd seen her daughter before she was positive the child wasn't hiding somewhere in the foliage? If the call came from a police station, of which there were several possible options, Carston could take a number of different routes.

So many things left to chance.

The BMW was heading down the correct street, the one she would have chosen as the quickest route to the zoo. He was driving a little erratically as well. She carefully moved up from behind two other cars. She didn't want to spook him.

It was the right car. The plates matched. It looked like the back of Carston's mostly bald head.

Alex watched for eyes in the rearview mirror, but he seemed to be focused on the road. She maneuvered into the parallel lane.

She supposed she should feel better that this part was going according to plan. But it felt like someone was drilling a wide hole into the bottom of her stomach; she thought she might gag as she pulled alongside his car. Because if this part worked, that meant she had to go forward with the rest of the plan.

The light turned yellow ahead. Cars streamed through, but Carston was slowing. He knew he was too far back to make it. The car in front of him braked, too. Alex could have pulled up to the line in her lane—the car in front of her had turned right. Instead, she stopped directly beside Carston.

She waved, her face pointed straight toward his profile. The motion was deliberately large, meant to catch his peripheral vision.

Carston glanced over automatically at the movement, his mind clearly far away, worry making a crinkled mess of his forehead. It took him a second to realize what he was seeing. In that instant of shock, before he could smash down the accelerator, pull a gun, or dial a number, she held up the phone in her hand. She had the image zoomed in on the girl's sleeping face.

He locked down his expression as the facts began falling into place.

Quickly, she hopped out of her car and reached for the passenger door of his. She didn't look back to watch Val slide over into the driver's seat, but she heard the door close behind her. Alex waited with her fingers on the BMW's passenger-door handle until she heard the locks click open. She climbed in next to him. The whole wordless exchange had taken less than two seconds. The cars behind them might be curious, but they would probably forget the transfer by the next light.

"Turn left," she told Carston as Val went right and headed east. The Jag disappeared around the corner.

Carston was quick to recover. He put on his blinker and pulled across the left lane, nearly hitting the van headed through the light. Alex took his phone out of the cup holder, powered it down, and shoved it in her pocket.

"What do you want?" he asked. His voice sounded calm, but she could hear the strain in his lack of inflection.

"I need your help."

He took a moment to digest that.

"Turn right at the next corner."

He complied carefully. "Who is your partner?"

"Someone for hire. Not your concern."

"I really believed you were dead this time."

Alex didn't respond.

"What have you done to Livvy?"

"Nothing permanent. Yet."

"She's only three." His voice quavered uncharacteristically.

She turned to give him an incredulous look, which was wasted, as he never glanced away from the road in front of them. "Really? You expect me to care about civilians at this point?"

"She's done nothing to you."

"What did three innocent people in Texas do to you, Carston? Never mind," she said when he opened his mouth to answer. "That was obviously rhetorical."

"What do you want from me?"

"Kevin Beach."

There was another long pause as he rearranged things in his mind.

"You're going to turn left at the next block," she instructed.

"*How* did you . . ." He shook his head. "I don't have him. The CIA does."

"I know who has him. And I know Deavers is following your direction in his interrogation," she bluffed. "Your specialist is the one leading the case. I'm sure you know where they're working on him."

He stared stone-faced through the windshield.

"I don't understand what is happening," he muttered.

"Let's talk about what you do understand, then," Alex said in a bleak voice. "Of course you remember a little concoction Barnaby and I created for you called *Deadline*."

His pasty skin started to mottle, blotches of puce blooming on his cheeks and neck. She held her phone out and his eyes flickered to it automatically. The photo was back to its original size now, and the

IV hooked into his granddaughter's arm was conspicuously in the foreground. There was a saline bag, the nutrition bag, and a smaller, dark green bag attached underneath it.

He stared at the photo for one long second, then his eyes were back on the road.

"How long?" he asked through his teeth.

"I was generous. Twelve hours. One hour has passed. This operation shouldn't take more than four, at most. Then Livvy is delivered safely back to her mother, no worse for wear."

"And I'm dead?"

"I'll be honest, the odds aren't good that either of us makes it through unscathed. A lot is riding on your acting abilities, Carston. Lucky for you, we both know how convincing you can be."

"What happens if, through no fault of mine, you die?"

"Bad luck for Livvy. And her mother, for that matter. Things have been set in motion. If you care about your family, you'll do your very, very best to get me out alive."

"You could be bluffing. You were never this cold-blooded."

"Policies change. People change. Shall I share a secret?"

She gave him a moment to respond, but he just stared straight ahead with his jaw locked.

"Kevin Beach wasn't in Texas when Deavers sent the kill squad. *I* was." She let those two words hang in the air for a moment before she went on. Carston wasn't the only one with acting abilities. "I'm not the person you used to know, Carston. You'd be surprised at the things I'm capable of now. Take the next right."

"I don't know what you hope to accomplish here."

"Let's get down to it," Alex said. "Where is Kevin?"

Carston didn't hesitate. "He's in a facility west of the city. It used to be a CIA interrogation suite, but they haven't used it in years. Officially, it's abandoned."

"The address?"

He listed it from memory without a pause.

"What kind of security?"

He glanced over, his eyes studying her for a second before he responded. "I don't have that information. But knowing Deavers, it's more than is necessary. He'll go overboard. He's terrified of Kevin Beach. That's why he came up with the whole charade with the brother. *No risk,* that's what he called it." Carston chuckled once. It was a bitter sound, in no way amused.

"Does he know my face?"

Carston's eyes jerked to her in surprise. "You're going in?"

"Will he recognize me?" she demanded. "How much of my file did he see? Did you show him the footage from the Metro?"

Carston pursed his lips. "We agreed from the beginning to keep our... situations separate. It was need-to-know. Years ago, he would have had access to your old recruitment file, your write-ups from a few interrogations. He might still have those, but nothing more current. The only picture in that old file was from your mother's funeral. You were very young, your hair was longer and darker..." He paused, seeming lost in thought. "Deavers isn't a detail guy. I doubt he'd be able to link you to the picture. You don't look that much like nineteen-year-old Juliana Fortis anymore."

She hoped he was right. "It's more than my life on the line," she reminded him.

"I'm aware. And... that much is a bet I'd take. But I don't know what you think you're going to do when you get inside."

"*We,* Carston, we. And, probably, we go down in a hail of bullets."

"And Livvy pays? That's not acceptable," he growled.

"Then give me more to work with."

He took a deep breath, and she glanced over at him. He looked exhausted.

"How about this," she suggested. She was going on intuition. She'd listened to Carston's aggravation with that one particular *him* in the phone calls, and she thought she could guess who it was. After all, it was Deavers's plan that had failed so spectacularly, over and over. "Would it be accurate to characterize you as unhappy with Deavers's management of this joint operation?"

He grunted.

"Have you and Deavers disagreed on how to proceed?"

"You could say that."

"Does he think that you trust him to handle the interrogation of Kevin Beach?"

"No, at this point, I would say he does not believe that I trust him to zip up his own fly correctly."

"Tell me about your interrogation specialist."

Carston made a sour face. "Not mine. He's Deavers's lackey, and he's an imbecile. I told Deavers that someone like Beach was going to die before he talked to an ordinary interrogator. You can rest easy, if that's your concern. They won't break him. Beach hasn't said anything about you, except that he killed you. I don't think they even followed up on that. To be fair, I believed it, too."

She was surprised. "So you never replaced me?"

Carston shook his head. "I've tried. I wasn't lying about that in the beginning—you remember? 'True talent is a limited commodity.'" He quoted himself and sighed. "Deavers has had a stranglehold on the department for a long time now, ever since I 'lost a dangerous asset.' The CIA has blocked my recruitment process and shut down all but the lab. The things we're producing now could be created by any halfway decent pharmacist." He shook his head. "They act as if they aren't the reason why you're dangerous in the first place."

"You still pretend you weren't part of that decision?"

"If I had been, I'm being punished for it now." Carston stared morosely through the windshield.

"Would Deavers be shocked to learn that you were developing talent on the side?"

Carston was always quick. He pursed his lips and nodded as he talked it through. "For about half a second, then he'll just be angry.

He's one hundred percent on board with the current program, but he knows my doubts have been increasing. No, he won't be that surprised."

"You don't like how Pace gets things done? He seems like a pragmatic person, I thought you'd get along."

"So you did put it together. I thought you might. But I'll bet you never would have if Pace hadn't overreacted in the first place. Machiavellianism doesn't bother me—stupidity does. Mistakes happen, but Pace has a penchant for compounding one error with a second that's worse. And then a third. He's put us all in this mess."

"What are you saying, Carston? That we're on the same side? Everybody makes mistakes, like you said, but you shouldn't rely on my gullibility again."

"I don't expect you to believe me, but it is what it is. I have nothing to gain from the current agenda. If Pace succeeds, Deavers's star will rise. He'll end up director of the CIA. My life's work is already being dismantled. We're more on the same side than you know."

"If it makes you happy to say so. It doesn't change the plan."

"We go in together," he mused. "You're my secret protégée. I insist that you take over for Deavers's butcher. It can work, up to that point. I don't know what you think happens then."

She tried to hide her flinch when Carston said the word *butcher*. So much depended on how much was left of Kevin.

"We'll see," she said, working to keep her voice smooth.

"No, don't tell me. That's smart. Just as long as you have a plan." She didn't answer. Her plan wasn't strong enough.

"Just out of curiosity," she asked, trying to distract Carston from her reaction. "When did Dominic Haugen die?"

"Two weeks after the lab in Jammu was destroyed."

She nodded. Then it was as she'd suspected. Barnaby had seen something and begun his preparations.

"I have an idea," Carston volunteered.

"This should be good."

"How do you feel about faking some injuries? A sling, maybe? We had a situation in Turkey nine days ago, got some good information from a quick-thinking corporal. Exactly the kind of person I would have been interested in recruiting, but the situation went dark. The corporal didn't survive the hostile force's rescue attempt. But maybe the information was actually acquired by my secret side project, who *did* make it out alive."

She stared at him.

He held a hand up, as if in surrender. "Okay, we don't have to do it my way. It was just an idea. Deavers knows the story; it would make my bringing you in feel anchored, less spur of the moment."

"I think I can manage some injuries," Alex said dryly.

• • •

THEY'D GONE OVER the story a few times before they reached the rendezvous point, and he'd described the interrogation room in detail. It wasn't a pretty picture, and she felt their chances for survival getting more bleak.

Carston pulled into the lot attached to the small municipal park and stopped the Bimmer next to the only other car in the lot, as directed. It gave Alex a start, even though she was expecting it, to see the big blond man waiting on the park bench.

This was the first test, and if Daniel didn't pass, she was pulling the plug. Carston had surely seen the photos of Daniel on the news, no matter how separate he and Deavers had kept their operations. She watched Carston from the corner of her eye, assessing his reaction. His face was a blank.

"Who's this?" he asked.

"Your new aide."

"Is that necessary?"

"Cut the engine."

Daniel got up and walked quickly toward them. Alex watched Carston for any change in expression as Daniel approached.

"I can't watch you every second, Carston," she said sweetly. "Pop the trunk."

She and Carston waited in silence as Daniel moved the gear from the back of the sedan into the BMW's cargo space. When he was done, he stood beside Carston's door, waiting.

"Get out," Alex said.

Slowly, always keeping his hands in view, Carston opened the door and stepped out. As Alex got out, she saw the way he was eyeing Daniel. She tried to appraise Daniel impartially. He was a large man and looked able to handle himself, even with the glasses and the extra paunch. It made sense under these circumstances that Carston would be cautious and probably frightened, though he hid it well.

As instructed, Daniel said nothing. He met Alex's eyes only briefly and kept his expression neutral. His jaw jutted out just a bit, the way it had when he'd intimidated the drunk boys in Oklahoma City. It made him look dangerous, but also slightly more like Kevin. Had Carston seen photos of Kevin?

Daniel stopped beside the driver's door, his arms loose at his sides, ready.

"Hands on the roof," Alex ordered Carston. "Don't move until I get back."

Carston assumed the position of a suspect braced against a police car. He kept his head down, but Alex could tell he was examining what he could see of Daniel in the window's reflection. There was no sign of recognition, but Alex couldn't be sure if Carston was hiding his response. Alex was distracted by the way the parking-lot lights glinted off their bald heads in the same spots.

"This is Mr. Thomas," she told Carston. "If you try to give me away, or escape, or hurt me, you'll be dead in approximately two and a half seconds."

A bead of sweat was forming at Carston's temple. If he was faking that, she was truly impressed.

"I'm not going to do anything to endanger Livvy," he snapped.

"Good. I'll be right back. I'm going to go give myself some injuries."

Daniel's bright blue eyes flickered to her when she said the word *injuries;* he forced them back to Carston.

All her things were neatly stowed in the cargo hold of the BMW. She unzipped the first-aid duffel bag and rummaged around quickly till she found what she needed, then cut off a short section of gauze and tape. She grabbed her handbag and turned away, leaving the trunk open. The public restroom was just on the other side of the little playground. She walked quickly to the ladies' room and turned on the lights.

There was no counter, and nothing had been cleaned in days, maybe weeks, so she kept the bag on her shoulder. She used the gritty powdered soap to scrub off Val's lovely makeup job. It was better this way. The makeup was out of character, and the patch of fake skin would have been a red flag to anyone who looked closely. Her bruises and bandages would draw attention, obviously, but they would also make her less recognizable. People would be less likely to examine the face underneath.

She was happy to see the remnants of her black eyes, the yellow shape of the lingering bruise on her cheek. The glue job on her jaw was too amateur, but a normal person would keep it bandaged regardless.

There were no towels, just a broken air drycr. She used her T-shirt to dry her face, then taped the gauze to her jaw and ear, taking the extra seconds to do the job right, so it looked like a doctor had done it. Her black T-shirt and thick leggings worked — comfortable clothes were part of the job, and the lab coat in the trunk would give her the professional appearance she wanted.

As she walked back to the car in the encroaching darkness, she could hear Carston trying to engage Daniel, but Daniel was staring down at the man with his lips tightly closed.

Alex retrieved the lab coat from the trunk and put it on, then ran her palms down the front of it to smooth out the folds. When she was satisfied, she shut the trunk and opened the back door.

"At ease, Lowell," she told Carston. He straightened up warily. "You'll ride with me in the back. Mr. Thomas will drive."

"Taciturn fellow," Carston commented as he ducked in through the open door.

"He's not here to entertain you; he's here to keep you in line."

Alex shut the door behind him, then walked around the car to climb in the other side. Carston stared at her.

"Your face...that's very realistic work, Jules. Subtle. It doesn't look like you're wearing any makeup at all now."

"I've developed many new skills, and the name is Dr. Jordan Reid. Please direct Mr. Thomas to our destination. When we're five minutes out, you get your phone back."

Her eyes met Daniel's in the mirror. He gave one tiny shake of his head. Carston hadn't said anything to make Daniel think he'd been recognized during the time they were alone.

Daniel started the engine. Carston gave him the address and a short set of directions. Daniel nodded once.

Carston turned to Alex and asked, "I assume someone is with Livvy now?"

"Assumptions are never a safe bet, you know that."

"If I do my best, Jules, if I do everything I can..." Carston began. His voice was suddenly raw. "Please. Please let Livvy go. Make the call, whatever you have to do. Even if...even if you're not getting out. I know you have every reason to hurt me, but, please, not the baby." He was only whispering by the end. She rather thought he was speaking from the heart, as much as he had one.

"I can't do anything for her if I don't make it out. I'm sorry, Carston, I wish I could have done things differently, but I didn't have the time or the resources."

He clenched his hands in his lap and stared at them. "You better know what you're doing."

She didn't answer. He probably could guess what that meant.

"If we go down," he said, his voice stronger, "at least take that bastard Deavers with us. Can you do that?"

"I'll make a point of it."

• • •

"WE'RE FIVE MINUTES out, approximately."

"Okay, here."

Alex handed Carston his phone. He turned it on, then, after a second, selected a number from his address book. The phone rang twice over the car's speaker.

"Why are you interrupting me?" a man answered. His voice was pitched to be quiet, almost a whisper, but Alex could hear that it was a deep baritone. He sounded annoyed.

Carston was annoyed, too. "I'm assuming there's been no progress."

"I don't have time for this."

"None of us have time for this," Carston snapped. "Enough is enough. I'll be at the gate in two minutes. Make sure they're expecting me and my assistants."

"What—" Deavers started, but Carston hung up.

"Combative," Alex commented.

"It's our normal form of interaction."

"I hope so."

"I'll do my part, Jules. If Livvy weren't involved, I think I would actually enjoy this. I am so *tired* of that pompous fool."

The building they pulled up to would have looked abandoned if there weren't two cars parked beside the entrance. The small lot was protected by steep, man-made hills that surrounded it on three sides, the unassuming, one-story concrete building taking up the fourth. The front of the building wasn't visible until you were already in the lot. The location was hidden in the middle of miles of warehouses and Soviet bloc–style office buildings, all certainly owned by some arm of the government and all seemingly empty. As was the maze of roads weaving through them. She doubted anyone would wander back here by accident, and she was glad she'd had Carston to guide them through the maze. She hoped Daniel had paid attention. She'd tried to memorize the route, but it was unlikely she'd be there to guide him back out.

There were no lights in the small, shaded windows, but that was expected. The ground floor was nothing but camouflage.

Carston got out and came around to hold the car door for her, already acting his role. She almost smiled, remembering what it had been like when she had been *the talent.* Well, that was her part to play tonight. She would have to get into character.

Daniel pulled the steel toolbox on rollers out of the trunk and brought it around to her. Someone was probably already watching, though she couldn't see where the cameras were hidden.

"Careful with that," she admonished in a stern tone, taking the handle from him. She straightened her left cuff, and brushed an imaginary speck of dust off her sleeve. Daniel went to stand just behind Carston's right shoulder. She noticed the gold pinkie ring. It didn't quite fit the picture, but the rest of him did—even in the dark lot, his black suit looked just right, conservative, not expensive; every FBI agent in the country had something exactly like it in his or her closet. No badge, but then, anyone working as an aide to *this* department wouldn't be expected to carry identification. It wasn't a badge kind of organization.

She squared her shoulders and faced the dark building, trying to come to terms with the fact that she'd probably never see this ugly parking lot again.

CHAPTER 30

his way, Dr. Reid," Carston said, and he led them to a blank gray door. Daniel stayed close on his heels, his back to Alex. She walked briskly behind them, struggling to keep up with her shorter legs.

Carston didn't knock on the door; he merely stood directly in front of it. Expectant, like he'd already rung the bell.

The door opened a second after Carston planted himself. The man who answered it wore a suit not unlike Daniel's, though this man's was so new it still had a sheen on it. He was shorter than Daniel and wider through the shoulders. There was an obvious bulge under his left arm.

"Sir," the man said, and saluted Carston. His hair was high and tight, and she guessed he'd feel more at home in a uniform. But his appearance was still part of the camouflage. The uniforms would be downstairs.

"I need to see Deavers immediately."

"Yes, sir, he informed us you'd be arriving. This way."

The soldier turned abruptly and paced inside.

She followed Daniel into a drab office space: gray carpet, a few tight cubicles, some uncomfortable-looking chairs. The door closed behind her with a solid-sounding thud and an ominous click. No doubt someone was still watching; she couldn't afford a glance back to look at the lock. She would have to hope it was meant to keep people out and not in. It hadn't taken the soldier long to open the door to them.

The soldier turned sharply down a dim hallway, took them past several darkened rooms with open doors, then stopped at the very end. There was a door there labeled JANITORIAL SUPPLIES. He reached into his left sleeve and pulled out a spiral cord with a key. He unlocked the door and led the way inside.

The room was dimly lit by an emergency exit sign over another door opposite the first. Mops and buckets lined the wall, presumably for show. The soldier opened the emergency door, revealing a featureless, metal-lined box. An elevator. She'd known to expect this; she hoped Daniel was controlling his expressions.

They joined the soldier in the elevator. When she turned to face the doors, she saw that there were only two buttons. He pressed the bottom one, and she felt the descent begin immediately. She couldn't be sure, but it felt like at least three floors. Not entirely necessary, but definitely disconcerting. Though this building had not been used for the same kind of interrogations she had conducted, it would still be part of the routine to make the subject feel alarmed and isolated.

It worked; she felt an increase in both.

The elevator came to an abrupt halt, and the doors opened on a brightly lit anteroom. It looked like an airport security post, only much less crowded and more colorless. There were two more men, these in dark blue army uniforms, and a standard metal detector with a short counter and even the little plastic trays for belt buckles and car keys. The uniforms made Alex think these must be Pace's men.

The surveillance cameras were very obvious in this room.

Carston moved forward, impatient and sure of himself. He put his phone in the tray, and a handful of change. Then he stalked through the square frame. Daniel moved quickly behind him, putting the car keys in another tray, then retrieving Carston's belongings and handing them back to him before reclaiming the keys for himself.

Alex wheeled the steel toolbox to the side of the detector.

"I'm afraid you'll have to search that by hand," she said as she walked through the frame. "I have a lot of metal tools. Please be careful, some of my things are breakable, and some are pressurized."

The two soldiers looked at each other, obviously uncertain. They looked at her damaged face, then at her toolbox. The taller one knelt down to open the top compartment while the shorter one stared at her face again.

"Please be careful," she repeated. "Those syringes are delicate."

The short soldier watched now as the tall soldier lifted the top tray of syringes, only to find an identical tray below it. He carefully replaced it, not checking the two trays beneath. He opened the second compartment, then looked up quickly at his companion. Then at Carston.

"Sir, we aren't supposed to let weapons past this point."

"Of course I'll need my scalpels," Alex said, letting some irritation bleed into her tone. "I'm not here to play Scrabble."

The soldiers looked at her again, understanding beginning to dawn in their eyes.

Yes, she wanted to say, *I'm* that *kind of guest.*

They might have read the words in her expression. The tall one straightened up.

"We're going to have to get authorization for this." He turned on his heel and strode through the metal double doors behind them.

Carston huffed out a big, exasperated breath and folded his arms across his chest. Alex schooled her expression into one of impatience. Daniel stood very still by Carston's right shoulder, his face blank. He was doing well. No one had paid him any attention at all. To the soldiers, he was just one of those anonymous briefcase holders, which was exactly what she'd hoped for. Val was right thus far—they would have paid much more attention to her.

It was only a few minutes before the doors opened again. The tall soldier was back with two other men.

It was easy to tell which was Deavers. He was smaller and more gaunt than the voice had suggested, but he moved with an obvious authority. He didn't watch to see where the other men walked; he expected them to move around him. He wore a well-cut black suit, several pay grades in price and style above what Daniel and the door guard were wearing. His hair was steel gray, but still thick.

From his lack of formality, Alex guessed the man behind Deavers was the interrogator. He was dressed in a rumpled T-shirt and black pants that looked like scrubs. His lank brown hair was greasy and disheveled; there were substantial bags under his bloodshot eyes. Though he'd obviously had a long day, there was fire in those eyes as he focused on her lab coat, then her toolbox, the scalpel tray still exposed.

"What is this, Carston?" he blustered.

Neither Carston nor Deavers looked at him. Their eyes were focused on each other.

"What do you think you're doing?" Deavers asked in an even voice.

"I'm not going to let that hack kill the subject when I have a better option."

Deavers looked at her for the first time. She tried to project calm, but she felt her heart racing as he examined her, his eyes lingering on the damage to her face.

He turned back to Carston. "And where did you suddenly get this better option?"

At least he hadn't recognized her immediately. And he hadn't so much as looked at Daniel. The two men were focused on each other again, antagonism running between them like an electric current.

"I've been developing alternatives to save the program. This alternative has already proven herself more than capable."

"Proven how?"

Carston's chin moved up an inch. "Uludere."

The current seemed to break on that word. Deavers took an unconscious step back and blew out an annoyed breath. He looked at Alex's bandaged face again, then at his adversary.

"I should have known there was more going on in Turkey. Carston, this is beyond your authority."

"I'm currently being underutilized. Just trying to make myself more valuable."

Deavers pursed his lips and glanced back at her again. "She's good?"

"You'll see," Carston promised.

"But I'm at a critical point," the interrogator protested. "You can't pull me off the case now."

Carston gave him a withering glance. "Shut up, Lindauer. You're out of your league."

"All right," Deavers said sourly. "Let's see if your better option can get us what we need."

. . .

THE ROOM WAS as Carston had described. Plain concrete walls, plain concrete floor. One door, a large one-way mirror between this and the observation room, a round overhead light flush with the ceiling.

At one time, there would have been a desk in this room, two chairs, and a very bright desk lamp. Subjects would have been questioned, harangued, threatened, and pressured, but that would have been the extent of it.

Now a surgical table took the place of the desk. It was like something from a World War I movie, one solid piece of unpadded stainless steel with the kind of wheels a gurney had. There was a folding chair in the corner. This facility was nowhere near as functional as the state-of-the-art suites back at the department, but clearly, this interrogation was off even the most covert section's records.

She kept her inspection clinical and prayed that Daniel would have the restraint necessary for this.

Daniel had accompanied Carston and the others into the observation room, and he was invisible to her behind the glass. Before the group divided, neither Deavers nor any of the others had looked at his face. She desperately hoped he would do nothing now to change their indifference to suspicion.

Kevin lay on the table under the one light, handcuffed and shackled in place. He was naked, his body gleaming wet with sweat and blood. Long burns blistered a multitude of uneven parallel lines down his chest. Thin slices ran up his ribs, ragged skin blanched at the edges—probably with acid. The soles of his feet were covered in blisters and bleached white as well. Lindauer had poured acid into those burns. Kevin was missing another toe on his left foot, the one next to the first stump.

Lindauer's tools littered the floor, messy with blood and his dirty handprints. She knew there was a toe down there, too, but she couldn't find it at first glance.

She'd expected a clean, clinical setup; that was what she was used to. This was savagery. Her nose wrinkled in disgust.

Kevin was alert. He watched her as she walked in behind the interrogator, his face tightly controlled.

With a precision meant to mock Lindauer's unprofessional work habits, she bent to her toolbox and carefully laid out a few of her syringe trays.

"What's this?" Kevin asked hoarsely. She glanced up automatically to see that he was addressing the mirror, not her. "You think a little girl can break me? I thought this flunky was the low. Honestly, you guys never cease to disappoint."

Lindauer, who had insisted on being in the room, leaned furiously over the table. He jammed one finger into a slash wound that cut across a burn on Kevin's chest. Kevin grunted and clenched his jaw.

"Don't worry, Mr. Beach. The *little girl* is just a nice rest period for you. Get your strength back. I'll return later, and then we'll have some productive conversations."

"Enough, *Doctor*," Alex snapped in a ringing tone. "I agreed to let you observe, but you will kindly step away from my subject now."

Lindauer glanced at the mirror as if expecting backup. When he got only silence in response, he frowned sullenly and went to sit in the lone chair. Once he was down, he seemed to collapse a little, whether from exhaustion or disgrace, she couldn't tell.

Alex turned her back on Lindauer and pulled on a pair of blue latex gloves. The small piece of metal she'd palmed in the process was invisible beneath the right glove.

She stepped to the edge of the table, gingerly clearing a swath in Lindauer's mess with one foot.

"Hello, Mr. Beach. How are you feeling?"

"Good to go a few more rounds, sweetheart. Looks like somebody already had a nice time with you, eh? Hope it was fun for him."

While he spit the words through his teeth, she began examining him, shining a small flashlight in his eyes and then assessing the veins in his arms and hands.

"A little dehydrated, I think," she said. She looked directly at the mirror while she put his right hand back on the table, leaving the thin key under his palm. "I assumed there would be an IV in place. Could I get a pole, please? I have my own saline and needles."

"I'll *bet* you know your way around a pole," Kevin said.

"No need to be crass, Mr. Beach. Now that I'm here, things will be much more civilized. I do apologize for the current conditions. This is all very unprofessional." She sniffed scornfully, giving Lindauer her most cutting side-eye. He looked away.

"Honey, if this is the good-cop routine, sorry, but you're not really my type."

"I assure you, Mr. Beach, I am not the good cop. I am a specialist, and I should warn you now, I won't play the same silly games this . . . *interrogator*" — the desire to use a less flattering word was clear in her inflection — "has wasted your time with. We'll get down to business immediately."

"Yeah, sugar, let's get down to business, that's what I'm talking about." Kevin tried to keep his voice loud and his tone derisive, but she could see the effort it was costing him.

The door opened behind her. She watched in the mirror as the tall soldier brought in an IV pole. So far she'd seen only four others besides Deavers and Lindauer, but there were probably more hidden from view.

"Just put that at the head of the table, thank you," she said without turning to look at him, voice dismissive. She bent to retrieve the syringe she wanted.

"You gonna dance for me now?" Kevin muttered.

She looked at Kevin coldly as she straightened. "This will be just a sample of what we'll be doing tonight," she told him as she circled the table. She placed the syringe by his head while she hung the saline bag and the tubing. The door closed, but she didn't look away from Kevin. She examined his veins again, then chose his left arm. He didn't resist. While she carefully inserted the needle, she tried to spy the key she'd given him, but it was nowhere in sight. She picked up the largest blade she could see on the floor and laid it next to his right arm. "You see, I don't need such crude weapons; I have something better. I always think it's fairer to let the subject understand what he's up against before I go full strength. Let me know what you think."

"I'll tell you what I think, you—" Kevin launched into an avalanche of profanity that put all his previous creative descriptions to shame. The man had a talent.

"I appreciate your bravery, really, I do," Alex said when he was done. She held the point of the syringe against the IV port. "But please know, it's a wasted effort. Playtime is over."

She stabbed the needle through the plastic and depressed the plunger.

The response was nearly immediate. She heard his breathing accelerate, and then he started shrieking.

Lindauer's head snapped up. She could tell he'd never gotten a reaction like this from Kevin, despite his best efforts. She heard movement behind the glass as the audience edged closer, and the faint murmur of voices. She thought she could pick out a surprised tone, and it was gratifying. Though, honestly, it was all due to Kevin's acting.

She knew how he would be feeling now as the strength raced through his veins and all the pain vanished. She'd used more than double the highest dose of *Survive* she'd ever used on herself, taking into account his greater mass and need. His screams were primal, almost triumphant. She hoped she was the only one to notice that nuance and that he'd remember that the damage done to his body was still very real, whether he felt it any longer or not.

She waited only five minutes — tapping her foot and watching him dispassionately — while he did his part, keeping his screams loud and constant. She wanted him to have as much time with the drugs in his system as possible. When they wore off, he would be incapacitated.

"There, Mr. Beach," she said as she shot ordinary saline into the IV line. She gave him the cue he would need. "I think we understand each other now, so I can let this end. Shall we talk?"

Kevin took longer to recover than he should have, but then, he didn't know her drugs. He pretended to come out of it slowly, and she was glad Daniel was standing close to Carston with the venom-coated ring ready. Only Carston would recognize the fraud.

Kevin was still breathing heavily after a minute, and he actually had tears streaming down the sides of his face. It was easy for her to forget he was an undercover professional, because she'd never seen him in the field, but she should have known he would nail this performance.

"Well, Mr. Beach, what now? Shall we continue to full strength, or would you like to talk first?"

He turned to stare at her, his eyes wide with convincing fear.

"Who are you?" he whispered.

"A specialist, as I told you. I believe the *gentleman*" — sarcastically, with a nod toward Lindauer — "had some questions for you?"

"If I talk," he said, still in a whisper, "do you go away?"

"Of course, Mr. Beach. I am merely a means to an end. Once you have satisfied my employers, you will never have to see me again."

Lindauer was openly gaping now, but Alex was worried. They had to keep moving forward, but at the same time, would anyone believe Kevin could fold so easily?

Kevin moaned and closed his eyes. "They won't believe me," he said.

She wasn't sure how, but she thought his right handcuff was no longer locked to his wrist. There was just the tiniest misalignment of the two halves of the bracelet. She didn't think anyone could see it but her.

"I'll believe you, if you tell me the truth. Just tell me what you want to say."

"I did have help...but...I can't..."

She took his hand in hers, as if she were soothing him. She felt the key drop into her palm.

"You *can* tell me. But please don't try to buy time. I have little patience."

She patted his hand, then walked around his head to examine the IV line.

"No," he mumbled weakly. "I won't."

"All right, then," she said, "what do you want to tell me?" She dropped her hand onto his left, inserting the key between his fingers.

"I had help...from a traitor on the inside."

"What?" Lindauer gasped out loud.

She shot him a dirty look, then turned to the mirror.

"Your man is unable to control himself. I want him removed from this room," she said severely.

An electronic crackle sounded through the room. She glanced up for the speaker but couldn't find it.

"Continue," Deavers's disembodied voice commanded. "He will be escorted out if there is any more misconduct."

She frowned at her own reflection, then turned to lean over Kevin.

"I need a name," she insisted.

"Carston," he breathed.

No!

Nerves already frayed and strained, she had to fight back the urge to slap him. But of course Kevin had no way of knowing how she'd gotten here.

She heard a commotion in the observation room and hurried on in a louder voice. "I find that very hard to believe, Mr. Beach, as Mr. Carston is the reason I am here with you. He wouldn't send me in if he wanted to avoid the truth. He knows what I'm capable of."

Kevin shot her one disgusted look under half-lowered lids, then groaned again. "That's the name my contact gave me. I can only tell you what he told me."

Nice save, she thought sarcastically.

The commotion hadn't ended with either her pronouncement or Kevin's. She could hear raised voices and some movement. Lindauer was distracted, too, staring at the glass.

She tried again, pulling a new syringe and slipping a small device from beneath it into her pocket. "Forgive me for thinking that was all a bit too easy—"

"No, wait," Kevin huffed, pitching his voice a little louder. "Deavers sent the guy; he knows who I'm talking about."

Well, maybe that would muddy the water a bit. Get both names on the table.

It wasn't stopping whatever was happening in the observation room, though. She had to make a move. The one good thing about the unanticipated situation on the other side of the glass was that they obviously weren't watching her very carefully. Time was up.

"Mr. Lindauer," she called sharply without looking in his direction. In the mirror, she could see that he was preoccupied with the other room as well. His head whipped around to her.

"I'm worried these ankle restraints are a little too tight. I need his circulation performing optimally. Do you have the key?"

Kevin could guess what this was about. His muscles tensed in readiness. Lindauer hurried to the foot of the table. One voice was raised above the others in the observation room, shouting.

"I don't know what you're talking about," Lindauer complained, his eyes on Kevin's ankles and mangled feet. "These aren't cutting off his circulation. It wouldn't be safe to have them any looser. You don't know what kind of man you're dealing with."

She stepped close to him, speaking softly so that he would have to lean in toward her. Inside her pocket, she pressed her thumb against the tiny flash capacitor of the electromagnetic-pulse emitter.

"I know exactly what kind of man I'm dealing with," she murmured.

She switched on the capacitor with her left hand and stabbed the syringe into Lindauer's arm with her right.

The light overhead flickered and popped; the shattered bulbs tinkled against the Plexiglas face of the fixture. Luckily the pulse didn't blow out the Plexiglas or it would have been bad for Kevin's exposed skin. The room went black.

The pulse wasn't strong enough to reach the other room. Muted light shone through the mirror, and she could see dark figures moving on the other side of the glass, but she couldn't tell who was who or what was happening.

Lindauer managed only half a scream before he was convulsing on the floor. She could hear Kevin moving, too, though those sounds were much quieter and more purposeful than Lindauer's thrashing.

She knew precisely where her toolbox was in the dark. She whirled and fell to her knees next to it, yanked the second-to-last drawer open, emptied the tray of syringes to the floor, and felt for the hidden compartment beneath.

"Ollie?" Kevin breathed. She could hear he was off the table now, near the IV pole.

She grabbed the first two guns she touched and lurched toward the sound of his voice. She collided with his chest, and his arms came up to keep her from falling backward. She shoved the guns against his stomach just as two shots rang out in the other room. There was no shatter of glass—they weren't shooting into the interrogation room. A third, and then a fourth shot.

"Danny's in there," she hissed as he yanked the guns out of her hands.

She fell back to her knees as he spun away and slid into the toolbox. She grabbed the other two guns, the familiar shape of her own PPK and another she didn't recognize by touch. She'd given Kevin her SIG Sauer by accident.

It didn't matter. She'd accomplished the main objectives of her strategy: free Kevin and get a loaded gun into his hands. Now she was primarily backup. She just had to hope that the star performer was in good enough shape to do what she needed him to do. If that sadist Lindauer had injured him too greatly . . . well, then they were all dead.

Lindauer had gotten his. He was probably still alive, but not for much longer. He wouldn't enjoy what was left of his life at all.

A full second hadn't passed when another shot echoed deafeningly through the small concrete room, and this time there was the muffled crunch of buckling safety glass.

Cracks of yellow light spider-webbed through the window as four shots responded back in quick succession. The answering shots didn't change the splintered pattern of light; again, they weren't aimed into the interrogation room. They were still shooting at each other inside the observation room.

She stayed low as she moved forward, guns pointed at the fractured square in case someone burst through it. But the movement came from her side; a dark shadow hurtled into the mosaic of glass fragments and crashed through it into the next room.

The men in the observation room were only ten feet away from her, so much closer than the hay bales she'd practiced on that it seemed too easy. She braced her hands against the steel table and fired toward the uniforms that filled the room. She didn't allow herself to react to the fact that she couldn't see Daniel or Carston. She'd told Daniel to get down when the shooting started. He was just following directions.

A storm of shots rang out now, but none of them were aimed at her. The soldiers were firing at the bloody, naked man who had exploded into their midst with a volley of bullets. There were six uniformed men still on their feet now, and she quickly dropped three before they could realize the attack was coming from two fronts. As they crumpled, they revealed the man in the suit they'd been protecting. His eyes were focusing toward her as she aimed, his body already in motion when the bullet left her gun; she wasn't sure she'd done more than just wing him as he ducked down out of her range.

She couldn't see Kevin's position, but the other three soldiers were now on the ground. She had nothing left to aim at from this vantage.

Alex darted to the edge of the open window, glass crunching beneath her shoes, and put her back against the wall beside it.

"Ollie?" Kevin called, his voice strong and controlled.

Relief flooded through her body in a hot rush at the sound of his voice. "Yes."

"We're clear. Get in here. Danny's down."

Ice washed down the same path the heat had just blazed.

She dropped the guns into her pockets, wrapped her hands in the folds of her lab coat, and boosted herself over the jagged ledge of the window. The floor was a mass of bodies in dark uniforms, with deep red splatters marking everything light enough to show it — the faces, the floor, the walls. Kevin was shaking off a body he'd evidently used as a shield. There was still movement, and more than one gasping murmur. So, not entirely clear, but he must feel it was under control, and, obviously, the need was urgent.

Daniel was in the back right corner — she could see the

white-blond hair ringing his pale scalp, but most of him was obscured by two bodies in uniform that looked to have crumpled on top of him. Carston was down a few feet away, blood blossoming across his white shirt from multiple wounds. His chest was still moving.

It took less than a second for her to absorb all this, already in motion as she assessed, heading straight for Daniel.

"Deavers is alive," she muttered as she passed Kevin, and in her peripheral vision, she saw him nod and start moving in a crouch toward the far left corner of the room.

There was very little blood on the soldier lying across Daniel's chest, but his face was an unhealthy shade of purple and there were pink bubbles on his lips. A quick glance at the man draped over Daniel's legs revealed the same manifestations. Both of these men were dying from the venom on Daniel's ring. A new froth of bloody bubbles foamed on the first man's lips as she tried to pull his paralyzed body off Daniel.

Part of her was very far away from what was happening—the part that needed to scream and panic and hyperventilate. She let the ice of her fear keep her focused and clinical. Later there would be time for hysterics. Now she had to be a doctor on the battlefield, quick and certain.

She finally rolled the man off Daniel's chest, and suddenly there was blood everywhere. She ripped Daniel's crimson-drenched shirt out of the way and found the source only too easily. All of her training, all of her time as a trauma doctor for hire, told her she was far too late.

It was a perfect kill shot, right through the upper left side of his chest. Whoever had placed that bullet knew exactly what he was doing. It was one of the few shots that would fell a person instantly, straight through the heart, dead before he hit the ground. Dead probably before he could even register the pain.

There was nothing she could have done, even if she'd never left his side. She'd let him come here to protect her, and that choice had killed him just as surely as the bullet in his heart.

CHAPTER 31

It wasn't supposed to have happened like this. The guns should have been pointed at Alex and Kevin. In the confusion, no one had shot at her—not even once; she was totally unscathed. Daniel was supposed to be in the background, invisible. There was no reason to waste such a perfect shot on an anonymous aide. That skilled shooter was supposed to be aiming for Alex.

She'd known the plan was deeply flawed, but she had never dreamed she'd walk through the firefight untouched. Daniel was supposed to be the survivor.

A line of nameless faces—gangsters she hadn't been able to save—flashed through her mind. One had a name—Carlo. He'd died exactly the same way. She hadn't been able to do anything. What had Joey G said? *You win some, you lose some.* But how did she live through this loss?

The shrieking part of her was very near the surface. Only shock kept the paroxysm of grief at bay. The frozen pause was endless, crystal clear, with every detail defined. She was aware of the sound of a struggle somewhere very far away from her, and Kevin shouting in his harshest voice, *"Where's your deep perimeter now, Deavers?"* She could smell the fetid musk of her ring's victims and the warm, *alive* scent of fresh blood. She could hear labored breathing at her back where Carston lay dying.

Then, suddenly, the sound of another shallow, sucking wheeze close beside her bowed head.

Her eyes, which she hadn't even realized were closed, snapped open. She knew that sound.

Frantically, she ripped the glove from her hand and stretched it tight over the hole in Daniel's chest. She watched incredulously as the pull of his struggling lung tried to suck air through the latex. She lifted the edge of the glove for the exhale, letting the air vent, and then strained the glove against his skin again for the inhale.

He was *breathing*.

How? The shot must have somehow missed his heart, though it seemed perfectly placed. She took stock quickly and realized that there wasn't actually as much blood as she'd first thought. Not enough to suggest a hole in his heart. And he was breathing, which he wouldn't have been if the bullet had gone true.

She thrust her other hand under his shoulder, searching frantically for an exit wound. Her fingertips found the tear in his jacket, and she shoved them through the hole, then into the hole in his back, trying to seal the airflow. It didn't feel any bigger than the hole in his chest. The bullet had passed straight through him.

"Kevin!" Her raw shriek held all the panic she was too numb to feel. "I need my toolbox. Now!"

Movement again, but she didn't look up to see if it was Kevin helping her or a victorious Deavers moving in for the kill. She found she didn't even care if it was Deavers; she wasn't afraid of anything he could do to her. Because if Kevin was down and unable to get her the things she needed immediately, Daniel could die in minutes.

She had more of what she needed in the car, but she had no idea how to get Daniel back to the surface.

A metallic crash sounded at her right elbow.

"Ziploc bags," she instructed frantically. "The bottom compartment, on the left, and tape—should be near the top."

Kevin laid the things she needed on Daniel's chest, next to her hand. Quickly, on the exhale, she traded her glove for the plastic bag and instructed Kevin to tape it down tightly on three sides. She didn't have anything that would work as a valve to vent the excess air, so she had to leave the fourth side open. It should suck against the hole as he inhaled, and then let the air release as he breathed out.

"Roll him toward me, I need to seal the exit wound."

Kevin carefully moved his unconscious brother onto his side. She hoped the position would take some of the pressure off Daniel's undamaged lung. She had to break contact with the wound briefly as Kevin moved him, and then another precious second as she used a scalpel to cut his shirt and jacket out of the way. She taped a second plastic bag against his skin while she analyzed the pool of blood beneath him. Not so much, really. The bullet had miraculously missed his heart entirely, and the major vessels as well. The exit wound looked clean and she didn't see any bone fragments. If she could just keep him breathing, she could get him through the next hour.

Kevin's voice interrupted her frantic planning. "Carston's still alive. What do you want me to do with him?"

"Can he be saved?" she asked while she checked Daniel's airway and pressure. He'd lost too much blood. He was in shock. She could still make out a pulse at his wrist, but it was weak and fading. She grabbed a syringe from the top tray and injected him with ketamine and a separate painkiller.

"Doubt it. Too much damage. He probably only has a few minutes. Oh, um, hey. Sorry, man."

His voice had changed at the end. He wasn't speaking to her anymore.

"Is he lucid?" she asked. She ran her hands down Daniel's arms and legs, searching for any other wounds.

"Jules?" Carston rasped weakly.

"Kevin, bring the operating table over here. We've got to get Daniel up to the car." She took a deep breath. "Lowell, it's okay. I never poisoned Livvy. Of course not. She's only sedated. She'll be with her mother by morning, whether I come home or not."

While she reassured Carston—her eyes never leaving Daniel—she heard Kevin leave and then return. There was a heavy metal groan as he shoved the table through the window and a moist thud when it hit the bodies on the floor. She bit her lip as she continued to work on Daniel, pulling the rubber pieces of his disguise out of his mouth so he couldn't choke on them, carefully wiping the contacts from his eyes. How long till Kevin collapsed? He still had a good fifty minutes to enjoy the drugs in his system, but that wouldn't affect how much his body could actually endure. She needed to try to remember that he wasn't the same Kevin, the one who could do anything. She had to go easier on him. But how? Daniel needed speed. If she could just get him to the car...

"Proud of you, Jules," Lowell Carston wheezed quietly. "You managed to hold on to your soul. Impressive..." The last word trailed off with a low, rattling exhalation. She listened for more, but it was silent behind her now.

She'd outlived Carston, a feat she never would have put money on. Instead of feeling the triumph she'd always expected, she was ambivalent. Perhaps the triumph would come later, when the panic gripping her was gone.

"Is it safe to lift him?" Kevin asked.

"Carefully. Try to keep his chest as immobile as possible. I'll get his legs."

Together they hefted Daniel carefully onto the silver tabletop. She took his wrist again, willing his pulse to stay discernible.

"Give me two seconds, Ollie," Kevin said as he began stripping the soldier who'd fallen over Daniel's legs, the one with the least blood on him. "How many more are upstairs?"

She glanced at the faces on the floor. She thought she recognized the shorter guard from the metal detector.

"At least one isn't here, for sure. He was at the door. It seemed empty up there, but I didn't see most of these guys beforehand."

He was already in the pants, pulling socks over his mangled feet and then trying the shoes. They were too small. He yanked another pair off the other poisoned soldier. Those looked a little big, but Kevin tied the laces tight.

"You're going to have to cut those off," she said.

He buttoned the white shirt, then threw the dark navy coat over the top, not bothering with the tie. "I'll do what I have to do when we live through this. Lose the lab coat, it's covered in blood."

"Right," she agreed, awkwardly shoving the guns into the elastic band at the back of her leggings. It was barely strong enough to hold them both in place. She shrugged out of the coat and let it drop to the floor.

"Okay, let's get this table past all the bodies, then you should be able to handle it in the hall. I'll sweep ahead and take out anybody who's left."

In seconds she was rolling Daniel down the hall, half running while Kevin disappeared into the darkness, somehow at a full sprint. Then she was in the metal-detector room, and Kevin was waiting, holding the elevator for her. The room was empty; everyone must have rushed to the observation room when the shooting started. She darted into the elevator.

Kevin reached out to hit the button as the doors shut silently behind her. She stared at his right hand on the button, his dominant hand, and a sudden burst of understanding had her coughing out one half-delirious laugh.

Kevin eyed her sharply. "Keep it together, Ollie."

"No, no, see, it's his *heart,* Kev. It's on the wrong side — the *right* side. That's why the shooter missed." She choked out another laugh. "He's alive because he's your opposite."

"Lock it up," he ordered.

She nodded once, taking a deep breath to steady herself.

The elevator stopped and the door opened to the supply closet. The outer door was closed. Kevin lifted the edge of the table over the lip of the elevator, then went to the door.

She expected him to ease it open, but instead he threw it wide with a loud bang.

"Help!" he yelled. "We need help down here!"

Then he was racing forward silently. She could hear louder footsteps coming for them from the other room—just one set, she was sure. She pushed Daniel forward as quietly as she could.

Kevin was in place before the guard came around the corner. The guard ran right past him, gun in hand but held low by his side, pointed at the ground. Kevin's gun was high. He shot the guard in the back of the head. The man crumpled to the floor. Kevin stepped forward and put one more bullet into his head to be thorough.

The hallway was too narrow to maneuver the gurney around the body. Kevin grabbed it with both hands and lifted it over. Alex did what she could to help, but she knew Kevin was taking most of the weight. She didn't know how he was still performing at this level, and she was afraid he was going to kill himself trying.

There was no other guard.

"Get him to the car," Kevin commanded. "Let me finish up here."

No one tried to stop her; no one shot at her from a darkened window while she ran into the parking lot. The sky was completely black now. The single streetlight near the front door cast only a dim yellow circle toward the parked cars. She fumbled in Daniel's pockets till she found Carston's keys. She popped the trunk and ran for her souped-up first-aid kit.

She knew exactly where the blowout gear was. She'd expected either she or Kevin—or both—would be shot, and she'd prepared accordingly. She didn't need the tourniquet or the QuikClot gauze, but she had several HALO seals, and they would work better than her plastic sandwich bags. She also had a Mylar survival blanket, more saline, and some strong intravenous antibiotics. Bullets were dirty things, and infection would be a concern...if she could keep Daniel alive that long.

She knew she couldn't. Maybe for twenty-four hours at most with what she had here. Despair made her hands shake as she ripped open the packages.

Then Kevin was right beside her. He threw a heavy black-and-silver square into the trunk.

"Hard drive the cameras recorded to," Kevin explained. "I'll get him into the back."

She nodded, filling her arms with stopgap measures.

When she crawled into the foot space of the backseat, she could see that Kevin had done everything right. Daniel was on his left side. His head was propped up on the driver's headrest, which Kevin had ripped out of place—violently, it appeared. She checked Daniel's airway again, his pulse. She could still just make it out in his carotid. The ketamine would keep him under for a while. He couldn't feel any pain. His system would remain as unstressed as possible under the circumstances.

The car started to move. She could feel Kevin was trying to keep the motion smooth for her, but it wouldn't be smooth enough.

"Stop," she said. "Give me a minute to get things in place."

He hit the brakes. "Hurry, Ollie."

It took only seconds to switch her makeshift seals for the real thing. She got the IV in quickly and then pinned the bag to the top of the seat back.

"Okay." As she spoke this time, she could barely recognize her own voice—she knew there wasn't anything more she could do, and the despair was starting to suck her down. "You can drive."

"Don't quit on me now, Oleander," Kevin growled. "You're stronger than that. I know you can do this."

"But there's nothing more I can do," she choked out. "I've done everything. It's not enough."

"He's going to make it."

"He needs a level-one trauma center, Kevin. He needs a thoracic surgeon and an operating suite. I can't clean his wounds or put in a chest tube in the backseat of a damn *Bimmer!*"

Kevin was silent.

Tears streamed down Alex's cheeks, but she didn't feel grief yet.

Just rage—at the injustice, at the limitations of their situation, at herself for this ultimate failure.

"If we dropped him off at an ER—" She sobbed.

"We'd be handing him over to the bad guys. They'll be looking at the hospitals."

"He's going to die," she whispered.

"Better that than he end up in a room like the one you just busted me out of."

"Didn't we just kill the bad guys?"

"Pace is still in charge, Ollie, till he slaps the right patch on, and given the current stress level, he might just start smoking again. If he doesn't die…even without his partners, he has no shortage of muscle at his command. The hospital is out."

She bowed her head, defeated.

The seconds ticked by. She marked them by the faint, steady pulse in Daniel's neck. She should probably be driving. She didn't know how Kevin was still going, but he didn't even seem fazed by his ordeal, not slowed in the slightest by his myriad of wounds. He was a machine. At least Daniel shared the same iron constitution… But finding any excuse for hope right now was kind of stupid.

"If…" Kevin began thoughtfully.

"Yes?"

"If I could get you to an operating space…if I could get you the things you needed…Could you fill in for the thoracic surgeon?"

"It's not my specialty, but…I could probably handle the basics." She shook her head. "Kev, how could we get a suite up and running? If we were in Chicago, sure, I might know a guy, but—"

Kevin laughed once—more of a bark, really.

"Ollie, I've got an idea."

• • •

ALEX HAD NO sense of what time it was. Maybe three a.m., maybe four. She was ragged with exhaustion, but also wired and jittery. The hand that held her seventh Styrofoam cup of coffee was trembling so badly that the surface of the liquid looked like a miniature storm at sea. Well, that was okay. She didn't need steady hands anymore.

Joey Giancardi. She never would have thought she could feel so much warmth toward her old Mafia handler, but tonight she blessed his name. If she hadn't done what amounted to an intensive trauma course with the Mob, she never would have been able to pull Daniel through. Each thug and gangster she'd repaired had given her just that much more experience, all of it adding up until she could play both EMT and surgeon tonight. Maybe she should send Joey a thank-you card.

She ran her quivering free hand through her hair and suddenly found herself wishing she were a smoker, like Pace. Smokers always seemed so serene with a cigarette in hand. She needed something to bring her down, to slow her agitated heart, but the only physical comfort she could find was the cup of strong black sludge she held, and that wasn't exactly helping her relax.

Dr. Volkstaff was snoring on a battered couch squeezed between two large storage cabinets against the back wall of his workspace. He'd been surprisingly capable — despite his age and specialty. They'd had to cobble together much of what they'd needed in his operating theater, but he was inventive and familiar with his tools, and she was inspired by desperation. Together, they'd made a potent team. They'd even done a decent job of patching together a make-shift Heimlich valve that appeared to be working perfectly. The gentle beeping of Daniel's heart monitor was the most soothing sound she'd ever heard. Not that it could do anything about the caffeinated overstimulation of her nervous system. Unthinkingly, she took another gulp of coffee.

Daniel's color was good, his breathing even. He did share all of Kevin's physical characteristics, it seemed; he was engineered to survive. Dr. Volkstaff said he'd never seen a smoother procedure, and he'd dealt with plenty of lung injuries in his time, though usually puncture wounds. It was possible that Daniel would be walking out of here tomorrow.

She carefully set her cup on the counter and then gripped her shaking hands into fists as she walked slowly back to the stool by Daniel's bed and sat. It was actually two operating beds bungeed together. Nothing here had been near long enough for Daniel.

After a second, she leaned her head against the thin, plastic-covered cushion and closed her eyes.

She thought about what they had accomplished tonight, what she had almost traded Daniel's life for.

Deavers and Carston were dead. There might not be another person alive—besides Wade Pace—who knew she existed. And his hours were numbered. Hopefully.

Kevin was snoring on the floor, an old dog bed under his head for a pillow. She'd given him the largest dose of painkillers that was safe, and Volkstaff had cleaned his wounds once Daniel was in the clear. Sleep was the best thing for Kevin now.

By this time, Val should have dropped Livvy at the urgent-care center—chosen for its lack of exterior cameras—with Alex's grammatically unsound, tearstained apology note. She wondered how seriously the police would continue their search for the kidnapper. Livvy was unharmed, with no memory of her time away from Erin. The DC police would surely have little time to track down a frenzied mother who'd thought the little girl looked exactly like an older version of her own child, stolen two years ago by an estranged father. There had to be several missing-children cases that would match the loose information she'd given them. It would keep the authorities focused in the wrong direction. Maybe they'd tie Livvy's kidnapping to the death of her grandfather on the same day, but probably they wouldn't. There was an entirely separate cornucopia of motives to sift through for Carston's violent death. It would look like nothing more than a horrible coincidence.

The shadowy powers that be, the people who pulled the puppet strings, would *have* to cover everything up. One fact was going to stand out to them—the CIA's second in command and the director of a black ops program that wasn't supposed to exist had shot each other and a handful of American soldiers. The puppet masters would probably demolish the entire complex before they'd even had time to make sense of the evidence there. They'd call it a horrible accident, a building collapse due to a structural flaw, what a shame.

She thought of the last things Kevin had said to her before he crashed.

"You can do this, Ollie. I know you'll save his life. Because you have to. And then we'll all be safe. This isn't going to happen to Danny again, so you *pull him through it.*"

She wondered if he really did have that much faith in her or if he was just trying to keep her from panicking. But would he have allowed himself to pass into unconsciousness if he hadn't believed his own words?

"Alex?"

Her head whipped up so fast the wheeled stool beneath her rolled back a few inches. She jumped off it and leaned over Daniel, taking the hand that was weakly groping for hers.

"I'm right here." She glanced at his IV. The ketamine must be out of his system now, but he had an intravenous painkiller that would keep him from feeling too much discomfort.

"Where are we?"

"Safe, for the moment."

His eyes slowly opened. It took them a moment to find her, and then another to focus.

She'd known with decent certainty for at least two or three hours now that he was going to open his eyes again, but the familiar gray-green nearly knocked the wind out of her anyway. She felt tears overflow her own eyes.

"Are you hurt?" he asked.

She sniffed. "Not a scratch on me."

He smiled slightly. "Kevin?" he asked.

"He's fine. That's him snoring you hear—not a buzz saw."

The corners of his mouth turned down as his eyes slipped closed again.

"Don't worry about him. He'll be fine."

"He looked . . . really bad."

"He's tougher than any person should be—kind of like you."

"Sorry." He sighed. "I got shot."

"Yeah, I noticed that."

"Carston took the gun from the guy next to me when Deavers pulled a gun on him," Daniel explained, his lids pulling back just a few millimeters. "He moved fast for an older guy. They were shouting at each other, but all the soldiers lined up with Deavers."

Alex nodded. "Those were their orders."

"Deavers gave the order, and one of them shot Carston and then me. Carston fell to his knees but started shooting. I didn't have a gun, so I grabbed the ankles of the people near me with your ring."

"You did good."

"I wanted to get to a gun, but the two guys I hit fell on me. I couldn't lift them. My arms weren't working right."

"The one on your chest probably saved your life, actually. He kept the wound covered till I could get there."

Daniel blinked his eyes open again. "I thought I was dead."

Alex had to swallow. "Honestly, so did I for a while."

"I wanted to stay until you got there. I wanted to tell you some things. It felt horrible when I knew I couldn't."

She stroked the side of his face. "It's okay. You did it. You stayed."

The comfort thing was coming to her more easily these days. She'd changed a lot since meeting Daniel.

"I just wanted you to know that I don't regret any of it. I'm grateful for every second I've had with you—even the bad ones. I wouldn't have missed it, Alex, not for anything."

She leaned her forehead against his. "Neither would I."

They didn't move for a long moment. She listened to the sound of his breathing, the sound of his evenly beeping monitors, and Kevin's robust snores in the background.

"I love you," he murmured.

She laughed once—a quick, jittery sound that matched the

tremors in her hands. "Yeah, I've sort of figured that one out, I think. Took me long enough, didn't it? Anyway, though, I love you, too."

"Finally speaking the same language."

She laughed again.

"You're shaking," he said.

"I've had so much caffeine, I need a detox."

It was still middle-of-the-night quiet outside, so the sound of a car pulling up to the back of the building was hard to miss. Alex was surprised by how little her nerves reacted—there wasn't much left in her, she could tell. She just felt weary as she straightened up and freed her hands. She pulled her PPK from the small of her back.

"I really hope that's Val," she muttered.

"Alex—" Daniel whispered.

"Don't move even a fraction of an inch, Daniel Beach," she whispered back. "I spent too long patching you up for you to go and tear something now. I'm just being cautious. I'll be back in a sec."

She hurried to the rear door and peeked past the side of the little curtain. It was the car she was expecting—the ugly green Jag—Val in the driver's seat. She could see Einstein standing up on the passenger side.

Alex knew she should feel more, knowing that all of it was over, that almost every loose end was wrapped up. She should be elated, relieved, grateful, possibly shedding tears of joy. But her body was completely done. Once the coffee wore off, she'd be comatose.

"It's Val, like I thought," she told Daniel quietly as she set the gun on the end of his improvised bed.

"You look like you're going to pass out."

"Soon," she agreed. "Not quite yet."

"Alex?" Val called quietly as she came through the door.

"Yes."

Einstein bounded into the room, head whipping back and forth as he searched for Kevin. He paused and made a little whimper when he found him on the floor. Einstein's head cocked to the side, and then he licked Kevin's face twice. Kevin's snore stuttered.

Alex expected Einstein would curl up with his best friend, but, his tail wagging vigorously, he turned and ran to her. He jumped both paws onto her hips so he could lick her face. She had to hold on to Daniel's bed to keep from being knocked over.

"Careful, Einstein."

He coughed a quiet bark, almost like an answer. Then he dropped back to all fours and trotted over to Kevin, nestled into his side, and licked his neck again and again.

Alex was shocked when Kevin spoke. The drugs she'd given him should have kept him out for ... well, she wasn't actually sure how long it had been. Her brain was too exhausted even for simple addition.

"Hey, buddy, hey there," he said, sounding just like he usually did — too loud. His voice seemed impossibly vigorous for the way his body must be feeling. "Did you miss me? Good boy. You told them what happened. I knew you would do it."

"Kev?" Daniel asked. Alex put her hand firmly on his forehead when he twitched like he wanted to sit up.

"Danny?" Kevin nearly shouted. Volkstaff snorted and rolled onto his side.

Kevin pulled himself up, wincing.

"You probably shouldn't move ..." Alex began, and then, when he completely ignored her, "Hey, at least keep off your feet!"

"I'm fine." Kevin grunted.

"You're an idiot," Val said harshly. "Just stay put for two seconds."

Val was out of the strange, avant-garde-runway sari-thing and in sweats and a T-shirt now. She strode out through a door marked LOBBY. Kevin waited, puzzled, kneeling on the linoleum with one hand braced against the wall. She was back almost immediately, pushing a wheeled office chair, her expression set in angry lines. If Alex had any energy left, she would have sighed with envy. Val looked absolutely ridiculous for someone in a ponytail and no makeup who'd gotten no more sleep than the rest of them.

"I'm fairly sure they don't keep wheelchairs here, but this ought to work for now," Val said. "Sit."

Though her voice sounded deeply annoyed, she offered both hands to pull him up. He hissed and staggered when the soles of his feet touched the ground, but as soon as he was seated, he was trying to use them to roll himself closer to Daniel.

"Ugh, stop it," Val complained. She guided the chair across the room while Kevin held his feet gingerly a few inches off the floor. Val stopped when Kevin was right beside Alex. Alex shuffled over a step to make room.

Kevin stared at Daniel's open eyes and good color with shock. Carefully, he patted Daniel's hair, obviously afraid to touch any other part of him.

"Looks like your poison woman got it done," Kevin said in a gruff voice. "I'm not sure about the balding Swede thing you've got going on, though."

"Val's idea."

Kevin nodded absently for a moment. "You shouldn't have come in after me. I didn't want you to do that."

"You would have done it for me."

"That's different." He shook his head when Daniel started to protest. "But you're going to be okay?" Kevin looked up at Alex for the answer.

She exhaled through her nose and nodded. "He looks like he's going to be totally fine. I don't know what it is with you two. Are you sure your mom didn't have a one-night stand with a genetically engineered superhuman?"

When Kevin's hand darted toward her, Alex's first instinct was that she'd crossed the line with the mother comment. But before she could brace for a blow, he'd grabbed her roughly and yanked her into an awkward bear hug. She found herself half on his lap, her arms pinned under his, and there was nothing she could do when he decided to kiss her full on the lips with a wet, resounding *smack*.

"Hey!" Daniel protested. "Get your face off my poison woman!"

Alex wrenched her head to the side, finally feeling something again—nausea. "Ugh, get *off* me, you psychopath." She heard Val laughing.

Kevin managed to spin the chair in a complete revolution. "You're a genius, Ollie. I can't believe you did it."

"Go make out with Volkstaff, he did half the work."

He wouldn't free her. It was like he didn't even notice that she was trying—violently—to wriggle away. "What a performance! I can't *believe* you just walked in there and busted me out! Never tell me you aren't black ops—honey, you're what black ops *dreams* about being!"

Einstein whined and Alex felt his jaws close lightly around her wrist. He yanked, trying to help her escape. Kevin didn't seem to notice.

She knew where Kevin's worst injuries were. She'd use that knowledge soon if she had to. "Let me go!"

"Kevin," Daniel said, his voice measured but icy. "If you don't set Alex down right now I'm going to shoot you with her gun."

Finally Kevin dropped his arms. She ducked free and they both spun anxiously to Daniel.

"Don't move," they said in unison.

Alex breathed again when she could see that Daniel hadn't actually tried to reach for the gun.

"Volkstaff?" Daniel asked. "I know that name...where are we?"

"You remember Dr. Volkstaff," Kevin said. "He saved my best friend's life in fifth grade—after he got caught in the bear trap. You can't have forgotten that."

Daniel blinked. "Tommy Velasquez got caught in a bear trap?" he asked, bewildered.

Kevin smiled. "Tommy wasn't my best friend." He stroked Einstein's head, and the dog rubbed his face against Kevin's leg, still delirious with joy.

"Wait...*Volkstaff?*" Daniel repeated, finally putting it together. "You took me to the *vet?*"

Alex laid a hand on his forehead. "Shh. It was the right place to go. Volkstaff is a rock star. He saved your life."

"Now, now," Volkstaff's gravelly voice broke in. "I was merely the assistant, Dr. Alex. Don't be trying to give me the credit for saving Danny."

Volkstaff was sitting up on the couch, patting the unruly tufts of white hair that were arrayed in a jagged halo around his head. It made her think of Barnaby, and she realized why she'd felt so comfortable working with the friendly old man who was apparently still quite devoted to the Beach family.

"It was an honor to work beside you, Doctor," Volkstaff continued as he tottered over to them. He appeared frail with age now, but he'd shown no feebleness during the long night. He smiled down at Daniel. "Good to see you awake, son." He dropped his voice into a stage whisper. "You've found a winner, kid. Don't mess things up with this one."

"Oh, I know it, sir."

Alex frowned. She hadn't said anything about her feelings for Daniel, and Daniel had been unconscious. How were they always so obvious?

Volkstaff turned. "What a gorgeous shepherd. This can't be Einstein, can it? It's been years."

"His grandson, actually," Kevin told him.

"Isn't that something!" He reached down to caress Einstein's ear. "Such a beauty."

Einstein licked his hand. The dog was full of goodwill for all mankind tonight.

"Now, Kevin," Volkstaff said, straightening, "would you like to walk again? Because if so, you'll need to get those feet elevated, and all of you needs to rest. Don't you dare give me that look, young man. You can use my couch over there. Er, Miss..." Volkstaff's eyes bugged a little as he took in Val for the first time. Alex had warned Volkstaff that the fourth member of their party would show up later, but he clearly hadn't expected a Victoria's Secret model.

"You can call me Valentine," Val purred.

"Yes, thank you, well. Miss Valentine, could you push Kevin over to the sofa and help him onto it? Exactly—thank you."

Alex watched, feeling numb again, her head disconnected from every part of her body, while Val half shoved Kevin from the chair to the couch. Her expression was irritated, her hands rough, but Alex saw her duck in suddenly to kiss his forehead.

"And you, Doctor..."

Alex turned slowly to look at Volkstaff.

"There are more couches in the waiting room. Go use one of them. That's an order."

She hesitated, swaying in place, staring at Daniel.

"Yeesh, you two," Val said as she stalked back across the room. "Sleep before you collapse, Alex. I've had a few hours. I'll keep an eye on him."

"If anything *at all* changes on his monitors, the slightest variation—"

"I'll drag you back in here by your much-improved hair," Val promised.

Alex bent down and kissed Daniel softly. "Volkstaff and I went through a lot of trouble to put you back together again," she murmured against his lips. "Don't screw up our work."

His lips brushed hers as he spoke. "Wouldn't dream of it. Be a good girl and get some sleep like my old family vet ordered you to."

"I'll have you know I'm in the prime of my life," Volkstaff objected.

"C'mon," Val said, suddenly right in Alex's ear. "Let's go while you can still walk. I'm sure I could carry you, but I don't *want* to."

Alex let Val guide her through the door and down the unlit hallway. She concentrated on moving her feet and nothing else. Her surroundings were just a dark blur. Val had to lower her to the couch, but Alex was sure she would have been just as happy on the floor. Unconsciousness took her while she was still falling.

CHAPTER 32

I t was a strange morning.

For Alex, it was also a very late morning. It was peaceful in the empty veterinary hospital, and no one disturbed her. She learned later that Volkstaff had called his office team, canceled all the appointments, and put a sign in the window that read CLOSED FOR FAMILY EMERGENCY.

It was an odd place to feel so safe — an unfamiliar place, a place where she'd prepared no traps or defenses.

But things had changed. She'd only really thought of rescuing Kevin, but their actions last night had also shifted their position significantly.

Kevin was as energetic as ever, despite the fact that he was stuck in the rolling office chair again, his gauze-wrapped feet elevated on the wheeled stool. Val disappeared as soon as she saw Alex to take her turn on the couch. Daniel had had his eyes closed to ignore his brother but quickly "woke up" when he heard Alex's voice. Volkstaff was apparently out getting lunch. The others had left her a bagel and cream cheese.

As soon as Alex had finished her examination of Daniel — who was recovering more quickly than anyone who hadn't worked with Kevin Beach would believe — Alex grabbed her breakfast and the newspaper Volkstaff had brought in with the bagels. She read furiously while she chewed. They'd made the front page — though only the people in the room knew that.

"This all feels anticlimactic, Ollie," Kevin complained, using a broom to push his chair in circles around the room. "It would have been more fun to shoot him."

The big headline for the day was Wade Pace's fatal aneurysm. The journalists had barely paused for a moment of silence before they were on to guessing what President Howland's strategy would be for finding his new running mate.

"Well, you did get to shoot Deavers."

"I was too stressed about Danny to really enjoy it, though," he mused.

Kevin had been terse in his explanation about how Deavers had gotten the upper hand. Alex could tell he was embarrassed, but she didn't think less of him. How could anyone have prepared for the extremes that Deavers's paranoia had pushed him to? More than forty men, deployed into three perimeters, one more than a mile out from Deavers's position. Once Deavers hit the panic button, the perimeters had collapsed in. Kevin maintained that if he hadn't ignored his gut and brought a rocket launcher along, he would have made it out.

There was nothing else in the news, nothing about a violent shootout in an underground bunker on the outskirts of town. No word about a missing CIA deputy director. No mention of Carston, not even the relatively public kidnapping of his granddaughter. Maybe in tomorrow's news.

Kevin didn't think so.

"It'll be a gas-line explosion or something like that. That real story is all going to get buried so deep, they'll name Jackie Kennedy as the Dallas shooter before any of it gets out."

He was probably right.

They couldn't be 100 percent sure, of course, and they would continue to behave with caution, but the pressure was significantly decreased. Alex knew she would feel the lightness like a layer of helium under her skin, if she could ever convince herself to believe in their good luck.

After lunch, Volkstaff removed the stitches from Alex's ear and complimented Daniel's even hand when she gave him the credit. Alex was bemused by how much the white-haired old man took in stride. None of them had tried to explain their unusual injuries or even make up a cover story, but Volkstaff asked no questions and showed no obvious curiosity. He didn't comment on the fact that Kevin was supposed to have died in prison, though apparently — Daniel informed her in a whisper — Volkstaff had been at the funeral. He asked only about old acquaintances from their childhood and, more particularly, the animals they'd known together. Though Alex had just barely learned to recognize love at all, she thought she might be falling for Volkstaff just a little, too.

Still, they couldn't live in the animal hospital forever. Volkstaff had other patients. After a few minutes of discussing options, Val surprised Alex by volunteering to house them again, back in her palatial penthouse, now that it was safe. For a fee, naturally. Kevin seemed the most shocked at her offer.

"Don't let it go to your head," she told him. "I want the dog. And I actually *like* Alex and Danny. Almost as much as I can't stand you." Then she'd kissed him — long enough that it got uncomfortable for everyone. Volkstaff politely turned his back, but Alex just stared. She would never understand what Val saw in Kevin.

• • •

"SOOO . . ." KEVIN BEGAN.

Alex turned from her organizing; it wasn't quite packing yet. Kevin was lounging in the doorway of the room Alex and Daniel had always shared in Val's home, his left arm braced against the top of the frame. For one second, Alex was irrelevantly jealous of tall people in general. It wasn't an uncommon feeling these days, always surrounded by giants as she was. She put it away.

"So what?"

"So how did the appointment go today? What did you and Volkstaff conclude?"

He didn't have to ask where Daniel was now — Daniel's normal shower-serenade volume would have gotten him in trouble if the other tenants were any closer. The Bon Jovi phase hadn't passed yet; he was particularly fond of "Shot Through the Heart" at the moment. Alex didn't find it so funny, but she tried not to let it irritate her.

"The vet thinks Daniel's good to go. I concur. You Beaches are a charmed breed." She shook her head, still a little incredulous at how quickly and thoroughly Daniel had healed. "Also, he wants to look at your feet."

Kevin scowled. "My feet are fine."

"Don't shoot the messenger. I mean that literally."

His frown faded into his normal expression, but he continued to stand there in the doorway, staring at her.

"Sooo . . . ?" she echoed.

"So . . . do you have any ideas about where you're heading now?"

Alex twitched her shoulders noncommittally. "Nothing too specific yet." Like a coward, she turned back to her worn duffel and looked over her stowed chemicals again, checking that they were all appropriately protected from jostling. She might have been going overboard with the organization, she admitted to herself. They probably didn't need to be alphabetized. But she'd had a lot of time on her hands, and other than surfing the web for possible new digs, she was at loose ends. Daniel had objected to being examined more than four times a day.

"Have you talked to Danny about it?"

She nodded with her back still turned to him. "He says wherever I want to go is fine by him."

"He's planning to tag along with you, I guess."

Kevin's voice was casual, but Alex knew it must be a strain to keep it that way.

"I haven't discussed that part specifically with him, but, yes, it does seem to be the assumption."

He didn't say anything for a moment, and she really had nothing left to do with the bag. She turned slowly to face him.

"Yeah," he said, "I could tell it was going to go that way." His expression was indifferent. Only his eyes revealed the depths of his hurt.

She didn't want to tell the full story, but she felt guilty holding it back. "If it makes you feel any better, he seems to be assuming you'll be there, too."

Kevin's eyebrows eased back from their normal compressed position.

"Really?"

"Yes. I don't think he's envisioned any more splitting up at this point."

Kevin inclined his chin. "I can understand that. Kid's been through a lot."

"He's bouncing back pretty well."

"True, but we wouldn't want to traumatize him again. Don't want him to have a setback."

Alex knew where Kevin was going with this. She suppressed both a sigh and a smile, keeping her face neutral.

"True," she said in her serious-doctor tone. "It might be best to keep his environment as stable as possible, aside from all the unavoidable changes."

Kevin didn't suppress *his* sigh. He blew out a huge breath and crossed his arms over his chest. "It'll probably be an enormous pain, but I guess I can stick close until he's adapted."

Alex couldn't resist pushing back just a tiny bit. "I'm sure he wouldn't want you to put yourself out. He'll survive."

"No, no, I owe the kid. I'll do what I have to."

"He'll appreciate that."

Kevin met her gaze for one long second, his expression candid, and then suddenly sheepish. The moment passed, and he grinned.

"What's the general area you're looking at?" he asked.

"I was thinking maybe the Southwest or the Rocky Mountains. Medium-size city, settle in the suburbs. The usual."

No one was looking for them, as far as they knew, but Alex was always a fan of playing it safe, just in case. She'd have to use a fake name regardless—Juliana Fortis was legally dead.

Daniel's singing cut off, then picked up again, muffled by a towel.

"I know a town that might work."

Alex shook her head slowly. He'd probably already rented a house and set up the new identities. She'd choose her own name no matter what he'd done. "Of course you do."

"How do you feel about Colorado?"

EPILOGUE

Adam Kopecky sat today's files on his desk and reached for the phone with a smile already in place. He had the best job in the world.

Working as an assistant producer for a famous chef's reality road show could have meant many things, but for Adam, it meant flexible hours, a quiet little office, and a near-constant stream of positivity.

He was in charge of managing the visits to the various mom-and-pop eateries his chef would be featuring on the show, and while he was sometimes jealous of Bess and Neil, who were always on the road trying out every hole-in-the-wall they could find, he believed what he was doing suited his temperament better. Plus, Bess and Neil had to eat a lot of garbage to find the diamonds in the rough, and Neil had gained at least twenty-five pounds in this past year with the show; Adam had cobbled together a standing desk so that his more stationary job would not start to affect him the same way. And then, out of necessity, no one knew who Bess and Neil were, so no one was particularly excited to hear from them.

Thursday afternoon was Adam's favorite. Today he would call the chosen ones.

The show was heading to the Denver region in a month, and the lucky winners were a barbecue place in Lakewood, a bakery right in downtown, and then the outlier, a bar and grill that was closer to

Boulder than Denver. Adam had been skeptical, but Bess insisted that the Hideaway would be the highlight of the episode. If possible, they should be there on a Friday night. The place was a local karaoke hot spot. Adam hated karaoke, but Bess was insistent.

"It's not what you're thinking, Adam," she'd promised. "This place is so cool, Chef'll need a parka. Doesn't look like much from the outside, but the style is there. *Je ne sais quoi* and all that. Plus the owners are seriously camera-ready. The cook's name is Nathaniel Weeks—so *fine*, let me tell you. I hate to admit to being unprofessional, but I did make a play. I got zero response. The waitress tipped me off that he was married. The good ones are always taken, right? But he's got a hot brother, apparently. Plays bouncer for the bar at night. I may tag along with Chef for this one."

She'd taken a bunch of pictures on her iPhone. As she'd mentioned, the outside was forgettable. It could have been anyplace in the West. Saloon-ish, dark wood, rustic. Most of the other photos were of plates of food that seemed to have too much style for such an unremarkable location. A few of the pictures must have been of the cook she liked so much—tall, full beard, thick curly hair. Adam didn't think he was especially attractive, but what did he know? Lumberjacks could be Bess's thing. A small woman with short dark hair was in a lot of the backgrounds, never facing the camera... maybe this was the chef's wife. He had the names of all the owners off the alcohol license. Nathaniel Weeks was the chef, so Kenneth must be the bouncer brother, and Ellis the wife.

Adam had remained hesitant, but the Hideaway had gotten Neil's enthusiastic thumbs-up as well. Best food he'd had in the past three seasons.

There were always a couple of backups—a coffee shop in Parker and a breakfast-only diner in Littleton were on this list—but Adam very rarely had to contact the backups. The show had a track record of boosting business by a healthy percentage for the first two months after an episode aired, with an ongoing lift for the rest of the year.

There were even a bunch of groupie types who tried to follow Chef's journey and eat at every place he featured. Chef was always complimentary, and the show regularly pulled in almost a million viewers every Sunday night. It was the world's best advertisement, and it was free.

So Adam was prepared for the reaction at the Lakewood barbecue place, Whistle Pig. As soon as he said the name of the show, the owner was screaming. Adam thought he could even hear her feet pounding against the floor as she jumped up and down. It was like showing up at someone's door with one of those huge Publishers Clearing House checks.

Once the owner had calmed down, Adam went through the usual spiel, getting the date on her calendar, giving her the contact info she would need, prepping her for the kinds of access the show would require, et cetera. All the while, she kept thanking Adam and occasionally shouting the good news to someone who'd just walked into the room.

Adam had made this same call over eight hundred times now, but it always left him grinning and feeling like Good Saint Nick.

The call with the bakery was similar, but instead of screaming, the head pastry chef had an infectious belly laugh that Adam couldn't help but laugh along with. This call took longer than the first, but eventually Adam was able to compose himself, even if the local chef never did.

Adam had saved the Hideaway for last, knowing that a Friday-night karaoke event would be a little more complicated to arrange. Adam thought it might be too much of a departure for the show, but he supposed they could get some footage from both the dinner hour and the performances, then cut it together to see what would work.

"This is the Hideaway," an alto female voice answered his call. "How can I help you?"

In the background, Adam could hear the expected sounds — the clinking of clean dishes being put away, the *chop, chop, chop* of the prep work, the murmur of a few conversations lowered for the sake of the phone call. Soon they'd be plenty loud.

"Hello," Adam greeted her heartily. "Could I please speak to Mrs. Weeks — Mrs. Ellis Weeks — or either of the Mr. Weekses?"

"This is Mrs. Weeks."

"Great. Hi. My name is Adam Kopecky, and I'm calling you on behalf of the show *The Great American Food Trip*."

He waited. Sometimes it took a minute to sink in. He wondered if Mrs. Weeks was a screamer or a gasper. Maybe a crier.

"Yes," Mrs. Weeks responded in a cool tone. "What can I do for you?"

Adam coughed out an awkward laugh. It happened sometimes. Not everyone was familiar with the show, though it really was a household name these days.

"Well, we're a cuisine-focused reality show that follows the food journeys of Chef —"

"Yes, I know the program." There was a hint of impatience in the voice now. "And what can I help you with?"

Adam was a bit thrown. There was the strangest sort of suspicion in her reaction, like she thought this was a scam. Or maybe something worse. Adam couldn't quite put his finger on it.

He hurried to set her straight. "I'm calling because the Hideaway has been chosen for our show. Our spies" — he laughed lightly — "came home raving about your menu and your entertainment. We hear you've become quite a local hot spot. We'd love to profile your establishment — get the word out to anyone who hasn't heard of you yet."

Surely now it would click for her. As one-third owner of the restaurant, she had to be adding up the financial possibilities in her head. He waited for the first squeal.

Nothing.

He could still hear the clinking, the chopping, the murmuring, and in the distance, a couple of dogs barking. Otherwise he would have thought the call had dropped. Or that she'd hung up on him.

"Hello, Mrs. Weeks?"

"Yes, I'm here."

"Well, then, um, congratulations. We plan to be in your area the first part of next month, and we can be somewhat flexible within that time frame to work with your schedule. I've heard that Friday nights are a highlight, so we might want to plan for that—"

"I'm sorry—Mr. Kopecky, did you say it was?"

"Yes, but call me Adam, please."

"I'm sorry, Adam, but while we're . . . flattered, I don't think it will be possible for us to participate."

"Oh," Adam said. It was half gasp, half grunt.

He'd had a few instances where schedules could not be made to fit, where exigent circumstances of the most weighty kind—weddings, funerals, organ transplants—had gotten in the way, but the dream had never died without a major effort on the part of the owners and major disappointment to follow. One poor woman in Omaha had sobbed into the receiver for a solid five minutes.

"Thank you so much for thinking of us . . ."

As if this were no more than an invitation to a distant relative's backyard birthday party.

"Mrs. Weeks, I'm not sure you realize what this could do for your business. I could send you some statistics—you'd be amazed at what a difference in your bottom line a spot on the show would mean."

"I'm sure you're right, Mr. Kopecky—"

"What is it, Ollie?" a voice interrupted. This one was deep, and very loud.

"Excuse me a moment," Mrs. Weeks said to Adam, and then her voice was slightly muffled. "I've got it," she said to the loud voice. "It's that show—the *American Food Trip* thing."

"What do they want?"

516

"To feature the Hideaway, apparently."

Adam took a slow breath. Maybe one of the other owners would respond appropriately.

"Oh," the deep voice said, and his tone reminded Adam of the woman's first response. Flat.

How was this bad news? Adam felt like he was being pranked. Was this Bess and Neil's idea of a joke?

"Really?" someone called out from a distance—another deep voice, but this one more enthusiastic. "They want to put us on their show?"

"Yes," Mrs. Weeks responded. "But don't—"

A few cheers interrupted whatever she was going to say. Adam didn't relax. He couldn't feel any change directly on the other end of the line.

"You want me to talk to him, Ollie?" the loud voice asked.

"No, go deal with *them*," Mrs. Weeks said. "Nathaniel might need a stiff drink. Maybe the waitstaff, too. I'll take care of this."

"Wilco."

"I apologize for the interruption, Mr. Kopecky," Mrs. Weeks said, her voice clear again. "And truly, thank you so much for the offer. I'm very sorry it won't work out."

"I don't understand." Adam could hear the deflation in his own tone and was sure she could, too. "We can be flexible, like I said. I've... I've never had anyone who didn't want this."

Now her voice was more animated—soothing, kind. "And we would want this, absolutely, if it was possible. You see..." A short pause. "There's an issue, a legal issue, that we're dealing with. A lien situation with my brother-in-law's former girlfriend. Was it a business loan, was it a personal gift? Yada yada; you get the picture. It's all very delicate—sticky, you know, and no press is good press for now. We have to keep a low profile. I hope you can understand. We *are* very flattered."

He could hear the loud brother arguing with someone in the

background, more barking, and some quieter mumbles that sounded like complaints.

This was more like it. A concrete reason, even if he didn't totally understand how a legal case would be negatively impacted by the restaurant's involvement with the show . . . unless they thought they were going to have to pay out some percentage of what the place was worth?

"I'm sorry to hear that, Mrs. Weeks. Maybe sometime in the future? I could give you my—"

"Absolutely. Thank you so much. I'll be in contact if we are ever in a position to accept."

The line went dead. She hadn't even let him give her his phone number.

Adam stared at the papers in front of him for a few seconds, trying to shake off what felt very much like being shut down after asking a charity date to the prom.

A few minutes passed while he stared at the phone. Finally, he shook his head and reached for the file with the backups. The coffee shop in Parker would be only too grateful to be chosen. Adam needed a few good screams.

ACKNOWLEDGMENTS

This story wasn't one I could have written by myself, and I'm immensely grateful to all the people who gave me so much of their time, patience, and expertise.

My MVP was Dr. Kirstin Hendrickson of Arizona State University's school of Molecular Sciences and her colleague Dr. Scott Lefler. Dr. Hendrickson spent an incredible amount of time working out realistic ways for me to kill, torture, and chemically manipulate fictional people, and I am so appreciative for her help.

My favorite RN, Judd Mendenhall, was also a huge help in keeping Daniel Beach alive by talking me through a sucking chest wound and coming up with the veterinarian solution.

Without Dr. Gregory Prince's brilliant help with molecular biology and monoclonal antibodies, I would not have been able to give Alex the backstory she deserved.

An enormous thank-you to each of the following awesome people: Tommy Wittman, retired special agent, ATF, who gave me an excellent crash course in gas masks; Paul Morgan and Jerry Hine, who were frighteningly helpful with the mechanics of building a functional death trap; Sergeant Warren Brewer of the Phoenix Police Department, who vetted my drug deals; S. Daniel Colton, former captain, USAF JAG Corps, for his expertise in the creation of Kevin's backstory; Petty Officer First Class John E. Rowe, who is always happy to talk guns with me or any other random thing I might be curious about.

And a huge thank-you also to my sources who preferred to remain anonymous. Your help is so appreciated.

All my love to the usual suspects: My very understanding family, who are so patient with my sleepless, manic writing spells; my brilliant and kind editor, Asya, who never tells me I'm crazy even when I am; my ninja agent, Jodi, who inspires fear in all who oppose her (and sometimes those who don't); my super-classy film agent, Kassie, whom I aspire to be when I grow up; my production partner, Meghan, who carries all the weight of Fickle Fish so it doesn't burn to the ground in my absence. And, of course, my heart is full of love for all the people who pick my books up and give them a chance — thank you for letting me tell you stories.

And finally, thank you to Pocket, my gorgeous and IQ-challenged German shepherd, who, at the very slightest hint of danger, immediately cowers behind my legs. Who will never love me the way he loves my husband. Who still doesn't understand the basic principles of the game of fetch. I love you, too, you big, dumb, beautiful chicken.

ABOUT THE AUTHOR

Stephenie Meyer graduated from Brigham Young University with a degree in English literature. She lives with her husband and three sons in Arizona. Read more about Stephenie and her other books at stepheniemeyer.com.